"A handy resource for anyone interested in the gay movement today...Comprehensive, concise and literate."

—**URVASHI VAID**,
Executive Director,
National Gay and Lesbian
Task Force

"Provides an essential road map to Gay America and will undoubtedly become the Bible of gay organizations for years to come."

—**RANDY SHILTS**

THE ESSENTIAL REFERENCE TO GAY CULTURE IN AMERICA TODAY

- Political Organizations
- Switchboards and Hotlines
- Gay Radio and Television
- Gay Film and Video
- Colleges and Universities Gay Students Should Consider
- Coming Out
- Gay Mensa
- Gay Youth
- Gay Horticulturists, Philatelists, and Railroaders
- Living with AIDS
- Safe Sex
- Athletic Organizations
- Resorts
- Religious Organizations
- Travel and Recreation
- PLUS much more interesting and important information for gay men

JOHN PRESTON is the former editor of *The Advocate,* a co-founder of the first gay community health center in the United States, and an official for several national gay rights organizations. He has lived in the nation's largest gay communities—Los Angeles, San Francisco, and New York—and for the last eight years in Maine. He is the co-author of *Safe Sex: The Ultimate Erotic Guide,* also available in a Plume edition.

EDITED BY
JOHN PRESTON

THE BIG GAY BOOK

A MAN'S SURVIVAL GUIDE FOR THE 90'S

A PLUME BOOK

This book is a resource guide and the listing of any individual or organization implies only that they possess information relevant to the subjects under discussion. The inclusion, mention, or photograph of any individual or group herein does not necesscarily imply anything about their sexual orientation.

PLUME

Published by the Penguin Group
Penguin Books USA Inc., 375 Hudson Street, New York, New York 10014, U.S.A.
Penguin Books Ltd, 27 Wrights Lane, London W8 5TZ, England
Penguin Books Australia Ltd, Ringwood, Victoria, Australia
Penguin Books Canada Ltd, 10 Alcorn Avenue, Toronto, Ontario, Canada M4V 3B2
Penguin Books (N.Z.) Ltd, 182-190 Wairau Road, Auckland 10, New Zealand

Penguin Books Ltd, Registered Offices: Harmondsworth, Middlesex, England

First published by Plume, an imprint of New American Libarary, a division of Penguin Books USA Inc.

Copyright © John Preston, 1991
All rights reserved

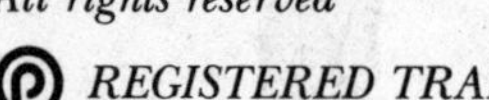

REGISTERED TRADEMARK—MARCA REGISTRADA

LIBRARY OF CONGRESS CATALOGING IN PUBLICATION DATA:

Preston, John.
The big gay book: a man's survival guide for the 90's/John Preston.
p. cm.
ISBN 0-452-26621-1
1. Gay men—United States—Life skills guides. I. Title.
HQ76.2.U5P74 1991 91-10375
306.76'62—dc20 CIP

Printed in the United States of America
Set in New Baskerville

Designed by Steven N. Stathakis

Without limiting the rights under copyright reserved above, no part of this publication may be reproduced, stored in or introduced into a retrieval system, or transmitted, in any form, or by any means (electronic, mechanical, photocopying, recording, or otherwise), without the prior written permission of both the copyright owner and the above publisher of this book.

To Robert Riger,
because he made me do it

▼

CONTENTS

PART THREE: GAY CULTURE

PART FOUR: CAMPUS LIFE

PART FIVE: HOW WE LEAD OUR LIVES

PART EIGHT: ENTERTAINING OURSELVES

ACKNOWLEDGMENTS

The first seed of the idea for this book was planted by Peter Ginsberg, my agent, and Arnold Dolin of NAL/Dutton. Gary Luke, the original NAL editor, and I took the next steps and began working on the concept that would eventually be this volume. Matt Sartwell took over some of Gary's duties when Gary moved on to another publishing house; it's an open question whether the overseeing of this project was one of the rewards of his position, or one of the crosses he has had to bear.

Once the idea of *The Big Gay Book* was established, Tom Hagerty took over his usual position in my enterprises, making up files and file categories (no small matter in an undertaking this size), and delivering constant cheers, which, toward the end, became moans: "Can't you please finish it?!"

Celeste DeRoche, coincidentally Tom's cousin, did much of the typing and her labors made the completion of this book possible. Amanda Coffin and Robert Riger both contributed volunteer typing services as well. If you calculate the hours they spent and then factored in the per diem rate these two consultants charge their clients—Amanda in computer networking, Robert in publishing—this may well be the most expensive manuscript ever delivered to an American publishing house.

I've tried to acknowledge the people who've given specific help in the area where I've used their expertise. There are, of course, many more people who have donated time, suggestions, and expertise beyond one area. While I can't name them all, Richard Labonté, manager of A Different Light in San Francisco, Robert Bray, formerly of The Human Rights Campaign Fund and now with The National Gay and Lesbian Task Force, Michael Bronski of *Gay Community News,* Jim Baxter of *The Front Page,* Essex Hamphill, Bob Summer, and Sami of Pride Products are some whose contributions have been beyond the call of duty. Agnes Bushell of The Portland School of Art, Jerry Banner of The University of Southern Maine, and Jane Troxell of Lambda Rising Bookstore all helped with bibliographic research. Robert Diamante worked on fact checking. And on any book this complicated, design is of particular importance, so thanks to Steven N. Stathakis for his patient contribution.

In more general terms: This book would never have been possible without the gay press. If there weren't a network of gay publications, the word about the organizations and activities that are cataloged in this book couldn't be heard. In fact, without a vibrant gay press, it's probable that this network of organizations couldn't even exist.

—JOHN PRESTON
Portland, Maine

INTRODUCTION

The most impressive aspect of this book is one simple fact: Twenty-five years ago, almost none of this existed. I don't think any of us who were involved in the first steps of activisim believed that our work would eventually generate a network of gay political, academic, community, athletic, and benevolent organizations as complete as that in the gay world today.

As I've compiled these listings, interviewed various people involved in these enterprises, and read the extensive literature that's been written in the past two decades, I couldn't help but experience great pride; I've felt a part of a collective accomplishment that is truly remarkable.

Before the Stonewall Riots of 1969, being gay in America was to inhabit a mostly arid closet. Only a very few organizations spoke up for gay life as a reasonable alternative existence. More common was self-hatred, societal disdain, if not outright hatred, and religious condemnation.

Building on the fragile foundation that the early pre-Stonewall pioneers had laid down, activists began to confront the mainstream with demands, to nurture one another in healing centuries of abuse, and to construct the framework of what would eventually become the gay community that begins the new decade, and, soon, the new millennium.

The struggles have required sacrifices, and often the costs have been high. People have succumbed to the emotional and physical violence of homophobia. There have been huge setbacks in the legislatures and the courts. The unforeseeable tragedy of AIDS, while it has in its own ways increased the moral perception of the gay world—our perceptions of ourselves as well as the perceptions of others—has produced that progress at an obscenely high cost.

Nor is the struggle over, at all. Many parts of society continue to perceive gay people as legitimate targets for mistreatment. Even as our visibility increases, so do the attacks on us for daring to leave the closet of silence.

But the beginnings are solid, manifest in the organizations and individuals who are in this book. They are proof that the vitality of the gay community is so great that it cannot be sapped. On the playing fields, in churches, in political circles, in our community centers, and on the pages of our newspapers, gay people have declared that we are here, we will not disappear, and we will be dealt with.

That leads me to the most essential aspiration I've had in putting this volume together. In one way, this is a kind of almanac. It tells you who is doing what and how you might benefit from those services. I hope you will go much further than simply consuming these services, though. I would also like to see you use the examples in this book as an inspiration to do something on your own. For that reason, I like to think of this as an *interactive* volume, not a passive reference work. *The Big Gay Book* is not just here to tell you what someone else will do for you, it's here to show you the possibilities in your own life and community. That there is a gay lending library in Winnipeg, Manitoba, should make you wonder why there isn't one in your hometown. That there can be a Gay Pride celebration in a place as small as Traverse City, Michigan, should make you question why you and your friends aren't celebrating your own pride in your own location. If your alma mater isn't one of those listed as being especially worth consideration for a gay student, why not? And what can you do about it?

All that exists in these pages and in our lives exists because people chose to act and took the risks that came with those actions. You, and all of us, who are taking part in the bounty that has become gay life in the United States and Canada also have an obligation to give something back, to return the efforts that have been made on our behalf. While you read this book, please don't just wonder at what people have accomplished. Ask yourself what you should be doing to match their accomplishments.

Some more thoughts about this book and how I've gone about putting it together:

One of the first issues that I and my editors had to face was that of gender. Gay men and lesbians have forged alliances in many fields. In politics, there's been no choice. Whatever differences we might perceive between ourselves, the legal establishment doesn't discern any difference between gay men and lesbians. Almost all political organizations working for legislative or judicial progress have had to be mixed-gender groups. Many community organizations also are made up of both gay men and lesbians, though with less success on the most part. While many of the organizations in this book list themselves as "gay and lesbian," a quick and informal survey showed that fewer than 25 percent actually had anything close to gender equality in administrative or board positions or memberships; they are essentially gay men's organizations. The integration of men and women in our world in not nearly so complete as we like to suppose.

Nor am I convinced that such an integration is always a positive or necessary step. Certainly there are many areas where we gay men have our own work to do, just as women have often found it necessary to separate certain parts of their own lives for their own priorities. Also, there are still differing sensibilities among us concerning sexuality and other issues.

In the end, the decision was made to make this book for gay men and to focus on the areas that gay men would find important and valuable and entertaining. Of course there are many listings which will be of interest to lesbians and I hope they're well served by those chapters, if they choose to look in these pages. I'm even more hopeful that NAL/Dutton will proceed with its plan to create a companion volume to this one. I hope that by the time *The Big Gay Book* is in your hands, *The Big Lesbian Book* is well under way. I've pledged to help whoever might undertake that project with as much information and as many contacts from my own work as I can.

Another of the problems in constructing this work has been getting to a place where I could say that it was done. Things happen quickly in a community as young as ours. Organizations are born, leaders change directions, resources are developed, all with an astonishing speed.

Too, many of the organizations in these pages are grass-roots-based. They have minimal amounts of money and they don't have paid staff to answer correspondence. That means that there are constant address changes involved. At some point, I had to stop changing the manuscript and move on.

That has meant many things:

First, there are movements just beginning as I finish this work. *Queer Nation* and *The Pink Panthers,* both groups originated to fight against violence toward the gay community, are just coming into being as I write. They appear to be spirited and dynamic efforts and I suspect they'll have a long life. But, they don't appear in these pages, only because they haven't set a structure yet. Look for information about them in the gay press and other means of gay communication.

Second, there are groups that are undergoing such dramatic

change that I can't be sure they'll survive the length of time it will take to go from a manuscript in my computer to a printed book in your hands. That's meant that *The Fund for Human Dignity,* an organization that certainly would have been in these pages if they were written even six months ago, is missing here. The Fund's board chose to hire a straight executive director, an action that led most staff and many volunteers to quit. According to press reports, the only activity the Fund continues at this point is raising money. I can't in good conscience recommend it to you; if you see that it is active in the future, investigate its activities and administration for yourself before you become involved with it.

That, of course, goes for every organization in this volume. You should investigate them thoroughly before you donate money, buy services, volunteer your time, or recommend them to others.

That leads to the question of how I myself went about constructing the entries in this book. I have worked hard not to allow my own prejudices and inclinations to dominate this work. I have striven to be as inclusive as possible. My having made mention of a religious organization says nothing about my own background or current faith. A political organization did not have to pass any litmus test of my own to be incorporated. I am not necessarily a Catholic or an atheist, an athlete or a naturalist. I have not embraced or rejected any organization solely on the measure of its being for-profit or nonprofit.

The basic criteria for entry in *The Big Gay Book* were simple: Did the organization identify itself as gay, or at least as serving gay men? Was it accessible? That is, could a reader find a way to make contact with an enterprise through the mail, computer modem, or telephone? I also needed to know that there was some stability, that a reader could, in fact, reach the organization. I wrote to every group in this volume. If there was no current address to which the postal services would deliver mail, the group was taken out of the listing.

This is a book born to be revised and I stand ready to do the work to update it extensively, if there's demand for it. With all the material presented to me, I know I must have overlooked some active, positive organizations. If you find that some group with which you're involved is not in these pages, please let me know. If your group's address has changed, tell me and put my name on your mailing list so I can keep track of changes. I hope *The Big Gay Book* is going to be of unique value to gay men; I also hope it will be even more constructive in the future. That will happen only if you lend a hand and tell me what's going on in your part of your country, or if you'll tell me what else you wished had been here. If you have any suggestions on the look, shape, content of a future edition of *The Big Gay Book,* please write and tell me.

John Preston
Box 5314
Portland, ME 04101

PART ONE

HOW WE ORGANIZE . . . AND WHY

In the beginning, isolation was the fact of gay life. Isolation didn't mean just loneliness, though. It also meant vulnerability and powerlessness. A population that isn't in touch with its own members can't advocate for itself, except as individuals. Once we began to join together and realize that we weren't only separate entities but members of a group, then we could champion our joint causes and articulate our common issues. When we understood that we faced common injustices, we could form organizations to protest those inequities. When we saw that we could gain strength by learning to know one another and broadening the definition of what it meant to be gay, we could increase our efforts to organize.

In this still early stage of gay organization and activism, any kind of organizing is important. There's a political need for our legislative and legal groups, and there's a social need for our other communal activities, from enjoying hobbies to exploring sexism. In many cases we need to break down further the segments of our world in order to explore important subgroups of gay men; those of some racial and ethnic categories need to spend time with one another, for instance, to understand how racism and other prejudices in addition to homophobia shape their lives.

POLITICAL ORGANIZATIONS

Civil rights is the most obvious arena for gay collective activity. We're all affected by laws that discriminate against us, denying us job protection, the right to live where we choose, the ability to select who we will love—and how we will do it—and the right to be free of assault.

The many political groups in the United States and Canada are all involved in dealing with those issues. They lobby the legislative and administrative branches of government and they are engaged in public education as well.

If you have any question about the legal status of gay people in your state or province, you should be in touch with the association in your area.

NATIONAL ORGANIZATIONS

There are three groups—two in the United States, one in Canada—that have essential functions in our world and in our struggle for rights and dignity. Their influence extends throughout the rest of our organizations and activity, both political and communal. They are often the major sources of consultative experience, help, and encouragement for the gay community and they are the first places that the mainstream press, legislators, and other people of influence go when they want to discover our point of view.

Their presence is utterly necessary, if we're ever going to have any major social change. If they provided only the single function of networking—of keeping the diverse elements of the gay and lesbian movement in touch with one another—they would be vital to our collective lives. But they do much more than that.

If you do nothing else, you are obliged to belong to one of these organizations. The cost of membership is minimal and there are often scaled fees for students or others who might not be able to pay full charges. You owe it to yourself and all other gay men to find out how you can help these groups.

UNITED STATES

THE HUMAN RIGHTS CAMPAIGN FUND
1012 14th Street NW, #607
Washington, DC 20005
Phone: 202 628 4160
Fax: 202 347 5323

THE NATIONAL GAY AND LESBIAN TASK FORCE
1517 U Street NW
Washington, DC 20009
Phone: 202 332 6483
Fax: 202 332 0207

CANADA

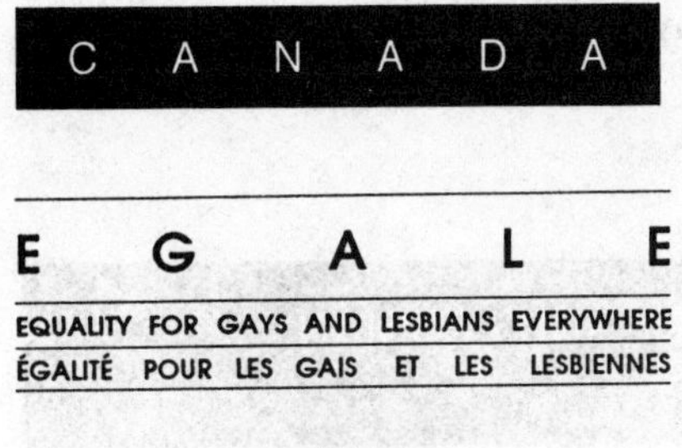

EGALE
Equality for Gays and Lesbians Everywhere
Égalité pour les Gais et les Lesbiennes
Box/C.P. 2891
Station D/Succursale D
Ottawa, ON K1P 5W9
Phone: 613 230 4391

HUMAN RIGHTS CAMPAIGN FUND COMPUTER BULLETIN BOARD

Gay and lesbian computer users can get up-to-the-minute information from the nation's capital by signing on to the Human Rights Campaign Fund (HCRF) computerized bulletin board. The bulletin board is called HCRF NET. Access HCRF NET for:

■ Legislative Updates. With current AIDS and civil rights bills, amendments, and other Capitol Hill happenings.
■ Voting Records. Are your congresspersons homophobes or homophiles? Check their voting records on the most recent gay-related legislation.
■ Press Releases. Get gay news released to the media.
■ HCRF Editorials. A monthly editorial from the desk of the HRCF executive director.
■ Field Division. Learn about gay and lesbian constituent mobiliza-

tion and sign up directly online for hard-hitting mailgrams to Congress.

■ Housekeeping. With HRCF NET Introduction, HRCF NET Policies, HRCF NET Instructions, HRCF NET Archives, and a short Log-On Questionnaire.

The HRCF NET access number is 202 639 8735. Modems must be at a minimum of 300 baud rate. Contact the system operator at 202 628 4160 (voice number) or write: HRCF, 1012 Fourteenth Street NW, Suite 607, Washington, DC 20005. Use of the bulletin board is free, except for phone line charges.

STATE AND PROVINCIAL GAY AND LESBIAN POLITICAL ORGANIZATIONS

These are political organizations that are involved in gay civil rights and operate in a state or provincial arena. Most are fairly sophisticated and are dedicated to lobbying and educational activities throughout their area. Others, usually in less-populated regions, are organizations which do the same job, even if this was not their original goal. The U.S. listings were compiled with the help of the staff of the National Gay and Lesbian Task Force.

UNITED STATES

■ ALABAMA ■

LAMBDA, INC.
516 27th Street S
Birmingham, AL 35233
Phone: 205 326 8600

PRO-PAC
Box 55913
Birmingham, AL 35225
Phone: 205 326 8600

■ ALASKA ■

IDENTITY, INC.
Box 200070
Anchorage, AK 99520

■ ARKANSAS ■

ARKANSAS GAY AND LESBIAN TASK FORCE
Box 45053
Little Rock, AR 72214

■ CALIFORNIA ■

LOBBY FOR INDIVIDUAL FREEDOM AND EQUALITY
926 J Street, Suite 1020
Sacramento, CA 95814
Phone: 916 444 0424

■ COLORADO ■

COLORADO GAY AND LESBIAN TASK FORCE
Box 18632
Denver, CO 80218

■ CONNECTICUT ■

CONNECTICUT COALITION FOR LESBIAN/GAY CIVIL RIGHTS
Box 141025
Hartford, CT 06114

■ DELAWARE ■

GAY AND LESBIAN ALLIANCE OF DELAWARE
214 N. Market Street
Wilmington, DE 19801
Phone: 302 655 5280

■ FLORIDA ■

FLORIDA TASK FORCE
Box 10565
Tallahassee, FL 32302

■ GEORGIA ■

LESBIAN AND GAY RIGHTS CHAPTER, ACLU OF GEORGIA
233 Mitchell Street SW, Suite 200
Atlanta, GA 30303
Phone: 404 523 6201

■ HAWAII ■

GAY COMMUNITY CENTER
Box 3224
Honolulu, HI 96801
Phone: 808 536 6000

GAY RIGHTS TASK FORCE
Box 8061
Honolulu, HI 96850

BOTH SIDES NOW
Box 5042
Kahului, Maui, HI 96732
Phone: 808 572 1884

GAYS AND LESBIANS OF HAWAII ISLAND
RR 2, Box 4500
Pahoa, HI 96778
Phone: 808 965 7828

■ IDAHO ■

IDAHO AIDS FOUNDATION
Box 421
Boise, ID 83701

■ ILLINOIS ■

ILLINOIS GAY AND LESBIAN TASK FORCE
615 West Wellington
Chicago, IL 60657
Phone: 312 975 0707

■ INDIANA ■

JUSTICE, INC.
Box 2387
Indianapolis, IN 46206
Phone: 317 634 9212

■ IOWA ■

GAY/LESBIAN RESOURCE CENTER
4211 Grand
Des Moines, IA 50312
Phone: 515 277 1454

IOWA CITIZENS ACTION NETWORK
415 10th Street
Des Moines, IA 50309
Phone: 515 244 9311

■ KANSAS ■

RIGHTFULLY PROUD
Box 674
Topeka, KS 66605

■ KENTUCKY ■

GREATER LOUISVILLE HUMAN RIGHTS COALITION
Box 2653
Louisville, KY 40201

■ LOUISIANA ■

LOUISIANA GAY POLITICAL ACTION CAUCUS
Box 53075
New Orleans, LA 70153
Phone: 504 523 3922

■ MAINE ■

MAINE LESBIAN AND GAY POLITICAL ALLIANCE
Box 232
Hallowell, ME 04347

■ MARYLAND ■

BALTIMORE JUSTICE CAMPAIGN
Box 13221
Baltimore, MD 21203

■ MASSACHUSETTS ■

MASSACHUSETTS GAY AND LESBIAN POLITICAL CAUCUS
Box 246
State House
Boston, MA 02133
Phone: 617 262 1565

■ MICHIGAN ■

MICHIGAN ORGANIZATION FOR HUMAN RIGHTS
Box 27383
Lansing, MI 48909
Phone: 517 887 2605

■ MINNESOTA ■

GAY AND LESBIAN COMMUNITY ACTION COUNCIL
310 East 38th Street
Sabathani Center, Room 204
Minneapolis, MN 55409

■ MISSISSIPPI ■

MISSISSIPPI GAY/LESBIAN ALLIANCE
Box 8342
Jackson, MS 39204
Phone: 601 435 1090

■ MISSOURI ■

PINK TRIANGLE POLITICAL COALITION
Box 411411
Kansas City, MO 64141

PRIVACY RIGHTS EDUCATION PROJECT
Box 24106
St. Louis, MO 63130

■ MONTANA ■

OUT IN MONTANA
Box 951
Helena, MT 59624

■ NEBRASKA ■

COALITION FOR GAY AND LESBIAN CIVIL RIGHTS
Box 94882
Lincoln, NE 68509

■ NEVADA ■

SILVER STATE GAY AND LESBIAN TASK FORCE
Box 50472
Reno, NV 89513

■ NEW HAMPSHIRE ■

CITIZENS ALLIANCE FOR GAY AND LESBIAN RIGHTS
Box 756
Contoocook, NH 03229
Phone: 603 228 9009

■ NEW JERSEY ■

NEW JERSEY LESBIAN AND GAY COALITION
Box 1431
New Brunswick, NJ 08903

■ NEW MEXICO ■

NEW MEXICO LESBIAN AND GAY POLITICAL ALLIANCE
Box 25191
Albuquerque, NM 87125
Phone: 505 243 2540

■ NEW YORK ■

NEW YORK STATE LESBIAN AND GAY LOBBY
Box 932
Albany, NY 12201

■ NORTH CAROLINA ■

NORTH CAROLINA COALITION FOR LESBIAN/GAY EQUALITY
Box 15533
Winston-Salem, NC 27113
Phone: 704 376 6352

NORTH CAROLINA HUMAN RIGHTS FUND
Box 19782
Raleigh, NC 27605
Phone: 919 829 0181

■ OHIO ■

STONEWALL CINCINNATI
Box 954
Cincinnati, OH 45201

STONEWALL UNION
Box 10814
Columbus, OH 43201
Phone: 614 299 7764

■ OKLAHOMA ■

TULSA OKLAHOMANS FOR HUMAN RIGHTS
Box 52729
Tulsa, OK 74152
Phone: 918 743 4297

■ OREGON ■

RIGHT TO PRIVACY PAC
2164 N.W. Aspen
Portland, OR 97210
Phone: 503 224 4369

■ PENNSYLVANIA ■

PHILADELPHIA LESBIAN AND GAY TASK FORCE
1501 Cherry Street
Philadelphia, PA 19102
Phone: 215 563 9584

■ RHODE ISLAND ■

RHODE ISLAND ALLIANCE FOR LESBIAN AND GAY CIVIL RIGHTS
Box 5758, Weybosset Hill Station
Providence, RI 02903

■ SOUTH CAROLINA ■

PALMETTO GAY AND LESBIAN ASSOCIATION
Box 10022, Federal Station
Greenville, SC 29603

■ SOUTH DAKOTA ■

SIOUX EMPIRE GAY COALITION
Box 220
Sioux Falls, SD 57101
Phone: 605 332 4599

■ TENNESSEE ■

TENNESSEE GAY AND LESBIAN ALLIANCE
Box 41305
Nashville, TN 37204
Phone: 615 292 4820

■ TEXAS ■

TEXAS LESBIAN AND GAY RIGHTS LOBBY
Box 2505
Austin, TX 78768
Phone: 512 474 5475

■ UTAH ■

DESERT/MOUNTAIN STATES LESBIAN AND GAY CONFERENCE
Box 1221
Salt Lake City, UT 84110

GAY AND LESBIAN COMMUNITY COUNCIL OF UTAH
Box 3832
Salt Lake City, UT 84110

■ VERMONT ■

VERMONT COALITION FOR LESBIANS AND GAY MEN
Box 1125
Montpelier, VT 05602

■ VIRGINIA ■

VIRGINIANS FOR JUSTICE
Box 342, Capitol Station
Richmond, VA 23202

■ WASHINGTON ■

PRIVACY FUND
1206 E. Pike, Suite 816
Seattle, WA 98122

■ WEST VIRGINIA ■

GAY/LESBIAN MOUNTAINEERS
SOW Mountainlair
West Virginia University
Morgantown, WV 26506

■ WISCONSIN ■

GALVANIZE
Box 310
Madison, WI 53703
Phone: 608 255 8061

CANADA

■ NEW BRUNSWICK ■

NEW BRUNSWICK COALITION FOR HUMAN RIGHTS REFORM
Box 1556, Station A
Fredericton, NB E3B 5G2

■ NEWFOUNDLAND ■

THE GAY ASSOCIATION IN NEWFOUNDLAND
Box 1364, Station C
St. John's, NF A1C 5N5
Phone: 709 739 7975

■ NOVA SCOTIA ■

LESBIAN AND GAY RIGHTS NOVA SCOTIA
Box 7067 North
Halifax, NS B3K 5I4
Phone: 902 455 5729

■ ONTARIO ■

COALITION FOR LESBIAN AND GAY RIGHTS IN ONTARIO
Box 822, Station A
Toronto, ON M5W 1G3

THE RIGHT TO PRIVACY COMMITTEE
428 Dudas Street E
Toronto, ON M5A 2A8

GAY AND LESBIAN DEMOCRATIC ORGANIZATIONS

The Democratic party in the United States has many gay groups within it. The Democrats, while not always on our side, have been much more likely to embrace gay civil rights and make appointments of gay people to administrations and the courts than have the Republicans. Many Republicans, especially those who have a libertarian philosophy, which is based on a strong stand on personal liberties, do find gay issues something they can support. While there may not be as many gay organizations in the Republican party, they are certainly growing in number.

UNITED STATES

■ ALABAMA ■

PRIVACY RIGHTS ORGANIZATION
PAC
P.O. Box 55913
Birmingham, AL 35205

■ ARIZONA ■

ARIZONA GAY/LESBIAN DEMOCRATS
9260 E. Summer Trail
Tucson, AZ 85749

DEMOCRATIC CAUCUS/ARIZONA GAY/LESBIAN TASK FORCE
3637 E. Monterosa, #12
Phoenix, AZ 85018

■ CALIFORNIA ■

EAST BAY LESBIAN/GAY DEMOCRATIC CLUB
P.O. Box 443
Berkeley, CA 94701

GAY & LESBIAN AREA DEMOCRATS
P.O. Box 139
Concord, CA 94522

LAMBDA DEMOCRATIC CLUB
P.O. Box 14454
Long Beach, CA 90803

CALIFORNIA ASSOCIATION OF LESBIAN/GAY DEMOCRATIC CLUBS
3212 Silverado Drive
Los Angeles, CA 90039

STONEWALL DEMOCRATIC CLUB
P.O. Box 38812
Los Angeles, CA 90038

RIVER CITY DEMOCRATIC CLUB
P.O. Box 161958
Sacramento, CA 95816

HARVEY MILK DEMOCRATIC CLUB
P.O. Box 33915
San Diego, CA 92103

SAN DIEGO COUNTY
HARVEY MILK DEMOCRATIC CLUB
P.O. BOX 33915, SAN DIEGO, CA 92103

SAN DIEGO DEMOCRATIC CLUB
P.O. Box 80193
San Diego, CA 92138

ALICE B. TOKLAS DEMOCRATIC CLUB
P.O. Box 11316
San Francisco, CA 94101

HARVEY MILK LESBIAN/GAY DEMOCRATIC CLUB
P.O. Box 14368
San Francisco, CA 94114

LESBIAN/GAY CAUCUS CALIFORNIA DEMOCRATIC PARTY
561 28th Street
San Francisco, CA 94131

STONEWALL LESBIAN/GAY DEMOCRATIC CLUB
473 Corbett Avenue
San Francisco, CA 94114

ELEANOR ROOSEVELT DEMOCRATIC CLUB
3941B Bristol Street, #420
Santa Ana, CA 92704

FREEDOM DEMOCRATIC CAUCUS
1214 King Street
Santa Cruz, CA 95060

SUSAN B. ANTHONY DEMOCRATIC CLUB
705 S. 11th Street
San Jose, CA 95112

GAY & LESBIAN DEMOCRATIC CLUB
P.O. Box 6201
Santa Rosa, CA 95406

WEST HOLLYWOOD DEMOCRATIC CLUB
7548 Lexington Avenue
West Hollywood, CA 90046

■ COLORADO ■

COLORADO LGDC
1029 E. 8th Avenue, #606
Denver, CO 80218

■ DELAWARE ■

ROOSEVELT-MILK DEMOCRATIC CLUB
608 W. 28th Street
Wilmington, DE 19802

■ DISTRICT OF COLUMBIA ■

GERTRUDE STEIN DEMOCRATIC CLUB
P.O. Box 21067
Washington, DC 20009

■ FLORIDA ■

CENTRAL FLORIDA GAY/LESBIAN DEMOCRATS
c/o Ford
1505 Shady Acres Lane
Apopka, FL 32703

ATLANTIC COAST DEMOCRATIC CLUB
618 N.W. 13th Street, #31
Boca Raton, FL 33486

DOLPHIN DEMOCRATIC CLUB
P.O. Box 39502
Ft. Lauderdale, FL 33339-9502

OLDE TOWNE DEMOCRATIC CLUB
P.O. Box 1708
Key West, FL 33040

DADE COUNTY COALITION FOR HUMAN RIGHTS
3775 Poinciana Avenue
Miami, FL 33133

DAN BRADLEY DEMOCRATIC CLUB
3775 Poinciana Avenue
Miami, FL 33133

FLORIDA TASK FORCE
411 Chapel Drive, #226
Tallahassee, FL 32304

BAY AREA RIGHTS COUNCIL
14450 Bruce Downs Boulevard
Tampa, FL 33613

■ GEORGIA ■

LEGAL
P.O. Box 54105
Atlanta, GA 30308-0105

■ HAWAII ■

HAWAII DEMOCRATS FOR GAY/LESBIAN CONCERNS
Box 8061
Honolulu, HI 96830

■ ILLINOIS ■

LGPDO
3225 N. Sheffield
Chicago, IL 60657

PRAIRIE STATE DEMOCRATIC CLUB
c/o Annex, 3160 N. Clark
Chicago, IL 60657

■ IOWA ■

LESBIAN/GAY DEMOCRATIC CAUCUS OF STORY COUNTY
708 Douglas
Ames, IA 50010

DES MOINES GAY/LESBIAN DEMOCRATIC CLUB
3500 Kingman Boulevard
Des Moines, IA 50311

GAY & LESBIAN DEMOCRATS OF IOWA
P.O. Box 611
Iowa City, IA 52244

■ KENTUCKY ■

GAY/LESBIAN DEMOCRATS OF KENTUCKY
P.O. Box 187
Lexington, KY 40584

■ MAINE ■

LESBIAN & GAY DEMOCRATIC CLUB OF MAINE
RFD #1, Box 697
Monmouth, ME 04259

■ MARYLAND ■

BALTIMORE LESBIAN/GAY DEMOCRATIC CLUB
c/o Walker
2277 Park Hill
Baltimore, MD 21211

MONTGOMERY COUNTY GAY DEMOCRATS
7608 Quincewood
Rockville, MD 20855

■ MASSACHUSETTS ■

BAY STATE LESBIAN/GAY DEMOCRATIC CLUB
P.O. Box 6191
JFK Station
Boston, MA 02114

■ MINNESOTA ■

LESBIAN/GAY CAUCUS MN DFL
2414 Stevens Avenue S
Minneapolis, MN 55404

■ MISSISSIPPI ■

MISSISSIPPI LESBIAN/GAY DEMOCRATIC CAUCUS
P.O. Box 8342
Jackson, MS 39204

■ MISSOURI ■

LESBIAN/GAY DEMOCRATS OF MISSOURI
2053 Alfred Street
St. Louis, MO 63110

■ NEW HAMPSHIRE ■

LESBIAN/GAY DEMOCRATS OF NEW HAMPSHIRE
9 Christopher Road
Merrimack, NH 03054

■ NEW MEXICO ■

NEW MEXICO LESBIAN AND GAY POLITICAL ALLIANCE
P.O. Box 25191
Albuquerque, NM 87125

■ NEW YORK ■

ELEANOR ROOSEVELT DEMOCRATIC CLUB
P.O. Box 2180
Albany, NY 12220-2180

BRONX GAY/LESBIAN INDEPENDENT DEMOCRATS
P.O. Box 736, Jerome Avenue Station
Bronx, NY 10468

LAMBDA INDEPENDENT DEMOCRATS
44 Fifth Avenue, #151
Brooklyn, NY 11217

CAUCUS OF LESBIAN/GAY DIST. LEADERS
80 8th Avenue
New York, NY 10011

GAY/LESBIAN INDEPENDENT DEMOCRATS
P.O. Box 7241
New York, NY 10150

STONEWALL DEMOCRATIC CLUB
P.O. Box 1750
Old Chelsea Station
New York, NY 10011

ROCHESTER LESBIAN & GAY POLITICAL CAUCUS
713 Monroe Avenue
Rochester, NY 14607

■ NORTH CAROLINA ■

LESBIAN/GAY DEMOCRATS OF NORTH CAROLINA
P.O. Box 307
Chapel Hill, NC 27514

■ OREGON ■

LESBIAN GAY CAUCUS OF THE OREGON DEMOCRATIC PARTY
1703 S.W. Montgomery Drive
Portland, OR 97201

■ PENNSYLVANIA ■

PHILADELPHIA EQUAL RIGHTS COALITION
4519 Osage
Philadelphia, PA 19143

■ TEXAS ■

LESBIAN/GAY DEMOCRATS OF TEXAS
201 Peach Street
Denton, TX 76201

HOUSTON GAY AND LESBIAN POLITICAL CAUCUS
Box 6664
Houston, TX 77006

■ UTAH ■

LESBIAN & GAY DEMOCRATS OF UTAH
P.O. Box 11213
Salt Lake City, UT 84147

■ VERMONT ■

LESBIAN/GAY CAUCUS OF THE VERMONT DEMOCRATIC PARTY
46 Crowley Street
Burlington, VT 05401

■ WASHINGTON ■

GAY DEMOCRATS OF GREATER SEATTLE
P.O. Box 1975
Seattle, WA 98111

Names and addresses provided by:

Gay and Lesbian Democrats of Americ
114 Fifteenth Street NE
Washington, DC 20002

GAY REPUBLICAN ORGANIZATIONS

The national gay Republican political action committee is:

CIRCL-PAC
Box 93462
Los Angeles, CA 90093
Phone: 714 494 6961

There are also *Log Cabin Clubs* made up of gay Republicans in California:

LOG CABIN CLUB OF ORANGE COUNTY
932 Rembrandt Drive
Laguna Beach, CA 92651

SAN DIEGO LOG CABIN CLUB
c/o Bob Fraas
2046 Camino Loma Verde
San Diego, CA 92084

LOG CABIN CLUB OF SAN FRANCISCO
Box 14174
San Francisco, CA 94114

▼ Money is the grease of politics. To make sure gay opinions are heard, you can contribute to one of the PACs (Political Action Committees) that exist nationally or locally.

The largest gay PAC is run by the Human Rights Campaign Fund. They can also tell you about organizations closer to home. For information:

Human Rights Campaign Fund
1012 14th Street NW, Suite 607
Washington, DC 20005
Phone: 202 628 4160
Fax: 202 347 5323

> *It is from the numberless diverse acts of courage and belief that human history is shaped. Each time a man stands up for an ideal, or acts to improve the lot of others, or strikes out against injustice, he sends a tiny ripple of hope, and crossing each other from a million different centres of energy and daring those ripples build a current which can sweep down the mightiest walls of oppression and resistance.*
>
> —*ROBERT F. KENNEDY*

CREATING CHANGE

▼ *Creating Change* is an annual conference, usually held in the autumn, put on by the National Gay and Lesbian Task Force. The weekend event is designed for gay and lesbian organizing and skill building. Recent conferences included special sessions for people of color and on fund-raising.

The conference offers everything from theoretical debates to informative workshops and keynote speeches, all designed to explore the challenges facing the movement today.

There are limited scholarship funds available.

For more information:

Creating Change Conference
National Gay and Lesbian Task Force
1517 U Street NW
Washington, DC 20009
Phone: 202 332 6483
Fax: 202 332 0207

BUT WHAT DO GAY POLITICAL GROUPS *DO*?

Every state and local political group has its own agenda and establishes its own priorities according to what it feels needs to be done in its locality. *The Gay and Lesbian Activists Alliance of Washington, DC* (GLAA) claims to be the oldest continuously active gay and lesbian civil rights organization in the United States. Here's their statement of purpose. It's indicative of the range of concerns that such groups embrace:

> GLAA is a dynamic organization committed to effecting changes in the perceptions, policies, and politics concerning lesbians and gay men within the community at large.
>
> Changing people's perceptions of lesbians and gays involves GLAA with a wide range of individuals and community groups.
>
> Changing the policies of government, business, education, and the media engages GLAA in a continual process of monitoring, advocating, and occasionally confronting these and other major institutions which impact upon the lives of lesbians and gay men.
>
> GLAA advocates full rights and privileges for all gay men and lesbians through activist participation in the political process. We work to abolish all discriminatory laws and practices, to make government respond to the interests and needs of gay men and lesbians, and to ensure that gays and lesbians are represented in and by the government.
>
> GLAA works with the media to promote fair and accurate portrayals of gay men, lesbians and their interest in press, radio, and television. We advocate for fairness of our cause in the justice system, in employment, housing, education, health services, and any other area which serves gays and lesbians.

GLAA has been very active in meeting the challenges of the current AIDS crisis. We lobby the District government to devote adequate resources for the prevention and treatment of AIDS. GLAA also worked hard to secure the passage of legislation prohibiting the use of antibody tests and any other discriminatory measures which could be used against people at risk for AIDS.

MAKING A POLITICAL ORGANIZATION WORK

Stewart Butler, secretary of ***Louisiana Gay Political Action Caucus,*** gives these reasons for the success of that organization after its founding in 1980.

1. LAGPAC wasn't formed in response to an immediate crisis but because it was time for it to exist.

2. Even though LAGPAC's initial strength was—and continues to be—centered in New Orleans, it was structured to provide for a statewide organization with local chapters wherever there was enough strength to have them. There could be little or no hope of changing things on the all-important state level with only a city base.

3. LAGPAC was established as a nonpartisan organization to allow for the inclusion of as many points of view as possible and to increase the possibility of presenting the only organized point of view. Although it usually endorses Democrats, it has been successful in electing openly gay/lesbian persons to both the Republican and Democratic Orleans Parish Executive Committees and State Central Committees.

4. *Most importantly:* By requiring female and male cochairpersons for both the state board of directors and the local chapters, LAGPAC was structured to decrease the likelihood of male domination. An ongoing effort is made to maintain some semblance of gender parity at all levels of the groups, to recognize the fact that lesbians comprise half of our strength.

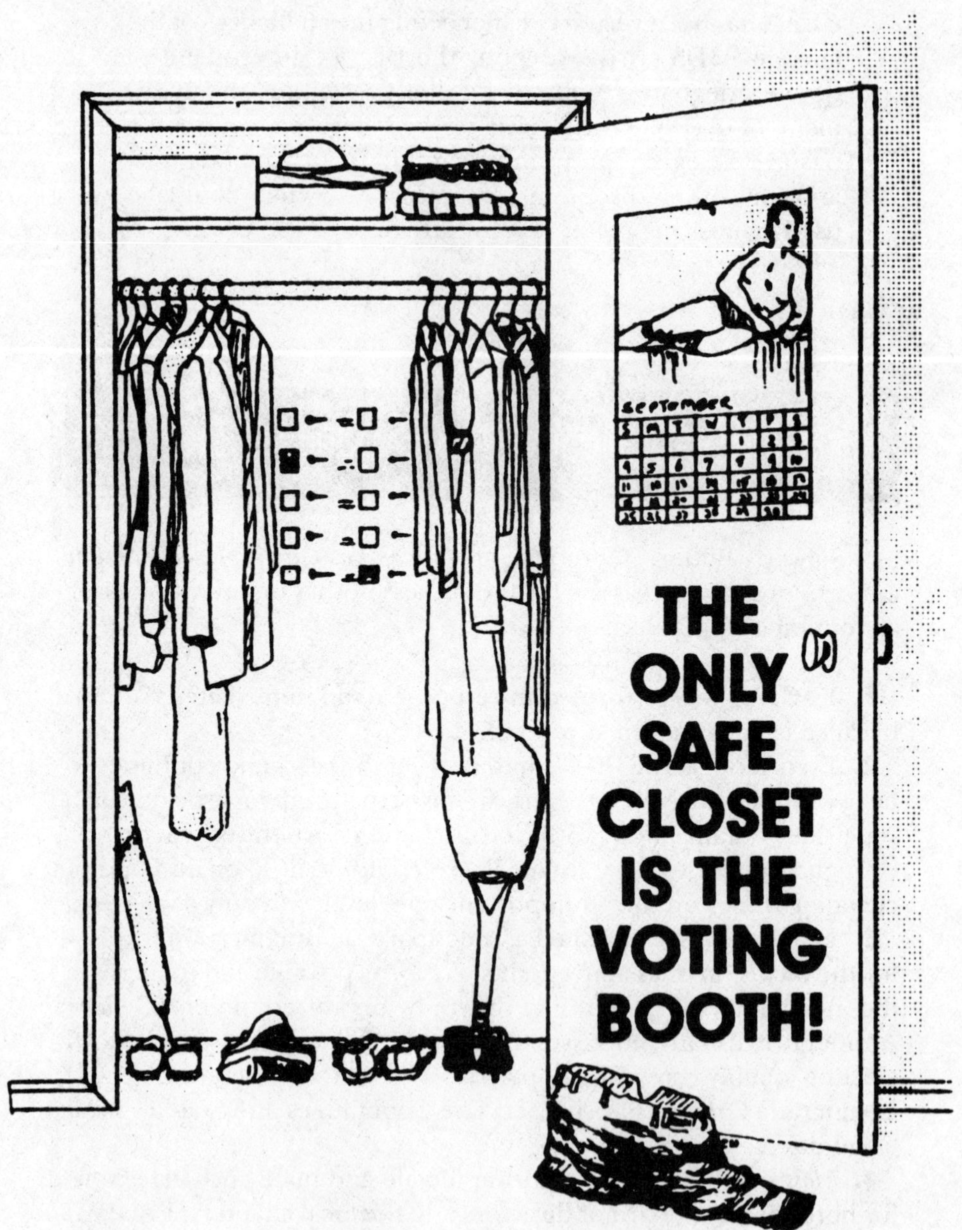

REPRINTED WITH THE PERMISSION OF THE LOUSIANA GAY POLITICAL ACTION CAUCUS.

THE VALUE OF ORGANIZING

Just how important is political activism? ***The Maine Lesbian/Gay Political Alliance*** and the ***Maine Civil Liberties Union*** cosponsored a survey of gay men and lesbians in their state to try to decide just how much discrimination people experienced. The survey included data from 323 respondents from urban and rural areas throughout the state. Similar surveys have been done by ***The National Gay and Lesbian Task Force*** and other organizations around the country with comparable results.

DISCRIMINATION IN EMPLOYMENT

Because of their sexual orientation:

■ 46 percent reported some type of employment discrimination (e.g., fired; not hired; denied raise, promotion, or benefits, apprenticeship or membership in a labor organization; demoted; or lost clients)—in addition, 67 percent have concealed their sexual orientation to avoid employment discrimination
■ 46 percent were questioned about their sexual orientation by an employer
■ 36 percent were the victims of violence at work
■ 19 percent were fired
■ 15 percent were never hired
■ 10 percent were denied promotions, raises, or benefits

DISCRIMINATION IN HOUSING

■ 28 percent reported discrimination in obtaining housing (e.g., denied purchase or rental), while 40 percent reported concealing their sexual orientation to avoid such treatment
■ 8 percent were refused for rental because they were gay

DISCRIMINATION IN PUBLIC ACCOMMODATIONS AND CREDIT

Because of their sexual orientation:

- 24 percent experienced discrimination in public accommodations (e.g., denied room in a hotel or service in a restaurant), while 46 percent reported concealing their sexual orientation to avoid this
- 7 percent were denied service in a restaurant
- 5 percent were denied hotel accommodations
- 4 percent of the respondents experienced credit discrimination (e.g., denial of loans, credit, or other), while 32 percent reported concealing their sexual orientation to avoid discrimination

ACTS OF VIOLENCE AGAINST GAY MEN AND LESBIANS

PHYSICAL VIOLENCE

Because of their sexual orientation:

- 54 percent experienced some kind of violence, while 79 percent reported concealing their sexual orientation to avoid violence; 85 percent knew people who were the victims of violence, and 77 percent anticipated harassment, intimidation, or violence in the future. Respondents reported the following acts of violence:

- 38 percent were chased or followed
- 26 percent had objects thrown at them

- 20 percent had property vandalized or set on fire
- 16 percent were punched, hit, kicked, or beaten
- 11 percent were spat at
- 9 percent were assaulted with an object or weapon

VERBAL ABUSE

Because of their sexual orientation:

- 84 percent of the respondents were called anti-gay/lesbian names
- 45 percent were threatened with physical violence
- 38 percent received verbal abuse from their families
- 14 percent were called names by the police

WHERE DID VIOLENCE AGAINST GAYS OCCUR?

The respondents reported harassment, intimidation, threats, or assault because of their sexual orientation:

- 37 percent in high school
- 31 percent in junior high school
- 39 percent in the family unit
- 48 percent by police (15 percent reported physical abuse)

RESPONDENT DEMOGRAPHICS

OPENNESS WITH OTHERS REGARDING SEXUAL ORIENTATION

- 81 percent were unlikely to be open with acquaintances
- 68 percent were unlikely to be open with coworkers
- 56 percent were unlikely to be open with family members
- 42 percent were unlikely to be open with health care workers

AGE WHEN FIRST AWARE OF SEXUAL ORIENTATION

- 50 percent—by age 13
- 77 percent--by age 18

WHAT TO DO ABOUT GAY BASHING

Gay-bashing—beating up gay men and lesbians—is an increasing problem. AIDS-phobia is only one reason why gay men and lesbians are more vulnerable. Our increased visibility is another. These and other motivations are intensified by a belief on the part of hoodlums that society will sanction their actions. Political pressure and education of police and other authorities are one important element in the struggle against this violence, but self-defense is another important component.

These guidelines are adapted from advice given in a pamphlet by *The Gay and Lesbian Community Action Council* of Minnesota to help reduce your chances of becoming a victim of crime. They're reprinted with permission.

Stay Alert
Awareness is your best self-defense.
Trust Your Feelings
If you think something is wrong, you're right.
Project Confidence
Don't look like an easy mark.

- Be aware of who is in front of you and who is behind you.
- Don't walk alone, especially if you are upset or intoxicated.
- Be aware of who gets off the bus with you.
- Choose busy, well-lit streets.
- Walk near the curb, avoiding doorways, alleys, construction sites, and parks after dark.
- If you feel threatened, cross the street, change direction, or run to a safe place.

■ Don't wear headphones.
■ Have your keys in hand when you reach your home or car.
■ Conceal your money and jewelry.
■ Carry a whistle or "screamer" or shout to attract attention.
■ If you decide to bring someone home, introduce him or her to a friend or acquaintance so that someone knows with whom you left.
■ Harassment is often a prelude to an assault. If you decide to answer back, do so from a safe distance and be prepared to run or fight.

If you are the victim of an attack, *report it!* Anti-gay crime is aided and abetted by a belief that we gay men won't claim our privileges by complaining to the police or our civic organizations. *Call the police!*

■ Call the police and report the details of the assault. Try to remember race, sex, age, height, weight, build, clothes, and other characteristics.
■ If an officer responds at this time, make sure that he/she files an incident report. In most cases, you must file within twenty-four hours to qualify for victim's compensation—another reason to make sure you report this incident.
■ If a police report is not taken at the time of the assault, go to your local police station and file one. Always ask for a copy of the report.

COMMUNICATING WITH YOUR LEGISLATORS

Congress seems remote to most of us, but the decisions made there have a profound impact on our rights, our privacy, our health, even our lives. Most of us mean to write to Congress, and a few actually do, but only once or twice. Often, our good intentions don't get translated into the letters to Congress that will help us win on AIDS and fairness.

The Human Rights Campaign Fund's *Speak Out* program helps bridge that gap of good intentions. You can authorize them to send brief telegram messages on your behalf to key senators and representatives. This system responds to the frequent legislative emergencies whenever key votes come up on short notice. Speak Out allows your messages to be coordinated with on-the-Hill priorities and strategies.

You can authorize a specific number of payments to cover Speak Out messages, usually about $3.25 each. For more information, contact:

Human Rights Campaign Fund
1012 14th Street NW, #607
Washington, DC 20005
Phone: 202 628 4160
Fax: 202 347 5323

HRCF NET (Computer Bulletin Board)
Phone: 202 639 8735

HOW TO WRITE AN EFFECTIVE LETTER

The most basic means of political action are still some of the most effective. Our mass society often makes us feel as though nothing we do could be effective against the size of political movements, but a simple letter to a legislator is still one of the most productive acts we

ILLUSTRATION BY DONELON, REPRINTED WITH PERMISSION OF THE HUMAN RIGHTS CAMPAIGN FUND.

can take to promote our causes. Don't think your letter will be lost in the rush. It can make all the difference.

When you do write to a member of your state legislature or the United States Congress, use these easy guidelines developed by *The Front Page* to make your words all the more forceful:

WHAT TO DO

1. Use your full name, address, and phone number for proper identification and credibility.

2. Sign your name legibly. Type your letter, if possible.

3. Be informed on the subject you are writing about.

4. Be courteous, and, when appropriate, personal.
5. Identify the subject of your letter by bill number, title, and issues, if possible.
6. State the reasons for the position you are taking. Give facts.
7. Indicate how you and others will be affected.
8. Use your own words.
9. Request a specific action.
10. When you receive a reply, follow up with a thank-you letter.
11. On state and local matters, send a copy of your letter to your local gay or lesbian publication.

On federal matters, send a copy of your letter to the National Gay and Lesbian Task Force and the Human Rights Campaign Fund. Send a copy of any response to these groups, as well.

WHAT NOT TO DO:

1. Do not make demands.
2. Do not send mimeographed or photocopied letters.
3. If you are using arguments from material provided by NGLTF, HCRF, or other organizations, *do not copy verbatim.* Change the wording, list the reasons in a different order, or pick one or two of them and relate them to your own experience.
4. Do not mention your membership in any particular organization. Spontaneous "grass roots" letters have much greater impact.

Reproduced with permission of *The Front Page.*

To address a letter to a legislator in Washington, D.C., use these formats:

Senator ——
Senate Office Building
Washington, DC 20510

Representative ——
House Office Building
Washington, DC 20515

On Lesbian/Gay Rights and Health Issues...

GRASSROOTS MAIL MEANS CLOUT.

And now the Campaign Fund makes it simple and easy.

Speak Out!

USING YOUR RIGHT TO PETITION

A basic right in a democracy is to be able to meet with the legislators who represent you at either the state or federal level. Meeting with your senators or representatives can be one of the most effective means of getting their support on gay and lesbian rights and AIDS and other health issues. Whether you are part of a small group or by yourself, your visit is solid evidence that these national issues affect people in the legislator's state or district.

Getting an appointment with your representatives or senators is easier than most people realize. Politicians are usually eager to meet with constituents, even if they disagree on some issues. Simply write or call to request a personal visit. Ask for the appointments secretary or scheduling coordinator. Briefly explain the nature of your visit and explore possible dates. There are times when upcoming legislative developments make this "constituent lobbying" time urgent and you may need to meet with an aide instead of the legislator. However, when possible, it's important to press to meet directly with the senators or representatives.

Your legislators likely return home often and meet with constituents in district offices, particularly on weekends. Or you can make the visits in their offices in Washington or your state capital if that's convenient and possible.

Begin the meeting by thanking the senators or representatives for taking a particular stance. Then let him or her know what you are going to ask.

Focus on how legislation affects people in your own district. For example: "Thousands of people in Des Moines live in fear that they will be fired if someone discovers that they are gay or lesbian. In fact, just last week my friend lost his job because . . ."

If possible, show that your position affects a broad cross-section of the community. Cite any significant support within the district (editorials, support from mayors, city councilors, ministers, labor leaders, etc.).

Anytime you personally visit your senators or representatives (or their staffs) you increase their awareness about issues. The effectiveness of your visits will increase in direct relationship to the amount of follow-up you do. Send letters thanking them for the opportunity to meet.

Use the follow-up letter to reemphasize the important points you discussed during the meeting. For instance, if they agreed to take the position you wanted, thank them for their stance and tell them you will publicize their support in the gay and lesbian community. If they were supportive, but noncommittal, use the letter to refine points and urge additional support. If they were opposed, use your follow-up letter to make points they do agree with and ask questions to further clarify the sources of their resistance. In all cases, ask questions which require a clear response in order to avoid a form letter reply.

If you promised to get back to them with information you didn't have during the meeting, be sure you do so.

Your activities can be even more effective if you coordinate them with one of the larger political groups. Let the Human Rights

Campaign Fund, the National Gay and Lesbian Task Force, and/or your local or state political organization know what you've done and what the results were. Send them photocopies of your correspondence and generally keep them up-to-date. They may be able to put you in touch with other people in your locality who are interested in doing the same work.

ADAPTED FROM *GRASSROOTS MEMO: VISITING YOUR U.S. SENATOR OR REPRESENTATIVE.* COPYRIGHT 1990 HUMAN RIGHTS CAMPAIGN FUND. USED WITH PERMISSION.

THE GAY VOTE

National organizations, including the National Gay and Lesbian Task Force, Dignity/USA, and the Human Rights Campaign Fund, have joined with many local organizations to support *The National Visibility Campaign for the Gay and Lesbian Vote.* The campaign, a nonpartisan effort, is aimed at registering as many gay and lesbian voters as possible and then getting them to the polls to show the strength of the gay electorate. If you're interested in working to have a local campaign, contact:

The National Visibility Campaign for the Gay and Lesbian Vote
c/o Eddie Marriott
330 E. 83rd Street, #27
New York, NY 10028
Phone: 212 737 2319

OPENLY GAY AND LESBIAN ELECTED OFFICIALS

As of this writing, the elected officials listed on the following pages have publicly acknowledged that they are gay or lesbian.

NATIONAL OFFICE

United States Representatives:
Barney Frank (D-Massachusetts)
Gerry Studds (D-Massachusetts)

STATE OFFICE

California Superior Court Judge
Donna Hitchens

Maine State Senator
Dale McCormick

Minnesota State Representative
Karen Clark

Minnesota State Senator
Alan Spear

New York State Assembly Member
Deborah Glick

Oregon State Legislator
Gail Shibley

Washington State Representative
Calvin Anderson

LOCAL OFFICIALS

■ CALIFORNIA ■

Laguna Beach City Council Member
Robert Gentry

Sacramento School Board Member
Gary Miller

San Francisco Supervisors
Harry Britt
Carole Migden
Roberta Achtenberg

San Francisco Board of Education Member
Tom Ammiano

San Mateo County Supervisor
Tom Nolan

Santa Cruz City Council Member
John Laird

Santa Monica City Council Member
Judy Abdo

West Hollywood City Council Member
John Heilman

■ CONNECTICUT ■

State Representative
Joe Graybarz

■ FLORIDA ■

Wilton Manors City Council Member
John R. Fiore

■ MAINE ■

Portland City Council Member
Barbara Wood

■ MASSACHUSETTS ■

Boston City Councilor
David Scondras

Fall River City Council Member
Steve Camara

■ MINNESOTA ■

Minneapolis City Council Member
Brian Coyle

■ MISSOURI ■

Bruncetown City Council Member
Gerald Ulrich

■ NEW YORK ■

Albany City Council Member
Keith C. St. John

Rochester City Council Member
Tim O. Mains

■ NORTH CAROLINA ■

Chapel Hill Town Council Member
Joe Herzenberg

■ WISCONSIN ■

Dane County Supervisors
Tammy S. G. Baldwin
Richard Wagner
D. Earl Bricker

Madison City Aldermen
Jim McFarland
Ricardo Gonzalez

CANADA

NATIONAL OFFICE

Member of the House of Parliament
Svend Robinson

LOCAL OFFICIALS

■ BRITISH COLUMBIA ■

Vancouver Alderman
Gordon Price

This list was compiled with the help of Portland (ME) City Councilor Barbara Wood.

> *I am very lucky to be able to have a profession that allows me to work on changing the status quo in areas that also happen to involve my sexual orientation. I am a lawyer who heads the city of Boston's civil rights office. One third of my office's caseload involves cases dealing with discrimination complaints based on a person's sexual orientation. I am also a policy advisor in the City Administration on the impact and prevention of AIDS in the minority community. This is very fulfilling to me both personally and professionally. I realize I am very lucky.*
>
> —*JIM WILLIAMS, attorney*

LEGAL ORGANIZATIONS

HOW GAY LEGAL GROUPS PROTECT YOUR RIGHTS

Lambda Legal Defense and Education Fund, Inc., is one of the oldest and largest gay legal organizations in the United States. According to its pamphlet "A Description of the Organization and Its Work," Lambda "was founded in 1973 to advance the rights of gay people and lesbians." In recent years, Lambda has also devoted considerable attention to the civil rights issues arising from AIDS, filing and then winning the very first case in the nation alleging discrimination on account of AIDS.

"Lambda pursues test-case litigation in all parts of the country, and in all areas of concern to gay men and lesbians. Case by case, its efforts strip away any respectability afforded sexual orientation discrimination, bringing gay people closer to equal citizenship under the law. The organization's work ultimately benefits all Americans, for it helps to fashion a society that is truly diverse and tolerant."

Here are some of the cases that Lambda lists among its accomplishments:

■ 1972. A state court in New York refused to give Lambda recognition as a "legal assistance corporation." The court said that Lambda was "neither benevolent nor charitable." Lambda appealed to New York's highest court and won a reversal, and its right to exist.
■ Lambda joined with others to challenge restrictions that the University of New Hampshire put on the newly formed Gay Students Organization. The courts nullified the limitations as an infringement of the students' First Amendment rights.
■ Lambda played a key role in the lawsuit that led to the invalidation of New York State's consensual sodomy statute in 1980.
■ Lambda brought the first case in the United States charging discrimination related to AIDS, helping to establish the principle

that laws prohibiting unequal treatment against those with disabilities also protect people with AIDS.

■ In 1986 Lambda became counsel to a Tennessee lesbian mother who was fighting to retain custody of her child. Lambda succeeded in dismissing the long-standing challenge brought against her by the woman's own parents.

GAY LEGAL ORGANIZATIONS

There are a growing number of gay legal organizations around the country. Whether they operate nationally or locally, their existence has meant a continuing presence in the courtroom and in the legislature, challenging archaic laws and promoting the rights of gay groups and organizations to exist.

BAR ASSOCIATION FOR HUMAN RIGHTS OF GREATER NEW YORK
Box 1899
Grand Central Station
New York, NY 10163

BAY AREA LAWYERS FOR INDIVIDUAL FREEDOM
Box 1983
San Francisco, CA 94101
Phone: 415 431 1444

EQUAL RIGHTS ADVOCATE
1370 Mission Street, #300
San Francisco, CA 94103

GAY AND LESBIAN ADVOCATES AND DEFENDERS (GLAD)
Box 218
Boston, MA 02112
Phone: 617 426 1350

LAMBDA LEGAL DEFENSE AND EDUCATION FUND, INC.
666 Broadway, 12th floor
New York, NY 10012
Phone: 212 995 8585

NATIONAL GAY RIGHTS ADVOCATES
540 Castro Street
San Francisco, CA 94114
Phone: 415 863 3624

and

8901 Santa Monica Boulevard
West Hollywood, CA 90069
Phone: 213 650 6200

TEXAS HUMAN RIGHTS FOUNDATION
1014-G N. Lamar Boulevard
Austin, TX 78703

▼ The year 1986, the centenary of the Statue of Liberty, was also a landmark for gay men and lesbians, in New York City and everywhere. In that year, the New York City Council finally approved a bill to extend equal treatment in employment, housing, and public accommodations to all the city's citizens—fifteen years after the introduction of the original bill. New York City, the home of the Statue of Liberty, became the most populous jurisdiction in the United States ever to approve a law protecting gay people.

George Stavrinos created a commemorative statement for Lambda Legal Defense and Education Fund, Inc. The museum-grade lithograph, measuring 18 by 24 inches, is available for $20, plus $2 postage and handling. The profits from the sale go to support Lambda.

Lambda Legal Defense and Education Fund, Inc.
666 Broadway
New York, NY 10012

GAYS AND LESBIANS IN PRISON

Gay Community News has established a *Prison Project.* Seeing gay and lesbian prisoners as a uniquely isolated and ignored population, the Prison Project reaches out to the weakest and least protected of us all. Here's part of their rationale, and information on one of the most important aspects of the project, *The Prison Book Program.*

"There are over half a million prisoners in the United States. The criminal 'justice' business, from cops through judges to prison bureaucrats, being as racist and money/property-oriented as it is, has little interest in providing legal, educational, and other reading material to those they keep in their cages. Often the most "spirited" (resistant!) are isolated (for their own 'protection'): jailhouse lawyers who are filing suits on prison conditions, organizers inside who are blunting the divide-and-rule racist/homophobic techniques of the administrations. Access to law or general libraries is sometimes limited especially for those in isolation who need them most. More and more what have passed for prison libraries (westerns and romances) are being converted into dormitories as overcrowding increases at a rate of a double-in-population every ten years.

"Prisoners *need* educational (GED, etc.), legal (rights, process, etc.), and stimulating political/cultural reading material desperately. What little is available to them is largely religious (Christian).

"Regional programs (your state, for example, or even just one prison) would be especially effective. Prisoners show their gratitude generously and teach you something about how *your* criminal justice system works.

"Prison Book Program has fifteen years of experience in sending reading material to prisoners. We're writing a brochure on the 'tricks' of getting books in, and getting started. Please send for a free copy of 'Books for Prisoners' ":

Prison Book Project
Gay Community News
62 Berkeley Street
Boston, MA 02116
Phone: 617 426 4469

▼ Another enterprise interested in working with prisoners is run by *Dignity*, the Roman Catholic gay organization. One of the main functions of the *Dignity Prison Ministry* is to put people on the inside of prison walls in touch with those on the outside. There is no expectation that those on the outside will or should send money or gifts. The exchange of personal perceptions and support is the real goal.

For information on how people are paired up, write:

Dignity Prison Ministry
1500 Massachusetts Avenue NW
Suite 11
Washington, DC 20005

LEGAL INFORMATION RESOURCES

The Section on Gay and Lesbian Legal Issues of the Association of American Law Schools publishes a newsletter, *Lesbian/Gay Law Notes*, which is circulated to members, all lesbian and gay law student groups in the country, and other interested people.

In addition to the newsletter, the group produces programs on legal issues of concern to gay men and lesbians at the association's annual meeting; advocates within the association for policies supportive of lesbian and gay people in law schools and the legal profession; conducts surveys and compiles information about law school policies relevant to gay issues; and shares information about teaching materials useful to those who wish to introduce those issues in their law school classes. Contact:

Arthur S. Leonard
Professor of Law
New York Law School
57 Worth Street
New York, NY 10013

Law & Sexuality: A Review of Lesbian and Gay Legal Issues, a new journal edited by students at Tulane Law School in New Orleans, Louisiana, is the first national law journal devoted exclusively to issues of concern to the lesbian and gay community. Its goal is to encourage creative legal approaches to issues of sexual orientation while keeping people informed of developments in lesbian and gay rights. The first issue is scheduled for publication in July 1991. Unsolicited manuscripts are welcome.

Here are the reasons the staff mention as proof of the need for such a law review:

"Lawyers defending lesbian and gay legal clients are currently hampered by the absence of a comprehensive source of information on legal issues affecting the lesbian and gay community. This lack of information also contributes to the misunderstandings underlying the discrimination and bigotry currently faced by lesbians and gay men in this country. The three major purposes of *Law & Sexuality* are:

1. To provide a legal research resource needed by lawyers to effectively represent lesbian and gay clients.
2. To disseminate thought-provoking analyses that will foster greater understanding of lesbian and gay concerns.
3. To offer Tulane Law School students an opportunity to learn about lesbian and gay legal issues while gaining valuable legal research and writing skills."

For information:

Law & Sexuality
Tulane Law School
6801 Freret Street
New Orleans, LA 70118

Immigration and emigration can be one of the most difficult issues for gay men. No one should try to enter the United States or Canada without firm and expert legal advice. In both countries, a bungled attempt at entry could lead to permanently being barred from reentering. Please, if you or your lover is interested in changing citizenship, getting proper documents for a long non-tourist, non-student stay, seek help from one of these organizations. If they don't have the expertise you need, they can help you find a source for it.

THE AMERICAN CIVIL LIBERTIES UNION

The ACLU is one non-gay organization that is committed to gay rights. The local ACLU may, in fact, function as the gay rights organization in some cities. The various chapters are all available to work with you on any case that might have gay civil rights or other libertarian implications.

If you have any questions about the law and gay people, check with the ACLU, if there's not a gay organization nearby to help you.

American Civil Liberties Union
132 W. 43rd Street, Fifth Floor
New York, NY 10036
212 944 9800

■ NATIONAL WASHINGTON OFFICE ■

ACLU
Mort Halperin
122 Maryland Avenue NE
Washington, DC 20002
Phone: 202 544 1681

■ ALABAMA ■

ACLU
P.O. Box 447
Montgomery, AL 36101
Phone: 205 262 0304

■ ALASKA ■

ACLU
P.O. Box 201844
Anchorage, AK 99520-1884
Phone: 907 276 2258

■ ARIZONA ■

ACLU
2021 N. Central, #301
Phoenix, AZ 85004
Phone: 602 252 7627

■ ARKANSAS ■

ACLU
209 W. Capitol
Suite 214
Little Rock, AR 72201
Phone: 501 374 2660

■ CALIFORNIA ■

Northern California
ACLU
1663 Mission Street
Suite 460
San Francisco, CA 94103
Phone: 415 621 2493

Southern California
ACLU
633 S. Shatto Place
Los Angeles, CA 90005
Phone: 213 487 1720

San Diego
ACLU
1202 Kettner Boulevard
Suite 6200
San Diego, CA 92101
Phone: 619 232 2532

■ COLORADO ■

ACLU
815 E. 22nd Avenue
Denver, CO 80205
Phone: 303 861 2258

■ CONNECTICUT ■

ACLU
32 Grand Street
Hartford, CT 06106
Phone: 203 247 9823

■ DELAWARE ■

ACLU
903 French Street
Wilmington, DE 19801
Phone: 302 654 3966

■ DISTRICT OF COLUMBIA ■

ACLU
1400 20th Street NW, #119
Washington, DC 20036
Phone: 202 457 0804

■ FLORIDA ■

ACLU
225 N.E. 34th Street
Suite 208
Miami, FL 33137
Phone: 305 576 2337

■ GEORGIA ■

ACLU
233 Mitchell Street SW
Suite 200
Atlanta, GA 30303
Phone: 404 523 6201

■ HAWAII ■

ACLU
P.O. Box 3410
Honolulu, HI 96801
Phone: 808 545 1722

■ ILLINOIS ■

ACLU
20 E. Jackson Boulevard
Suite 1600
Chicago, IL 60604
Phone: 312 427 7330

■ INDIANA ■

ACLU
445 N. Pennsylvania Street
Suite 911
Indianapolis, IN 46204
Phone: 317 635 4059

■ IOWA ■

ACLU
409 Shops Building
Des Moines, IA 50309
Phone: 515 243 3988

■ KANSAS & WESTERN MISSOURI ■

ACLU
106 E. 31 Terrace
Kansas City, MO 64111
Phone: 816 531 7121

■ KENTUCKY ■

ACLU
425 W. Muhammad Ali Boulevard
Suite 230
Louisville, KY 40202

■ LOUISIANA ■

ACLU
921 Canal Street
Suite 1237
New Orleans, LA 70112
Phone: 504 522 0628

■ MAINE ■

ACLU
97A Exchange Street
Portland, ME 04101
Phone: 207 774 8087

■ MARYLAND ■

ACLU
Equitable Building
Suite 405
10 N. Calvert Street
Baltimore, MD 21202
Phone: 301 576 1104

■ MASSACHUSETTS ■

ACLU
19 Temple Place
Boston, MA 02111
Phone: 617 482 3170

■ MICHIGAN ■

ACLU
1701 David Whitney Building
1553 Woodward Avenue
Detroit, MI 48226-2003
Phone: 313 961 7728

■ MINNESOTA ■

ACLU
1021 W. Broadway
Minneapolis, MN 55411
Phone: 612 522 9734

■ MISSISSIPPI ■

ACLU
921 N. Congress Street
Jackson, MS 39202
Phone: 601 355 6464

■ EASTERN MISSOURI ■

ACLU
4557 Laclede Avenue
St. Louis, MO 63108
Phone: 314 361 2111

■ MONTANA ■

ACLU
P.O. Box 3012
Billings, MT 59103
Phone: 406 248 1086

■ NEBRASKA ■

ACLU
633 S. 9th Street, Lower Level 10
Box 81455
Lincoln, NE 68508
Phone: 402 476 8091

■ NEVADA ■

ACLU
1824 Goldring Avenue
Las Vegas, NV 89106
Phone: 702 387 0320

■ NEW HAMPSHIRE ■

ACLU
11 S. Main Street
Concord, NH 03301
Phone: 603 224 5591

■ NEW JERSEY ■

ACLU
2 Washington Place
Newark, NJ 07102
Phone: 201 642 2086

■ NEW MEXICO ■

ACLU
130 Alvarado Drive NE
Albuquerque, NM 87108
Phone: 505 266 5915

■ NEW YORK ■

ACLU
132 W. 43rd Street, 2d floor
New York, NY 10036
Phone: 212 382 0557

■ NORTH CAROLINA ■

ACLU
P.O. Box 28004
Raleigh, NC 27611
Phone: 919 834 3466

■ OHIO ■

ACLU
360 S. Third Street
Suite 150
Columbus, OH 43215-5463
Phone: 614 228 8951

Cleveland Chapter
ACLU
1223 W. 6th Street, 2d floor
Cleveland, OH 44113
Phone: 216 781 6278

■ OKLAHOMA ■

ACLU
P.O. Box 799
Oklahoma City, OK 73101
Phone: 405 525 3831

■ OREGON ■

ACLU
705 Board of Trade Building
310 S.W. Fourth Avenue
Portland, OR 97204
Phone: 503 274 8257

■ PENNSYLVANIA ■

ACLU
P.O. Box 1161
Philadelphia, PA 19105-1161
Phone: 215 592 1513

Pittsburgh Chapter
ACLU
237 Oakland Avenue
Pittsburgh, PA 15213
Phone: 412 681 7864

■ RHODE ISLAND ■

ACLU
212 Union Street, Room 211
Providence, RI 02903
Phone: 401 831 1230

■ SOUTH CAROLINA ■

ACLU
533-B Harden Street
Columbia, SC 29205
Phone: 803 771 6520

■ TENNESSEE ■

ACLU
P.O. Box 120160
Nashville, TN 37212
Phone: 615 320 7143

■ TEXAS ■

ACLU
1611 E. First Street
Austin, TX 78702-4455
Phone: 512 477 5849

Dallas Chapter
ACLU
P.O. Box 215135
Dallas, TX 75221
Phone: 214 528 5654

Houston Chapter
ACLU
1236 West Gray
Houston, TX 77019
Phone: 713 524 6021

■ UTAH ■

ACLU
Boston Building
9 Exchange Place, Suite 701
Salt Lake City, UT 84111
Phone: 801 533 8206

■ VERMONT ■

ACLU
100 State Street
Montpelier, VT 05602
Phone: 802 223 6304

■ VIRGINIA ■

ACLU
6 N. 6th Street
Suite 2
Richmond, VA 23219-2419
Phone: 804 649 8140

■ WASHINGTON ■

ACLU
1720 Smith Tower
Seattle, WA 98104
Phone: 206 624 2184

■ WEST VIRGINIA ■

ACLU
P.O. Box 1509
Charleston, WV 25325
Phone: 304 342 5066

■ WISCONSIN ■

ACLU
207 E. Buffalo Street, #325
Milwaukee, WI 53202
Phone: 414 272 4032

■ WYOMING ■

ACLU
P.O. Box A
Laramie, WY 82070
Phone: 307 742 0945

STATES WITH PUBLIC EMPLOYMENT PROTECTION FOR GAY MEN AND LESBIANS

STATE	DATE ENACTED
California	April 1979
Illinois	November 1981
Maryland	N.A.
Massachusetts	December 1989
Michigan	March 1981
Minnesota	November 1986
New Mexico	April 1985
New York	November 1983
Ohio	December 1983
Pennsylvania	September 1978
Rhode Island	August 1985
Washington	December 1985
Wisconsin*	March 1982

*FULL EQUAL RIGHTS FOR HOMOSEXUALS

Source: NATIONAL GAY AND LESBIAN TASK FORCE

MUNICIPALITIES AND COUNTIES WITH EMPLOYMENT PROTECTION

Municipality	Public Employment	Employment	Union Practices
Alexandria, VA	■	■	
Alfred, NY	■	■	■
Amherst, MA	■	■	■
Ann Arbor, MI	■	■	■
Aspen, CO	■	■	
Atlanta, GA	■		
Austin, TX	■	■	■
Baltimore, MD	■	■	
Berkeley, CA	■	■	■
Boston, MA	■	■	■
Boulder, CO	■	■	
Buffalo, NY	■		
Burlington, VT	■	■	
Cambridge, MA	■	■	■
Champaign, IL	■	■	■
Chapel Hill, NC	■		
Chicago, IL	■	■	
Columbus, OH	■	■	
Cupertino, CA	■		
Davis, CA	■	■	■
Dayton, OH	■		
Denver, CO	■		
Detroit, MI	■	■	■
East Hampton, NY	■	■	
East Lansing, MI	■	■	■
Evanston, IL	■		
Gaithersburg, MD	■	■	■
Harrisburg, PA	■	■	■

Hartford, CT	■		
Honolulu, HI	■		
Houston, TX	■		
Iowa City, IA	■	■	■
Ithaca, NY	■	■	■
Laguna Beach, CA	■	■	■
Los Angeles, CA	■	■	■
Madison, WI	■	■	■
Malden, MA	■	■	■
Marshall, MN	■	■	
Milwaukee, WI	■		
Minneapolis, MN	■	■	■
Mountain View, CA	■		
New York, NY	■	■	■
Oakland, CA	■	■	■
Olympia, CA	■		
Philadelphia, PA	■	■	■
Portland, OR	■		
Pullman, WA	■		
Raleigh, NC	■		
Rochester, NY	■		
Sacramento, CA	■	■	■
San Francisco, CA	■	■	■
Santa Barbara, CA	■		
Santa Cruz, CA	■		
Seattle, WA	■	■	■
Troy, NY	■		
Tucson, AZ	■	■	■
Urbana, IL	■	■	
Washington, DC	■	■	■
West Hollywood, CA	■	■	■
Yellow Springs, OH	■	■	■

County			
Arlington County, VA	■		
Clallam County, WA	■		
Cuyahoga County, OH	■		
Dane County, WI	■		
Essex County, NJ	■		
Hennepin County, MN	■		
Howard County, MD	■	■	■
Ingraham County, MI	■		
Minnehaha County, SD	■		
Montgomery County, MD	■	■	■
Northampton County, PA	■		
San Mateo County, CA	■	■	
Santa Barbara County, CA	■		
Santa Cruz County, CA	■		
Suffolk County, NY	■		

Source: NATIONAL GAY AND LESBIAN TASK FORCE

SPECIAL INTEREST ORGANIZATIONS

There's a need for special interest organizations whenever there's a racial, ethnic, or other commonality that exists between some gay men. Certainly racial organizations are an obvious example. There are times and places where gay men of color need to be together, to work on the site where racial and sexual politics come together and affect them in a profoundly unique manner. Too, most general gay organizations are dominated by whites in our society and are too willing to overlook their own racism and the effect their attitudes have on current or potential members of color.

AFRICAN-AMERICAN ORGANIZATIONS

NATIONAL COALITION FOR BLACK LESBIANS AND GAYS
Box 19248
Washington, DC 20036

THE BLACK GAY AND LESBIAN LEADERSHIP FORUM
Box 29812
Los Angeles, CA 90027
Phone: 213 667 2549

Black Gay & Lesbian Leadership Forum

■ CALIFORNIA ■

BAY AREA BLACK LESBIANS AND GAYS
437 Webster Street
San Francisco, CA 94117

BLK
BLK Publishing Company
Box 83912
Los Angeles, CA 90083
Phone: 213 410 0808

BLK is a monthly publication for the black gay community. It offers news, reviews, essays and general reportage.

THIRD WORLD CAUCUS
Alice B. Toklas Lesbian/Gay Democratic Club
Box 11316
San Francisco, CA 94101

■ DISTRICT OF COLUMBIA ■

D.C. COALITION OF BLACK GAY WOMEN AND MEN
Box 50622
Washington, DC 20004

FAITH TEMPLE
Box 386
Howard University
Washington, DC 20059

■ GEORGIA ■

GAY ATLANTA MINORITY ASSOCIATION
Box 3381
Atlanta, GA 30302

■ ILLINOIS ■

CHICAGO COALITION OF BLACK LESBIANS AND GAYS
c/o Max Smith
5633 North Winthrop
Chicago, IL 60660

COMMITTEE ON BLACK GAY MEN
Box 7209
Chicago, IL 60611

■ LOUISIANA ■

LANGSTON/JONES
c/o Kohn
Box 5061
New Orleans, LA 70150

■ MARYLAND ■

BALTIMORE COALITION OF BLACK LESBIANS AND GAYS
Box 22575
Baltimore, MD 21203

■ MASSACHUSETTS ■

BLACK MEN'S ASSOCIATION
Box 196, Astor Station
Boston, MA 02123

■ MICHIGAN ■

DETROIT COALITION OF BLACK LESBIANS AND GAYS
Box 31-5177
Detroit, MI 48231

■ MINNESOTA ■

IRUWA
Box 19146
Minneapolis, MN 55419

■ NEW YORK ■

GAY, BISEXUAL, LESBIANS OF COLOR
Cornell University
535 Willard Straight Hall
Ithaca, NY 14853

GAY MEN OF AFRICAN DESCENT
Box 2519
New York, NY 10185
Phone: 718 802 0162/718 756 1548

OTHER COUNTRIES
Box 3142, Church Street Station
New York, NY 10008

■ NORTH CAROLINA ■

TRIANGLE COALITION OF BLACK LESBIANS AND GAYS
604 W. Chapel Hill Street
Durham, NC 27701

■ PENNSYLVANIA ■

ADODI
Box 19312, Kingsessing Station
Philadelphia, PA 19143

■ TENNESSEE ■

MEMPHIS BLACK GAY SUPPORT
1285 Niese
Memphis, TN 38106

THIS LIST WAS COMPILED WITH THE HELP OF ESSEX HEMPHILL.

STATEMENT OF PURPOSE: NATIONAL COALITION OF BLACK LESBIANS AND GAYS

Black Pride and Solidarity:
The New Movement of Black Lesbians and Gays

As a national organization, we are committed to building solidarity between black lesbians and gays, transpersons, and with our heterosexual sisters and brothers, with the understanding that an end to the oppression of black people requires the full participation, dedication, and commitment of us all.

We are committed to fighting for an end to lesbian and gay oppression, racism, sexism, class oppression, militarism, and all the barriers which interfere with our right to live in peace and harmony. We stand in solidarity with movements for liberation and social justice.

We condemn the increasing racist attacks against the black community, and other people of color. We condemn the increasing right wing attacks against the lesbian and gay community.

We are the National Coalition of Black Lesbians and Gays, a national political and educational organization, providing support and advocacy for individuals and organizations on issues affecting the black lesbian and gay community.

Purposes:

1. To actively work against racism, sexism, ageism, classism, homo-

phobia, and any other form of discrimination with the black community and the gay community.

2. To create positive attitudes between and among black non-gays and black gays.

3. To improve the working and social relationship between and among black lesbians and black gay men.

4. To raise the consciousness of black lesbians and black gay men on major local, national, and international issues.

5. To stimulate wholesome and soulful sociopolitical atmospheres for black lesbians and black gay men.

6. To work cooperatively with other national and local lesbian/gay organizations in pursuit of human/civil rights.

7. To work cooperatively with other national and local black organizations in pursuit of human/civil rights.

8. To support the struggles for human and civil rights for all including—but not limited to—women, youth, physically challenged, senior citizens, prisoners, Native Americans, Asians, Latin Americans et al.

9. To promote coalition building and unity among and between black lesbians and black gay men.

LOOKING FOR LANGSTON (SANKOFA FILM & VIDEO, 1989) DIRECTED BY ISAAC JULIEN IS A POWERFUL CINEMATIC EXPRESSION OF THE AFRO-AMERICAN GAY EXPERIENCE. COPYRIGHT 1989, THIRD WORLD NEWSREEL.

10. To pursue political power and recognition in non-partisan, non-violent, but aggressive ways for the survival and growth/ acceptance of ourselves as black lesbians and gay men.
11. To maintain and stress the beauty of black culture and lesbian/ gay culture, thereby projecting our motto: "As Proud of Our Gayness as We Are of Our Blackness."

▼ A common—and usually valid—complaint by many African-Americans is that there are not enough people of color helping to fill the ranks of gay and lesbian leaders. WIM Publications, a black-owned, women-owned publishing house, has taken up the baton to fill the need. They're creating a "Black List" of people and organizations that are willing to appear, organize, and otherwise serve as liaisons for organizations that have little outreach to the African-American community. WIM invites all black gay and lesbian people to send in a statement of their skills and talents, addresses and phone numbers. The listing will be made available for a small fee as soon as it's complete.

WIM Publications
3601 Crowell Road, Suite 100
Turlock, CA 95380

▼ *The National Black Gay and Lesbian Leadership Conference* is an annual event designed to promote leadership skills and networking for black gay and lesbian pioneers and administrators in the fields of politics, education, and the arts. For information on the next conference:

The Black Gay and Lesbian Leadership Forum
Box 29812
Los Angeles, CA 90027
Phone: 213 667 2549

ASIAN ORGANIZATIONS

The following list of organizations for gay and lesbian people of Asian descent and their friends was compiled with the help of Asian/Pacific Lesbians and Gays, Inc., of Los Angeles.

UNITED STATES

■ CALIFORNIA ■

APL NETWORK
P.O. Box 2594
Daly City, CA 94017-2594

GARP—GAY ASIAN RAP
P.O. Box 461104
Los Angeles, CA 90046

GLASS
c/o Jim Mitsuo Cua
P.O. Box 89174
San Diego, CA 92138-9174

LAVENDAR GODZILLA
P.O. Box 421884
San Francisco, CA 941142-1884

LONG YANG EAST (OF MALAYSIA)
c/o Pacific Friends
544 Clipper Street
San Francisco, CA 94114

PACIFIC FRIENDS
246 Faxon Avenue
San Francisco, CA 94112

PACIFIC FRIENDS—SOUTH BAY
P.O. Box 8262
San Jose, CA 95155

A/PLG INC.
Box 443, Suite 109
7985 Santa Monica Boulevard
West Hollywood, CA 90046-5111

■ ILLINOIS ■

ASIANS & FRIENDS—CHICAGO
P.O. Box 11313
Chicago, IL 60611

■ MASSACHUSETTS ■

ALLIANCE FOR MASSACHUSETTS ASIAN LESBIANS & GAY MEN
P.O. Box 543
Prudential Station
Boston, MA 02199

■ NEW YORK ■

ASIAN/PACIFIC STUDENTS ALLIANCE
Hunter College
Box 221 DSSG
695 Park Avenue
New York, NY 10021

ASIANS & FRIENDS—NEW YORK
P.O. Box 6628, Grand Central Station
New York, NY 10163-6023

■ PENNSYLVANIA ■

ASIAN LESBIAN AND GAY ASSOCIATION OF PHILADELPHIA
P.O. Box 58815
Philadelphia, PA 19102

■ VIRGINIA ■

"SILK ROAD" ASIANS & FRIENDS—WASHINGTON
P.O. Box 1695
Falls Church, VA 22041

■ WASHINGTON ■

APLG—PACIFIC NORTHWEST
1218 Third Avenue, #2010
Seattle, WA 98101-3016

CANADA

■ BRITISH COLUMBIA ■

GAY ASIANS OF VANCOUVER
3-1230 W. 12th Street
Vancouver, BC W6H 1M1

■ ONTARIO ■

GAY ASIANS TORONTO "CELEBRASIAN"
Box 752, Station F
Toronto, ON M4Y 2N6

INTERRACIAL ORGANIZATIONS

Race is such an overwhelming factor in the United States and Canada that it has had to become a focus for the work of some people in our community. These organizations exist to help overcome some of the barriers between whites and blacks and members of other racial minorities.

THE NATIONAL ASSOCIATION OF BLACK AND WHITE MEN TOGETHER

Local chapters of this organization sometimes use names different than Black and White Men Together (BWMT) to reflect their multi-racial and multi-cultural membership. Those local chapters that use the initials MACT call themselves Men of All Colors Together. Those which use the initials MACCT call themselves Men of All Colors and Cultures Together.

UNITED STATES

■ CALIFORNIA ■

BWMT-LOS ANGELES
7985 Santa Monica Boulevard
#109-136
West Hollywood, CA 90046
Phone: 213 664 4716

BWMT-SAN FRANCISCO
2261 Market Street, #506
San Francisco, CA 94114
Phone: 415 931 2963

■ CONNECTICUT ■

MACT-CONNECTICUT
P.O. Box 12332
Hartford, CT 06112

■ DISTRICT OF COLUMBIA ■

BWMT-WASHINGTON, DC
P.O. Box 73111
Washington, DC 20056

■ FLORIDA ■

MACT-JACKSONVILLE
1231 King Street
Jacksonville, FL 32204

BWMT-TALLAHASSEE/BIG BEND
c/o Ollie Lee Taylor
411 Chapel Drive, #226
Tallahassee, FL 32304
Phone: 904 222 0684

■ GEORGIA ■

BWMT-ATLANTA
P.O. Box 1334
Atlanta, GA 30301
Phone: 404 794 2968

■ ILLINOIS ■

BWMT-CHICAGO
P.O. Box 14622
Chicago, IL 60614
Phone: 312 334 2012

■ INDIANA ■

BWMT-INDIANAPOLIS
P.O. Box 88784
Indianapolis, IN 46205

■ KENTUCKY ■

BWMT-LOUISVILLE
1321 S. Preston Street
Louisville, KY 40208

■ MARYLAND ■

BWMT-BALTIMORE
P.O. Box 22472
Baltimore, MD 21203

■ MASSACHUSETTS ■

MACT-BOSTON
c/o GCN Box 1
62 Berkeley Street
Boston, MA 02116

■ MICHIGAN ■

BWMT-DETROIT
P.O. Box 8831
Detroit, MI 48224

■ MISSOURI ■

BWMT-KANSAS CITY
P.O. Box 412432
Kansas City, MO 64141

■ NEW YORK ■

MACT-NEW YORK
P.O. Box 1518, Ansonia Station
New York, NY 10023
Phone: 212 245 6366/212 222 9794

■ OHIO ■

MACT-CINCINNATI
P.O. Box 19421
Cincinnati, OH 45219
Phone: 513 751 7659/513 242 2761

BWMT-CLEVELAND
P.O. Box 5144
Cleveland, OH 44101

YOUNGSTOWN ASSOCIATION BWMT
P.O. Box 1346
Youngstown, OH 44501
Phone: 216 782 3483/216 747 3624

■ PENNSYLVANIA ■

BWMT-PHILADELPHIA
P.O. Box 42257
Philadelphia, PA 19101

■ TENNESSEE ■

BWMT-MEMPHIS
P.O. Box 41773
Memphis, TN 38174
Phone: 901 272 3705/901 278 7092/901 726 1461

■ TEXAS ■

MACT-DALLAS
c/o Al Kennon
9409 Thornberry
Dallas, TX 75220
Phone: 214 357 7897

■ WASHINGTON ■

MACCT-SEATTLE
P.O. Box 12348
Seattle, WA 98111
Phone: 206 325 9833

■ WISCONSIN ■

BWMT-MILWAUKEE
P.O. Box 12292
Milwaukee, WI 53212

OTHER ETHNIC ORGANIZATIONS

Gay Native Americans and gay Native Canadians are among the most ignored parts of our world, even though many of the icons and symbols of gay male life come from our romantic image of Indian life and lore.

Living the Spirit: A Gay American Anthology, compiled by Gay American Indians with the help of coordinating editor Will Roscoe (New York: St. Martin's Press, 1988), is an attempt to let gay Native Americans and Native Canadians speak in their own words. The anthology is a vital contribution to the completeness of our self-image.

▼ *Two Eagles: An International Native American Gay and Lesbian Quarterly* is the publication of American Indian Gays and Lesbians.

The quarterly reports on AIGL's activities and also publishes poetry, fiction, and essays by gay and lesbian Native Americans.

American Indian Gays and Lesbians
Box 10229
Minneapolis, MN 55458

▼ *The Gay and Lesbian Arabic Society* (GLAS) is the first such group in the world—including the Middle East. The group is open to gays and lesbians of Arabic descent and their supporters. Its purpose is to provide a support network for Arab men and women and a vehicle for gay Arab visibility.

GLAS sponsors social events in its DC base and publishes a newsletter for more formal communication with other people around the country and the world.

The Arabic Society
Box 4971
Washington, DC 20008

THE HEARING IMPAIRED

The deaf haven't been recognized as a special interest organization for long. While they've often fought against the dehumanization and stereotyping that society has laid on them, we've not often paid attention to their issues.

Only recently have deaf protests against their treatment in the educational system and at the hands of professionals who claimed their world as their own private work made a difference in the society's perception.

The gay deaf have organized themselves around the United States and Canada. They offer supportive situations for the newly coming out and also a place where the deaf can meet one another and construct mutually important relationships.

The Rainbow Alliance is the national umbrella organization for these groups.

UNITED STATES

RAINBOW ALLIANCE OF THE DEAF
P.O. Box 14182
Washington, DC 20044-4182

■ CALIFORNIA ■

ORANGE COUNTY RAINBOW SOCIETY OF THE DEAF
4412 S. Constitution Avenue
Orange, CA 92669

SOUTHERN CALIFORNIA LAMBDA ASSOCIATION OF THE DEAF
c/o Lee Ellis
4192 33rd Street, #1
San Diego, CA 92104

RAINBOW DEAF SOCIETY
P.O. Box 1606
San Francisco, CA 94101

SAN JOSE LAMBDA SOCIETY OF THE DEAF
P.O. Box 90035
San Jose, CA 95109-3035

SOUTHERN CALIFORNIA RAINBOW SOCIETY OF THE DEAF
P.O. Box 2686
Van Nuys, CA 91404

■ COLORADO ■

MILE HIGH RAINBOW SOCIETY OF THE DEAF
P.O. Box 86
Denver, CO 80201

■ DISTRICT OF COLUMBIA ■

CAPITAL METROPOLITAN RAINBOW ALLIANCE
P.O. Box 33257
Washington, DC 20033

■ FLORIDA ■

COCONUT CITY SOCIETY OF THE DEAF
P.O. Box 15681
Plantation, FL 33318

■ MARYLAND ■

MARYLAND LAMBDA DEAF ALLIANCE
P.O. Box 4479
Baltimore, MD 21223

■ NEW JERSEY ■

NEW JERSEY RAINBOW ALLIANCE OF THE DEAF
c/o Don Smith
48 Hill Street, Apt. #504
Bloomfield, NJ 07003

■ OHIO ■

BUCKEYE RAINBOW SOCIETY OF THE DEAF
P.O. Box 6253
Cleveland, OH 44101-1253

■ OREGON ■

NORTHWEST RAINBOW ALLIANCE OF THE DEAF
c/o Tim Amundson
7518 S.W. Barnes Road, #A
Portland, OR 97225

■ TEXAS ■

CEN TEX RAINBOW SOCIETY OF THE DEAF
P.O. Box 2555
Austin, TX 78768

DALLAS RAINBOW ALLIANCE OF THE DEAF
P.O. Box 225661
Dallas, TX 75222

ASTRO RAINBOW SOCIETY OF THE DEAF
P.O. Box 501951
Houston, TX 77250

CANADA

■ ONTARIO ■

TORONTO RAINBOW ALLIANCE OF THE DEAF
Postal Station "F" P.O. Box 671
Toronto, ON M4Y 2N6

ASSOCIATION DES BONNES GENS SOURDS
C.P. 875, Succ. "C"
Montreal, QU H2L 4L6

THE NATIONAL ORGANIZATION FOR MEN AGAINST SEXISM

NOMS was founded in 1982 to establish and coordinate community and regionally based efforts of men working to change male roles. Activists, educators, human service providers, and artists realized the need for a national forum to address masculinity and the need for change.

NOMS publishes a newsletter, *Brother,* which keeps members informed of national, regional, and local events and which offers a forum for addressing issues affecting men's lives. NOMS sponsors an annual national conference, "Men and Masculinity."

There are many areas that the members of NOMS identify as needing change in their lives:

- excessive involvement in work
- fear of being vulnerable or out of control

© 1989, HOWARD CRUSE. REPRINTED WITH PERMISSION.

- limited self-awareness of emotional needs and potential
- high rates of alcoholism, drug abuse, suicide
- isolation from other men and loved ones
- fear of being perceived as being other than heterosexual
- high incidence of accidents and death due to unnecessary risk-taking
- loss of opportunity for child custody rights

If you're interested in pursuing any of these topics or others which you think are a part of your masculinity, NOMS has long had a gay component. You would not be out of place in any of their gatherings. For more information:

National Organization for Men Against Sexism
794 Penn Avenue
Pittsburgh, PA 15221
Phone: 412 371 8007

▼ *The Campaign to End Homophobia* began in 1986 as an offshoot of the National Organization for Men Against Sexism. The Campaign offers a multidimensional response to homophobia in our society, including workshops, publications, and conferences. The steering committee is not only made up of equal numbers of men and women, it is also racially balanced. The Campaign has been especially active in working on issues of discrimination among adolescents. It publishes a magazine, *Empathy,* and maintains a resource library which is producing bibliographies on discrimination.

A leader's guide on how to structure and run workshops on homophobia is available for $10.

The Campaign to End Homophobia
Box 819
Cambridge, MA 02139

RADICAL FAERIES

The *Radical Faeries* have a long tradition in gay life. These gender-bending, pre–New Age New Agers find a spiritual center in their communal gay lives. It's hard to even describe them as a group. One man who's involved gave me this description: "Is it correct to call the faeries a group? I see it more as a life-style, a loose philosophy, a mixture of gayness, feminism, and paganism. In some ways faerie circles are much like the leather/Levi's club networks in terms of fostering brotherhood, obtaining friends and places to stay in distant places, etc. 'Gatherings' are much like bike club runs, perhaps with a bit less leather, alcohol, and sex, perhaps with more political or ecological consciousness.

"Most faerie doings have extra emphasis on sissyhood, sisterhood, drag, etc. Faerie circles attempt to be nurturing environments of total freedom, perfect love, and perfect trust. They can fall short of that, but I'm still attracted to them for their rurality and their freedom. They're not perfect, but certainly more than we enjoy in the outside world, be it gay or straight."

Harry Hay, the founder of *The Mattachine Society,* one of the original gay rights organizations in the United States, was also in on the beginning of the faerie movement. For a delightful glimpse at his experiences, read his biography, *The Trouble with Harry Hay: Founder of the Modern Gay Movement* (Boston: Alyson, 1990).

The various components of the movement are often anarchistic and even less likely to have glossy promotional brochures or to do advertising about their events. There are some contacts you can use if you'd like to learn more about activities near you:

■ CALIFORNIA ■

SOUTHERN CALIFORNIA FAERIES
Harry Hay/John Burnside
5343 La Cresta Court
Los Angeles, CA 90030

NOMENUS
Box 11655
San Francisco, CA 94101

■ ILLINOIS ■

CHICAGO FAERIES
c/o Midwest Men's Center
Box 2547
Chicago, IL 60690

■ LOUISIANA ■

L'AFFARIE
David Givens
Rt. 1, Box 614
Pollack, LA 71469

■ MINNESOTA ■

NORTHWOODS
John Sutton
2440 Garfield Avenue S
Minneapolis, MN 55405

■ MISSOURI ■

MIDWEST MEN'S FESTIVAL
David Hubert
1523 S. 10th, #108
St. Louis, MO 63104

■ NEW YORK ■

BLUE HERON FARM
Rt. 2, Box 144
Dekalb, NY 13630

NEW YORK CITY FAG GATHERING
Box 1251, Canal Street Station
New York, NY 10013

NORTHEASTERN FAERIES
Tom Seidner
90 Lieb Road
Spencer, NY 14883

GANOWUNGO SANCTUARY
Jay Stratton
121 Union Street
Westfield, NY 14787

■ NORTH CAROLINA ■

WILLOW HOLLOW RANCH
P.O. Drawer 70
Purlear, NC 28665

■ **TENNESSEE** ■

SHORT MOUNTAIN SANCTUARY
Rt. 1, Box 84-A
Liberty, TN 37095

■ **TEXAS** ■

GRAY LADY PLACE
Box 6111
Blum, TX 76627

■ **WASHINGTON** ■

NORTHWESTERN FAERIES
1206 1st Avenue, #23
Seattle, WA 98101

Thanks for *R.F.D.,* Jason Serinus, and Richard Labonté for their help in constructing this list.

▼ *Touch Circle* is a faerie listing and referral project dedicated to facilitating communication between people who are interested in the movement. You can reach them at:

Touch Circle
Box 3350
Berkeley, CA 94703

Information on Bay Area and national faerie events can be heard by calling *Tel-a-Fairy,* a twenty-four-hour event and message bulletin. It's updated at least once a week: 415 626 3369.

Another resource, if you have a computer modem, is *Fey Dish,* a computer bulletin board that can be reached at 415 861 4221.

WHAT'S MISSING?

There are numerous gay business organizations around the country. In fact, it seems that almost every metropolitan area has one. However, this is the one area of gay organizing that hasn't been tied together. There is no national clearinghouse for these names and addresses. It's a shame, and it seems strange as well, since business should be the one area where there could be some money to support a national council. There certainly would be enough work for such a national group, and a newsletter and other publications could be a forum for exchanging information and experience. An attempt to put together a national organization was made a few years ago, but it's fallen by the wayside. I hope it'll be a project someone can pick up before the next edition of *The Big Gay Book.*

> *Every person who is gay should join some gay organization. Because he must prove to the world that he cares about his own freedom. People will never fight for your freedom if you have not given evidence that you are prepared to fight for it yourself.*
>
> —*BAYARD RUSTIN*

PHILATELISTS

The study of history and geography and the simple pleasures of socializing with other gay men all come together in *Gay and Lesbian History on Stamps Club*.

The club was founded in 1981, based on the work of founder Paul Hennefeld. It produces a quarterly journal, *Lambda Philatelic Journal,* with articles, fee ads of philatelic interest to members, games, etc. They have been accepted as an American Topical Association Study Unit Charter since 1985.

The club handbook lists over two hundred people who have been portrayed on stamps of countries all around the globe, with sources documenting evidence of their sexual orientation. The club is also interested in collecting male nudes on postcards.

Gay and Lesbian History on Stamps Club
Box 3940
Hartford, CT 06130

HORTICULTURISTS

The Lavandula Society says its purpose is "to provide support and to promote networking and good will among gay and lesbian plant enthusiasts and professionals in horticulture, botany, and landscape architecture."

The various chapters meet occasionally and produce newsletters about ongoing activities in the organization and in the general area as well. As a recent issue of the *Lavandula-Midwest Newsletter* says, "Theatre, dance, art, music, letters; these are fields that have provided an abundance of documented lesbian and gay personalities. And why not? We have long been recognized for our originality, and our 'flair.' Well, those of us fiscally entangled with our love for plants have no less originality, no less flair—simply less access to the press." The way to rectify that? Create your own press.

To make contact with gay plant lovers, write whichever of the following chapters is closest to you:

LAVANDULA MIDWEST
Box 2641, Station A
Champaign, IL 61825

LAVANDULA WEST
41370 S.E. Thomas
Sandy, OR 97055

THE LAVANDULA SOCIETY
318 E. Davie Street
Raleigh, NC 27601

LIATRIS INTERNATIONAL
Box 1336
Davis, CA 95617

SCIENCE FICTION AND FANTASY FANS

"Out of the Closet and into the Universe." That's the cry of *The Gaylactic Network,* an organization of gay science fiction and fantasy fans and their friends (membership is not limited to gay people). The national organization works with a sibling association, *The Gaylaxians,* which is made up of fans in central New England. They share the same address:

The Gaylactic Network
Box 1051
Back Bay Annex
Boston, MA 02117

Other local groups are being formed.

RAILROADING

"Do you fantasize about tugging firmly on the throttle of a U.P. 'Big Boy'? Did you, as a kid, lock yourself in the bathroom with Builder's Erection Photos? Are your loins stirred by a rushing train erupting from a tunnel? Are muscular gandy dancers high on your list of railroad favorites?"

No, those aren't questions from a classified ad. It's a tongue-in-cheek come-on for a gay railroader's organization. *Hotbox* presents itself as "A life-style enhancement for the discriminating railfan." It's a social network of people who like train trips, are looking for travel companions, and want to share dinner and hot rail conversation.

If you're interested in more information on the group:

Hotbox
Box 171135
Memphis, TN 38187

MENSA

Elitism is a naughty word in the gay world. Inclusivity is the usual goal for most organizations. The gay SIG (Special Interest Group) of

Mensa is an exception to the rule. To gain admission, applicants have to score at or above the 98th percentile on the IQ test.

The gay SIG is a fine little group, if you can get in. They maintain a presence at the national Mensa convention and there are numerous chapters of the SIG around the country. Their newsletter, *Le Gambit*, is a challenge to your intelligence.

For more information:

Le Gambit
Box 35822
Dallas, TX 75235

LEATHER

While much gay organizing and identity building has been around the central idea that we are more than just sexual entities, it doesn't mean that we have given up sex! Nor that there aren't many times and places where gay men gather together to talk about and learn about sex.

The National Leather Association is the largest national network of sexual organizations, with member chapters in most states and many foreign countries. It also sponsors an annual Living in Leather Conference. For more information on the conference or on organizations in your own locality, you can contact their headquarters:

The National Leather Association
Box 5161
Portland, OR 97208

The Leather Journal is a bi-monthly publication that reports on the activities of the National Leather Association and other sexually active and sexually responsible organizations. It carries updated listings of groups in many places throughout the United States, Canada, and other countries. For information:

The Leather Journal
7985 Santa Monica Boulevard, #214
West Hollywood, CA 90046

COMMUNITY ORGANIZATIONS

The most fundamental complaint of gay men has always concerned the experience of being alone, of being "the only one." Community organizations serve a vital role in our well-being by eroding the isolation we feel before we come out.

GAY COMMUNITY CENTERS

Community centers are the essential building blocks of this movement. They offer a safe space where gay organizations of all kinds can meet. The centers are places where new groups can be born and nurtured.

UNITED STATES

■ ALASKA ■

IDENTITY, INC.
Box 8200070
Anchorage, AK 99520

■ CALIFORNIA ■

BILLY DEFRANK COMMUNITY CENTER
1040 Park Avenue
San Jose, CA 95216

THE CENTER
2017 E. 4th Street
Long Beach, CA 90814
Phone: 213 434 4455

GAY AND LESBIAN CENTER
12832 Garden Road Boulevard
Garden Grove, CA 92643
Phone: 714 534 0862

GAY AND LESBIAN COMMUNITY SERVICES CENTER
1213 N. Highland Avenue
Los Angeles, CA 90038
Phone: 213 464 7400
Fax: 213 463 1702

GAY AND LESBIAN COMMUNITY CENTER
Box 6333
San Bernardino, CA 92412
Phone: 714 824 7618

GAY AND LESBIAN RESOURCE CENTER
126 E. Haley, Suite A18
Santa Barbara, CA 93101
Phone: 805 963 3636

GAY AND LESBIAN SERVICE CENTER
3780 Fifth Avenue, Suite 2
San Diego, CA 92103
Phone: 619 294 4635

■ COLORADO ■

GAY AND LESBIAN COMMUNITY CENTER OF COLORADO
Drawer E
Denver, CO 80218
Phone: 303 831 6268

PIKE'S PEAK GAY COMMUNITY CENTER
Box 574
Colorado Springs, CO 90801
Phone: 719 471 4429

■ DELAWARE ■

GRIFFIN COMMUNITY CENTER
214 N. Market Street
Wilmington, DE 19801
Phone: 302 655 5280

■ GEORGIA ■

ATLANTA GAY CENTER
63 12th Street
Atlanta, GA 30309
Phone: 404 876 5372

■ HAWAII ■

GAY COMMUNITY CENTER
1154 Fort Street Mall, Suite 415
Honolulu, HI 96801
Phone: 808 536 6000

■ ILLINOIS ■

HORIZONS COMMUNITY SERVICES, INC.
961 West Montana Street
Chicago, IL 60614
Phone: 312 472 6469
Fax: 312 472 6643

■ INDIANA ■

NEW WORLD CHURCH
Outreach Center
222 E. Leith Street
Fort Wayne, IN 46806
Phone: 219 456 6570

■ IOWA ■

THOREAU CENTER
3500 Kingman Boulevard
Des Moines, IA 50311

CLEARSPACE GAY COMMUNITY CENTER
Box 1313
Fairfield, IA 52556

■ LOUISIANA ■

ST. LOUIS COMMUNITY CENTER
1022 Barracks Street
New Orleans, LA 70116
Phone: 504 524 6932

■ MARYLAND ■

BALTIMORE GAY AND LESBIAN COMMUNITY CENTER
231 Chase Street
Baltimore, MD 21201
Phone: 301 837 5445

■ MASSACHUSETTS ■

GAY AND LESBIAN COMMUNITY CENTER
338 Newbury Street
Boston, MA 02101
Phone: 617 426 1350

■ MICHIGAN ■

DETROIT LESBIAN/GAY COMMUNITY CENTER
195 West Nine Mile Road
Detroit, MI 48220
Phone: 313 398 7105

■ MINNESOTA ■

GAY AND LESBIAN COMMUNITY ACTION COUNCIL
310 E. 38th Street
Minneapolis, MN 55409
Phone: 612 822 0127
Fax: 612 822 8786

■ MISSISSIPPI ■

GAY AND LESBIAN ALLIANCE
Box 1271
Biloxi, MS 39533
Phone: 601 435 1029

■ MONTANA ■

OUT IN MONTANA RESOURCE CENTER
Box 7223
Missoula, MT 59807
Phone: 800 366 4297

■ NEW MEXICO ■

COMMON BOND COMMUNITY CENTER
107 Tulane SE
Albuquerque, NM 87106

■ NEW YORK ■

THE LESBIAN AND GAY COMMUNITY SERVICES CENTER
208 W. 13th Street
New York, NY 10011
Phone: 212 620 7310
Fax: 212 620 7383

GAY AND LESBIAN COMMUNITY CENTER
2316 Delaware Avenue, Suite 267
Buffalo, NY 14205
Phone: 716 883 4750

THE LOFT
255 Grove Street
White Plains, NY 10605
Phone: 914 948 4922

■ OHIO ■

GAY/LESBIAN COMMUNITY CENTER
1418 W. 29th Street
Cleveland, OH 44113
Phone: 216 522 1999

■ OKLAHOMA ■

OASIS COMMUNITY CENTER
2135 N. 39th Street
Oklahoma City, OK 73112
Phone: 405 525 2437

■ OREGON ■

PHOENIX RISING
333 S.W. Fifth Avenue, Suite 404
Portland, OR 97204
Phone: 503 223 8299

■ PENNSYLVANIA ■

PENGUIN CENTER
201 South Camac Street
Philadelphia, PA 19107
Phone: 215 923 7505

■ TEXAS ■

GAY COMMUNITY CENTER
2701 Reagen
Dallas, TX 75219
Phone: 214 528 4233
Fax: 214 528 8436

MONTROSE ACTIVITY CENTER
Box 66684
Houston, TX 77266
Phone: 713 529 1223

■ WASHINGTON ■

LESBIAN/GAY MEN'S RESOURCE CENTER
CAB 305, Evergreen State College
Olympia, WA 98505
Phone: 206 866 6000, extension 6544

■ WISCONSIN ■

GAY/LESBIAN CENTER
310 E. Wilson Street
Madison, WI 53701
Phone: 608 255 8582

CREAM CITY FOUNDATION
Box 204
Milwaukee, WI 53201
Phone: 414 265 0880

CANADA

■ BRITISH COLUMBIA ■

VANCOUVER GAY AND LESBIAN COMMUNITY CENTER
Box 2259
Vancouver, BC V6B 3W2
Phone: 604 684 5307

■ MANITOBA ■

WINNIPEG GAY/LESBIAN COMMUNITY CENTRE
222 Osborne Street, Suite 1
Winnipeg, MB R3L 1Z3
Phone: 204 284 5208

■ ONTARIO ■

GO CENTRE
c/o Gays of Ottawa
Box 2919, Station D
Ottawa, ON K1P 5W9
Phone: 613 233 1324

HALO CLUB
649 Colbourne Street
London, ON N6A 3Z2
Phone: 519 433 3762

■ QUEBEC ■

CENTRE COMMUNAUTAIRE
1355 Rue Ste. Catherine East
Montreal, QU H2G 2H7
Phone: 514 528 8424

WHAT HAPPENS AT A COMMUNITY CENTER?

A community center offers a place for a wide range of activities in the gay world. The variety of events and organizational meetings that can take place in a community center is almost limitless. Here's a listing of groups who hold their gatherings at *The Gay and Lesbian Community Services Center of New York.* This listing is only to show you the scope of a major community center's activities. These organizations hold regular events at the Center, but they do not have their offices there. Do not send mail to these organizations in care of the Center. You can call the Center if you want to get their mailing addresses: 212 620 7310.

ACT UP (AIDS Coalition to Unleash Power)

Adult Children of Alcoholics (ACOA)

11th Step Workshop

Gay/Lesbian/Bisexual

GAYLESBI ACOA Alanon

Gender/Sex/Sexuality (Gay/BI/Non-Gay)

Lesbians

Literature Meeting

Relationships

Struggle for Intimacy

Topic Meeting (Food)

Topic Meeting

Al-Anon

Gay Men Double Winners

Gay Men

Gay Men Beginners

GLAD Gay & Lesbian discussion

Alcoholics Anonymous

High Noon

Lesbian & Gay Grupo Identidad

NY Women's Discussion Group

Topics Discussion

Village Agnostics

Westwingers

Women Now

Women Together
Beginners
Step Meetings

Arts Anonymous
Open 12-step support group for artists

Asian Lesbians of the East Coast

Asians & Friends of NY

Axios, Eastern & Orthodox Christians

Bar Association for Human Rights

Bisexual Dominance & Submission Group

Bisexual Pride Group

Bisexual Support Group

Body Positive of NY

Bronx Lesbians United in Sisterhood
Support and social networking group

Chapter 9
12-step program for committed couples in 12-step recovery programs

Chinese Healing for Today
Lecture/demonstration

Christian Science Group

Cocaine Anonymous
Gay/Lesbian Open Meeting

Co-Dependents Anonymous

Committee of Outraged Lesbians (COOL)
Consciousness-raising group for lesbians in multicultural/racial relationships

Community of the Inner Light
Men & women using metaphysical principles of the Science of Mind for self-empowerment and freedom

Community Republican Club

Conference for Catholic Lesbians

Debtors Anonymous
Gay Topics Meeting

Dignity/Big Apple
Liturgy and social for lesbian and gay Catholics

Dignity/New York

EDGE (Education in a Disabled Gay Environment)
Gay & Lesbian Alcoholism Services

Gay & Lesbian Alliance Against Defamation

Gay & Lesbian Independent Democrats

Gay & Lesbian Italians

Gay & Lesbian Justice Project
Counseling and referrals for ex-offenders

Gay & Lesbian Reading Group

Gay & Lesbian Writers
Discussion group/workshop for fiction and nonfiction writers

Gay & Lesbian Youth of NY

Gay Circles
Eight-week cycles of discussion groups for gay men

Gay Fathers Forum

Gay Male S/M Activists

Gay Men of African Descent

Gay Men Together
Discussion group

Gay Men's Chorus

Gay Men's Health Crisis

Gay Officers Action League

Friends of GOAL

Gay Performances Company

Gay Teachers Association

Gay Veterans Association

Girth & Mirth Club of NY

Greater Gotham Business Council

Health/Education/AIDS Liaison (HEAL)
Drop-in information and support group for alternative and holistic approaches to AIDS-related conditions

Heritage of Pride
Organizers of Gay Pride Week-end

Hispanic United Gays & Lesbians

Incest & Sexual Abuse Survivors Anonymous—Gay Men

Knights Wrestling Club

Las Buenas Amigas
Latina Lesbians

Lavender Bytes
Lesbians in computers

Legal Clinic
Bar Association for Human Rights drop-in free legal consultations

Lesbian & Gay Labor Network

Lesbian Feminist Liberation

Lesbians in Government

Mad Dykes Support Group
Ex-psychiatric inmates, victims, survivors

Magickal Study Group
Witchcraft and history of ancient mystery

Men of All Colors Together

Moonfire Women's Spirituality Circle

Nar-Anon

Narcotics Anonymous

National Lesbian Agenda Conference, NYC Area Planning Group

Natural History Group

New York Advertising & Communications Network

New York Association of Gay & Lesbian Psychologists

New York Bankers Group

Other Countries: Black Gay Men Writing

Overeaters Anonymous
Gay Men

Open Gay Meeting

Open Lesbian Meeting

West Side Gay Meeting

People with ARC Support Group

Positive Action of NY
HIV+ support groups

Salsa Soul Sisters

Sexaholics Anonymous

Sexual Compulsives Anonymous (SCA)
For those who want to stop having compulsive sex

SCA-Anon

Sexually Abused Anonymous (SAA) (Women)

Sundance Outdoor Adventure Society

Support Group for Single Lesbians

Survivors of Transsexuality Anonymous

Times Squares
Square dancing

Tri-State Gaylaxians
Social group for science fiction fans (literature, film video, cartoons); open to gays, lesbians, and friends

Village Dive Club
Gay and lesbian scuba club

Village Playwrights

Water of Life
Support group for those practicing or interested in urine therapy

WBAI Union

Women About
Quarterly planning meetings; call for dates: 212 874 2104

A community center also allows for special events, times for the community to come together for celebration, action, education, or appreciation of one another's art and crafts. This is a list of some of the events held in *The New York Lesbian and Gay Community Services Center* in January and February of 1990:

Center Kids

Are You a Single Parent? Planning to Be One?
A social event for single parents and their friends

Afro-American Celebration
A special event sponsored by Center Kids' Multi-Cultural Committee

Alternative Insemination 101
Another in an on-going series of forums at the Center

Women & Friends Dance

2nd Saturday Dance
Cosponsored by Front Runners

In Our Own Write

Ancestors Within Us: Dorothy Randall Gray Writing Workshop.

Focus on past life, music imagery, time and place, and inanimate animation writing exercises. For writers of all levels

National Museum of Lesbian and Gay History

A Hundred Legends
Exhibition of artwork in various media by persons with AIDS from across the country

LAVA (Lesbians About Visual Arts)
Group show featuring the work of lesbian artists, coinciding with The Women's Caucus for Art Conference

Orientation

Young or old, new or native, your best introduction to New York's lesbian and gay community. Forty groups represented; literature available from four hundred more. Presentations, socializing, entertainment

Project Connect—12-week Connecting Groups

Connecting Groups for Gay Men
Early recovery support groups

Connecting Group for Lesbians
Early recovery support group

Relax and Recover Group
On-going recovery strategies and stress management for lesbians and gay men

Speech

Vanessa Ferro, NYPD Liaison to the Lesbian and Gay Community

Hon. David N. Dinkins
Celebrating Black History Month—the mayor's first scheduled appearance at a lesbian and gay community event.

Volunteer Placement

Meet other volunteers and find out how you can be part of the team that makes the Center run. Choose from a host of committees or find an independent project.

YES Youth Enrichment Services

For lesbian and gay youth under twenty-two years old. Free

Lesbian and Gay Youth Discussion Group
General discussion of issues important to lesbian and gay youth

Alternate Visions: Improv Theatre Workshop

Coming Out Group
Support group for dealing with issues of coming out

Gay Men of African Descent
"Stressed Out." Discussion of the stresses involved in being black and gay in the workplace

Knights Wrestling Club Exhibition
Over twenty wrestlers compete in individual, free-style matches to raise money to send wrestlers to the 1990 Gay Games.

"Pumpkins" Staged Reading by Gay Performances Company

GMHC Workshop: Men Meeting Men
Enhance your self-confidence and ability to negotiate safer sex with potential partners

Scrabble-Players Club
Newcomers, please bring a board!

Open Circle, Full-Moon Celebration of the God/dess

National Lesbian Agenda Conference, Local Planning
Develop working committees for fund-raising, media, mobilization, and program for 1991 conference in Atlanta.

Gay Men of African Descent
"He's Got to Have It." Discussion of "sexual addiction" in the black/Latino gay community

GMHC Workshop: Keep It Up!
Reaffirm the importance of safer sex and feel confident about saying "yes."

Boricua Gay & Lesbian Forum, Orientation
General introduction plus social with members

Axios
Sixth Anniversary and Christmas Celebration with ethnic food and dance

"Metamorphosis" by Eric Booth
Stage production. A slice of black gay life

Benefit Cabaret for Manhattan Center for Living
A potpourri of performers to help raise funds for this nonprofit organization dedicated to helping those affected by life-threatening illness and grief

Two-Week Self-Defense Class
(Brooklyn women's Martial Arts). Basic physical self-defense with special attention to concerns of lesbians and gay men

GMHC Workshop: Eroticizing Safer Sex
Learn how to play safely while meeting other men

At Home with the Archives
Lesbian Herstory Archives presents video about the Resistance-Conspiracy-Case defendants who speak about their experiences as political prisoners. Two of the women are lesbians active in the anti-imperialist movement.

"All My Avatars: The Pagan Soap Opera" by John Yohalem
Staged reading. In the New Age when natural religion conquers the world, what soap operas will we be watching?

Physique Exhibition sponsored by New York in '94
See women and men athletes training for Gay Games III in Vancouver. Benefit to bring Gay Games IV to New York City in 1994, the twenty-fifth anniversary of Stonewall

Two-Week First Aid Class
Be prepared! Learn basic first aid from a licensed medical technician. Includes rescue breathing, treating bleeding, shock, burns, fractures, seizures.

Medical Powers of Attorney
Discussion and workshop sponsored by the New York Committee to Free Sharon Kowalski. Choose who you want to care for you in case of accident or illness. A lawyer will discuss problems and help you fill out these important forms.

Women's Circle, Line and Square Dance
Live musicians, and an instructor calling the moves

Maintaining Your Financial Health, a Workshop
Sponsored by Body Positive of New York for HIV+ people and their loved ones to plan for the financial health that is the necessary underpinning for physical health.

Learning from ACT-UP
Community Organizing in the Nineties. Discussion and video presentations on ACT-UP organizing strategies and direct action tactics. Speakers Maxine Wolfe and Gregg Bordowitz. Presented by the Bertha Capen Reynolds Society and the Lesbian/Gay Alliance at the Hunter School of Social Work.

"The Lemon Tree" Staged Reading by New York Theatre Group
Poetic drama about love and AIDS, set simultaneously in Sicily, the American South, and on the set of a film-in-progress. NYTG is a nonprofit

theater entering its second season. This reading is part of its New American Plays Series, a developmental process for new works by emerging and established U.S. playwrights.

"Leonardo" Staged Reading by New York Theatre Group

After a not-so-fictional encounter with Machiavelli, Leonardo da Vinci and his young assistants awaken to the realities of Renaissance court politics and ultimate betrayal.

Boricua Gay & Lesbian Forum Poetry Reading

Commemorating the birthday of the late Puerto Rican poet Julia de Burgos.

▼ Gay organizations serve many functions. As a rule of thumb, the smaller the community, the broader the range of interests a group will have. After all, San Francisco and New York City can afford a level of specialization that isn't possible in other parts of the country.

Friends North is the gay organization in Traverse City in northwestern Michigan. Richard Tuxbury describes the breadth of interests for this association:

"Our group has been active since 1986. The inspiration originated with a long-ago dissolved chapter of Dignity. Traverse City is a small (20,000) resort city surrounded by lakes and has an increased summer population. We service the surrounding rural areas, which stay busy with farming and, again, resort-oriented activity.

"Friends North is involved with social activities, sponsoring about fourteen dances per year that are attended by 200–250 persons on the average. The Gay Pride picnic last June saw a turnout of 190. Other 'open parties' are encouraged to integrate new persons into the community. The activities are attended by an interesting mix of people, from age eighteen to eighty, about an equal number of men and women.

"Educational activities are also organized in the form of seminars and workshops. We also sponsored a highly visible ad ("When was the last time you talked to someone gay . . .?) for National Coming Out Day, which generated over 200 inquiries. Our newsletter mailing list, though not all local, is up to 760 subscribers.

"Besides this we have a semi-active, but growing Political Awareness task force and a pushy financial project. Our primary goal is to provide networking connections to those who inquire, while referring crisis calls to a local hotline or gay-oriented counselors.

"In a nutshell, that's us. If anyone wants to contact us:"

Friends North
Box 562
Traverse City, MI 49685
Phone: 616 946 1804

▼ When a community is well organized and has a large base of population, it can seem as though the number of organizations it contains can get out of hand. Certainly there can be a problem with communication between groups and frequent conflict of interest over dates, fund-raisers, and just a plain lack of communication.

The Metropolitan Atlanta Council of Gay and Lesbian Organizations (MACGLO) is a model of how a region can overcome those problems. The council holds regular monthly meetings, all of them open to the public. The meetings serve as a forum for the exchange of ideas and information and friends, and coordinates many of the major gay and lesbian community activities and outreach programs.

For more information on how this coordinating council works:

MACGLO
Box 900142
Atlanta, GA 30329
Phone: 404 242 2342

> *I am a committed supporter of the Gay and Lesbian Community Service Center, here in New York (and others like it). The Center is a great start to building a more permanent history of our community for future generations of gay men and lesbians. It is a wonderfully positive reaction to who and what we are.*
>
> —*NORMAN LAURILA, literary agent*

GAY PRIDE ORGANIZATIONS

Gay Pride has become the great holiday of gay life. The parades, picnics, concerts, and speeches are usually held in June to celebrate the anniversary of the Stonewall Riots. (Though some cities use other dates. The Vancouver, British Columbia, pride celebration is held on BC Day, a provincial holiday in August of each year.) The June celebrations are tiered. The smallest cities, like Portland, Maine, tend to hold their celebrations in the beginning of the month. Then the second level of celebrations takes part in mid-June in regional centers such as Boston. All of these lead up to the largest festivities in the major cities: Chicago, New York, Los Angeles, and San Francisco. You need to check with each city's organizers to make sure of the date.

The following list was constructed with the help of Marsha Levine, the Executive Director of *The International Association of Lesbian/Gay Pride Coordinators, Inc.* Levine founded the IAL/GPC in 1982 to facilitate networking and information-sharing between the committees in various cities that coordinate lesbian/gay–pride events that commemorate the 1969 Stonewall Riots or similar historic milestones. In addition to an annual meeting, the group supports and sponsors regional meetings and they publish a quarterly newsletter, free to anyone who asks.

The International Association of Lesbian/Gay Pride Coordinators, Inc.
c/o M. H. Levine
746 Fourteenth Street, Apartment 1
San Francisco, CA 94114
Phone: 415 861 0779

UNITED STATES

■ ARIZONA ■

PHOENIX PRIDE COMMITTEE
1617 West Village Way
Tempe, AZ 85282
Phone: 602 631 0350

OLD PUEBLO BUSINESS & PROFESSIONAL ASSOCIATION
P.O. Box 44033
Tucson, AZ 85733
Phone: 602 883 8823

■ CALIFORNIA ■

GAY & LESBIAN UNION
415 Eschleman Hall
University of California
Berkeley, CA 94720
Phone: 415 642 6942

LONG BEACH LESBIAN & GAY PRIDE, INC.
Box 2050
Long Beach, CA 90801
Phone: 213 435 5530

ORANGE COUNTY CULTURAL PRIDE
Box 8167
Orange, CA 92664
Phone: 714 831 1732

LAMBDA FREEDOM FAIR
P.O. Box 163654
Sacramento, CA 95816
Phone: 916 442 0185

SAN DIEGO GAY PRIDE, INC.
P.O. Box 34352
San Diego, CA 92103
Phone: 619 692 2077

LESBIAN/GAY FREEDOM DAY PARADE & CELEBRATION
584 Castro Street, #513
San Francisco, CA 94114
Phone: 415 864 3733

GAY PRIDE CELEBRATION
Box 34352
San Diego, CA 92103

GPW COMMITTEE
c/o G & L Action Alliance
P.O. Box 828011
Santa Cruz, CA 95061

CHRISTOPHER STREET WEST/LOS ANGELES
7985 Santa Monica Boulevard
Suite 109-24
West Hollywood, CA 90046
Phone: 213 656 6553

■ COLORADO ■

GAY PRIDE COORDINATOR
P.O. Drawer E
Denver, CO 80218

■ DISTRICT OF COLUMBIA ■

GAY & LESBIAN PRIDE OF DC
c/o T. Adams
4427 39th Street
Brentwood, MD 20722
Phone: 301 783 1828

■ FLORIDA ■

SOUTH FLORIDA GAY & LESBIAN PRIDE COMMITTEE
P.O. Box 2048
Ft. Lauderdale, FL 33301
Phone: 305 989 8364

■ GEORGIA ■

ATLANTA GAY CENTER
63 12th Street
Atlanta, GA 30309
Phone: 404 876 5372

■ HAWAII ■

PRIDE COMMITTEE
c/o Gay Community Center
P.O. Box 3224
Honolulu, HI 96801
Phone: 808 536 6000

■ ILLINOIS ■

GAY/LESBIAN PRIDE WEEK PLANNING COMMITTEE
P.O. Box 14131
Chicago, IL 60614
Phone: 312 348 8243

■ INDIANA ■

JUSTICE
P.O. Box 2387
Indianapolis, IN 46206
Phone: 317 634 9212

■ KANSAS ■

PRIDE CELEBRATION
c/o K. Streips
2126 S.E. Carnahan
Topeka, KS 66605

WICHITA PRIDE COMMITTEE
Box 21106
Wichita, KS 67208
Phone: 316 681 2766

■ MAINE ■

PRIDE COMMITTEE
Box 5122, Station A
Portland, ME 04112
Phone: 207 883 6934

■ MARYLAND ■

BALTIMORE GAY/LESBIAN COMMUNITY CENTER
241 W. Chase Street
Baltimore, MD 21201
Phone: 301 837 5445

■ MASSACHUSETTS ■

BOSTON PRIDE CELEBRATION
Gay/Lesbian Community Center
338 Newbury Street
Boston, MA 02114
Phone: 617 426 1350

■ MICHIGAN ■

LESBIAN-GAY MALE PROGRAMS OFFICE
3118 Michigan Union
University of Michigan
Ann Arbor, MI 48109
Phone: 313 763 4186

FRIENDS NORTH
Box 562
Traverse City, MI 49685
Phone: 616 946 1804

■ MINNESOTA ■

TWIN CITIES LESBIAN/GAY PRIDE
Box 89442
Minneapolis, MN 55408
Phone: 612 824 3591

■ MISSISSIPPI ■

MISSISSIPPI GAY ALLIANCE
Box 8342
Jackson, MS 39204
Phone: 601 355 7495

■ MISSOURI ■

GALA
Box 411411
Kansas City, MO 63156

ST. LOUIS GAY PRIDE CELEBRATION COMMITTEE
P.O. Box 23260
St. Louis, MO 63156
Phone: 314 776 7138

■ NEW MEXICO ■

COMMON BOND
P.O. Box 26836
Albuquerque, NM 87125
Phone: 505 266 8041

■ NEW YORK ■

HERITAGE OF PRIDE
123 W. 44th Street #52
New York, NY 10011
Phone: 212 691 1774

■ OHIO ■

COLUMBUS STONEWALL UNION
P.O. Box 10814
Columbus, OH 43201
Phone: 614 299 7764

■ OREGON ■

PORTLAND GAY/LESBIAN PRIDE
P.O. Box 6611
Portland, OR 97228
Phone: 503 232 8233

■ PENNSYLVANIA ■

MCC PHILADELPHIA
P.O. Box 8174
Philadelphia, PA 19101-8174
Phone: 215 563 6601

■ RHODE ISLAND ■

RHODE ISLAND PRIDE
5671 Waybosset, Hill Station
Providence, RI 02903
Phone: 401 751 3322

■ TENNESSEE ■

MEMPHIS GAY COALITION
P.O. Box 3038
Memphis, TN 38173
Phone: 901 276 4651

TENNESSEE GAY COALITION
Pride Committee
P.O. Box 41305
Nashville, TN 37204
Phone: 615 292 4820

■ TEXAS ■

PRIDE COMMITTEE
c/o Political Caucus
Box 822
Austin, TX 78767

DALLAS GAY PRIDE ASSOCIATION
Box 190412
Dallas, TX 75219
Phone: 214 522 1713

MONTROSE ACTIVITY CENTER
(HGPW)
P.O. Box 66684
Houston, TX 77266
Phone: 713 529 1223

SAN ANTONIO PRIDE COMMITTEE
Box 12063
San Antonio, TX 78212
Phone: 512 733 8315

■ UTAH ■

SALT LAKE CITY GAY COMMUNITY COUNCIL
P.O. Box 3832
Salt Lake City, UT 84110
Phone: 801 595 0052

■ VIRGINIA ■

ALEXANDRIA GAY COMMUNITY ASSOCIATION
200 S. Van Dorn
Alexandria, VA 22304
Phone: 703 751 3037

GAY/LESBIAN PRIDE COALITION
Box 14747
Richmond, VA 23221
Phone: 804 353 4133

■ WASHINGTON ■

FREEDOM DAY COMMITTEE
Box 95687
Seattle, WA 98145
Phone: 206 328 1902

SEATTLE PRIDE FESTIVAL COMMITTEE
Box 694
Seattle, WA 98122
Phone: 206 682 4612

■ WISCONSIN ■

GALVANIZE
P.O. Box 14032
Madison, WI 53703
Phone: 608 255 8061

MILWAUKEE LESBIAN/GAY PRIDE COMMITTEE
Box 93852
Milwaukee, WI 53203
Phone: 414 327 7433

TWIN PORTS LESBIAN/GAY PRIDE COMMITTEE
1708 N. 17th Street
Superior, WI 54880
Phone: 715 392 1756

CANADA

■ BRITISH COLUMBIA ■

PRIDE FESTIVAL ASSOCIATION
c/o Dr. Malcolm Crane
1018 Ironwork Passage
Vancouver, BC V6H 3P1

■ ONTARIO ■

LESBIAN AND GAY PRIDE DAY
c/o P.O. Box 1215, Station F
Toronto, ON M4Y 2U8
Phone: 416 658 6834

> *At the top of a long list of gay organizations I value is New York's Lesbian & Gay Community Services Center. Why? Why is any community center valuable? It embodies a promise that no gay need feel alone.*
>
> —*HOWARD CRUSE, cartoonist*

SETTING UP AND NURTURING AN ORGANIZATION

Many organizations begin as grass-roots movements. A few people see a need and want to fill it. They become aware of other groups doing the same work in other parts of the country. They begin to network, learning more about each other's experiences and successes and failures.

If the need is a real one that's also perceived as being important by the community, support for the group increases. Members start to congregate; businesses and individuals with disposable income start to provide financial support; local gay and non-gay foundations are willing to provide support.

Often this growth almost seems spontaneous, it happens so quickly. And most often the organizational structure of the group is too small, too loose to handle the increased needs for financial accountability, communicative services, and fund-raising.

If you're involved in starting an organization, be smart and allow for the group's future growth. Avoid, as soon as possible, wherever possible, overdependence on individuals and lay the groundwork for the organization's own life. That means:

■ Start with the group's own mailbox. The rent is cheap and it provides a continuity that's important. Even if the group goes into hiatus for a period, the rent of a mailbox is minimal; you can keep alive the potential for the organization to continue. Realize that much of the publicity your organization will receive will be published far into the future in periodicals and books such as this one. A group post office box, located in a central location, protects against an organizer's moving and other unforeseen events that will mean that your advertised whereabouts might not be a viable address for you.

■ Consider doing the same thing in terms of a telephone number. Many groups use answering services as a publicized phone contact.

■ Incorporate. The cost of incorporating as a nonprofit organization can be minimal, either through a do-it-yourself packet or with the help of a law firm willing to offer you *pro bono* services. Incorporation protects individuals from tax liability and creates a legal structure for your group. You can also, if you're not involved in strictly political activities, investigate the possibilities of donations being tax deductible.

■ Keep records, not just meeting notes. Have someone start an archive of all your publications and activities. Contact your local public or university library. No matter what you may think of your regional political climate, libraries have a vested interest in sustaining the records of the community. They may well be willing to start a file or archive for you.

▼ *The Southern California Center for Nonprofit Management* publishes an excellent handbook: *Get Ready—Get Set: A Guide to Launching a Nonprofit Organization.* Get a copy by contacting:

Southern California Center for Nonprofit Management
315 W. 9th Street, Suite 1100
Los Angeles, CA 90015

Once you're set up, you can take advantage of *The Support Centers of America.* They publish numerous booklets and pamphlets on the administration of nonprofit organizations of all kinds and sponsor workshops for board members, officers, and staff throughout the year. The costs are kept at a minimum. You can contact the national office or the chapter nearest you:

Support Centers of America, National Office
1410 Q Street NW
Washington, DC 20009
Phone: 202 462 2000

■ CALIFORNIA ■

Support Center
3052 Clairmont Drive, Suite H
San Diego, CA 92117
Phone: 619 275 0880

Support Center
75 Lily
San Francisco, CA 94102
Phone: 415 552 7584

■ ILLINOIS ■

Support Center
166 W. Washington, Suite 530
Chicago, IL 60602
Phone: 312 606 1530

■ MASSACHUSETTS ■

Support Center
14 Beacon Street, Suite 408
Boston, MA 02108
Phone: 617 227 5514

■ NEW JERSEY ■

Support Center
17 Academy Street, Suite 1101
Newark, NJ 07102
Phone: 201 643 5774

■ NEW YORK ■

Accountants for the Public Interest/Support Center
36 W. 44th Street, Suite 1208
New York, NY 10036
Phone: 212 302 6940

■ OKLAHOMA ■

Support Center
515 N.W. 13th Street
Oklahoma City, OK 73103

Support Center
c/o First Tulsa
Box 1
Tulsa, OK 74193
Phone: 918 586 5112

■ RHODE ISLAND ■

Support Center
57 Eddy Street, Suite 504
Providence, RI 02903
Phone: 401 521 0710

■ TENNESSEE ■

Support Center
1755 Lynnfield Road, Suite 244
Memphis, TN 38119
Phone: 901 685 2175

■ TEXAS ■

Support Center
1301 McKinney, Suite 3800
Houston, TX 77010
Phone: 713 739 1211

▼ If you're an executive of a nonprofit organization, you're eligible for a free subscription to *The Nonprofit Times*, a publication designed to help administrators of nonprofit corporations. For more information:

The Nonprofit Times
Box 7286
Princeton, NJ 08543

▼ If you ever need proof of how many gay and lesbian organizations are clustered in New York City, you have only to take a look at the 450-plus entries in *The New York Metropolitan Area Lesbian and Gay Directory of Services and Resources.* The guide is published by the office of the New York City comptroller; your tax dollars at work!

You can get a copy by writing:

Alan Fleishman
Office of the Comptroller
1 Centre Street, Room 839
New York, NY 10007

THE WOMEN IN OUR LIVES

How should gay men relate to lesbians? What do we know about lesbian issues and concerns? How often do we treat the women who are an indispensable part of our political coalitions as though they were intruders on our own turf?

Gay men can, in fact, establish lives composed almost entirely within a male world. There are, especially in the larger cities, neighborhoods, organizations, bars, and support groups of all kinds that are available only to men.

The decision to live in such a male-centric world is one that

A few things gay men have always wanted to know about lesbians *

*but were too afraid of being called **sexist clods** to ask...

MOST LESBIANS HAVE **BETTER** THINGS TO DO THAN SIT AROUND **SCRAPING OFF** THEIR **BODY HAIR**. AND THE **FEW** OF US WHO **DO** PERSIST IN THIS **BIZARRE PATRIARCHAL CUSTOM** ALMOST **ALWAYS** HAVE A GOOD **EXCUSE**.

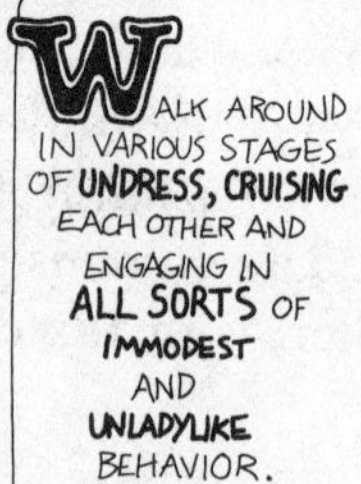

INNATELY **RE-SOURCEFUL** CREATURES, LESBIANS CANNOT **BEAR** TO SPEND HARD-EARNED MONEY ON SOMETHING AS **FRIVOLOUS** AS **FURNITURE** WHEN PERFECTLY **USEFUL** ITEMS CAN BE HAD FOR NEXT TO **NOTHING**.

YES. MOST LESBIANS DELIBERATELY CHOOSE THE **DEEP INTIMACY** BRED OF A **TRUSTING, MONO-GAMOUS** RELATIONSHIP, OVER THE **CHEAP** AND **TRANSITORY THRILLS** OF **PROMISCUITY**.

THERE! WASN'T THAT **BROADENING**? ISN'T CULTURAL EXCHANGE **FUN**?

ANY MORE QUESTIONS?

©1988 BY Alison Bechdel

some people might choose, at least for a part of their lives as they deal with issues of masculinity. But it's not very realistic.

Meeting women on their own ground, talking to them seriously, working with them as real compatriots in our mixed-gender organizations should all be part of the personal agenda of gay men.

Before entering into these serious discussions, a bit of self-deprecating humor might be appropriate. Alison Bechdel, one of the most creative and wise artists working in the gay and lesbian press, did the cartoon on the opposite page. Read it and wonder at your own stereotyping of women.

WHAT WOMEN WOULD LIKE MEN TO KNOW

One of the great frustrations lesbians have with gay men is our lack of knowledge and interest about their lives. Jane Troxell, the editor of *Lambda Book Report* and a columnist for *Feminist Bookstore News,* has put together this annotated listing of the essential reading that a gay man might do to learn more about lesbians:

Zami: A New Spelling of My Name by Audre Lorde. Crossing Press, 1982.

"I have always wanted to be both man and woman, to incorporate the strongest and richest parts of my mother and father within/into me—to share valleys and mountains upon my body the way the earth does in hills and peaks." In Lorde's work lies wisdom and eloquence.

On Lies, Secrets, and Silence: Selected Prose 1966–78 by Adrienne Rich. W. W. Norton, 1979.

Fundamental works from one of America's foremost lesbian/feminist thinkers.

Another Mother Tongue: Gay Words, Gay Worlds by Judy Grahn. Beacon Press, 1984.

An excellent and entertaining account of our collective history. *Another Mother Tongue* will enlighten members of both sexes about their own lives as well as those of their gay brothers and sisters.

Woman's Reality: An Emerging Female System in a White Male Society by Anne Wilson Schaef. Harper & Row, 1985.

Buzz Bryan, a white male colleague at Lambda Rising, recommends this book as "excellent" reading for men and women alike.

"Answer to a Man's Question, 'What Can I Do about Women's Liberation?'" by Susan Griffin, anthologized in ***Gay and Lesbian Poetry in Our Time,*** edited by Carl Morse and Joan Larkin. St. Martin's Press, 1988.

This work is simple, witty, and timeless.

Women of Brewster Place by Gloria Naylor. Viking Penguin, 1982.

In this novel of survival and triumph about *all* women, the subplot of the lesbian lovers, Theresa and Lorraine, is harrowing and unforgettable.

Desert of the Heart by Jane Rule. Naiad Press, 1964.

Of all lesbian literature, this is truly a classic.

WHAT DO THE TERMS MEAN?

If you're new to the gay world, you may not recognize some of the recurring terms that have the status of icons in gay male language: Here are the sources for some of the most important and often used.

Gay is a word with an ancient, if unclear, heritage. Used mainly to refer to people who lived in the sexual underground, it became the word of choice for members of our community who were rebelling against the term *homosexual,* itself a recent invention. Homosexual, which was coined by European academics at the end of the nineteenth century, pointed only to a person's sexual behavior. Gay came to be more inclusive and to encompass a wider range of meaning. The term, one chosen by us rather than applied to us as a label by others, refers to a person's identity and life-style, not just his sexuality.

The Lambda was designated the symbol of gay liberation by the Gay Activists Alliance of New York in 1970. It was adopted as the

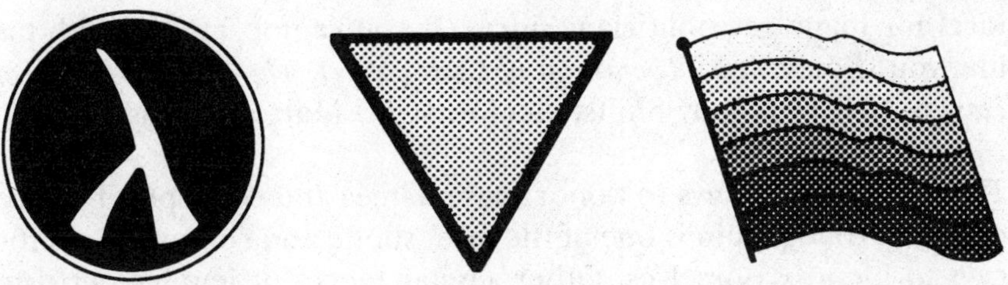

international symbol of gay liberation by the Gay Rights Congress in Edinburgh, Scotland, in 1974. The symbol was chosen because it stands for synergy—the concept that the whole is greater than its independent parts—according to some sources, or, according to others, because it is the letter "L" (for Liberation) in the Greek alphabet.

The Pink Triangle was worn by homosexual prisoners in the Nazi concentration camps. The triangle has come to stand for gay men's and lesbians' vow that the Holocaust will never happen again. Its great value is that those of us who might "pass" as not being gay use the triangle to mark ourselves as the brothers of others who were considered one of the lowest forms of humanity by the Nazis.

The Rainbow flag represents the diversity of the gay community. It's also used by many progressive political movements such as the Rainbow Coalition to signify the joining of all aspects of American society.

Stonewall refers to the night of June 29, 1969, when patrons of the small gay bar in New York City, having long suffered police harassment, fought back when the bar was raided. Their uprising went on for two nights and captured the imagination of gay men and lesbians around the world. Stonewall has become the symbol of united gay action against the general society and it is the event that most Gay Pride celebrations commemorate.

Harvey Milk was a member of the San Francisco Board of Supervisors. He was assassinated on November 27, 1978, as was Mayor George Moscone, by another politician, Dan White. Milk was one of the most charismatic figures the gay world has produced and his progressive, community-based political ideals have become an ideal for many gay politicians since. (If you're not familiar with his life, you should read *The Mayor of Castro Street: The Life and Times of Harvey Milk* by Randy Shilts, New York: St. Martin's Press, 1982.)

There are lots of ways to honor these names and concepts. The use of a pink triangle pin is one of the most subtle and common ways for gays to identify ourselves. Other similar pieces of jewelry perform the same function. Lambda Rising Bookstore carries a full line of pins and bumper stickers, as do many other gay bookstores. It also sells rainbow flags in different sizes. Write to them for costs and details.

Pride Products is a lesbian/gay/feminist jewelry maker that sells jewelry of all sorts using the pink triangle, the lambda, and joined male symbols. Their high-quality goods include everything from lapel pins to rings, money clips to earrings. Many of their goods double as religious symbols, combining the gay emblems with the cross or the star of David. Some other wares include sunglasses with gay symbols discreetly embedded in the lenses and a line of T-shirts that celebrate being out.

Lambda Rising Bookstore
1625 Connecticut Avenue NW
Washington, DC 20009
Phone: 800 621 6969
Fax: 202 462 7257

Pride Products
3449 Orchid Trail
Calabasas, CA 91302
Phone: 818 710 9292
Fax: 818 716 6276

PART TWO

HOW WE COMMUNICATE WITH OURSELVES AND OTHERS

One of the reasons gay people had been so isolated for so long was the ugly perception of our lives. The few glimpses of what it might be like to be gay involved loneliness, mental illness, emotional instability, and grotesque unhappiness. What was needed for us, and for the rest of society, were visions of alternatives to that image. One of the first services of gay activism was talking to the larger population about the variety and value of our gay lives. We set about convincing people that we could see ourselves as something other than victims and as something more than stereotypes. We learned to communicate to one another and to others the broad types of gay experiences and potential.

Once the basic identity of our community began forming, we had to learn how to communicate with one another, to share experiences that would establish a commonality between us, and to alert one another about events that would increase our awareness and involvement. These communications take many forms; they can be simple messages on a telephone answering machine or they can be involved analysis in a journal; they can be advertisements in the mainstream press, or they can be the establishment of our own publications.

SWITCHBOARDS AND HOT LINES

When someone's making an initial contact with the gay world, or reaching out to ask for help in an emergency, community switchboards are often the most efficient and the easiest means of communication. Staffed by volunteers, these services provide peer counseling services, or have referrals to other organizations that do. They usually have a listing of events and activities in their region or area and can provide the phone numbers of political, social, or other community organizations.

UNITED STATES

■ ALABAMA ■

Montgomery
Gay Helpline
205 264 7887

■ ARIZONA ■

Phoenix
Lesbian/Gay Community Switchboard
602 234 2752

■ CALIFORNIA ■

Fairfield
Solano County Gay & Lesbian Info Line
707 448 1010

Garden Grove
Gay & Lesbian Community Services
714 534 3261

Los Angeles
Gay & Lesbian Services Center
213 464 7400

San Bernardino
Gay & Lesbian Community Hotline
714 824 7618

Santa Rosa
Hotline
707 544 HELP

Santa Barbara
Gay & Lesbian Resource Center
805 963 3636

Santa Rosa
Hotline
707 544 HELP

■ COLORADO ■

Aspen
Aspen Gay Community
303 925 9249

Denver
Gay Community Center
303 831 6268

■ CONNECTICUT ■

Danbury
GLAD Helpline
203 426 4922

New Haven
Gay Switchboard
203 624 6869

■ DISTRICT OF COLUMBIA ■

Washington
Gay & Lesbian Switchboard
202 429 4971

Washington
Gay Hotline
202 833 3234

■ FLORIDA ■

Gainesville
Gay Switchboard
904 332 0700

Miami
Gay & Lesbian Hotline
305 759 3661

St. Petersburg
The Line
813 586 4297

■ GEORGIA ■

Atlanta
Gay Center Helpline
404 892 0661

■ HAWAII ■

Maui
Hotline
808 572 1884

■ ILLINOIS ■

Champaign
Lesbian/Gay Switchboard
217 384 8040

Chicago
Lesbian/Gay Helpline
312 929 HELP

■ INDIANA ■

Bloomington
Gay/Lesbian Switchboard
812 855 5688

■ IOWA ■

Ames
Open Line
515 292 7000

■ KANSAS ■

Topeka
Gay Rap Line
913 233 6558

■ KENTUCKY ■

Louisville
Gay and Lesbian Hotline
502 454 6699

■ MAINE ■

Caribou
Gay Phoneline
207 498 2088

■ MARYLAND ■

Baltimore
Gay and Lesbian Switchboard
301 837 8888

GAY AND LESBIAN
COMMUNITY
ACTION
COUNCIL

HELPLINE

■ MICHIGAN ■

Lansing
Michigan Lesbian and Gay Hotline
517 372 8519

■ MINNESOTA ■

Minneapolis
Helpline
612 822 8661

■ MISSOURI ■

Kansas City
Gay Talk
816 931 4470

St. Louis
Gay and Lesbian Hotline
314 367 0084

■ NEVADA ■

Las Vegas
Gay Switchboard
702 733 9990

■ NEW HAMPSHIRE ■

Concord
Gay Helpline
603 595 2650

■ NEW JERSEY ■

S. Hackensack
Gay Activist Alliance Helpline
201 692 1794

■ NEW MEXICO ■

Albuquerque
Common Bond
505 266 8041

■ NEW YORK ■

Albany
Lesbian/Gay Community Council
518 462 6138

Buffalo
Gay and Lesbian Community Center
716 886 1274

New York
Gay and Lesbian Switchboard
212 777 1800

Rochester
Gay Alliance of Genesee Valley
716 244 8640

Syracuse
Gayphone
315 443 3599

White Plains
Hotline
914 948 4922

■ NORTH CAROLINA ■

Charlotte
Gay/Lesbian Switchboard
704 525 6128

Wilmington
Gay Help Line
919 675 9222

■ OHIO ■

Cincinnati
Gay/Lesbian Community Switchboard
513 221 7800

Cleveland
Hotline
216 781 6736

Dayton
Lesbian and Gay Center Hotline
513 228 4875

Toledo
PRO Line
419 243 9351

■ OKLAHOMA ■

Oklahoma City
Oasis Resource Center
405 525 2437

■ OREGON ■

Eugene
Gay & Lesbian Alliance
503 686 3360

■ PENNSYLVANIA ■

Harrisburg
Gay Switchboard
717 234 0328

Lancaster
Gay/Lesbian Helpline
717 397 0691

Philadelphia
Gay Switchboard
215 546 7100

Reading
Lambda Alive
215 374 3000

State College
Gay and Lesbian Switchboard
814 237 1950

■ RHODE ISLAND ■

Providence
Gay Help Line
401 751 3322

■ TENNESSEE ■

Knoxville
Gay Helpline
615 521 6546

Nashville
MCC
615 320 0288

■ TEXAS ■

Dallas
Gayline
214 368 6283

Dallas
Gay Alliance
214 528 4233

Houston
Gay and Lesbian Switchboard
713 529 3211

San Angelo
Gay Community Lifeline
915 942 8115

San Antonio
Gay and Lesbian Switchboard
512 733 7300

■ VIRGINIA ■

Charlottesville
Helpline
804 971 4942

Richmond
Gay Information Line
804 353 3626

■ WASHINGTON ■

Spokane
Gay and Lesbian Community Services
509 489 2266

■ WISCONSIN ■

Milwaukee
Gay Hotline
414 562 7010

CANADA

■ MANITOBA ■

Winnipeg
Gay/Lesbian Info Line
204 284 5208

■ ONTARIO ■

London
Gayline
519 433 3551

PHONE TREES

Phone trees are a highly effective form of grass-roots organizing. One of the most effective is run by The Gay and Lesbian Alliance Against Defamation. Within forty-eight hours of a homophobic incident, GLAAD can marshal hundreds of angry letters and phone messages as a response. When the GLAAD phone tree is activated, you receive a call. You call the GLAAD hot line for details. You call three other people recruited by yourself or else people whose names and addresses have been given you by GLAAD. (Each of them will, in turn, call three more, constantly multiplying the number of people being mobilized.) You write or call whomever is being pressured, whichever is more comfortable for you.

The same kind of process is used by many political groups when they feel it's important to activate a large number of people. If you're involved with another political organization, find out if they have their own phone tree.

For more information:

GLAAD
80 Varick Street, 3E
New York, NY 10013
Phone: 212 966 1700

MAGAZINES AND NEWSPAPERS

The Advocate is the major American gay periodical. Published every two weeks, it is the most widely circulated of the gay press. It carries the normal content of a news magazine—features, news shorts, arts and book reviews, and personality interviews.

It also has one of the most extensive personal advertising sections in the world. Many people who are isolated geographically, or in other ways, are able to make contact with one another through these ads.

Personals are a basic form of advertising for almost all the gay newspapers; *The Advocate* isn't unique in carrying them. Far from it, most gay papers couldn't exist without the income from these ads, and from the circulation that comes from people seeking them out. While the ads carry a perhaps unfair onus because they increase the perception that the periodical is no more than a base sexual marketplace, they perform a much more extensive function, putting people with like minds and similar interests in touch with one another. Many of the organizations listed in this volume were begun when a person placed an ad seeking others who were interested and willing to work in a specific area of concern.

The Advocate
6922 Hollywood Boulevard, 10th floor
Los Angeles, CA 90028

THE ADVOCATE

UNITED STATES

■ ARIZONA ■

WESTERN EXPRESS
Box 5950
Phoenix, AZ 85010
Phone: 602 254 1324

■ CALIFORNIA ■

EDGE
6434 Santa Monica Boulevard
Hollywood, CA 90038
Phone: 213 962 6994
Fax: 213 962 2917

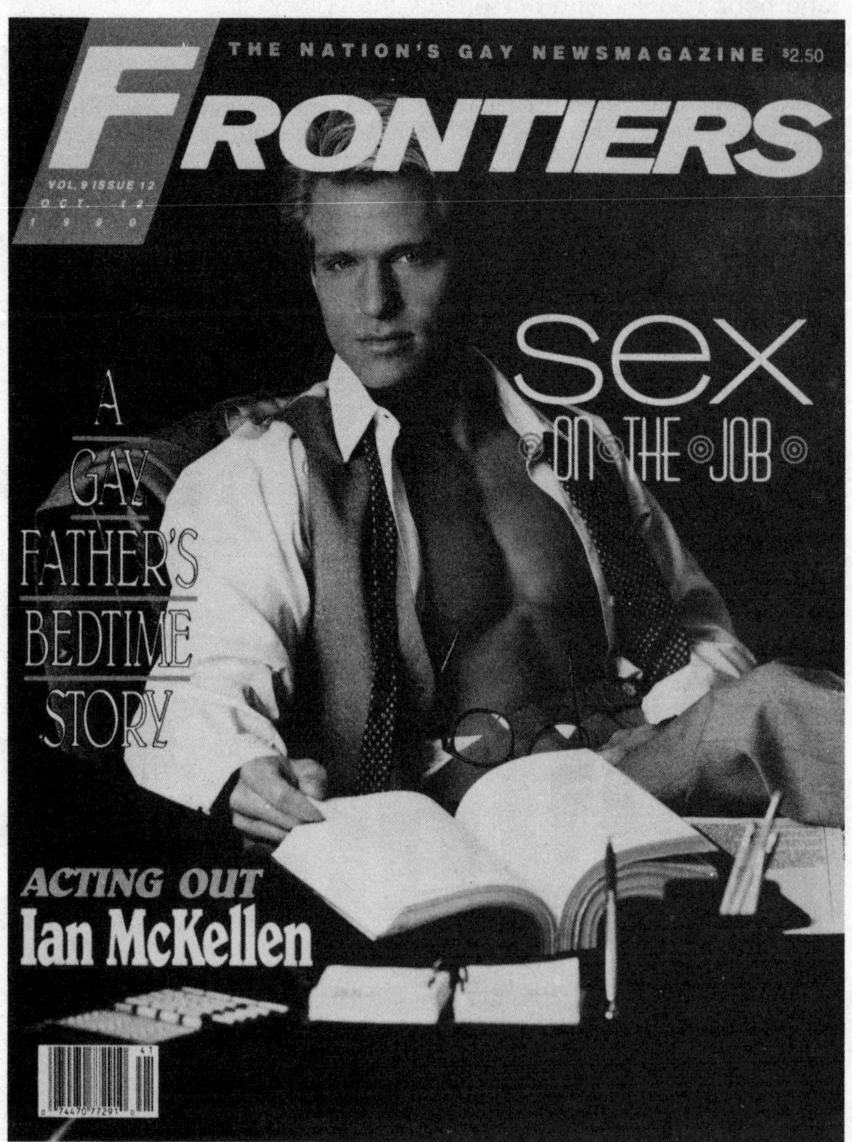

BAY AREA REPORTER
395 9th Street
San Francisco, CA 94103
Phone: 415 861 5019

FRONTIERS
7985 Santa Monica Boulevard,
Suite 109
West Hollywood, CA 90046
Phone: 213 654 7782
Fax: 213 656 8784

MOM . . . GUESS WHAT!
1725 L Street
Sacramento, CA 95814
Phone: 916 441 6397
Fax: 916 552 7921

SAN FRANCISCO SENTINEL
500 Hayes Street
San Francisco, CA 94102
Phone: 415 861 8100
Fax: 415 861 8431

UPDATE
Box 7762
San Diego, CA 92167
Phone: 619 225 0282
Fax: 619 225 0617

■ COLORADO ■

OUT FRONT
Box 18Z
Denver, CO 80218
Phone: 303 778 0470

■ CONNECTICUT ■

METROLINE
495 Farmington Avenue
Hartford, CT 06105
Phone: 203 236 7813
Fax: 203 231 8503

■ DISTRICT OF COLUMBIA ■

THE WASHINGTON BLADE
724 9th Street NW, 8th floor
Washington, DC 20001
Phone: 202 347 2038
Fax: 202 393 6510

■ FLORIDA ■

SOUTHERN EXPOSURE
Box 2226
Key West, FL 33045
Phone: 305 294 6303

THE WEEKLY NEWS
901 N.E. 79th Street
Miami, FL 33138
Phone: 305 757 6333
Fax: 305 756 6488

■ GEORGIA ■

SOUTHERN VOICE
Box 18215
Atlanta, GA 30316
Phone: 404 876 1819
Fax: 404 377 8829

■ HAWAII ■

GAY COMMUNITY NEWS
Box 3224
Honolulu, HI 96801
Phone: 808 536 6000

■ ILLINOIS ■

CHICAGO OUTLINES
3059 N. Southport Avenue
Chicago, IL 60657
Phone: 312 871 7610

GAY CHICAGO
3121 N. Broadway
Chicago, IL 60657
Phone: 312 327 7271
Fax: 312 327 0112

WINDY CITY TIMES
970 W. Montana Street
Chicago, IL 60614
Phone: 312 935 1790
Fax: 312 935 1853

■ INDIANA ■

THE NEW WORKS NEWS
4120 N. Keystone Avenue
Indianapolis, IN 46205
Phone: 317 545 1409

■ LOUISIANA ■

AMBUSH MAGAZINE
Box 71291
New Orleans, LA 70172
Phone: 504 552 8049

IMPACT
Box 52079
New Orleans, LA 70152
Phone: 504 948 9244

■ MAINE ■

OUR PAPER
Box 10744
Portland, ME 04104
Phone: 207 761 0733

■ MARYLAND ■

BALTIMORE GAYPAPER
Box 22575
Baltimore, MD 21203
Phone: 301 837 7748

■ MASSACHUSETTS ■

BAY WINDOWS
1523 Washington Street
Boston, MA 02118
Phone: 617 266 6670
Fax: 617 266 5973

GAY COMMUNITY NEWS
62 Berkeley Street
Boston, MA 02116
Phone: 617 426 4469

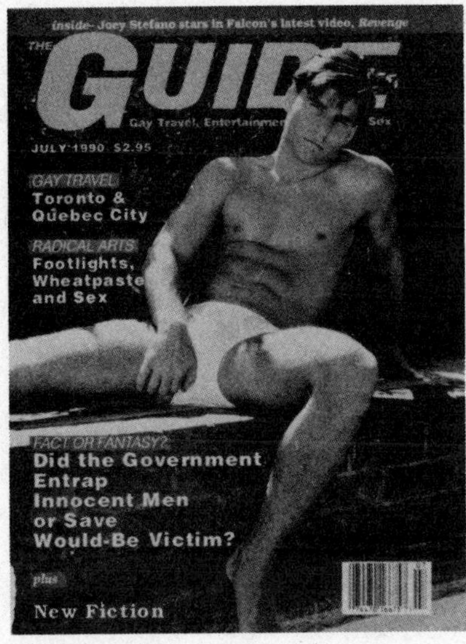

■ MINNESOTA ■

EQUAL TIME
310 E. 38th Street, #207
Minneapolis, MN 55409
Phone: 612 823 3836

GLC VOICE
1624 Harmon Place, #206
Minneapolis, MN 55403
Phone: 612 338 1411

TWIN CITIES GAZE
9 N. 4th Street
Minneapolis, MN 55401
Phone: 612 338 4045
Fax: 612 338 5292

THE GUIDE
Box 593
Boston, MA 02199
Phone: 617 266 8557
Fax: 617 266 1125

ILLUSTRATION BY ALISON BECHDEL.

■ MISSISSIPPI ■

THIS MONTH IN MISSISSIPPI
Box 8342
Jackson, MS 39284
Phone: 601 353 7611

■ MISSOURI ■

ALTERNATE NEWS
3946 Troost
Kansas City, MO 64110
Phone: 816 531 1339

LESBIAN AND GAY NEWS-TELEGRAPH
Box 14229A
St. Louis, MO 63178
Phone: 314 361 0066

■ NEVADA ■

BOHEMIAN BUGLE
Box 19360
Las Vegas, NV 89132
Phone: 702 737 7780

■ NEW MEXICO ■

OUT!
Box 27237
Albuquerque, NM 87125
Phone: 505 243 2540

■ NEW YORK ■

EMPTY CLOSET
179 Atlantic Avenue
Rochester, NY 14607
Phone: 716 244 9030

NEW YORK NATIVE
Box 1475, Church Street Station
New York, NY 10008
Phone: 212 627 2120
Fax: 212 727 9321

OUTWEEK
159 W. 25th Street,
7th floor
New York, NY 10001
Phone: 212 337 1200
Fax: 212 337 1220

■ NORTH CAROLINA ■

FRONT PAGE
Box 27926
Raleigh, NC 27611
Phone: 919 829 0181

■ OHIO ■

GAYBEAT MAGAZINE
Box 11470
Cincinnati, OH 45211
Phone: 513 662 2328

GAY PEOPLES CHRONICLE
Box 5426
Cleveland, OH 44101
Phone: 216 621 5280

■ OKLAHOMA ■

GAYLY OKLAHOMAN
Box 60930
Oklahoma City, OK 73146
Phone: 405 528 0800

■ OREGON ■

JUST OUT
Box 15117
Portland, OR 97214
Phone: 503 236 1252

■ PENNSYLVANIA ■

AU COURANT
222 N. 11th Street
Philadelphia, PA 19107
Phone: 215 592 4615

OUT
747 South Avenue
Pittsburgh, PA 15221
Phone: 412 243 3350
Fax: 412 243 4067

PHILADELPHIA GAY NEWS
254 S. 11th Street
Philadelphia, PA 19107
Phone: 215 625 8501
Fax: 215 925 6437

■ TENNESSEE ■

DARE
Box 40422
Nashville, TN 37204
Phone: 615 327 3273

■ TEXAS ■

DALLAS VOICE
3100 Caryle, Suite 216
Dallas, TX 75204
Phone: 214 521 3230
Fax 214 969 7271

MONTROSE VOICE
408 Avondale
Houston, TX 77006
Phone: 713 529 8490
Fax: 713 524 7587

THIS WEEK IN TEXAS
811 Westheimer, Suite 106
Houston, TX 77006
Phone: 713 527 9111

■ WASHINGTON ■

THE GUIDE
Box 23070
Seattle, WA 98102
Phone: 206 323 7374

SEATTLE GAY NEWS
704 E. Pike
Seattle, WA 98122
Phone: 206 324 4297

■ WISCONSIN ■

IN STEP MAGAZINE
225 S. 2nd Street
Milwaukee, WI 53204
Phone: 414 278 7840

CANADA

■ BRITISH COLUMBIA ■

ANGLES
1170 Bute Street
Vancouver, BC V6E 1Z6
Phone: 604 688 0265

■ ONTARIO ■

RITES
Box 65, Station F
Toronto, ON M4Y 2L4
Phone: 416 964 7577

XTRA
Box 7289, Station A
Toronto, ON M5W 1X9
Phone: 416 925 6665
Fax: 416 925 6674

▼ *The International Directory of Gay and Lesbian Publications* lists all known periodicals. It is available in many libraries, or it can be purchased from:

Orxy Press
2214 N. Central Avenue
Phoenix, AZ 85004

BEFORE YOU TRUST YOUR NEWSPAPER OR NEWS MAGAZINE TOO MUCH . . .

▼ You might want to remember this quote from *Time,* June 21, 1966. Here's what the venerable publication thought of homosexuality, not so long ago:

"It is a pathetic little second-rate substitute for reality, a pitiable flight from life. . . . It deserves no encouragement, no glamorization, no rationalization, no fake status as minority martyrdom, no sophistry about simple differences in taste—and, above all, no pretense that it is anything but a pernicious sickness."

▼ *Paz y Liberación* is a unique newsletter with an international angle. The monthly carries information about gay organizations and movements around the world. Parts of each issue are in Spanish; a major focus of the publication is Latin America.

Paz y Liberación
Box 66450
Houston, TX 77266

▼ *The Gay and Lesbian Press Association* is the coordinating body that works with publishers of all gay and lesbian periodicals. Their annual conventions are a major site for networking. They also hold regional gatherings and workshops and present annual awards for the best in gay and lesbian journalism. Their regular newsletter, *The Media Reporter,* serves as a sounding board for issues and interests of people who are involved in gay publications.

For membership information and more information on the resources they can offer you in your community:

Gay and Lesbian Press Association
Box 8185
Universal City, CA 91608

THE MOST ESSENTIAL NEWSPAPERS?

It would be difficult—and foolhardy—to try to determine which newspapers are better than others. Each one has a different audience and a distinct mission. But to which of these many gay newspapers would a well-read gay man subscribe?

Here are some capsule views of the best known and most widely circulated gay papers:

Gay Community News (Boston) is one of the more leftist (progressive) gay publications in the country. Adamantly inclusive in terms of gender, race, and class, *GCN* has a wide circulation beyond its Boston base and lays legitimate claim to being a national paper.

Philadelphia Gay News is one of the most activist gay liberationist papers. While it is certainly a local paper, *PGN* regularly covers national and international gay politics.

OutWeek (New York City) is one of the newest papers. Its editorial position originated, at least in part, with ACT-UP. A radically pro-gay paper, it's rapidly becoming one of the major publications and is beginning to circulate outside its New York City base.

Our Paper (Maine) has been called one of the best examples of a purely regional newspaper. It has extensive features about Maine and its personalities. Run by a nonprofit collective, it's not bound by commercial considerations that sometimes lead many other papers to spend too much editorial space on bars and their promotional contests.

The Front Page (North Carolina) is a regional paper for both Carolinas and parts of neighboring states. It regularly runs in-depth features on the gay world in its area and has a fine reputation for its other major articles. It does a superb job in providing a bulletin board for activists in a wide geographic region.

THE LESBIAN AND GAY NEWS MAGAZINE NO. 61
OUTWEEK
$2.95 USA $1.95 in NYC
PAT CALIFIA'S
BIKER DYKES

Can
Deborah
Glick
Get to
Albany?
The Gay
Guerrillas
PINK PANTHERS
SEIZE THE STREETS

36
0 74470 77824 0
EWS • SEXUAL POLITICS • HEALTH • THE ARTS

GAY COVERAGE IN MAINSTREAM NEWSPAPERS

The American Society of Newspaper Editors has published an incredible look at the inside of newspaper reporting. *Alternatives: Gays and Lesbians in the Newsroom* includes extensive interviews with gay and lesbian employees. In addition to the attributed essays about what it's like to work on a newspaper, there are also extensive polls on what a number of gay and lesbian reporters and editors—both named and anonymous—think about their papers' coverage of our issues.

Most reporters think that their newspapers do an adequate job of covering AIDS, but they aren't so enthusiastic about the handling other gay topics receive. Eighty-three percent of the respondents to the poll thought their newspaper did not devote enough space to issues of concern to gays and lesbians (other than medical issues). And 46 percent thought what coverage existed was only "fair"; 27 percent thought it was "poor."

On specific subjects, here's what the respondents thought of the coverage their publications gave:

Violence against gays, lesbians	23 percent Good/excellent 73 percent Fair/poor
Life-styles	17 percent Good/excellent 81 percent Fair/poor
Civil rights	27 percent Good/excellent 74 percent Fair/poor
Rights legislation	27 percent Good/excellent 72 percent Fair/poor
Politics	19 percent Good/excellent 81 percent Fair/poor
Community events	10 percent Good/excellent 85 percent Fair/poor

> *"Apart from AIDS and the occasional public restroom bust, our paper, like many others, has virtually no coverage of the gay and lesbian community. Little wonder then that the heterosexual public has so little understanding of the gays and lesbians living among them.*
>
> *"I have experienced no overt discrimination [at my job]. Since it is known that I am gay, I wonder to what extent people self-censor their biased comments. I think it is important for the gay 'cause' for straight people to know gays and lesbians and know their orientation."*
>
> —*MICHAEL HALLINAN, news editor*
> The Everett [WA] Herald
> *quoted in* Alternatives

▼ Anyone interested in gays and the media needs to get a copy of this excellent report. *Alternatives* is available for $3.95 from:

American Society of Newspaper Editors
Box 17004
Washington, DC 17004

THE GAY AND LESBIAN PRESS ASSOCIATION

The most complete listing of gay and lesbian media is compiled by *The Gay and Lesbian Press Association.* It contains hundreds of entries, including newspapers, other publications, and broadcasting outlets. The sale of the list is a major source of income for the association; they aren't able to give it out without a fee. For more information:

Gay and Lesbian Press Association
Box 8185
Universal City, CA 91608
Phone: 818 880 4139

INDEXES

The Alternative Press Index includes some gay newspapers and other periodicals. The *Index* creates its work so that alternative voices will be heard and collected.

Here are the publications that are included. (*Note:* Not all are still being published.)

The Advocate
Black/Out
Fag Rag
Gay Community News (Mass.)
Lambda Book Report
RFD
Rites

The Alternative Press Index is available in most larger libraries. For more information:

Alternative Press Center
Box 33109
Baltimore, MD 21218
Phone: 301 243 2471

▼ *Stephen Hunt* describes himself as an "inference reader." He regularly reads midwestern mainstream newspapers and the gay and lesbian press from across the country. Then he mails a weekly composite clipping sheet and other materials to apprise national news editors and various gay and lesbian "thought-leaders" of what's happening in the heartland.

The service is nonprofit; there's no charge. Hunt describes the operation as a kind of clipping service with special New Age values of insight, intuition, and sensitivity to gay and lesbian issues.

Materials that Hunt collects are routinely handed over to the Gerber-Hunt Library in Chicago.

Stephen Hunt
Inference Reader
1235 W. Loyola Avenue, #420
Chicago, IL 60626

COMPUTER BULLETIN BOARDS

The following is a listing of gay and lesbian and mixed electronic Bulletin Board Systems (BBS) provided by:

Joh Stamford-Chew
Harbor Communications
337 E. Lorraine Avenue
Baltimore, MD 21218
Phone: 301 366 8423 (Voice)/
301 235 6753 (Harbor Bytes BBS)

ILLUSTRATION © 1990, HARBOR BYTES, INC., REPRINTED WITH PERMISSION.

UNITED STATES

■ ARIZONA ■

602 345 8635 Twilight Zone

■ CALIFORNIA ■

Los Angeles Area

818 508 5178	SM Board (system password BIG BOOK)
818 358 6968	"Other" Ball
818 508 6482	Motherboard
818 509 9681	Oracle (system password LEATHER)
818 764 1739	Skinner Jack's Bath House
818 785 3340	The Board with No Name
818 842 9554	Foxxnet (system password SPANK)
818 592 1311	Joystick BBS
213 461 9899	Kings and Queens of Hearts
213 849 4048	Star Chat

Orange County Area

714 622 3174	Men's Room
714 779 2761	Foxhole

Sacramento Area

916 967 5817	Acropolis

San Diego

619 292 1184	Genesis (system password GAY)
619 444 7099	Bill Blue's PMS (mixed straight and gay)

San Francisco

415 349 6969	Wally's World
415 550 7377	New Kinky Komputer
415 552 8268	Kinky Komputer 1
415 647 3199	Byte It
415 756 6235	T-room
415 572 9563	PC Bear Lair
415 759 0521	Lambda
415 769 0918	Daddy's BBS
415 863 9697	Fog City BBS
415 864 1522	All My Modems
415 864 6535	Rough and Ready
415 864 7955	Local Talent (system password GAY)
415 922 5489	Alternatives (lesbian/feminist)

■ COLORADO ■

303 795 1215	G.C. FIDO

■ CONNECTICUT ■

203 644 5959	Billy's

■ FLORIDA ■

Miami

305 662 1748	The Eclectic

Orlando

407 351 6320 Compu-Who?

■ GEORGIA ■

404 321 5586 Hotlanta
404 350 0308 K. Scot's

■ ILLINOIS ■

312 281 6887 Coconut Club
312 337 2410 Cockpit
312 561 2382 Bear Link
312 674 2282 Closet
312 975 6546 Manhole

■ KANSAS ■

Topeka

913 362 6603 Male Exchange

Wichita

316 529 2688 Land of Awes (system password ADVOCATE)

■ KENTUCKY ■

606 252 3330 Kentucky BBS

■ MARYLAND ■

301 235 6753 Harbor Bytes BBS (oldest and largest in MD)
301 561 3983 Rendezvous BBS (mixed straight and gay)
301 661 8861 Purple Haze BBS

■ MASSACHUSETTS ■

618 235 9464 Doug's Den
617 265 4155 The Boston Connection
617 395 8866 Eagle's Nest BBS
617 923 3255 Luv Connection East

■ MINNESOTA ■

313 348 7854 Fountains of Pleasure

■ NEW JERSEY ■

Newark

201 431 1216 Backroom II
201 968 4349 Super Stud
201 992 5660 Christopher Street

Trenton

609 886 6818 Inferno

■ NEW MEXICO ■

505 265 4882 Buddy Board

■ NEW YORK ■

212 821 4180 NYC BBS
212 787 4787 Hard Candy
718 526 8184 Park BBS
718 531 9475 Pier
718 849 1614 Backroom

The BACKROOM
America's Largest Gay/Lesbian Computer Information Service
(718) 849-1614 (modem)

© 1990, BACKROOM, INC., REPRINTED WITH PERMISSION.

■ NORTH CAROLINA ■

704 568 6124 Metrolink

■ OKLAHOMA ■

918 744 9456 Ike's (gay section—"ALT LIFESTYLES")

■ PENNSYLVANIA ■

215 691 0491 The Locker Room (Hot!)

■ TEXAS ■

Dallas

214 288 7929 Texas Lambda

Houston

813 621 4951 Network

■ VIRGINIA ■

Arlington

803 578 4542 Gay/Lesbian Information Board (GLIB)

■ WASHINGTON ■

206 286 1850 Stage BBS

■ WISCONSIN ■

Madison

608 258 9555 The Party Board (ask for access to gay sections)

Milwaukee

414 447 4360 Western Star

CANADA

■ ONTARIO ■

416 979 3765 Glad Club
416 944 0178 Pink Flamingo
416 778 5346 Toronto Fag Exchange
416 882 1744 Gay Blade

▼ *The Pink Triangle Computer Alliance* is a Washington-based organization of lesbians and gay men who work with computers and use bulletin boards. Their activities include a Clip Art project that will collect images of gay men and lesbians that can be downloaded by computer users, a newsletter on activities, a local skill bank of volunteers who are willing to help other lesbian and gay nonprofit organizations with their computer expertise, and the creation of a Software Award to stimulate interest in creating lesbian- and gay-friendly computer games, databases, and so on.

While most activities appear to be in the Washington area, others can join and probably benefit from the contact with like-minded computer nuts.

Pink Triangle Computer Alliance, Inc.
Box 7336
Silver Spring, MD 20907

AIDS INFORMATION BULLETIN BOARDS

UNITED STATES

■ CALIFORNIA ■

Los Angeles

213 825 3736 UCLA DAIMP Drug Abuse and AIDS

San Francisco

415 626 1246 AIDS Info BBS

■ DELAWARE ■

302 731 1998 Black Bag BBS

■ GEORGIA ■

404 377 9563 AIDS Infoline

■ MARYLAND ■

301 235 8530 PAAINE BBS

■ TEXAS ■

San Antonio

512 444 9908 HEALTH-LINK

Dallas

214 247 2367 AIDS Info Exchange

HOW TO USE A COMPUTER BULLETIN BOARD

If you decide to enter the world of computer bulletin boards, here are a few tips from Joh Stanford-Chew, the SysOp of *Harbor Bytes.*

1. When you first "log-on" (call a system), you are usually asked to fill out a short questionnaire, asking your real name, your address, and your telephone number. This is used for a process known as "validation." The SysOp (short for System Operator) will usually make either voice or mail contact with you. On systems that require validation, you are usually blocked from seeing the complete system until you have been validated; the process usually takes only a day or so.

2. Larger, legitimate systems require you to pay a small fee for use of the board, and will usually give you complimentary time in which to assure them that you do indeed wish to subscribe. Do not think of the subscription as a requisite fee. Instead, it allows the SysOp (of which very few are independently wealthy) to expand and maintain the system in a professional manner, thereby providing you, the user, with a much better forum than can usually be found on "free" systems. There are exceptions to this rule, of course. Be prudent with your subscription dollars. The "BBS Bug" bites hard, right in the wallet. After a couple of months of $300 long-distance bills and numerous subscriptions, you may find yourself in over your head.

3. On the subject of long-distance bills, there are companies which allow you to make data (modem contact with most major cities) for a flat fee each month. While they are clumsy to use, limit you to evening hours, and are very busy, they can save you up to 60 percent off the charges of your usual long-distance carrier. One such service is P.C. Pursuit, offered by Telenet, Inc., at 1-800 TELENET.

4. If you have been validated for a system which does not seem to have any areas for gays, do not hesitate to ask the SysOp for such areas. On some systems, a special request must be submitted for access to these areas. On other systems, they are simply not present, but your request shows the SysOp that there is interest in such a section.

5. If you have any problems while on-line, do not hesitate to ask the SysOp for help. Many new BBSers have the impression that if they bother the SysOp too much s/he will "get mad" at them. Your interest in the system is what keeps it going, and the SysOp is more than happy to help.

6. By all means . . . have fun. Don't take yourself or others too seriously while on-line. Remember, you have no facial expressions, body language, or inflections to accent your messages, so many times a cute, flip comment can be misconstrued as a vicious attack. Keep it light, use lots of punctuation (screw the rules of grammar!) and try some of these symbols in your text:

:-) is a grin.

:-(is a frown.

:-() is a scream.

:-O is a yawn

GAY RADIO

Radio is one of the easiest ways for gay men to communicate with one another and with our community. Many college campus stations and public radio stations sponsor gay programming.

Unfortunately, this is one of the most difficult areas of gay communication to document. Also, since the programming can be done with a very small amount of money or investment, it's one of the least stable fields of gay contact. It's nearly impossible to make up a list of all the gay radio programs that will be around for any length of time. Call your gay switchboard, check with your gay community center or political organization, or check your local gay newspaper for current radio listings in your area.

LOCALLY PRODUCED RADIO PROGRAMS

UNITED STATES

■ CALIFORNIA ■

IMRU
Overnight Productions
KPFK-FM
3729 Cahuenga Boulevard W
North Hollywood, CA 91604
Phone: 213 833 0283

■ MINNESOTA ■

FRESH FRUIT
KFAI
1518 E. Lake Street, Suite 209
Minneapolis, MN 55407
Phone: 612 721 5011

■ MISSOURI ■

THE GAYDAR SHOW!
KOPN-FM
915 E. Broadway
Columbia, MO 65201

■ OHIO ■

ALTERNATING CURRENTS
c/o WAIF-FM
2525 Victory Parkway
Cincinnati, OH 45209

GAYWAVES
WRUW
11220 Bellflower Road
Cleveland, OH 44106

■ PENNSYLVANIA ■

GAYDREAMS
WXPN
3905 Spruce Street
Philadelphia, PA 19104
Phone: 215 898 6677

■ TENNESSEE ■

GAY ALTERNATIVE
WEVL
Box 41773
Memphis, TN 38104

CANADA

■ BRITISH COLUMBIA ■

THE COMING OUT SHOW
CFRO
337 Carrall Street
Vancouver, BC V6B 2J4
Phone: 604 684 8494

GAY WAVES
CKUV
Box 3035
University of Victoria
Victoria, BC V8W 3P3
Phone: 604 721 7211

■ NOVA SCOTIA ■

THE WORD IS OUT
c/o Student Union Building, Enquiry Desk
6136 University Avenue
Halifax, NS B3H 4J2

NATIONALLY DISTRIBUTED RADIO PROGRAMS

This Way Out is an internationally produced and distributed weekly lesbian and gay radio program currently on the air on over forty community radio stations in six countries.

This Way Out has won many prizes, including a 1988 Outstanding Achievement Award from the Gay and Lesbian Press Association. Satellite transmission of *This Way Out,* originating in Los Angeles, is underwritten by The Chicago Resource Center, making the show free of charge to any member of the National Public Radio Network. It is also distributed on reel-to-reel or cassette tape to stations in the United States and Canada unable to receive the NPR signal. There is a minimal cost for the tapes and postage and handling.

Stations with no locally produced gay and lesbian programs schedule *This Way Out* in a regular weekly time slot. Local gay and lesbian shows use selected segments of the program.

This Way Out has also become a "sound archive" for the gay movement, preserving the voices and issues of concern to the lesbian and gay communities for future historians.

If no radio station in your area carries *This Way Out,* ask why. There's every reason to have this program on every noncommercial radio station possible.

This Way Out is supported by some grants, but it also needs individual support. The 25 Club is made up of people who donate at least $25 a month to ensure the continuation of this vital gay and lesbian programming.

the international
gay and lesbian radio magazine

▼ *Naming Names* is a weekly program produced by GLAAD (Gay and Lesbian Alliance Against Defamation) and WBAI-FM in New York. The seven-minute show reports on recent defamation of the gay and lesbian community and provides names and addresses so that listeners may respond to what they have heard. *Naming Names* is sent up onto the National Public Radio satellite every other week and any station that has the capacity to pull it down for broadcast may do so. Or, any station that's interested can receive the program on cassette directly from GLAAD.

If no radio station in your area carries *Naming Names,* find out why.

Naming Names
GLAAD
80 Varick Street, Suite 3E
New York, NY 10013
Phone: 212 966 1700

GAY HAM RADIO

Lambda Amateur Radio Club is an alliance of gay ham radio operators. Ham operators, who must be licensed by their governments, operate two-way radio stations from their homes or cars, talking with other hams across town or across the world. Special sets of radio frequencies, or bands, are set aside for use only by amateur radio operators. Hams are not CB'ers (Citizen Band Operators). CB is intended for local business or personal use, and does not require a license. Ham radio is a worldwide service, for noncommercial use only, and a license is necessary. Ham radio is primarily a hobby, but in times of emergency or disaster, it serves as a valuable public service communications network.

Lambda Amateur Radio has been in existence since 1975. The club has a lending library of licensing materials for interested prospective members. It sponsors an awards ceremony and publishes *Lambda Net News,* a monthly publication. Active local chapters of the group have been formed and operate independent social programs.

For more information:

Lambda Amateur Radio Club
Box 24810
Philadelphia, PA 19130

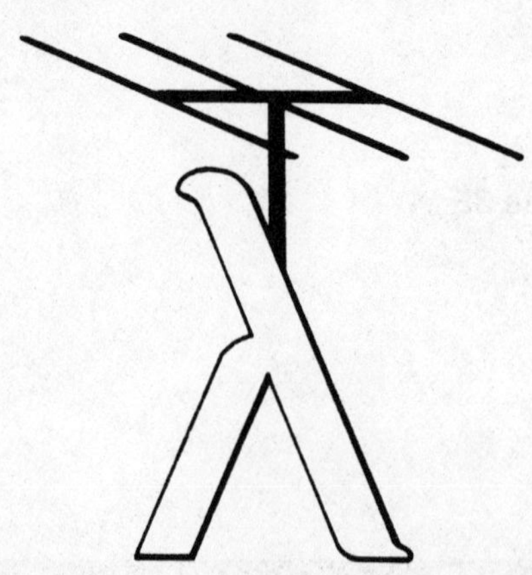

GAY TELEVISION

CABLE TELEVISION PROGRAMS

Mark Behar of Milwaukee Gay/Lesbian Cable Network maintains a networking list of gay and lesbian television producers in North America. The following names and addresses are provided by him. For more information, or to have your address added, contact:

Mark Behar
Co-Executive Producer
Milwaukee Gay/Lesbian Cable Network
Box 239
Milwaukee, WI 53201
Phone: 414 277 7671

UNITED STATES

■ CALIFORNIA ■

MCC-SAN DIEGO
Box 33291
San Diego, CA 92103
Phone: 619 280 0875

MCC-San Diego produces two regular programs. *Reflections of MCC* is composed of religious services. *Homosexuality and the Scriptures* is theological.

BEING GAY TODAY
Ron Hatch
5951 Riverside Boulevard, Suite 306
Sacramento, CA 95831
Phone: 916 392 7025

Live one-hour studio show.

OUTLOOK: GAY AND LESBIAN VIDEO MAGAZINE
Phil Tuggle
1519 Mission Street
San Francisco, CA 94103
Phone: 415 621 5619

Monthly half-hour magazine-style program in the South Bay area.

COMMUNITY ACTION NETWORK
Allen McClain
Box 146937
San Francisco, CA 94114
Phone: 415 285 1533

This biweekly half-hour cable show is a Gay & Lesbian Press Association Award winner.

FRAMELINE PRESENTS
Frameline
Box 14792
San Francisco, CA 94114
Phone: 415 861 5245

■ GEORGIA ■

GAY CABLE NETWORK
Jeffrey Laymon, Program Director
1519 Oakridge Street
Decatur, GA 30033
Phone: 404 633 4754

A one-hour-a-week program on local programs that's supported with grants both from the private sector and the City of Atlanta.

■ ILLINOIS ■

THE 10% SHOW
John Ryan
606 W. Barry, #234
Chicago, IL 60657
Phone: 312 348 6374

A one-hour program, aired monthly on five area cable systems. The program is rebroadcast many times in a month and has a potential audience of over a million viewers.

■ INDIANA ■

YOUR CHILDREN TOO
Michael Drudge
222 E. Leith Street
Fort Wayne, IN 45806

GAY TV
Gregg McDaniel
Box 2181
Indianapolis, IN 46206
Phone: 317 635 8397

■ LOUISIANA ■

JUST FOR THE RECORD
Box 3768
New Orleans, LA 70177
Phone: 504 948 4505

■ MICHIGAN ■

THE LAMBDA REPORT
The Michigan Organization for Human Rights
Box 27383
Lansing, MI 48909
Phone: 517 887 2605

The MOHR produces a statewide program shown in thirty-five cities. (It's banned in eleven other cities; Detroit still doesn't have cable.)

The Lambda Journal airs separate programs featuring single topics. MOHR also produces *The Lambda Report,* a quarterly investigative magazine show, shown on at least a half-dozen stations. Within the *Lambda Report* is the *AIDS Report,* a discrete learning module which is funded by a grant from the state for AIDS education.

■ MINNESOTA ■

GAZE
Brad Theissen
9 N. 4th Street, #212
Minneapolis, MN 55401
Phone: 612 338 4045

■ NEW YORK ■

GAY BROADCASTING SYSTEM
2264 Creston Avenue, 1G
Bronx, NY 10453
Phone: 212 562 3229

Out in the 90s is a one-hour weekly live news and information talk studio program broadcast on many cable systems in the three-state metropolitan area.

GAY CABLE NETWORK
32 Union Square East, Suite 1217
New York, NY 10003
Phone: 212 477 4220

Produces three programs: *Pride and Progress,* about news, sports, and health; *The Right Stuff,* about entertainment, reviews, and interviews; *Men and Films,* about reviewing male sex videos.

LIVING WITH AIDS
Gay Men's Health Crisis
Box 274
132 W. 24th Street
New York, NY 10011
Phone: 212 807 7517

A half-hour weekly program on AIDS-related issues.

■ OHIO ■

OUTFRONT
3000 W. McMicken
Cincinnati, OH 45225
Phone: 513 751 7808

STONEWALL LESBIAN/GAY PRIDE REPORT
Box 10814
Columbus, OH 43201
Phone: 514 299 7764

A twice-weekly program includes local and national gay and lesbian news, a calendar of upcoming events, and interviews with local, state, and national gay and lesbian leaders.

■ OREGON ■

BENT COMMUNICATIONS
1108 N.E. Going Street
Portland, OR 97211
Phone: 503 284 6807

■ TENNESSEE ■

GAY CABLE NETWORK/NASHVILLE
Box 22011
Nashville, TN 37202

■ VIRGINIA ■

SIGNIFICANT OTHERS

Russell Snider
Box 10629
Arlington, VA 22210
Phone: 703 532 4497

Produces a video news magazine that includes headline news, documentaries, and interviews of interest to the gay community.

GAY FAIRFAX

Fairfax Lesbian and Gay Citizens Association
Box 2322
Springfield, VA 22152
Phone: 703 451 9528

■ WISCONSIN ■

NOTHING TO HIDE

David Runyon
4701 Judy Lane
Madison, WI 53704
Phone: 608 241 2500

MILWAUKEE GAY/LESBIAN CABLE NETWORK

Box 239
Milwaukee, WI 53201
Phone: 414 277 7671

Past productions have included *Tri-Cable Tonight,* a prizewinning half-hour monthly magazine format studio program. Planned productions: *Yellow on Thursday,* a gay and lesbian community humor and comedy program, and documentaries.

CANADA

■ MANITOBA ■

COMING OUT!
Winnipeg Gay Media Collective
Box 1661
Winnipeg, MB R3C 2Z6

A radio program begun in 1977 became a television show in 1981. The weekly program reaches 225,000 homes. This organization has an extensive library of previously broadcast programs that they're anxious to trade for other gay and lesbian programming.

■ ONTARIO ■

THUNDER GAY MAGAZINE
Doug Broman
c/o AIDS Committee of Thunder Bay
Box 3586
Thunder Bay, ON P7B 6E2
Phone: 807 345 1516

▼ *The National Federation of Local Cable Programmers,* a general community organization, has also collected a networking list of gay and lesbian programmers. They sponsor an annual Hometown USA Video Festival, the largest video competition in the world, open to, but not limited to, gay and lesbian programming.

For more information:

National Federation of Local Cable Programmers
Box 27290-7290
Washington, DC 20038
Phone: 202 829 7186

HOW A GAY VIDEO COMPANY STARTS

The first broadcast of *Just for the Record* was in May of 1987. The program was fueled by a defeat of a New Orleans city ordinance that would have banned discrimination on the grounds of sexual orientation. The defeat served as a compelling reminder of the fear, hatred, and ignorance in the public attitude toward homosexuality.

Just for the Record is intended to be educational, informative, and entertaining. It's targeted directly at the gay community, but strives to be of value to the community as a whole.

Since 1987, there have been more than forty programs, each thirty minutes long, aired on the New Orleans Public Access Channel. The programs aim at keeping people informed of relevant events, workshops, and organizations. They have covered national topics such as the march on Washington and the NAMES Project. They have also covered various issues concerning the AIDS crisis. They collaborated with other gay cable companies to cover the 1988 National Republican Convention.

To get out word about their programs, *Just for the Record* publishes a monthly newsletter. Programs are marketed as home videos and sold through local gay businesses and bookstores for those without a cable hookup or for those who miss the original broadcast.

Just for the Record has begun selling advertising to local gay businesses to increase revenue to help improve the quality of its programming. It also has won Municipal Endowment Cable Grants for the past few years.

Male Entertainment Network

MEN is a unique utilization of video communication. The company makes video tapes of gay community events all around the country. The topics include everything from male beauty contests to the 1987 march on Washington. The videos are available for purchase by mail order, but the company has another system of distribution in addition to private sales.

MEN has created a network of video outlets, most of them in gay bars, which show their programs on television screens. The system is underwritten by advertisers, whose commercials go out on the same tapes for popular viewing in gay gathering spots.

For information on either the individual tapes available or on the commercial network MEN has set up, write:

Male Entertainment Network
One United Nations Plaza
San Francisco, CA 94102

GLAAD also published *The Media Guide to the Lesbian and Gay Community.* Designed to inform journalists and other reporters who are interested in covering the gay community, the guide includes a list of contacts at lesbian and gay advocacy, social service, and media organizations; a glossary of terms and a listing of "do's and don'ts"; a chronology of the American gay and lesbian movement; a primer on gay and lesbian history and culture, political and legal issues, and sociological issues; advice on covering the AIDS epidemic; and ideas for stories about the lesbian and gay community.

Any writer could benefit from this resource. If you know someone who's covering our community—whether he or she is straight or gay or lesbian—you should turn the reporter on to this important book.

It's available for $15 (there are discounts for bulk purchases) from GLAAD's national office.

OTHER RESOURCES

THE COMMUNITY CARDPACK

As the number of gay men and lesbians coming out increases, they provide a more coherent market for advertisers. Strub-Dawson is a gay-owned direct mail company that's put together a mailing list of over 100,000 gay and lesbian households in the country. Using this list, they've created *The Community Cardpack,* a direct mail "response deck" that's mailed periodically announcing the availability of goods and services directed to the gay and lesbian communities and, often, solicitations for funds or political action. Magazine and book publishers, AIDS organizations, artists, travel promoters, and other entrepreneurs have used the service, including such mainstream firms as Book-of-the-Month Club.

If you'd like to receive the Cardpack, or if you'd like to investigate advertising through it, contact:

Strub-Dawson
One Bridge Street
Irvington, NY 10533
Phone: 914 591 5900
Fax: 914 591 5918

GAYELLOW PAGES

Gayellow Pages offers over 8,000 entries on self-adhesive mailing labels. Deletions and additions are performed daily, so the lists on labels are always more current than the printed book. They will buy back for 25 cents each address that bounces within sixty days of your purchase, provided the front of the envelope, complete with any post office endorsements and corrections, is returned. Contact them for extracts from the list: they can select entries by gender, geographical region, specific category, etc. They can sort by name, city, zip, etc. Below are classifications from *Gayellow Pages* to give you an idea of what is available, and a rough idea of the number of addresses. Let them know what you need, and subject to a $20 minimum they will try to meet your request. Prices are about 10 cents per label. Contact the company to find out the cost of the list you might want to buy.

The entire list—8,000-plus businesses, organizations, publications, resources, etc., in USA and Canada:

Not-for-profit groups, publications, organizations, etc., in USA and Canada: 3,500

Businesses in USA and Canada: 4,500

Media labels: Gay, feminist, and receptive alternative publications and broadcast media: 750

Gay, feminist, erotica, and receptive general bookstores, with some gift and card stores and a handful of other businesses interested in buying gay-related items: 900

Gay, feminist, and general bookstores; no exclusively erotica ("adult") businesses: 450

Health care: Includes physical and mental health professionals, AIDS resources, plus community centers, hot lines, organizations and publications having a particular interest in gay health and/or AIDS: 1,200

Resources specifically concerned with AIDS, ARC, etc. Over 1,300 movement, political, social and support groups: 1,300

Religious groups: 600

Accommodations: Hotels, resorts, guest houses, etc.: 350

Bars, restaurants, discos, clubs: 2,000

Student and academic groups: 200

Renaissance House
Box 292 Village Station
New York, NY 10014
Phone: 212 674 0120

FIGHTING MEDIA STEREOTYPES

GLAAD

The Gay and Lesbian Alliance Against Defamation (GLAAD) has been our national voice against hate in the media since it was founded in 1985. GLAAD monitors media portrayals of gay concerns and responds quickly and loudly and effectively whenever negative images or dangerous stereotypes are used in newspapers, television, radio, or film.

GLAAD works in many ways. It educates media executives about violence and discrimination provoked by defamation and produces public service advertising to counter stereotyping. It mobilizes community responses to defamation through protests, picket lines, letter writing campaigns, and phone trees. It works with reporters, editors, programmers, and producers to generate positive coverage of the gay and lesbian community.

Participation in GLAAD at any level is one of the easiest and least time-consuming forms of gay activism you can find. Contact your local office or write to the New York chapter office, which functions as the national headquarters.

GLAAD

GAY & LESBIAN ALLIANCE AGAINST DEFAMATION

UNITED STATES

■ CALIFORNIA ■

GLAAD/LOS ANGELES
Box 741346
Los Angeles, CA 90004
Phone: 213 931 9429

GLAAD/ORANGE COUNTY
105 E. Wilkin Way, #A
Anaheim, CA 92802

GLAAD/SACRAMENTO
Box 188421
Sacramento, CA 95818
Phone: 916 552 1935

GLAAD/SAN FRANCISCO BAY AREA
347 Dolores Street, Room 312
San Francisco, CA 94110
Phone: 415 861 4588
Fax: 415 863 4740

■ DISTRICT OF COLUMBIA ■

GLAAD/NATIONAL CAPITOL AREA
Box 57044
Washington, DC 20036
Phone: 202 429 9500

■ ILLINOIS ■

GLAAD/CHICAGO
Box 148282
Chicago, IL 60614

■ MARYLAND ■

GLAAD/BALTIMORE
Gay and Lesbian Community Center of Baltimore
241 Chase Street
Baltimore, MD 21201
Phone: 301 837 8639

■ MASSACHUSETTS ■

GLAAD/BOSTON
Lesbian & Gay Community Services Center
338 Newbury Street
Boston, MA 02116
Phone: 617 492 4639

■ NEW YORK ■

GLAAD/NEW YORK
80 Varick Street, #3E
New York, NY 10013
Phone: 212 966 1700
Fax: 212 966 1701
Phone tree: 212 966 1702

■ TEXAS ■

GLAAD/Dallas
Box 190712
Dallas, TX 75219
Phone: 214 526 4523

GLAAD/HOUSTON
c/o 306 Stratford, #12
Houston, TX 77006

> *I'm proud to live in this great, free country. I'm proud of our commitment to free speech . . . and I'm proud of our country's commitment to protecting the rights of its citizens to work and live free from bigotry and violence. That's why I was amazed to discover that many people die each year in anti-gay attacks and thousands more are left scarred, emotionally and physically. Bigotry has no place in this great nation and violence has no place in this world. But it happens. Prejudice hurts . . . kills. Please don't be part of it.*
>
> —*BOB HOPE*

▼ At the request of the *Gay and Lesbian Alliance Against Defamation (GLAAD),* Bob Hope has filmed a public service announcement condemning anti-gay/lesbian violence. The thirty-second video features Mr. Hope—in a tux and standing in front of a blue sequined curtain—commenting that anti-gay violence violates the American traditions of free speech and respect for minorities.

The tape has been carried as a news item on "Entertainment Tonight" and in *People* magazine, and several broadcast and cable TV stations have agreed to air it.

The Hope public service announcement is available to groups around the country who want to try to get local TV stations to carry it, and for other purposes. Groups in Washington, D.C., and New York State have already used the PSA when lobbying for legislation related to anti-gay violence.

GLAAD will provide copies of the tape in VHS format for $25 (and will consider special pleas of poverty). When TV stations express an interest in broadcasting it, GLAAD can then provide a tape in the three-quarter-inch or one-inch formats stations typically need. Along with the tape, GLAAD will send an agreement imposing minor restrictions on resale of the tape and changing the end-of-tape credits. Groups may edit in their own credits if resources allow.

Copies on VHS format cost $25; three-quarter-inch format, $50; one-inch format, $50. For a copy of the tape, contact:

GLAAD
99 Hudson Street, 14th floor
New York, NY 10013
Phone: 212 966 1700

OTHER ORGANIZATIONS

The Lesbian and Gay Public Awareness Project is one of many organizations working to increase public visibility of gay life and issues around the country. Such organizations raise money to place advertisements in daily newspapers and to produce public service announcements on television.

This is one of the ads placed in Southern California media. (The ad was originally developed by *Alexandria (VA) Gay Community Association* which placed it in *The Washington Post.*)

Lesbian & Gay Public Awareness Project
Box 65603
Los Angeles, CA 90065
Phone: 213 281 1946

Alexandria Gay Community Association
Box 19401
Alexandria, VA 22320

The Gay and Lesbian Education Fund is a local Washington, D.C., organization that might be a model for other communities. The fund is particularly interested in awarding grants for projects designed to educate the heterosexual community about gay and lesbian concerns.

The fund tends to give money to those DC-area organizations that are involved in education and consciousness-raising, including providing material for religious and parents' organizations and conducting gay and lesbian awareness training for the DC police department.

The Gay and Lesbian Education Fund
Box 14055
Washington, DC 20044

▼ When Jay MacDonald, who is living with AIDS, decided he wanted to make a difference, the first idea that came to mind became his obsession.

MacDonald wanted to have a billboard in downtown Atlanta that sent out a positive message to the general community from the gay community. *Gay America Loves You* was the theme. He got Southeastern Arts, Media and Education Project (SAME) to help collect the money. The culturally oriented gay and lesbian nonprofit worked with MacDonald and helped him meet his goal. The billboard went up June 1, 1990. T-shirts and posters were made to commemorate its presence. When the billboard came down after a few months, MacDonald announced his new goal: "The billboard is going national!"

For more information:

SAME
Box 54719
Atlanta, GA 30308
Phone: 404 584 2104

ARE YOU ABUSING YOUR CHILD WITHOUT KNOWING IT?

1 in 10 Children Is Homosexual

If you could listen to the inner thoughts of a homosexual child, you might hear something like this:

*"I can't ever let anyone find out that I'm not straight. It would be so humiliating. My friends would hate me, I just know it. They might even want to beat me up. And my family? I've overheard them lots of times talking about gay people. They said, they hate gays, and that God even hates gays too. Gays are bad, and God sends bad people to hell. It really scares me now, when I hear my family talk that way, because now, they are talking about me. I guess I'm no good to anyone . . . not even God. Life is so cruel, and unfair. Sometimes I feel like disappearing from the face of this earth . . . "

No one chooses their sexual identity. If you are teaching your child to hate homosexual people, you might be teaching one of them to hate themself.

THAT ISN'T RIGHT. THAT IS A FORM OF EMOTIONAL CHILD ABUSE.

*These are the feelings of a 16 year old boy. Bobby Griffith committed suicide at the age of 20. Correct education about homosexuality would have prevented this tragedy.

LESBIAN AND GAY PUBLIC AWARENESS PROJECT

People United To End Homophobia

Enclosed is my tax deductible contribution (non-profit 501(c)3.
I want to help LGPAP increase understanding about homosexuality.

☐ $25 ☐ $50 ☐ $100 ☐ ____________
☐ Tell me how I can help.

LGPAP
P.O. Box 65603, Los Angeles, CA 90065
(213) 281-1946

© 1988 Lesbian & Gay Public Awareness Project

PART THREE

GAY CULTURE

Theater, the arts, books and literature have been taken out of the closet in the past two decades. The work of our authors, artists, and playwrights, even when it's sometimes discredited by the powers that be in the American cultural establishment, have become a meaningful way in which we examine our lives and develop our identity.

If other critics won't identify and value gay work for what it is, we are often the ones who have to establish our own prizes, books, and presses.

LITERARY MAGAZINES AND JOURNALS

These publications are the major vehicles for developing ideas and showcasing literary talent in the gay world.

AMETHYST: A JOURNAL FOR LESBIANS AND GAY MEN
SAME
Box 54719
Atlanta, GA 30308
Phone: 404 584 2104

Amethyst is published by the Southeastern Arts, Media and Education Project, Inc. It publishes prose, poetry, visual art, and essays that express gay liberation and gay aesthetics. It's published with support from a grant by the Georgia Council for the Arts.

BLK
BLK Publishing Company
Box 83912
Los Angeles, CA 90083
Phone: 213 410 0808

BLK is a monthly publication for the black gay community. It offers news, reviews, essays, and general reportage.

BLACK/OUT
The National Coalition of Black Gay
Women and Men
Box 19248
Washington, DC 20036

Black/Out is the quarterly publication of the National Coalition of Black Gay Women and Men. It reflects the political and cultural priorities of that group in its nonfiction essays and other articles.

CHANGING MEN: ISSUES IN GENDER, SEX AND POLITICS
306 N. Brooks Street
Madison, WI 53715

Changing Men is a publication for those interested in investigating gender roles, feminism, and sexism, as well as homophobia in our society. Its content usually consists of nonfiction essays and reviews with occasional art included.

CHRISTOPHER STREET
That New Magazine, Inc.
Box 1475, Church Street Station
New York, NY 10008

Christopher Street was the first serious literary magazine in the modern gay world. It featured many of the writers who would go on to become well known as gay authors, including Andrew Holleran (who still writes a regular column for the magazine) and Edmund White.

DRUMMER
Desmodus Publishing, Inc.
Box 11314
San Francisco, CA 94101

Drummer has a very heavy leather and sex content, and it stretches the definition of literary magazine, but it is a publication with readers who take it very seriously.

EMPATHY
Gay and Lesbian Advocacy Research Project
Box 5085
Columbia, SC 29250

This is an interdisciplinary journal for people working to end oppression on the basis of sexual identity.

THE EVERGREEN CHRONICLES
Box 8939
Minneapolis, MN 55408

Evergreen Chronicles is a gay and lesbian literary magazine that publishes quarterly. While open to submissions from anywhere, the roots of the publication are obviously in the Midwest.

THE JAMES WHITE REVIEW
Box 3356, Traffic Station
Minneapolis, MN 55403

The James White Review is one of the most highly regarded vehicles for short fiction and poetry by gay men.

LAMBDA BOOK REPORT
1625 Connecticut Avenue NW
Washington, DC 20009

Lambda Book Report is the major review vehicle for gay and lesbian books. The bimonthly publication covers trends in the development of gay literature and includes bestseller lists, reviews, and other information on books of special interest to gay men.

NORTHWEST GAY AND LESBIAN READER
1501 Belmont Avenue
Seattle, WA 98122
Phone: 206 322 4609

This bi-monthly publication is a book reviewing vehicle as well as a journal of opinion.

HOW TO GET THE WORD OUT?

If you acknowledge one or more of these magazines or newspapers as important, you might consider donating a subscription to your local school or college library.

MANDATE
FDC 58420
NOVEMBER 1990
$4.95 U.S.
$6.95 CAN.
FEATURING MARK BRANDON
ALL AMERICAN MEAT
COAST TO COAST STUD PIX
TURNING PRO
OBSESSIVE COMPULSIVE
0 71658 58420 4
11

MANDATE

Mavety Publications, Ltd.
462 Broadway, Suite 4000
New York, NY 10013

Mandate was one of the first nationally distributed publications. Its glossy pictures of male nudes and often sexual fiction puts it squarely into the realm of sex magazines, but it's always had a greater intent than to just turn on its readers. Book reviews, frequent nonfiction essays on politics and travel, and often humorous articles on the fads and fashions of the moment make it a favorite read for many gay men.

OUT/LOOK

Box 460430
San Francisco, CA 94146

Backed by a nonprofit foundation set up precisely to support it, *Out/Look* has quickly become one of the most respected gay and lesbian publications in the country. The politics are to the left, but the magazine is indispensable to anyone taking gay literature and thought seriously. It also sponsors the annual Out/Write literary conference.

THE PYRAMID PUBLICATION: THE PROVOCATIVE JOURNAL FOR LESBIANS AND GAY MEN OF COLOR
Box 1111, Canal Street Station
New York, NY 10013

Pyramid is a quarterly that is highly respected in the black gay world. It carries interviews, nonfiction essays, poetry, and fiction.

THE
PYRAMID
PERIODICAL

THE PROVOCATIVE JOURNAL FOR LESBIANS AND GAY MEN OF COLOR

RFD
Box 68
Liberty, TN 37095
Phone: 615 536 5176

RFD calls itself "a country journal for gay men everywhere." The publication focuses on gay life in rural Canada and the United States. Because of that focus and a general interest in the environment and new alignments of relationships between gay men, *RFD* is often considered the journal of the Radical Faerie movement.

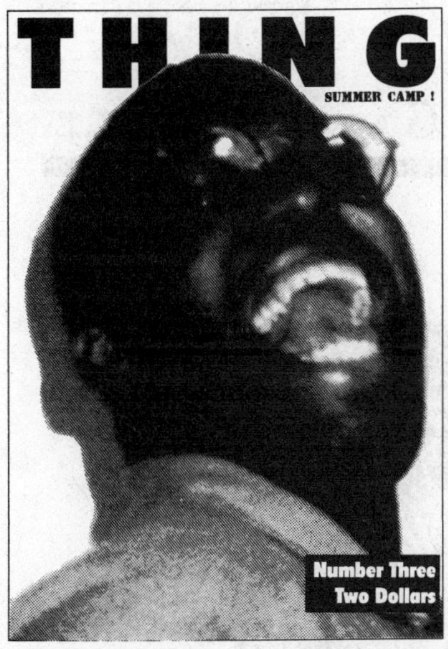

THING
Direct Communications
2151 W. Division Street
Chicago, IL 60622

There's a new movement of underground magazines (often called "'Zines") that chronicle the edges of gay life. They're involved in the latest music, the hippest camp fashions, and local personalities. *Thing* is by far the best of these often amateurish publications. It widens our experience by focusing on Chicago, a major city often neglected by the gay press, and on black gay life. It's raucous and iconoclastic, and a delight to read.

TRIBE: AN AMERICAN GAY JOURNAL

Columbia Publishing Company
234 E. 25th Street
Baltimore, MD 21218

Tribe is a quarterly journal devoted to the best of gay male literature. It includes a regular "books received" feature which announces the publication of as many gay-themed books as possible every quarter.

TRIBE

AN AMERICAN GAY JOURNAL

VOL. I, NO. I $6

Monk is one of the most fantastic magazines being produced. It's done by two men who travel the country in a run-down van, stopping wherever the spirit moves them to write about whatever and whomever they like. The eclectic style is part radical faerie, part ultra-environmentalist, and all-out complex.

The magazine is a valuable resource for its advertising, which includes New Age spirituality, organic goods-by-mail, and holistic medicines. This is definitely information you'll never find in other gay periodicals.

The magazine costs $10 for four quarterly issues. The Monks, as they call themselves, keep a base for subscriptions and for advertising information. Write:

Monk
369 Montezuma, Suite 137
Santa Fe, NM 87501

▼ If you want to create gay-friendly communications, art is important. Clip art is a term used to describe copyright-free illustrations that are available for the cost of the book. Many bookstores and art stores carry these books. One of particular interest is *Body Language: A Gallery of Recyclable Art.* Drawings and photographs of homoerotic themes are available in many different sizes and any or all can be used in newsletters, advertisements, or pamphlets.

For more information:

AD-Venture Apprentices, Inc.
Box 61186
Oklahoma City, OK 73146

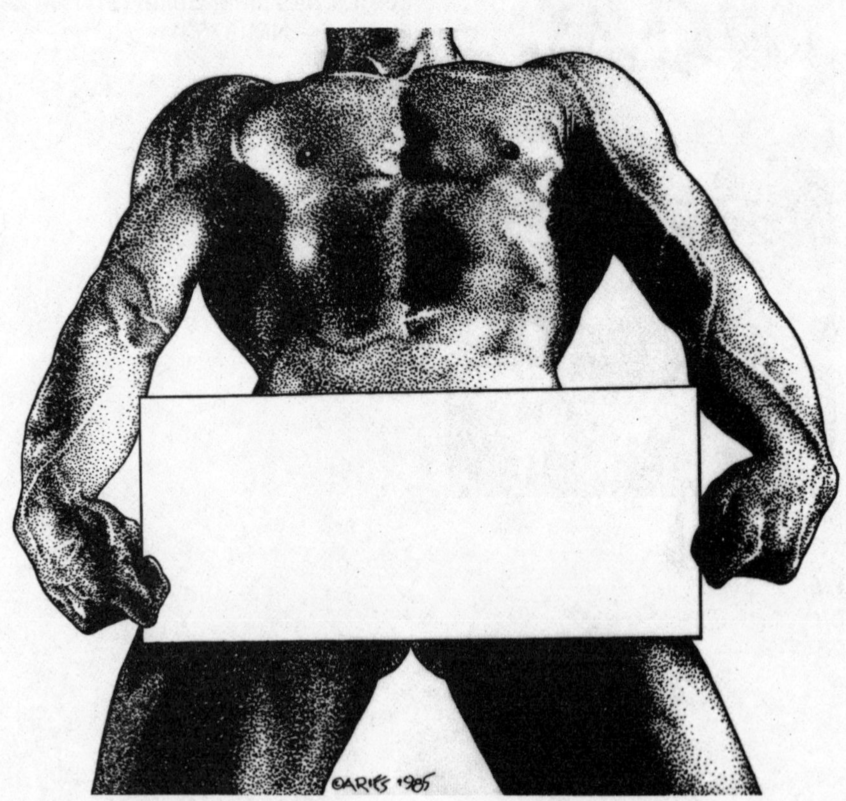

▼ *Alice in Rubberland* provides another option for illustration. The collection of hundreds of different rubber stamp images is available for a slight cost. Characters from artists Gerard Donelan, Howard Curse, and Tom of Finland are among the featured rubber stamps the company offers. Write for a catalog:

Alice in Rubberland
Box 2735
Los Angeles, CA 90078

▼ *The Lesbian and Gay Almanac and Events* is an annual publication that provides monthly lists of special social, athletic, cultural, and political events of the coming year. The front of the book has a series of changing feature articles, making the volume look and feel like an almanac.

To list your organization's activities, or to find out how to get a copy if your local bookstore doesn't carry *Events:*

Envoy Enterprises
740 N. Rush Street, Suite 609
Chicago, IL 60611

WILDE

Gay literature isn't a specific enough definition for some people. They want to know even more about a certain topic. One example of this literary compulsion is *Wild about Wilde,* a journal published twice yearly devoted to information about the (in)famous Irish gay poet and playwright.

Wild about Wilde
c/o Carmel McCaffrey
2542 Vance Drive
Mt. Airy, MD 21771

GAY BOOKSTORES

Gay bookstores are probably the one single most consequential element in the development of gay culture. These stores have been willing to stock our books when others wouldn't have them. They represent a distribution system for our journals and newspapers. They are often the first stop that isolated gay men make when they get to a major city, desperate for a gay cultural fix. The stores that follow are not necessarily exclusively gay; some are mainstream stores which have long been supportive of the gay and lesbian world. They are all tremendously vital parts of our community.

UNITED STATES

■ ALABAMA ■

LODESTAR BOOKS
2020 Eleventh Avenue S
Birmingham, AL 35205
Phone: 205 939 3356

TRADE 'N' BOOKS
5145 Atlanta Highway
Montgomery, AL 36109
Phone: 205 277 0778

■ ARIZONA ■

HUMANSPACE BOOKS
1617 N. 32nd Street, #5
Phoenix, AZ 85008
Phone: 602 220 4419

■ CALIFORNIA ■

A DIFFERENT DRUMMER
1027 North Coast Highway, #A
Laguna Beach, CA 92651
Phone: 714 497 6699

CIRCUS OF BOOKS
4001 Sunset Boulevard
Los Angeles, CA 90029
Phone: 213 666 1304

A DIFFERENT LIGHT
4014 Santa Monica Boulevard
Los Angeles, CA 90029
Phone: 213 668 0629

A**DIFFERENT**LIGHT

A DIFFERENT LIGHT
489 Castro Street
San Francisco, CA 94114
Phone: 415 431 0891

A DIFFERENT LIGHT
8853 Santa Monica Boulevard
West Hollywood, CA 90069
Phone: 213 854 6601

■ COLORADO ■

CATEGORY SIX BOOKS
1029 E. 11th Street
Denver, CO 80218
Phone: 303 832 6263

■ DISTRICT OF COLUMBIA ■

LAMBDA RISING
1625 Connecticut Avenue NW
Washington, DC 20009
Phone: 202 462 6969/800 621 6969

■ FLORIDA ■

LAMBDA PASSAGES
7545 Biscayne Boulevard
Miami, FL 33138
Phone: 305 754 6900

TOMES AND TREASURES
202½ S. Howard Avenue
Tampa, FL 33606
Phone: 813 251 9368

■ ILLINOIS ■

PEOPLE LIKE US BOOKS
3321 N. Clark Street
Chicago, IL 60657
Phone: 312 248 6363

UNABRIDGED BOOKS
3251 N. Broadway
Chicago, IL 60657
Phone: 312 883 9119

■ LOUISIANA ■

FAUBOURG MARIGNY BOOKSTORE
600 Frenchman Street
New Orleans, LA 70116
Phone: 504 943 9875

■ MAINE ■

NEW LEAF BOOKS
438 Main Street
Rockland, ME 04841
Phone: 207 596 0040

■ MARYLAND ■

LAMBDA RISING/BALTIMORE
241 W. Chase Street
Baltimore, MD 21201
Phone: 301 234 0069

■ MASSACHUSETTS ■

GLAD DAY BOOKSHOP
673 Boylston Street, 2d floor
Boston, MA 02116
Phone: 617 267 3010

PROVINCETOWN BOOKSHOP
246 Commercial Street
Provincetown, MA 02657
Phone: 508 487 0964

■ MICHIGAN ■

CHOSEN BOOKS
120 W. 4th Street
Royal Oak, MI 48067
Phone: 313 543 5758

■ MINNESOTA ■

A BROTHER'S TOUCH
1931 Nicollet Avenue
Minneapolis, MN 55403
Phone: 612 872 1412

■ MISSOURI ■

OUR WORLD TOO
11 S. Vandeventer
St. Louis, MO 63108
Phone: 314 533 5322

■ NEW MEXICO ■

FULL CIRCLE BOOKS
2205 Silver Avenue SE
Albuquerque, NM 87106
Phone: 505 266 0022

■ NEW YORK ■

A DIFFERENT LIGHT
548 Hudson Street
New York, NY 10014
Phone: 212 989 4850

OSCAR WILDE MEMORIAL BOOKSTORE
15 Christopher Street
New York, NY 10014
Phone: 212 255 8097

■ NORTH CAROLINA ■

WHITE RABBIT
1833 Spring Garden Street
Greensboro, NC 27403
Phone: 919 272 7604

WHITE RABBIT
309 W. Martin Street
Raleigh, NC 27603
Phone: 919 856 1429

■ OHIO ■

BOOKSTORE ON WEST 25TH
1921 W. 25th Street
Cleveland, OH 44113
Phone: 216 566 8897

■ PENNSYLVANIA ■

GIOVANNI'S ROOM
345 S. 12 Street
Philadelphia, PA 19107
Phone: 215 923 2960 (inside PA)/
800 222 6996 (outside PA only)

■ RHODE ISLAND ■

VISIONS AND VOICES
255 Harris Avenue
Providence, RI 02909
Phone: 401 273 9757

■ TEXAS ■

LIBERTY BOOKSTORE
1014-B N. Lamar Boulevard
Austin, TX 78763
Phone: 512 495 9737

LOBO AFTER DARK
4008-C Cedar Springs
Dallas, TX 75219
Phone: 214 522 1132

LOBO AFTER DARK
1424-C Westheimer
Houston, TX 77006
Phone: 713 522 5156

■ WASHINGTON ■

BEYOND THE CLOSET
1501 E. Belmont Avenue
Seattle, WA 98122
Phone: 206 322 4609

BAILEY/COY
414 Broadway Avenue E
Seattle, WA 98102
Phone: 206 323 8842

■ BRITISH COLUMBIA ■

LITTLE SISTER'S BOOKS AND ART
1221 Thurlow Street
Vancouver, BC V6E 1X4
Phone: 604 669 1753

■ ONTARIO ■

AFTER STONEWALL
103 Fourth Avenue
Ottawa, ON K1S 2L1
Phone: 613 567 2221

GLAD DAY BOOKSTORE
598-A Yonge Street
Toronto, ON M4Y 1Z3
Phone: 416 961 4161

■ QUEBEC ■

L'ANDROGYNE
3636 Boulevard St. Laurent
Montreal, QU H2X 2V4
Phone: 514 842 4765

▼ This list was compiled with the aid of "Bookstores and Mail Order Firms Specializing in Books for Gays/Lesbians/Feminists," a publication of the Gay and Lesbian Task Force of the American Library Association. For information on this listing and other publications, contact:

GLTF Clearinghouse
American Library Association
50 E. Huron Street
Chicago, IL 60611

▼ It's not always easy to find a gay library or bookstore if you live on the plains of either Canada or the United States or in other isolated locales.

The Winnipeg Gay/Lesbian Resource Centre Library has a special procedure for people in Manitoba, Saskatchewan, and northwestern Ontario. Their *Members-By-Mail* program allows people to borrow, who, because of physical disability or geographic remoteness, can't easily get to their library.

Members-By-Mail
Winnipeg Gay/Lesbian Resource Centre Library
222 Osborne Street, Suite 1
Winnipeg, MB R3L 1Z3

BOOKS BY MAIL ORDER

If you don't live near a bookstore, you can still have access to the large stock these businesses carry. Almost any of the stores listed here will be glad to fill a phone or mail order. Some even have 800 numbers, which means your long-distance calls are free.

Lambda Rising (DC), *A Different Light* (NY and all CA stores), *White Rabbit* (NC), and *Giovanni's Room* (PA) all have regular newsletters or other mailings to keep you up-to-date on what's being published that will be of interest to you.

Lambda Rising also publishes *Lambda Rising News,* an annual directory of books, videos, and other items it sells via mail order. A copy is available for $2 from:

Lambda Rising
1625 Connecticut Avenue NW
Washington, DC 20009
Phone: 202 462 6969/800 621 6969

▼ *Liberation Book Club* is another mail order option for buying gay books. You can join without the usual cost or obligations of a book club.

Liberation Book Club
Box 453
South Norwalk, CT 06856

HARD-TO-FIND BOOKS

While most gay bookstores strive to have inclusive stock—they try to keep all gay books in print on hand—inevitably there are titles that are no longer available from publishers. Two companies specialize in locating, collecting, buying, and selling gay titles that are no longer in print. They also issue brochures and catalogs. For information, including the costs of catalogs, contact either or both of them:

BOOKS BOHEMIAN
Box 17218
Los Angeles, CA 90017
Phone: 213 385 6761

ST. MAUR BOOKSELLER
820 N. Madison
Stockton, CA 95202
Phone: 209 464 3550

While many independent general bookstores suffer from the encroachment of the chain stores, A Different Light *has flourished as a specialty store selling only gay and lesbian literature. Through the stores I dedicate much of my life to educating, entertaining, and supporting our community. I've always been a firm believer that knowledge equals power and I consider it an honor that as a professional bookseller I can also help to keep our community strong, well informed, and visible.*

—NORMAN LAURILA,
bookstore owner

READING AND WRITING GAY

A PLACE TO START

Reading lists of modern gay literature are highly individual, of course. But a critic's register of his favorite works can inform other readers. Novelist and Brown University professor Edmund White created this list of "Some Favorite Works of Gay Literature" for *The Reader's Catalog.*

The Pure and the Impure by Colette. Out of print.

The Family of Max Desir by Robert Ferro. New York: New American Library, 1988.

Concerning the Eccentricities of Cardinal Pirelli (in five novels) by Ronald Firbank. New York: New Directions.

Dancer from the Dance by Andrew Holleran. New York: New American Library, 1986.

The Swimming-Pool Library by Alan Hollinghurst. New York: Random House, 1988.

A Single Man by Christopher Isherwood. New York: Farrar, Straus & Giroux, 1964.

Death in Venice by Thomas Mann. New York: Vintage, 1989.

Cities of the Plain by Marcel Proust. Included in ***Remembrance of Things Past,*** translated by C. K. Scott-Moncrieff and Terence Kilmartin. New York: Vintage, 1982.

A Voice Through a Cloud by Denton Welch. Out of print.

Orlando: A Biography by Virginia Woolf. New York: Harcourt Brace Jovanovich, 1956.

COPYRIGHT 1989 BY EDMUND WHITE. REPRINTED WITH PERMISSION.

GAY ART, GAY POETRY

Poet and editor David Groff has put together a listing of some of the most influential works of gay visual arts and gay poetry.

If you're still looking for a definition of the "gay aesthetic," start with the books on this list.

AUDEN, W. H. (WYSTAN HUGH). *Collected Poems.* Edited by Edward Mendelson. New York: Random House, 1976. "Includes all the poems that W. H. Auden wished to preserve, in text that represents his final revisions." Out of print. Being replaced by *Complete Poems* by Princeton University Press.

BIDANT, FRANK. *The Sacrifice.* New York: Random House, 1983.

CAVAFY, CONSTANTINE (1863–1933). *Collected Poems.* Princeton: Princeton University Press, 1975.

CLATTENBURG, ELLEN FRITZ. *Photographic Work of F. Holland Day.* Wellesley, Mass.: Wellesley College Museum, 1975.

COOPER, EMANUEL. *The Sexual Perspective: Homosexuality and Art in the Last 100 Years in the West.* New York: Routledge & Kegan Paul, 1986.

EAKINS, THOMAS. *The Photographs of Thomas Eakins.* New York: Grossman Publishers, 1972.

ELIASOPH, PHILIP. *Paul Cadmus, Yesterday & Today.* Oxford, Ohio: Miami University Art Museum, 1981.

GINSBERG, ALLEN. *Howl, and Other Poems.* San Francisco: City Lights, 1956.

GOODRICH, LLOYD. *Thomas Eakins.* Cambridge, Mass.: Harvard University Press, 1982.

GRAHN, JUDY. *The Work of a Common Woman: Collected Poetry (1964–1977).* Freedom, Calif: Crossing Press, 1984.

GUNN, THOM. *The Passages of Joy.* New York: Farrar, Straus & Giroux, 1982.

HASKELL, BARBARA. *Charles Demuth.* New York: Whitney Museum of American Art, 1987.

HIBBARD, HOWARD. *Michelangelo.* New York: Harper & Row, 1974.

HOCKNEY, DAVID. *Cameraworks.* New York: Alfred A. Knopf, 1984.

KIRSTEIN, LINCOLN. *Paul Cadmus.* New York: Imago Imprint, 1984.

KLEIN, MICHAEL. ed. *Poets For Life: 74 Poets Respond to AIDS.* New York: Crown, 1989.

LESLIE, CHARLES. *Wilhelm von Gloeden, 1856–1931.* Innsbruck: Allerheiligen-presse, 1980. Text in German, photos in "universal" language.

LIVINGSTONE, MARCO. *David Hockney.* New York: Holt, Rinehart & Winston, 1981.

MAPPLETHORPE, ROBERT. *Black Book.* New York: St. Martin's Press, 1986.

MARSHALL, RICHARD. *Robert Mapplethorpe.* Boston: Whitney Museum of American Art in association with New York Graphic Society/Little, Brown, 1988.

MERRILL, JAMES INGRAM. *The Inner Room.* New York: Alfred A. Knopf, 1988.

MONETTE, PAUL. *Love Alone: 18 Elegies for Rog.* New York: St. Martin's Press, 1988.

MORSE, CARL, AND JOAN LARKIN, eds. *Gay and Lesbian Poetry in Our Time.* New York: St. Martin's Press, 1988.

ORMOND, RICHARD. *John Singer Sargent: Paintings, Drawings, Watercolors.* New York: Harper & Row, 1970.

The Penguin Book of Homosexual Verse. New York: Penguin, 1983.

POPE-HENNESSY, JOHN W. *Cellini.* New York: Abbeyville, 1985.

RICH, ADRIENNE CECILE. *The Fact of a Doorframe: Poems Selected and New, 1950–1984.* New York: W. W. Norton, 1984.

SASLOW, JAMES M. *Ganymede in the Renaissance: Homosexuality in Art and Society.* New Haven: Yale University Press, 1986.

SCHUYLER, JAMES. *The Morning of the Poem.* New York: Farrar, Straus & Giroux, 1980.

TURNBAUGH, DOUGLAS BALIR. *Duncan Grant and the Bloomsbury Group.* Secaucus, N.J.: Lyle Stuart, 1987.

WEIERMAIR, PETER. *The Hidden Image: Photographs of the Male Nude in the Nineteenth and Twentieth Centuries.* Cambridge, Mass.: MIT Press, 1988.

WHITMAN, WALT. *Leaves of Grass.* New York: New American Library.

RECIPIENTS OF THE AMERICAN LIBRARY ASSOCIATION'S GAY/LESBIAN BOOK AWARD

1971 ***Patience and Sarah*** by Isabel Miller. New York: McGraw-Hill, 1969.

1972 ***Lesbian/Woman*** by Del Martin and Phyllis Lyon. New York: Glide Publications, 1972.
The Gay Mystique by Peter Fisher. New York: Stein & Day, 1972.

1973 (No award)

1974 ***Sex Variant Women in Literature: A Historical and Quantitative Survey*** by Jeanette Foster. New York: Vantage Press, 1956.

1975 ***Homosexuality: Lesbians and Gay Men in Society, History, and Literature,*** edited by Jonathan Katz. New York: Ayer Publications, 1975.

1976 (No award)

1977 ***Familiar Faces, Hidden Lives: The Story of Homosexual Men in America Today*** by Howard Brown. New York: Harcourt Brace Jovanovich, 1976.

1978 ***Our Right to Love,*** edited by Ginny Vida. New York: Prentice-Hall, 1978.

1979 ***Now That You Know: What Every Parent Should Know about Homosexuality*** by Betty Fairchild and Nancy Howard. New York: Harcourt Brace Jovanovich, 1979.

1980 ***Now the Volcano: An Anthology of Latin American Gay Literature,*** edited by Winston Leyland. San Francisco: Gay Sunshine Press, 1979.

1981 ***Christianity, Social Tolerance, and Homosexuality: Gay People in Western Europe from the Beginning of the Christian Era to the 14th Century*** by John Boswell. Chicago: University of Chicago Press, 1980.

1982 ***Black Lesbians: An Annotated Bibliography,*** compiled by J. R. Roberts. Tallahassee: Naiad Press, 1981.
The Celluloid Closet: Homosexuality in the Movies by Vito Russo. New York: Harper & Row, 1981.
Surpassing the Love of Men: Romantic Friendship and Love Between Women from the Renaissance to the Present by Lillian Faderman. New York: Morrow, 1981.

1983 (No award)
1984 ***Sexual Politics/Sexual Communities: The Making of a Homosexual Minority in the United States, 1940–1970*** by John D'Emilio. Chicago: University of Chicago Press, 1983.
1985 ***Another Mother Tongue: Gay Words, Gay Worlds*** by Judy Grahn. Boston: Beacon Press, 1984.
1986 ***Sex and Germs: The Politics of AIDS*** by Cindy Patton. Boston: Beacon Press, 1986.
1987 ***The Spirit and The Flesh: Sexual Diversity in American Indian Culture*** by Walter Williams. Boston: Beacon Press, 1986.
1988 ***A Restricted Country*** by Joan Nestle. Ithaca: Firebrand Books, 1987.
And the Band Played On: Politics, People, and the AIDS Epidemic by Randy Shilts. New York: St. Martin's Press, 1987.
1989 ***After Delores*** by Sarah Schulman. New York: E. P. Dutton, 1988.
The Swimming-Pool Library by Alan Hollinghurst. New York: Random House, 1988.
1990 ***Eighty-Sixed*** by David Feinberg. New York: Viking, 1989.
In Search of Gay America by Neil Miller. New York: Atlantic Monthly Press, 1989.
SERVICE AWARD: Armistead Maupin

THE LAMBDA LITERARY AWARDS

Also known as "The Lammies" and awarded by judges selected by the editors of *Lambda Book Report,* these have become some of the most recognized prizes in gay publishing. They're presented at a dinner held in conjunction with the annual convention of the

American Booksellers Association convention. (The same award categories are not necessarily used each year, which explains those listings where there are different categories for different years.) For more information, write:

Lambda Book Report
1625 Connecticut Avenue NW
Washington, DC 20009

GAY MEN'S NONFICTION:

1989: ***Borrowed Time*** by Paul Monette. New York: Harcourt Brace Jovanovich.

1990: ***In Search of Gay America*** by Neil Miller. New York: Atlantic Monthly Press.

GAY MEN'S ANTHOLOGIES:

1990: ***Hidden from History***, edited by M. Duberman, M. Vicinus, and G. Chauncey. New York: New American Library.

LESBIAN FICTION:

1989: ***Trash*** by Dorothy Allison. Ithaca: Firebrand Books.

1990: ***The Bar Stories*** by Nisa Donnelly. New York: St. Martin's Press.

LESBIAN SMALL PRESS BOOK AWARD:

1989: ***Trash*** by Dorothy Allison. Ithaca: Firebrand.

GAY MEN'S SMALL PRESS BOOK AWARD:

1989: (tie)
Goldenboy by Michael Nava. Boston: Alyson Publications; and ***The Delight of Hearts*** by Ahmad Al-Tifashi. San Francisco: Gay Sunshine Press.

GAY AND LESBIAN SMALL PRESS AWARD:

1990: ***My Life as a Mole*** by Larry Mitchell. New York: Calamus Press.

GAY MEN'S FICTION:

1989: ***The Beautiful Room Is Empty*** by Edmund White. New York: Knopf.

1990: ***Eighty-Sixed*** by David Feinberg. New York: Viking.

GAY MEN'S MYSTERY/SCIENCE FICTION:

1989: ***Goldenboy*** by Michael Nava. Boston: Alyson Publications.

GAY MEN'S SCIENCE FICTION/FANTASY:

1990: ***Somewhere in the Night*** by Jeffrey McMahan. Boston: Alyson Publications.

GAY MYSTERY

1990: ***A Simple Suburban Murder*** by Mark Richard Zubro. New York: St. Martin's Press.

LESBIAN NONFICTION:

1989: ***Lesbian Ethics*** by Sarah Hoagland. Palo Alto: Institute of Lesbian Studies.

1990: ***Really Reading, Gertrude Stein*** by Judy Grahn. Freedom, Calif.: Crossing Press.

LESBIAN ANTHOLOGIES:
1990: (Three-way tie)
Intricate Passions, edited by Tee A. Corinne. Austin, Tex.: Banned Books.
Out the Other Side, edited by Christian McEwen and Sue O'Sullivan. Freedom, Calif.: Crossing Press.
Hidden from History, edited by M. Duberman, M. Vicinus, and G. Chauncey. New York: New American Library.

LESBIAN MYSTERY/SCIENCE FICTION:
1989: ***Skiptrace*** by Antoinette Azolakov. Austin, Tex.: Banned Books.

LESBIAN SCIENCE FICTION/FANTASY:
1990: ***What Did Miss Darrington See?: An Anthology of Feminist Supernatural Fiction,*** edited by Jessica Amanda Salmonson. New York: Feminist Press.

LESBIAN MYSTERY:
1990: ***Beverly Malibu*** by Katherine V. Forrest. Tallahassee: Naiad Press.

GAY MEN'S FIRST NOVEL:
1989: ***The Swimming-Pool Library*** by Alan Hollinghurst. New York: Random House.
1990: ***The Irreversible Decline of Eddie Socket*** by John Weir. New York: Harper & Row.

LESBIAN FIRST NOVEL:
1989: ***Bird-Eyes*** by Madelyn Arnold. Seattle: Seal Press.
1990: ***The Names of the Moons of Mars*** by Patricia Roth Schwartz. Norwich, Vt.: New Victoria.

GAY AND LESBIAN POETRY:
1989: ***Gay & Lesbian Poetry in Our Time,*** edited by Carl Morse and Joan Larkin. New York: St. Martin's Press.
1990: ***Poets for Life,*** edited by Michael Klein. New York: Crown Publishers.

STONEWALL INN EDITIONS
GAY & LESBIAN POETRY IN OUR TIME
An Anthology
STONEWALL INN
SNP
EDITIONS
CARL MORSE & JOAN LARKIN
editors

AIDS (A SPECIAL CATEGORY):

1989: ***Borrowed Time*** by Paul Monette. New York: Harcourt Brace Jovanovich.

1990: ***Reports from the Holocaust*** by Larry Kramer. New York: St. Martin's Press.

GAY AND LESBIAN HUMOR:

1990: ***Gay Comics,*** edited by Robert Triptow. New York: New American Library.

EDITOR'S CHOICE AWARD:

1989: ***Why Can't Sharon Kowalski Come Home?*** by Karen Thompson and Julie Andrzejewski. San Francisco: Spinsters/Aunt Lute.

1990: ***Lifting Belly by Gertrude Stein,*** edited by Rebecca Mark. Tallahassee: Naiad Press.

PUBLISHER'S SERVICE AWARD:

1989: Sasha Alyson of Alyson Publications for his work on the industry-wide book project, ***You Can Do Something About AIDS.***

1990: Carol Seajay of Feminist Bookstore News for developing the major communications network for feminist bookstores.

YOUNG ADULT AND CHILDREN

1990: ***Losing Uncle Tim*** by Mary Kate Jordon. Albert Whitman & Co., 1989.

THE NEXT STEPS

LISTENING TO GAY AUTHORS

Readings are a way to help writers meet and charm their constituencies. Many bookstores sponsor regular readings, as do many community organizations.

If you're interested in setting up a program of readings in your community, "How to Start a Reading Series," a general, not-gay specific booklet will be a great help. It's one of many publications of *Poets and Writers,* a magazine and publishing house dedicated to the literary arts and publishing science. For more information on this booklet and others:

Poets and Writers
72 Spring Street
New York, NY 10012

TALKING ABOUT GAY BOOKS

Literacy means more than just knowing how to read. It means understanding the power of words and the impact of books. Many gay men aren't brought up to read and they feel separated from the literature that's such an important component in the creation of our culture. One of the ways to get more people involved in our books is to create book groups, circles of people who regularly gather together and discuss titles they've all read.

"How to Start a Book Group and Keep It Interesting" is a short pamphlet that gives great tips on how to find people with common interests, arrange a place to meet, get group discounts on titles, and many other facets of creating an ongoing book circle. For a copy, send $3.00 for the initial copy and $2.50 for each additional copy to:

Arbor Seminars
3409 Newark Street NW
Washington, DC 20016

THE PUBLISHERS

Almost every major publisher produces at least one book every year that is of special interest to gay men. There are some small presses that focus on gay publishing and a few mainstream publishers which have significant numbers of gay books. If you're looking for companies with sizable numbers of gay titles, here are some of the majors. Those firms which do have a mail-order catalog are marked with an asterisk. Most larger publishers do not encourage direct mail order; their catalogs are available only to retailers or others who will buy in large quantities. If you're looking for a single title of a book from one of those publishers, you're best off shopping through one of the gay bookstores that do encourage direct mail order from their customers.

ALYSON PUBLICATIONS*
40 Plympton Street
Boston, MA 02118

AMETHYST PRESS
6 W. 32nd Street,
Penthouse
New York, NY 10001

BANNED BOOKS
Box 33280
Austin, TX 78764

BEACON PRESS
25 Beacon Street
Boston, MA 02108

CALAMUS PRESS*
Box 294, Village Station
New York, NY 10014

CANADIAN GAY ARCHIVES
Box 639, Station A
Toronto, ON M5S 1V5

CATALYST
315 Blantyre Avenue
Scarborough, ON M1N 2S6

CELESTIAL ARTS/TEN SPEED PRESS
Box 7327
Berkeley, CA 94707

CROSSING PRESS*
Box 1048
Freedom, CA 95019

GAY PRESSES OF NEW YORK*
Box 294, Village Station
New York, NY 10014

GREY FOX PRESS*
Box 31190
San Francisco, CA 94140

HARPERCOLLINS PUBLISHERS
10 E. 53rd Street
New York, NY 10022

HARRINGTON PARK PRESS*
and
THE HAWORTH PRESS*
10 Alice Street
Binghamton, NY 13904

KNIGHTS PRESS*
Box 454
Pound Ridge, NY 10576

LIBERATION BOOKS
Box 453
S. Norwalk, CT 06856

MANROOT*
Box 762
Boyes Hot Springs, CA 95416

NAL/DUTTON
375 Hudson Street
New York, NY 10014

PINK TRIANGLE PRESS*
Box 639, Station A
Toronto, ON M5W 1G2

ST. MARTIN'S PRESS
175 Fifth Avenue
New York, NY 10010

STUBBLEJUMPER PRESS
Box 1203, Station F
Toronto, ON M4Y 2V8

SUMMERHILL PRESS
52 Shaftesbury Avenue
Toronto, ON M4T 1A2

TIMES CHANGE PRESS*
Box 1380
Ojai, CA 93023

DISTRIBUTORS

This is a list of companies who handle gay books and sell them to stores and libraries. While these are not gay companies, and while there are other large distributors who do handle gay titles, these companies have made gay books a priority:

ALTERNATIVE DISTRIBUTION
Box 29627
Philadelphia, PA 19144

BOOKPEOPLE
2929 5th Street
Berkeley, CA 94710

INLAND BOOK COMPANY
22 Hemingway Avenue
East Haven, CT 06512

The American Library Association has a more complete listing of "Publishers of Gay and/or Lesbian Books" which you can get by sending a stamped, self-addressed envelope to: GLTF Clearinghouse, American Library Association, 50 E. Huron Street, Chicago, IL 60611.

SELF-PUBLISHING

The existence of the network of gay bookstores offers a great possibility for the aspiring author. It's estimated that as many as half of all the sales of a gay-themed book take place in these stores. That means that, if you're willing to cover the expense of printing, you don't have to wait for acceptance from anyone else. You can publish your own work. You will have to learn about publicity and self-promotion, but the stores make it a viable risk, much more so than ever before.

It's the technology that allows the possibility. Besides paper itself, the other great cost of publishing is typesetting. With the advent of desk-top publishing and with new technology that allows some printing firms to translate a computer disc to typesetting, you can do a great part of the work of the production of the book by yourself.

If you're interested in pursuing this option, or if you're interested in being a book writer in any fashion, the single best text is *How to Get Happily Published* by Judith Appelbaum (New York: New American Library, 1988).

WRITERS GROUPS

Anyone interested in seriously pursuing writing as a career or even as a serious avocation should consider making contact with one of the major writers organizations. *PEN* and *The Authors Guild* offer many publications that will be of general interest. *The National Writers Union* is more activist and some of its chapters have active gay caucuses. All three have many different resources that would be of service to any writer in any field.

Authors Guild
234 W. 44th Street
New York, NY 10036

National Writers Union
13 Astor Place
New York, NY 10003

PEN/American Center
568 Broadway
New York, NY 10012

▼ *Out/Look* sponsors Out/Write, an annual gay and lesbian writers conference. Send for information about future events and also the availability of audio tapes of past presentations whose topics might be of interest to you.

Out/Look
Box 460430
San Francisco, CA 94146

▼ *Word Project AIDS* is a national organization that's involved in promoting writing about AIDS. The group makes various awards and sponsors readings in various regions.

You should contact them if you're interested in AIDS literature or if you're interested in starting any kind of group that will be dealing with writing and AIDS, such as a group of people living with AIDS or a study group of any other sort.

Word Project AIDS
Box 691133
Los Angeles, CA 90069

GAY THEATER

THEATER COMPANIES

These companies are involved in gay theater, though they are not necessarily gay companies nor do all their productions involve gay themes. This listing comes from a directory published by *The Purple Circuit,* an informal network of gay and lesbian theaters, production companies, producers, and "kindred spirits." For an updated listing, including lesbian theater companies and some international companies, send a donation of any size along with a stamped, self-addressed envelope to:

Artists Confronting AIDS
684½ Echo Park Avenue
Los Angeles, CA 90026

UNITED STATES

■ ALASKA ■

OUT NORTH THEATER COMPANY
Box 100140
Anchorage, AK 99510
Phone: 907 279 8099

■ CALIFORNIA ■

THE CAST THEATER
804 El Centro Avenue
Hollywood, CA 90038

MYNA BIRD PRODUCTIONS
1759 Orchid, Apt. #109
Hollywood, CA 90028

OUT THEATER
4102 E. 7th Street, #615
Long Beach, CA 90804

APOLLO'S MICE
1836 Lucretia
Los Angeles, CA 90026
Phone: 213 482 1329

ARTISTS CONFRONTING AIDS
684½ Echo Park Avenue
Los Angeles, CA 90026
Phone: 213 250 4187

CELEBRATION THEATER
4470–107 Sunset Boulevard, #353
Los Angeles, CA 90027
(Theater: 426 Hoover)
Phone: 213 666 8669

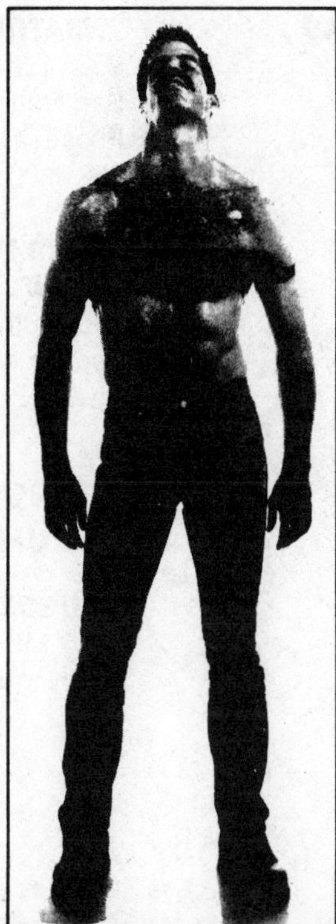

Soul Survivor

A Romance For The 80's *dammit*

SOUL SURVIVOR: A ROMANCE FOR THE 80'S, DAMMIT BY ANTHONY BRUNO IS ONE OF THE BEST KNOWN PRODUCTIONS OF KALIYUGA ARTS. PHOTO REPRINTED WITH PERMISSION.

THE ENTERTAINERS
1428 Kellum Avenue
Los Angeles, CA 90026
Phone: 213 850 6509

HEY WANNA DANCE PRODUCTIONS
4317 Nesho Avenue
Los Angeles, CA 90066
Phone: 213 390 8531/213 656 5688

L.A. THEATER ARTISTS
1318 N. Crescent Heights, Suite 101
Los Angeles, CA 90046
Phone: 213 509 8225

LATINO ENSEMBLE
P.O. Box 26A28
Los Angeles, CA 90026
Phone: 213 484 9005

TEATRO VIVA! ENSEMBLE
c/o Viva!
1022 N. Virgil Avenue, #444
Los Angeles, CA 90029
Phone: 213 232 8482

LAMBDA PLAYERS OF SACRAMENTO
1931 L Street
Sacramento, CA 95814
Phone: 916 442 0185

DIVERSIONARY THEATER/PRODUCTIONS
1345 28th Street
San Diego, CA 92102
Phone: 619 232 2333

KALIYUGA ARTS
141 Albion Street
San Francisco, CA 94110
Phone: 415 431 8423

THEATRE RHINOCEROS
2926 16th Street
San Francisco, CA 94103
Phone: 415 861 5079 (Box Office)/415 552 4100 (Administration)

HIGHWAYS PERFORMANCE SPACE
1651 18th Street
Santa Monica, CA 90404
Phone: 213 453 1755

■ DISTRICT OF COLUMBIA ■

SOURCE THEATER
1835 14th Street NW
Washington, DC 20009
Phone: 202 462 1073

CAFE HOMOPHOBE, A PRODUCTION OF LIONHEART GAY THEATRE OF CHICAGO.

FLORIDA

ASOLO CENTER FOR THE PERFORMING ARTS
5555 N. Tamiami Trail
Sarasota, FL 34243
Phone: 813 351 9010

GEORGIA

SAME (SOUTHEASTERN ARTS, MEDIA, AND EDUCATION PROJECT, INC.)
P.O. Box 54719
Atlanta, GA 30308
Phone: 404 584 2104

ILLINOIS

DAVID DILLON [independent producer]
3825 N. Pine Grove, #522
Chicago, IL 60613
Phone: 312 348 8894

LIONHEART GAY THEATER OF CHICAGO
P.O. Box 601
Wilmette, IL 60091

IOWA

GAY COALITION OF DES MOINES
P.O. Box 851
Des Moines, IA 50304
Phone: 515 279 2110

LOUISIANA

THEATER MARIGNY & ASSOCIATES
616 Frenchmen Street
New Orleans, LA 70116
Phone: 504 944 2653

MASSACHUSETTS

TRIANGLE THEATER
Box 174, 105 Charles Street
Boston, MA 02114

NEW YORK

WINGS THEATER COMPANY, INC.
154 Christopher Street
New York, NY 10014
Phone: 212 627 2961

GAY PERFORMANCES COMPANY
Box 1647
Old Chelsea Station
New York, NY 10011
Phone: 212 595 1445

THE GLINES
240 W. 44th Street
New York, NY 10036
Phone: 212 354 8899

3-DOLLAR BILL THEATER
530 W. 23rd Street, Suite 429
New York, NY 10011
Phone: 212 989 3750

WOW CAFÉ
c/o Shaw
75 E. 4th Street
New York, NY 10003
Phone: 212 460 8067

■ OREGON ■

CIRCA NOW PRESENTS
P.O. Box 14912
Portland, OR 97214
Phone: 503 236 2536

■ PENNSYLVANIA ■

AVALANCHE: THE MULTI-RACIAL GAY AND LESBIAN THEATRE TROUPE
248 S. 23rd Street
Philadelphia, PA 19103
Phone: 215 545 5247

THE DAYLIGHT ZONE
526 N. 19th Street
Philadelphia, PA 19130
Phone: 215 854 0112

■ TEXAS ■

THE GROUP (THEATER WORKSHOP)
436 Hawthorne, #2
Houston, TX 77006
Phone: 713 522 2204

THEATRE GEMINI
Box 191225
Dallas, TX 75219
Phone: 214 521 6331

SOULS IN A VOID WAS A 1990 PREMIER OF THEATER GEMINI. PHOTO BY CARL DAVIS.

■ WASHINGTON ■

ALICE B. THEATER
1535 11th Avenue, Suite 200
Seattle, WA 98122
Phone: 206 322 5723

SWEET CORN PRODUCTIONS
Box 9685
Seattle, WA 98109
Phone: 206 784 1519

CANADA

■ ALBERTA ■

SUN ERGOS: A COMPANY OF THEATER AND DANCE
2203–700 9th Street SW
Calgary, AB T2P 2B5
Phone: 403 264 4621

■ ONTARIO ■

BUDDIES IN BAD TIMES THEATRE
736 Bathurst Street, #213
Toronto, ON M5S 2R4
Phone: 416 588 7230

▼ The *American Library Association Gay and Lesbian Task Force* published a brochure, "Gays and Lesbians on Stage: Finding Gay/Lesbian Plays," which lists indexes, bibliographies, and buying guides. For price information:

GLTF
American Library Association
50 E. Huron Street
Chicago, IL 60611

PUPPETRY, MIME, AND MUSIC ARE ALL PARTS OF THE GAY THEATER SCENE. HERE STEVE BRYANT STARS IN SEATTLE'S SWEET CORN PRODUCTION OF *VOICE OF AN ANGEL: A CASTRATO REMEMBERS.* PHOTO BY DEMIAN, COPYRIGHT 1990, REPRINTED WITH PERMISSION.

PLAYS THAT EVERY GAY MAN SHOULD KNOW

This list of seminal gay theater was created and annotated by Laurence Senelick, Fletcher Professor of Drama at Tufts University.

The Merchant of Venice by William Shakespeare. 1594? Available in many editions.

The Bard's most intense depiction of one man's love for another. Antonio (who, people forget, is the title character) serves as a prototype of the tormented, unrequited lover willing to sacrifice his all for his beloved's happiness, even if that means giving up his beloved to a woman.

Sodom, or the Quintessence of Debauchery. Attributed to the Earl of Rochester. 1684? North Hollywood, Calif.: Brandon House, 1966.

A high-spirited pornographic fantasia in rhymed couplets about a kingdom where buggery is decreed by law, although, in fact, anything goes. Restoration comedy at its most liberated, it makes sodomy seem as jolly as lawn tennis, until VD takes its toll.

The Scarlet Princess of Edo (***Sakura Hime Azuma Bunsho***) by Tsuruya Namboku IV and others. 1817. In *Kabuki, Five Classic Plays,* edited by James Brandon. Cambridge, Mass.: Harvard University Press, 1975.

In this Kabuki classic, a priest and the acolyte he loves swear a suicide pact which only the boy honors. But his fate and the priest's remain entangled when he is reincarnated as a beautiful princess, whose mishaps eventually reduce her to whoredom and murder. In performance both the boy and the princess are played by the same actor.

The Importance of Being Earnest by Oscar Wilde. 1895. Available in many editions.

A masterpiece of nonsense writing, informed by a camp sensibility that revels in paradox and cool demolition of the social code. The

"Bunburying" of the two male leads has been read as a cipher for adventures in the gay demimonde.

The Green Bay Tree by Mordaunt Shairp, 1933, in *Gay Plays,* Michael Wilcox, ed. New York: Methuen, 1984.

A feline and polished melodrama about a young boy whose tastes and outlook are molded by an epicene older man. Politically deplorable by present-day standards, the depiction of a certain kind of ultra-refined aesthete has never been bettered.

A Streetcar Named Desire by Tennessee Williams. 1947. Available in many editions.

So many drag queens have modeled themselves on Blanche DuBois that many assume she was one. Equivocal elements, such as the irresistible allure of the brute and the alienation of the hypersensitive in a coarse world, open it to interpretation that an all-male cast production might some day illuminate.

Death Watch by Jean Genet. (*Haute Surveillance.*) 1949. Translated by Bernard Frechtman in *Death Watch and The Maids.* New York: Grove Press, 1961.

Without having to be as graphically explicit as later prison plays, this short lyrical drama of power relationships on Death Row potently puts across Genet's equation of sexual attraction and murder. It might also be seen as the "talkie" equivalent of his short film *Chant d'amour.*

Entertaining Mr. Sloane by Joe Orton. 1966. In *Complete Plays of Joe Orton,* edited by John Lahr. New York: Grove Press, 1986.

This jet-black comedy, Orton's tightest play, redraws the eternal triangle, situating an enigmatic bully-boy between predatory brother and sister. The language is especially juicy in its innuendo and double entendre and the overall tone joyously amoral.

Conquest of the Universe or When Queens Collide by Charles Ludlam. 1967. In *The Complete Plays of Charles Ludlam.* New York: Harper & Row, 1989.

Ludlam's authentic flavor and originality are best tasted in his early plays, when he was a countercultural phenomenon, not yet flattered into a *salonfähig* prodigy. Combining high art, low camp, down-market transvestism, and just plain bawdry, he levels Western civilization to anarchic rubble while challenging audiences to get all the jokes.

The Boys in the Band by Matt Crowley. 1968. (Out of print.)

Sodden with self-pity and populated by stereotypes, this tear-jerking comedy still surpasses such later crowd pleasers as *Torch Song Trilogy* in the neatness of its Albeean structure and its quotable bitchery. Besides, it was the ground-breaker that proved gay themes and characters to be commercially viable.

Chinchilla by Robert David Macdonald. 1977. Newark, Del: Proscenium Press, 1980.

Ostensibly based on the Diaghilev years of the Ballets Russes, this is an elegant and eloquent exploration of why artists make art. On the surface it seems as glancingly witty as Ronald Firbank, but is informed by deep experience and unpretentious wisdom.

Cloud Nine by Caryl Churchill. 1979. New York: Routledge, Chapnan and Hall, 1985.

Still the best play about gender roles and sexual identity because it is the least preachy and most open-ended and is not afraid to cast a jaundiced eye on gay lib and militant feminism along the way. Act One mixes caricatures of Victorian colonialism and sexism; Act Two complicates the issue with the dilemma of modern society's sensual smorgasbord. Roles are cast across gender lines.

Forty-Deuce by Alan Bowne. 1981. New York: Sea Horse Press, 1983.

Lurid but well-observed *Grand Guignol* about the boy hustlers of Times Square, with pithy dialogue and no bows to conventional sensibilities. The critics hated it for all the wrong reasons, yet Bowne's is a more authentic dramatic voice than those of many safer, playhouse-broken writers, just as his later AIDS-inspired work, *Beirut,* is a more genuine piece of theater than the tendentious thesis plays that overshadow it.

One of the best collections of gay plays is ***Out Front: Contemporary Gay and Lesbian Plays,*** edited with an informative introduction by Don Shewey. New York: Grove Press, 1988.

GAY FILM AND VIDEO

GAY FILMS FOR EDUCATION AND FOR PRIVATE ENJOYMENT

This list of films about the gay experience is culled from a longer list of suggested titles on both gay and lesbian themes which was

THE GLINES IS ONE OF MANY GAY THEATERS TO ORIGINATE PRODUCTIONS THAT HAVE MOVED ON TO BROADWAY AND HOLLYWOOD. PROBABLY THE BEST KNOWN IS *TORCH SONG TRILOGY* BY HARVEY FIERSTEIN. THE AUTHOR/ACTOR IS PICTURED HERE (*CENTER*) WITH FISHER STEVENS (*LEFT*) AND ESTELLE GETTY (*RIGHT*). PHOTO BY GERRY GOODSTEIN. REPRODUCED WITH PERMISSION OF THE GLINES.

compiled by the *National Gay and Lesbian Task Force* with the help of *Frameline.* The listing was originally devised to help college organizations and other community groups develop film showings as part of their educational efforts.

Inclusion on this list does not imply any endorsement of a film by the author or by NGLTF. This is only a starting point. If you intend to use a film or video from this list for a public audience, you should review it first by renting it from a video store, if possible, or by asking a distributor for a review copy, which most will give you. You can also get more information by writing to distributors (listings follow) and asking for a copy of their catalogs.

Costs of renting films from distributors change too rapidly to include them here. Contact the company listed to find out the current fee for a film's use.

If you have any other questions about film or video availability, contact the program director:

Frameline
Box 14792
San Francisco, CA 94114
Phone: 415 861 5245

Frameline has accumulated expertise in gay-themed films as the organizers of the San Francisco International Lesbian and Gay Film Festival and has helped many community and college groups organize gay and lesbian film festivals.

A Man Like Eva. Eva Mattes offers a portrayal of her former director, Rainer Werner Fassbinder. The story follows "Eva" and his cast and crew producing *La Dame aux Camelias.* Rental in 16mm available from Kino International, 250 W. 57th Street, New York, NY 10019.

Another Country. An examination of the sexual and political life of 1930s English public schools. Video version can be purchased from many gay bookstores or rented at local video stores.

Before Stonewall: The Making of a Gay and Lesbian Community. This film, a standard on local PBS stations during Gay Pride Week, uses interviews and archival material to trace the social, political, and cultural development of the gay and lesbian community. The 16mm version can be rented from Cinema Guild, 1697 Broadway, New York, NY 10001; telephone: 212 629 6222.

The Best Way. A macho athletic director catches a sensitive drama coach in drag and a teasing game of cat and mouse develops. The 16mm version can be rented from Cinema Guild, 1697 Broadway, New York, NY 10001; telephone: 212 629 6222; a video version is available for purchase from Lambda Rising (see page 211).

The Black Lizard. The story of a jewel thief played by a female impersonator, from a screenplay by Yukio Mishima. The 16mm version can be rented from Shochuku Films, 8230 Beverly Boulevard, Suite 9, Los Angeles, CA 90045.

Carravagio. A reexamination of the life of Carravagio, a seventeenth century painter who influenced and scandalized his contemporaries with the controversial nature of his art and his resistance to the social mores of his time. The 16mm or 35mm versions of the film are available from Kino International, 250 W. 57th Street, New York, NY 10019. The film is on video, available from Cinevista (see page 209).

The Clinic. This comedy is about the comings and goings in a VD clinic. Available from Lambda Rising (see page 211).

The Consequence. A middle-aged actor is jailed for "unnatural activities" and sent to prison where he falls in love with the teenage son of one of his guards. The 16mm version is available for rent from Almi Pictures, 1900 Broadway, New York, NY 10023; telephone: 212 769 2255.

Death in Venice. This film version of Thomas Mann's classic novel of sexual obsession is available for rental from most video stores and for purchase from most gay bookstores.

El Diputado. This Spanish film is the story of the illicit one-night stands of a prominent politician. The video version can be purchased from Lambda Rising and the Insider Video Club (see page 211).

Ernesto. A sexually inexperienced youth in Yugoslavia confronts his feelings, first with a dock worker, and then with a fellow violin student. Video version is for sale at Lambda Rising and through Insider Video Club (see page 211).

Improper Conduct. This documentary presents an important aspect of the homophobia of the Cuban Revolution. The 35mm film can be rented from Cinevista (see page 211).

Kissing Booth. This short film about the search for the perfect kiss stars Quentin Crisp. Available for rental from Co-Directions, 276 Riverside Drive, #4C, New York, NY 10025.

Kiss of the Spider Woman. This widely available film stars William Hurt in an Oscar-winning role about an effeminate prisoner in an Argentine jail and his bonding with another outcast, a political detainee. Available for rental at most video stores, or for purchase from Lambda Rising (see page 211).

La Cage aux Folles and *La Cage aux Folles II* are both farces involving a gay couple who own a nightclub on the French Riviera. Made into a Broadway hit musical, the films are widely available for rental at mainstream video stores and for purchase from Lambda Rising (see page 211).

Mala Noche. Already an underground classic, though it's only a few years old, the story portrays a young gay man's love for teenage illegal aliens and how they respond to his advances. The 16mm film can be rented from Frameline (see page 211).

Maurice. Based on the classic E. M. Forster novel, this film shows the lives of two homosexual lovers in Edwardian England. Rent the 16mm version (for public performances only) from Cinecom, 1250 Broadway, Suite 802, New York, NY 10001; telephone: 212 629 6222. The video version is available for sale from Lambda Rising (see page 211), and many other gay bookstores.

My Beautiful Laundrette. This delightful movie is the love story of two gays in the United Kingdom, one from an English background, the other from Pakistani roots. The film won much well-deserved praise. The video is available from Insider Video Club (see page 211), and available for rental at many bookstores and video stores.

Naked Civil Servant. This is the autobiography of gay wit Quentin Crisp. Available for sale from Lambda Rising (see page 211).

Not All Parents Are Straight. This film explores children who live in gay and lesbian households. The 16mm version can be rented from Cinema Guild, 1697 Broadway, Suite 802, New York, NY 10018.

Outrageous. A Canadian film that won the hearts of viewers with its portrayal of two characters, one a male transvestite, the other a mentally disturbed woman. The film version can be rented from Almi Pictures, 1900 Broadway, New York, NY 10023; telephone: 212 769 2255. The video version is available at most gay bookstores and many video rental stores.

The Outsiders. A Taiwanese film about a young man, thrown out by his family, who goes to live with other rejected gays in a park in Taipei, the capital. The 35mm version is available for rent from Oriental Films, Limited, 2025 W. Chestnut Street, Alhambra, CA 98103.

Parting Glances. One of the first films about AIDS, this story about a man who must say good-bye to both a lover who is moving abroad and a friend who is dying of AIDS, is still one of the best. The video version can be purchased from Lambda Rising (see page 211).

Pink Triangles. This half-hour-long historic documentary examines homophobia from the Nazi era to the present. Either a 16mm or a video version can be rented from Cambridge Documentary Films, Box 385, Cambridge, MA 02139; telephone: 617 354 3677.

Silent Pioneers. There are two version of this film—30 minutes and 42 minutes—which documents the lives of older gay men and lesbians. The 16mm version and the video version are available for rent from Filmmakers Library, 124 E. 40th Street, #901, New York, NY 10016; telephone: 212 355 6545.

Taxi zum Klo. This frank film about a sexually active Berlin schoolteacher recalls another time when erotic activity was free and easy. The 16mm version can be rented from Almi Pictures, 1900 Broadway, New York, NY 10023; telephone: 212 769 2255. A video version is available from Inside Video Club (see page 211).

The Times of Harvey Milk. This Oscar-winning documentary recalls the life of San Francisco City Supervisor Harvey Milk, who was assassinated after his rise to power as an advocate for gay rights. The 16mm film version and a video version are available for rent (public performances only) from Cinecom, 1250 Broadway, Suite 802, New York, NY 10001; telephone: 212 629 6222. The video is available for purchase from Lambda Rising (see page 211).

Urinal. This work by innovative and controversial Canadian filmmaker John Greyson includes a retelling of the legend of Dorian Gray. The 16mm version is available for rental from Frameline (see page 211).

Tongues United. A film about an African-American gay man's relationship to America. Rental available from Frameline (see page 206).

PHOTO BY RON SIMMONS

Whoever Says the Truth Shall Die. An Italian-language documentary of the art, politics, and homosexuality of Pier Paolo Pasolini. The 16mm film can be rented from Kino International, 250 W. 57th Street, New York, NY 10019.

Word Is Out: Stories of Some of Our Lives. One of the real classics of gay liberation film, this moving, evocative, and well-made series of interviews with gay men and lesbians is probably the best nonfiction introduction to issues of gay and lesbian life available. The 16mm version can be rented from New Yorker Films, 16 W. 61st Street, New York, NY 10023; telephone: 212 247 6110.

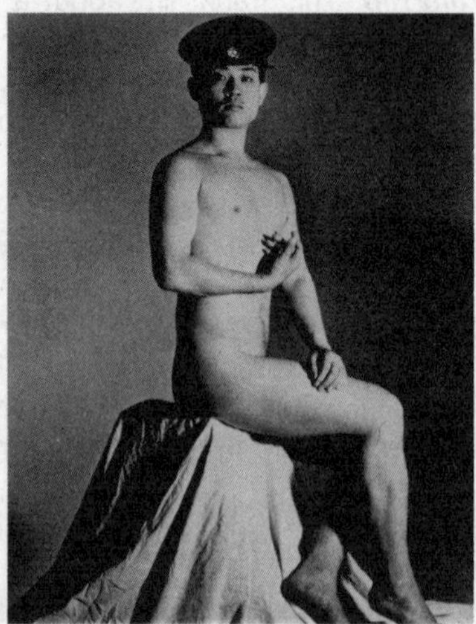

FROM JOHN GREYSON'S FILM *URINAL* (1988.) A FRAMELINE RELEASE.

▼ Of course, with the growth in video distribution, many of these productions are also available on videotape for home use. Many gay bookstores carry videotapes and may have some of these titles in stock for purchase. *Lambda Rising,* in Washington, D.C., has made a special effort to maintain a wide line of gay-themed videotapes. If your local store does not have a title that you're interested in purchasing, you should contact:

Lambda Rising
1625 Connecticut Avenue NW
Washington, DC 20009
Phone: 202 462 6969

▼ *Cinevista* is a video mail-order distributor which has many gay-themed titles for sale, including many on this list.

Cinevista
353 W. 39th Street
New York, NY 10018
Phone: 212 947 4373/fax: 212 947 0644

▼ *Insider Video Club* is another mail-order firm that will sometimes have these films for sale, often at discount prices. You can send for their catalog to check current offerings. Be aware that the catalog will probably include erotic films as well as mainstream titles. You will have to state that you are twenty-one years of age in order to get this catalog:

Insider Video Club
Box 93399
Hollywood, CA 90039
Phone: 800 634 2242/within California call, collect: 213 661 8330

TIPS ON ORDERING FILMS

The National Gay and Lesbian Task Force makes these suggestions about ordering films from distributors. Some films are easier to get than you may realize, and may be much cheaper. Check with your library to see what's in their selection. Also, see what's available through interlibrary loans. When ordering from a distributor, ask for a contract that clearly spells out their obligations and yours. Ask these specific questions:

■ What is the current price, including shipping and handling costs?
■ Is the film available on your chosen date?
■ How long is the rental period?
■ Is there a fine for returning the film late? How much is it?
■ In what format is the movie available? (VHS or BETA? three-quarter-inch or half-inch video? 8mm, 16mm, or 35mm film?)
■ Is the movie subtitled or dubbed? What is the original language?

NGLTF also suggests you get this information from the distributor to help publicize the film:

■ What is the length of the film?
■ What is the date of release?
■ Who are the key actors/actresses?
■ What awards, if any, has it won?

▼ For more information on choosing and ordering films for public events and a discussion of how to specifically organize a college or other film festival, contact:

Campus Project
National Gay and Lesbian Task Force
1734 14th Street NW
Washington, DC 20009
Phone: 202 332 6483

FILMS INDISPENSABLE TO ANY GAY VIDEO LIBRARY

Vito Russo is the acknowledged expert on gay images in film. His book *The Celluloid Closet: Homosexuality in the Movies* (New York: Harper & Row, 1981) is the best work on the subject. Russo put together this list of home videos along with a short commentary on each for *The Big Gay Book.* All are easily accessible, most through local video rental stores. If your store doesn't have them in stock, ask for them to get copies. It's only when there's a proven demand that such outfits become responsive.

Parting Glances. 1986. Directed by Bill Sherwood. Superbly written and directed independent film which captures a certain kind of New York gay life in the age of AIDS.

Desert Hearts. 1986. Directed by Donna Dietsch. Adapted from Jane Rule's novel about the love affair between a divorcee and a free spirit, set in Reno in the 1950s. One of the few films about a lesbian relationship in which the women end up together at the end.

Sunday Bloody Sunday. 1971. Directed by John Schlesinger. Literate, adult story of a gay doctor (Peter Finch) and his bisexual lover (Murray Head). The first screen kiss between two male lovers shocked audiences when the film was released.

The Times of Harvey Milk. 1985. Directed by Robert Epstein. Powerful and moving Oscar-winning documentary on the life of the San Francisco city supervisor who was assassinated in 1976.

The Boys in the Band. 1970. Directed by William Friedkin. Landmark screen version of Matt Crowley's hit play about homosexual self-hatred. The first Hollywood film in which most of the major characters were gay. Valuable as history and as a reminder to young gay people how far we've come in such a short time.

Abuse. 1983. Directed by Arthur J. Bressan, Jr. Partly autobiographical story of an abused gay teenager who falls in love with a thirty-five-year-old filmmaker. Issues of child abuse and intergenerational sex are dealt with expertly in this widely acclaimed low-budget feature.

My Beautiful Laundrette. 1986. Directed by Stephen Frears. Originally shot for British television, this film about racism and Thatcher's England became a surprise art house hit. One of the few films to integrate a gay couple into a story not "about" homosexuality.

Maurice. 1987. Directed by James Ivory. Based on the long-suppressed E. M. Forster novel, it's sort of a pretentious coffee table movie but refreshingly insistent on its anti-closet philosophy.

Novembermoon. 1985. Directed by Alexandra von Grote. Engrossing, well-made feature about a lesbian couple trying to survive in Nazi-occupied France.

Victim. 1961. Directed by Basil Dearden. Breakthrough thriller starring Dirk Bogarde as a London barrister fighting a ring of blackmailers who prey on homosexuals. The first major film to use the word "homosexual," a move which promptly got it banned in several countries.

Victor/Victoria. 1982. Directed by Blake Edwards. A genuinely funny throwback to the innocent comedies of the thirties when the gay character was everyone's best friend. Not particularly radical, but a relief from the *Making Love* genre.

This Special Friendship. 1964. Directed by Jean Dellanoy. Tragic tale of a gay love affair in a repressive Catholic school; based on the novel by Roger Peyrifitte.

Taxi zum Klo. 1980. Directed by Frank Ripploh. A refreshingly funny look at the kind of promiscuity that typified the fast-lane gay life in the 1970s.

COPYRIGHT © 1991 BY THE ESTATE OF VITO RUSSO. USED BY PERMISSION OF JED MATTES, INC.

EXPERIMENTAL VIDEO

Video not only allows a wide distribution of films that could be seen only in theaters a while ago, it also permits an inexpensive and creative new medium for artists.

The Video Data Bank, while not an officially gay or lesbian organization, is a major source of information and material in this field. It is the largest distributor of tapes by and about contemporary artists in the United States and Canada. The Data Bank collection consists primarily of independently produced experimental videos and documentaries, alternative and guerrilla television, early works from the annals of video history, curated series of video art as well as interviews with contemporary critics and artists. Their primary venues consist of art museums, educational institutions, film/video festivals, broadcast and cablecast programs, alternative spaces and media centers. They carry an extensive number of gay videos and are

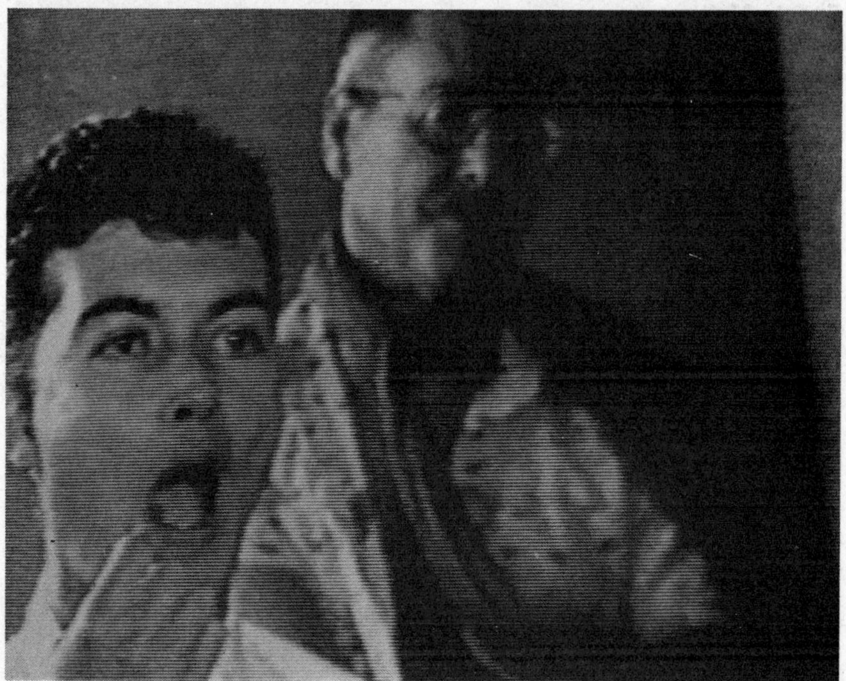

JOHN GREYSON'S *THE KIPLING TRILOGY* (1984–1985) IS IN THE COLLECTION OF VIDEO DATA BANK. REPRINTED WITH PERMISSION.

happy to help you choose an appropriate selection for a gay-themed program in any of those situations.

Recently they've also ventured into the home market. Videos are available for purchase from the Video Data Bank or for rental through *Facets Multimedia.* Facets also has an extensive catalog of films and videos with gay themes, "The Movie Lover's Guide."

Satellite Video Exchange Society is another organization that isn't really gay or lesbian, but that does have an extensive program of great interest to gay men. It is an artist-run center that includes production facilities, postproduction, an extensive video library, a video distribution facility, and more. It publishes *Video Guide,* a magazine that regularly reviews art and documentary works by gay and lesbian artists.

Video Data Bank
School of the Art Institute
280 S. Columbus Drive
Chicago, IL 60603

Facets Multimedia
1517 W. Fullerton Avenue
Chicago, IL 60614
Phone: 312 281 9075

Satellite Video Exchange Society
1102 Homer Street
Vancouver, BC V6B 2X6
Phone: 604 688 4336

EROTIC VIDEOS

The line between erotica (socially accepted sexual art) and pornography (socially unacceptable sexual art) is a difficult one to draw. Certainly there are many gay erotic films which deserve serious consideration, just as many are made without any aesthetic intent. The decision is up to you.

▼ If you are interested in gay video, *Bijou Video Sales* is the largest mail-order firm in the country. They publish a constantly up-dated catalog of gay videos. For a sales-oriented organization, their catalog is remarkably honest in its evaluation of the products. Write or call for information.

Bijou Video Sales
1363 N. Wells Street
Chicago, IL 60610
Phone: 800 932 7111

▼ *The Adam Film World Directory of Gay Adult Video* is another guide with rankings of the best—and worst—of gay video. The catalog is packed with advertisements from individual companies, if you're inclined to order the videos after reading the descriptions. Each copy of the directory is $7.95.

Adam Film World Directory of Gay Adult Video
Knight Publishing Corp.
8060 Melrose Avenue
Los Angeles, CA 90046

▼ "Pornography" is a very tricky term, full of social innuendo and relativity. The work of *Tom of Finland* is an example. The heavily stylized and often hard-core images of the famed craftsman (he really is Finnish, by the way) has had a major impact on gay art and self-image. In fact, his pictures are closer to being icons of gay life rather than easily dismissed sexually obvious porn. The Finnish government evidently agrees; they've just funded "Daddy and the Muscles Academy," a documentary film to be produced on the man and his work.

It's only fitting that an artist of his stature has a foundation formed for the sole purpose of promoting his work. The *Tom of Finland Foundation* believes that "sexuality in art is a legitimate expression of free speech." The foundation is working to collect and preserve Tom's artwork. Its newsletter announces shows around the world featuring his drawings and other activities.

Tom of Finland Foundation, Inc.
Box 26658
Los Angeles, CA 90026

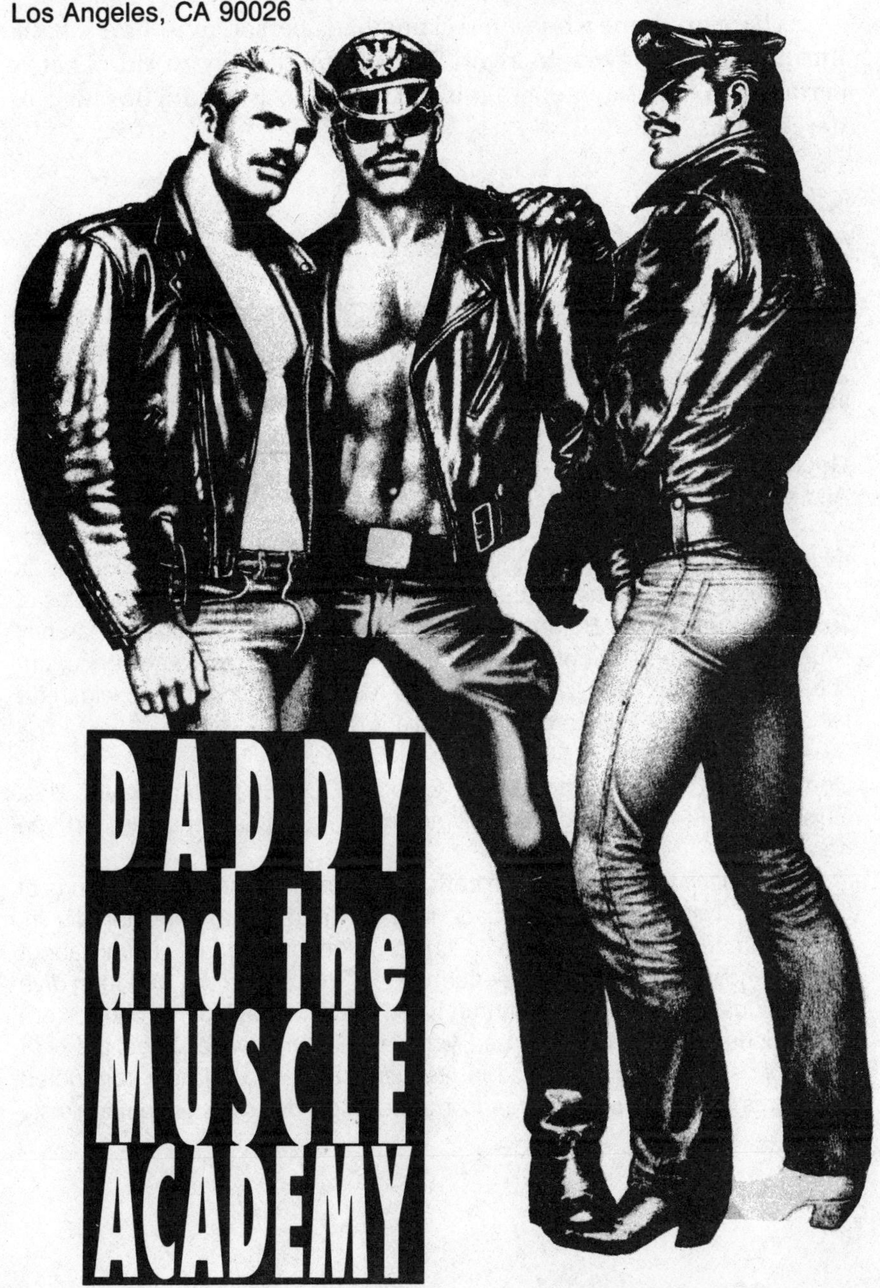

OPERA

Opera has a special place in the cultural lives of many gays. Michael Bronski chronicled some of that gay fascination with opera in his book *Culture Clash* (Boston: South End Press, 1987).

There are some who would claim that a person must have a basic introduction in opera to really be part of the gay world. That is certainly an overstatement, but it still led me to ask Walta Borawski to develop this list.

THE ESSENTIAL OPERA RECORDINGS FOR GAY MEN

Georges Bizet. *Carmen* (Angel AVB-34061). Maria Callas, Nicolai Gedda, Andrea Guiot, Robert Massard. Cond. Georges Prêtre

Perhaps the most accessible of grand operas, ***Carmen*** has rich melodies that will probably ring bells in the minds of nonopera folks. Callas never brought her Carmen to the stage; known for the great soprano roles of ***Tosca, Norma, Anna Bolena, Il Pirata,*** and ***Medea,*** she was apparently reluctant to perform one of the rare mezzo leads before a live audience, but she breathed fury and warmth into the doomed and dynamic cigarette factory worker in a Paris recording studio in 1964.

Donizetti. *Lucia di Lammermoor* (Melodram CD MEL26004). Maria Callas, Guiseppe Di Stefano, Rolando Panerai, Nicola Zaccaria. Cond. Herbert von Karajan

It is difficult to have to decide between the many wondrous recordings of this opera. This live recording made in Berlin in 1955 is remarkable for its clarity and the beauty of Callas's Lucia. Although I've no qualms about recommending so many Callas performances (she revived the very term ***diva*** in the middle of the twentieth century), I do feel odd that half my choices are productions conducted by Herbert von Karajan, who twice joined the Nazi party, once in Vienna and once in Germany, and who willingly conducted orchestras that had been purged of Jews and "political nonconformists," presumably including gay musicians. I obviously do not personally boycott his records, but people would be justified in deciding to.

Engelbert Humperdinck. ***Hansel and Gretel*** (EMI 153-03 382 3). Elisabeth Grümmer, Elisabeth Schwarzkopf, Josef Metternich. Cond. Herbert von Karajan

A mean stepmother with no maternal leanings, two children driven into the dark, brooding forest dropping breadcrumbs as markers, mere crumbs that will disappear into the mouths of insensitive birds, a colorful mezzo witch that everyone gets to eat in the end: all this and music that soars to heaven or drops gently as dew. You will recognize much of it, as its lovely melodies were often adapted for elementary school productions. Produced by the legendary Walter Legge, this recording has been in constant demand since its first appearance in 1953.

Leoš Janáček. ***Věc Makropulos*** [The Makropulos Case or Business or Secret or Affair] (London OSA-12116). Elisabeth Söderström. Cond. Sir Charles Mackerras

Elina Makropulos is 337 years old. It's 1922, she's been calling herself Emilia Marty for the last twelve years, she's a singer who's had centuries to perfect her vocal technique, and now she needs the formula for the elixir devised by her father, a long-dead Cretan physician, or she will soon show her age and then die. She also knows too much about the earlier stages of a 100-year-old court case for her own good. Like in other Eastern European operas there are no arias ***per se,*** just incredibly lush music that keeps on coming. Based on a play by Karel (***R.U.R.***) Capek. Totally haunting.

Giacomo Puccini. ***Madama Butterfly*** (EMI SLS 5128). Victoria de los Angeles, Jussi Björling. Cond. Gabriele Santini

Arguably the opera with more beautiful melodies than any other (although one suspects the competition would all come from the pen of Puccini). Here East meets West and East decidedly loses. The character of the teenage Butterfly, so eager to give up her culture and take on that of her lover the American Pinkerton, is very painful to witness. But for a soprano, few things can be more enthralling than her duets with Pinkerton and with her serving woman, and her own mesmerizing aria of expectation, "Un bel dí." There are wondrous recordings by Renata Scotto, Renata Tebaldi, and Maria Callas—but Victoria de los Angeles has a full, warm, powerful voice that enjoys immense chemistry with Puccini.

Richard Strauss. ***Salome*** (Angel SBLX-3848). Hildegard Behrens, José Van Dam, Karl-Walter Böhm, Agnes Baltsa. Cond. Herbert von Karajan

If you've ever wanted to dance naked for your stepfather so that he'll behead that special guy who won't put out for you, this spectacularly noisy setting of Oscar Wilde's play is a must. Superimposed tonalities, unrelated keys strung together, the whole tone scale—a pre-Jane Fonda workout for over a hundred musicians, their instruments, your speakers, and you. Some aficionados prefer Ljuba Welitsch's 1944 performance—for she manages to sound like a spoiled child with great diction. There are also great performances on record by Montserrat Caballé and Birgit Nilsson. But Behrens has an emotional force that serves her well here and on the later recorded Strauss's *Elektra.*

Richard Strauss. ***Der Rosenkavalier*** (EMI SLS 810). Elisabeth Schwarzkopf, Christa Ludwig, Teresa Stich-Randall. Cond. Herbert von Karajan

For people who avoid opera because of outlandish situations, this gorgeous look at a grand woman's final fling offers no beheadings, live entombments, or mass executions of an order of nuns. All that happens is she gives up her lover to a younger woman. She herself is in her thirties, but in a pre-Elizabeth Arden (and pre-Gloria Steinem!) society. Strauss so loved the female voice that he brought three of them to new orgiastic heights in the famous trio near the end—but then brings the ecstasy down to one of the quietest and most delicious denouements in opera. Don't forget your handkerchief.

Guiseppe Verdi. ***La Traviata*** (Angel ZBX-3910). Maria Callas, Alfredo Kraus, Mario Sereni. Cond. Franco Ghione

This is the legendary performance given March 27, 1958, at the San Carlos Opera House in Lisbon; it is the reason Terrence McNally's play is called ***The Lisbon Traviata.*** It is Callas in her prime (those glorious years from 1952 to 1959), singing Violetta with so much passion it could be embarrassing if there wasn't so much artistic control. If you are curious as to why Callas is known as "La Divina," listen to her "E strano! . . . Ah! fors'è lui" or "Addio del passato." The combination of enormous voice, total conviction, and brilliant acting ability just never happened again. The constant aural appearance of the prompter and the audience din might ruin the experience for some—but it is too classic to avoid, and too heartfelt not to be shared. A magic moment in opera's history.

Jaromír Weinberger. ***Schwanda*** (CBS Masterworks 79344). Lucia Popp, Siegfried Jerusalem, Hermann Prey. Cond. Heinz Wallberg

Weinberger escaped Hitler in 1938, and died of sedatives in 1967. His opera ***Schwanda,*** set in Czechoslovakian folklore, is about a bagpiper, his wife Dorotka, the legendary Babinsky, and an icy queen who wants to marry—or behead—the bagpiper . . . until Babinsky, a Czech Robin Hood figure, turns the executioner's ax into a broom—and puts the bagpipes in the doomed musician's capable hands. Schwanda goes to hell on a technicality—but the devil himself loves his playing, and helps provide a happy ending.

PRESERVING OUR CULTURE

Respecting our heritage means taking care of the materials that will become our history in the future. Archives and libraries are collecting books, periodicals, brochures, pamphlets, and other evidence of contemporary gay life. One of the easiest mistakes to make is to disvalue what of today's world might be important to historians in the future. If you or your organization are producing any writing, audio, video, film, or other materials that reflect our lives today, make sure you're sending copies of that information to a library that will care for what might well become treasures.

COMMUNITY ARCHIVES AND LIBRARIES

UNITED STATES

■ CALIFORNIA ■

BAKER MEMORIAL LIBRARY/ONE, INC.
3340 Country Club Drive
Los Angeles, CA 90019
Phone: 213 735 5252

HOMOSEXUAL INFORMATION CENTER
6758 Hollywood Boulevard
Suite 208
Los Angeles, CA 90028

INTERNATIONAL GAY/LESBIAN ARCHIVE
Natalie Barney/Edward Carpenter Library
626 N. Robertson
West Hollywood, CA 90038
Phone: 213 854 0271

GAY AND LESBIAN ARCHIVES
Box 4186
San Diego, CA 92104
Phone: 619 280 7411

CENTER FOR RESEARCH AND EDUCATION IN SEXUALITY
San Francisco State University
San Francisco, CA 94132
Phone: 415 338 1137

SAN FRANCISCO BAY AREA GAY/LESBIAN HISTORICAL SOCIETY
Box 42332
San Francisco, CA 94191
Phone: 415 626 0980

GAY AND LESBIAN ARCHIVE PROJECT
Lesbian, Gay and Bisexual Community Center at Stanford
Box 8265
Stanford, CA 94309
Phone: 415 725 4222

■ DELAWARE ■

DELAWARE LESBIAN AND GAY ARCHIVES
Box 974
Wilmington, DE 19899

■ FLORIDA ■

STONEWALL LIBRARY
c/o Holy Spirit Metropolitan Community Church
330 S.W. 27th Street
Ft. Lauderdale, FL 33315
Phone: 305 462 2004

■ ILLINOIS ■

CHICAGO GAY/LESBIAN HISTORY PROJECT
Box 60046
Chicago, IL 60660

HENRY GERBER/PEARL M. HART LIBRARY
Midwest Lesbian/Gay Resource Center
3238 N. Sheffield Avenue
Chicago, IL 60657
Phone: 312 883 3003

■ KANSAS ■

TOBY SCANLAND LIBRARY
Box 1144
Topeka, KS 66601

■ KENTUCKY ■

KENTUCKY GAY AND LESBIAN EDUCATION CENTER
Box 4264
Louisville, KY 40204

■ LOUISIANA ■

HOMOSEXUAL INFORMATION CENTER
115 Monroe Street
Bossier, LA 71111
Phone: 318 742 4709

■ MINNESOTA ■

QUATREFOIL LIBRARY
1619 Dayton Avenue
St. Paul, MN 46856
Phone: 612 641 0969

■ MONTANA ■

OUT IN MONTANA RESOURCE CENTER
Box 7223
Missoula, MT 59807

■ NEW YORK ■

AIDS ARCHIVES
Gay Men's Health Crisis
132 W. 12th Street
P.O. Box 274
New York, NY 10011
Phone: 212 807 7660

NATIONAL MUSEUM OF LESBIAN AND GAY HISTORY
New York Gay and Lesbian Community Center
208 W. 13th Street
New York, NY 10011
Phone: 212 807 0197

GAY ALLIANCE OF THE GENESEE VALLEY LIBRARY
713 Monroe Avenue
Rochester, NY 14607
Phone: 716 244 8640

■ OHIO ■

SOCIETY FOR INDIVIDUAL RIGHTS
26500 Wildcat Road
Rockbridge, OH 43149

■ PENNSYLVANIA ■

BLACK GAY ARCHIVES
Box 30004
Philadelphia, PA 19103

GAY AND LESBIAN LIBRARY/ARCHIVES OF PHILADELPHIA
P.O. Box 15748
Philadelphia, PA 19103

■ TEXAS ■

DALLAS GAY/LESBIAN HISTORIC ARCHIVES
Gay Community Center
2701 Reagan
Dallas, TX 75219
Phone: 214 528 4233

METROPOLITAN COMMUNITY CHURCH LIBRARY
1919 Decatur
Houston, TX 77007
Phone: 713 991 6766

CANADA

■ BRITISH COLUMBIA ■

GAY ARCHIVES COLLECTIVE
Box 3130, MPO
Vancouver, BC V6B 3X6

■ MANITOBA ■

WINNIPEG GAY/LESBIAN ARCHIVE
222 Osborne Street, Suite 1
Winnipeg, MB R3L 1Z3
Phone: 204 284 5208

■ NEW BRUNSWICK ■

ARCHIVES FOR THE PROTECTION OF GAY HISTORY AND LITERATURE
Box 6368, Station A
St. John, N.B. E2L 4R8

■ ONTARIO ■

HAMILTON-WENTWORTH GAY ARCHIVES
Box 44, Station B
Hamilton, ON L8L 7T5

HALO LIBRARY
649 Colbourne Street
London, ON N6A 3Z2
Phone: 519 433 3762

CANADIAN GAY ARCHIVES
(Incorporates the James Fraser Library)
Box 639, Station A
Toronto, ON M5W 1G2

The Canadian Gay Archives publishes a newsletter. *The Gay Archivist* is an irregular publication each issue of which includes special bibliographies, manuals, and historical sketches.
Phone: 416 921 6310

LESBIAN AND GAY HISTORY GROUP OF TORONTO
Box 639, Station A
Toronto, ON M5W 1G2
Phone: 416 921 6310

■ QUEBEC ■

ARCHIVES GAIES DU QUEBEC
CP 395 suc Place du Parc
Montreal, QU H2W 2N9

▼ This list was compiled with the help of "Archives and Special Collections of Gay/Lesbian Materials in North America." The complete list is available for a small fee from:

GLTF Clearinghouse
American Library Association
50 E. Huron Street
Chicago, IL 60611

QUATREFOIL LIBRARY

Quatrefoil Library is named for the 1950 novel by James Barr, one of the first gay novels to portray homosexual characters positively. What the title meant to Barr isn't known, but legend tries to attach meaning to the number four, and its conventionalized representation, the quatrefoil, has come to mean completion, solidarity, stability, order, and justice. The whole of the quatrefoil is unified and complete, but each part, too, has its own unity and completeness. The quatrefoil has also been equated with the four-leaf clover, which, either because of its rarity or because of its resemblance to a Maltese Cross, has become a symbol of good luck.

The library was inspired by David Irwin and Dick Hewetson, who started collecting gay books in the mid-1970s. Their dream was to start a lending library and they eventually saw it fulfilled when Quatrefoil was incorporated in 1984. The library went public on February 4, 1986, when space became available in a building housing other nonprofit organizations.

The collection immediately grew, once its services and collection were easily accessible, and by June 1987 the library reopened in its own space.

The library currently receives local, national, and international periodicals and houses a vast collection of memorabilia, clippings, historic erotica, and periodicals going back to the 1950s. In addition to those materials, which are not allowed to circulate, Quatrefoil has a wide variety of fiction and nonfiction books which are available to members. There is also a growing number of records, audio and video tapes, and games in the library's selection.

The goal of Quatrefoil is to collect, preserve, disseminate, and document materials and information relevant to sexual minorities and to develop educational and other appropriate community services. The library also has a goal of networking with other libraries and archives specializing in materials relevant to sexual minorities.

Like most other libraries, Quatrefoil solicits donations of suitable materials and is able to offer a tax deduction, depending on their value.

Quatrefoil Library
1619 Dayton Avenue
St. Paul, MN 55104

It may not be the *Encyclopedia Britannica* yet, but Garland Publishing has made a start. *The Encyclopedia of Homosexuality,* edited by Hunter College professor Wayne R. Dynes, is a two-volume straightforward reference book on the subject. The five thousand entries go from Achilles to Zoroastrianism, with Buggery and Nameless Sin in between.

Garland Publishing, Inc.
136 Madison Avenue
New York, NY 10016

▼ GAY PROMP flashes on your IBM screen events from gay history relevant to the day you run the program. Put GAY PROMP in your AUTOEXEC.BAT file, and you will automatically pause to celebrate gay history each time that you turn on your computer. Available for $7.50 from Louie Crew, P.O. Box 1545, Orangeburg, SC 29116-1545.

An easy and enjoyable way to celebrate the heroes of gay life and letters is looking at and either collecting or mailing postcards from Crossing Press. The company has a whole series of famous figures in our lives available. For a complete listing:

Crossing Press
Box 1048
22D Roache Road
Freedom, CA 95019

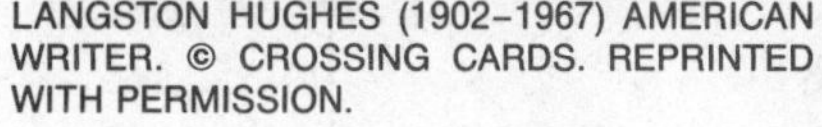

LANGSTON HUGHES (1902–1967) AMERICAN WRITER. © CROSSING CARDS. REPRINTED WITH PERMISSION.

FEDERICO GARCIA LORCA (1899–1936), SPANISH POET AND DRAMATIST. © CROSSING CARDS. REPRINTED WITH PERMISSION.

> *The preservation of Lesbian and Gay History—the fact of our existence—is the most vital legacy . . . and the various Gay Archives around the country are the institutions I value the most. The health, social, and political groups matter now; a gay archives will matter for generations to come, as we rediscover ourselves.*
>
> —*RICHARD LABONTÉ,*
> *bookstore manager*

▼ The visual arts are one of the means through which our history can be captured. There are two major projects under way:

The Mariposa Portraits are a series of paintings by Don Bachardy commissioned by the Mariposa Foundation. The first set of twelve portraits is completed and has been displayed often. For more information:

Mariposa Education and Research Foundation, Inc.
Box 36 B 35
Los Angeles, CA 90036
Phone: 818 704 4812

THIS PORTRAIT OF THE REVEREND TROY PERRY, FOUNDER OF THE METROPOLITAN COMMUNITY CHURCH, IS ONE OF A SERIES BY ARTIST DONALD BACHARDY COMMISSIONED BY THE MARIPOSA FOUNDATION. REPRINTED WITH PERMISSION FROM THE MARIPOSA FOUNDATION.

NOVELIST JAMES PURDY PHOTOGRAPHED BY ROBERT GIARD. © 1987 ROBERT GIARD. REPRINTED WITH PERMISSION.

Robert Giard has undertaken an archival project, capturing the spirit of gay and lesbian writers on film. His many photographic portraits have been widely exhibited. Giard hopes they will be published in book form.

For more information:

Robert Giard
Box 1011
Amagansett, NY 11930

ACADEMIC COLLECTIONS

Academic institutions are also collecting gay and lesbian materials in special collections. The following are cited in "Archives and Special Collections of Gay/Lesbian Materials in North America," a brochure by the Gay and Lesbian Task Force of the American Library Association, as having major collections. For a complete copy write to the GLTF, American Library Association, 50 E. Huron Street, Chicago, IL 60611.

BOWLING GREEN STATE UNIVERSITY
Popular Culture Collection
William T. Gerome Library
Bowling Green, OH 43403
Phone: 419 372 2450

CALIFORNIA STATE UNIVERSITY, SACRAMENTO
Library
Dissent and Social Change Collections
Sacramento, CA 95819
Phone: 916 278 6466

UNIVERSITY OF CALIFORNIA
Bancroft Library
Social Protest Project
Berkeley, CA 94720
Phone: 415 642 3781

CORNELL UNIVERSITY
Collection on Human Sexuality
John M. Olin Library
Ithaca, NY 14853
Phone: 607 255 3530

The Cornell University Libraries Collection on Human Sexuality was established with the help of a major bequest by David Goodstein, former publisher of *The Advocate.* The collection was founded with a basis of research material which had been housed in the archives of the Mariposa Foundation.

UNIVERSITY OF CONNECTICUT LIBRARY
Alternative Press Collection
Special Collections Department
Storrs, CT 06268
Phone: 203 486 2524

INDIANA UNIVERSITY
Kinsey Institute for Research in Sex, Gender and Reproduction
Room 313, Morrison Hall
Bloomington, IN 47405
Phone: 812 335 7686

INSTITUTE FOR ADVANCED STUDY OF HUMAN SEXUALITY
Research Library
1523 Franklin Street
San Francisco, CA 94109
Phone: 415 928 1133

UNIVERSITY OF MICHIGAN
Ladabie Collection
Department of Rare Books and Special Collections
Ann Arbor, MI 48109
Phone: 313 764 9356

In addition to over 300 gay periodicals, the Ladabie Collection includes the personal papers of Louie Crew, gay academic and activist who was especially involved with the founding of Integrity, and Lon G. Nungesser, AIDS activist and author.

NEW COLLEGE OF CALIFORNIA
Humanities Library
777 Valencia
San Francisco, CA 94110
Phone: 415 626 1694

NORTHWESTERN UNIVERSITY LIBRARY
Special Collections Department
1937 Sheridan Road
Evanston, IL 60201
Phone: 708 491 3635

OAKLAND MUSEUM
History Department
1000 Oak Street
Oakland, CA 94607
Phone: 415 273 3842

SAN FRANCISCO STATE UNIVERSITY
Center for Research and Education in Sexuality
San Francisco, CA 94132
Phone: 415 469 1137

STATE HISTORICAL SOCIETY OF WISCONSIN
816 State Street
Madison, WI 53706
Phone: 608 262 3421

TEMPLE UNIVERSITY
Contemporary Culture Collection
Samuel Paley Library
Berks and 13th Streets
Philadelphia, PA 19122
Phone: 215 787 8231

UNIVERSITY OF TEXAS
Humanities Research Center
2114 Harry Ransom Center
Austin, TX 78713
Phone: 512 471 9119

TULANE UNIVERSITY
Contemporary Culture Collection
Howard-Tilton Memorial Library
7001 Freret Street
New Orleans, LA 70188
Phone: 504 787 8667

SCHOLARLY NEWSLETTERS AND JOURNALS

ASSOCIATION OF GAY AND LESBIAN PSYCHIATRISTS NEWSLETTER
c/o David Scasta
1721 Addison Street
Philadelphia, PA 19146

ASSOCIATION OF LESBIAN AND GAY PSYCHOLOGISTS NEWSLETTER
2336 Market Street, #8
San Francisco, CA 94114

CENTRE/FOLD
Toronto Centre for Lesbian and Gay Studies Newsletter
2 Bloor Street W
Suite 100-129
Toronto, ON M4W 3E2

JOURNAL OF THE HISTORY OF SEXUALITY
Bard College
Annandale-on-Hudson, NY 12504
Phone: 914 758 7542
Fax: 914 758 7544

LESBIAN AND GAY STUDIES NEWSLETTER
(Published by the Lesbian and Gay Studies Caucus for the Modern Languages)
c/o Michael Lynch
Department of English
University of Toronto
7 King's College Circle
Toronto, ON M5S 1A1

MEN'S STUDIES REVIEW
Box 32
Harriman, TN 37748

OURSTORIES
(Published by The Gay and Lesbian Historical Society of Northern California)
Box 42126
San Francisco, CA 94142

SOCIETY FOR LESBIAN AND GAY PHILOSOPHY NEWSLETTER
c/o John K. Pugh
Department of Philosophy
John Carroll University
University Heights, OH 44118

SOCIOLOGISTS' LESBIAN AND GAY CAUCUS NEWSLETTER
Box 415
Claremont, CA 91711

SODOMA: RIVISTA OMOSESSUALE DI CULTURA
Fondazione Sandro Penna
via Accademia della Scienze, 1, 10123
Torino, ITALY

SOLGA NEWSLETTER: SOCIETY OF LESBIAN AND GAY ANTHROPOLOGISTS
c/o Arnold Pilling
Department of Anthropology
Wayne State University
Detroit, MI 48202

FORUM HOMOSEXUALITAT AND LITERATUR
c/o Wolfgang Popp and Dietrich Molitor
Universität Gesamthochschule Siegan
Fachbereich 3
Postfach 10 12 40, D5900
Siegen, GERMANY

GAY AND LESBIAN STUDIES DEPARTMENT NEWSLETTER
City College of San Francisco
50 Phelan Avenue
San Francisco, CA 94112

HOMOLOGIE
Dokumentatiecentrum Homostudies
University of Amsterdam
Oudezijds Achterburgwal 185
NL 1012 DK
Amsterdam, THE NETHERLANDS

LEGACY: NEWSLETTER OF THE LESBIAN AND GAY STUDIES CENTER AT YALE
Box 2585
Yale Station
New Haven, CT 06520

NEWS FROM CLAGS: THE COMMITTEE FOR LESBIAN AND GAY STUDIES AT CUNY
c/o Center for the Study of Women and Society
City University Graduate Center
33 W. 42nd Street
New York, NY 10036

THANKS TO MICHAEL LYNCH OF THE UNIVERSITY OF TORONTO FOR SUPPLYING THESE NAMES AND ADDRESSES.

▼ Columbia University Press is publishing *Between Men—Between Women: Lesbian and Gay Studies,* a series of academic books that intends to publish scholarship on lesbian and gay culture in the Humanities and Social Sciences. The series has been established to contribute an increased understanding of lesbians and gay men; it also aims to provide through that understanding a wider comprehension of culture in general.

Between Men—Between Women: Lesbian and Gay Studies
Columbia University Press
562 W. 113th Street
New York, NY 10025

▼ *The Haworth Press* is the publisher of two gay academic journals, *The Journal of Homosexuality* and *The Journal of Gay and Lesbian Psychotherapy*. Special themed issues of the journals are often republished as anthologies, making Haworth one of the major publishers of books of gay academic interest. For a complete catalog of their titles:

Haworth Press
10 Alice Street
Binghamton, NY 13904

▼ Continuing education is important in any community. An example of one effort comes from the Gay and Lesbian Community Center of Baltimore. Their *William Wolfe Institute* offers courses at low cost to people who are interested in learning more about our history and culture. They offer approximately four courses a season with such topics as "Black Gay and Lesbian Writers," "AIDS: From Hope to Health and Wellness," and "History and Politics of the U.S. Lesbian and Gay Movement."

For more information on how they've organized themselves, write:

William Wolfe Institute
GLCCB
Box 22575
Baltimore, MD 21203

PART FOUR

CAMPUS LIFE

COLLEGES AND UNIVERSITIES GAY STUDENTS SHOULD CONSIDER

A gay student today doesn't have to contract for a closet in order to get a college education. On many campuses there are active gay organizations and supportive, open gay faculty. Before a student enrolls in a college or university, he should seriously look at the quality of gay life he might find. And not just on campus. For instance, what is the legal status of gay people in that city or state? What are the laws about sexual harassment?

Any list of "the best" colleges is always going to be subjective. But, taking into consideration legal protection for gay people, availability of gay studies courses, visibility of gay faculty, and support of the administration, the following twenty-five schools fit that definition. They represent a cross-section of working-class and elite private universities as well as state universities. One of the major criteria for inclusion in this list is the existence and vibrancy of a student organization. If a student is considering attending college as a gay person, he should correspond with the student group and find out for himself the quality of life.

College is a time to assert one's independence, when the confusion of adolescence is moving into the sharper focus of adulthood. Because there are so few resources available to gay youth under college age, this is a time when many people have their first encounters with conscious and articulated gay activism and gay culture. The result can be exciting, especially for those who knew they were gay at an earlier age and who were able to choose a setting that would support their desire to know about themselves and their community.

College instructors are increasingly aware of the importance of providing that supportive atmosphere on their campuses. That's one of the reasons many of them have chosen to come out, so they could present themselves as role-models for the students who are attending their institutions.

CAMPUS LIFE

As we understand the importance of training future leaders for the gay world, and as we acknowledge that the experience of having been gay on campus was not necessarily a pleasant one for those of us who matriculated earlier, gay alumni have a desire to influence how gay students—and gay studies—are handled at their alma maters.

The open influence of gay students, faculty, and alumni on American and Canadian campuses is producing great change.

UNITED STATES

■ CALIFORNIA ■

UNIVERSITY OF CALIFORNIA AT SAN DIEGO
Lesbian and Gay Organization
UC, SD
Q-077 B-18
La Jolla, CA 92093
Phone: 619 534 4297

STANFORD UNIVERSITY
Lesbian, Gay and Bisexual
Community Center at Stanford
Box 8265
Stanford, CA 94309
Office: 415 725 4222
Events Tape: 415 723 1488

■ CONNECTICUT ■

YALE UNIVERSITY
Gay and Lesbian Co-operative at Yale
Box 2031
Yale Station
New Haven, CT 06520

■ DISTRICT OF COLUMBIA ■

GEORGE WASHINGTON UNIVERSITY
Gay People's Alliance
George Washington University
Box 16
Marvin Center
Washington, DC 20052

■ MASSACHUSETTS ■

AMHERST COLLEGE
Amherst College Gay, Lesbian,
Bisexual Alliance
Box 809
Amherst, MA 01002
Phone: 413 542 01002

HARVARD UNIVERSITY
Harvard-Radcliffe Gay and Lesbian
Student Association
197 Memorial Hall
Harvard University
Cambridge, MA 02138

MASSACHUSETTS INSTITUTE OF TECHNOLOGY
Gays at M.I.T. (GAMIT)
50–306 Walker
Massachusetts Institute of
Technology
Cambridge, MA 02139
Phone: 617 253 5440

NORTHEASTERN UNIVERSITY
Northeastern University Alternative Lifestyles
Room 260, Ell Center
360 Huntington Avenue
Boston, MA 02115
Phone: 617 437 2738

■ MICHIGAN ■

UNIVERSITY OF MICHIGAN
Lesbian-Gay Male Programs Office
3118 Michigan Union
University of Michigan
Ann Arbor, MI 48109
Phone: 313 763 4186

■ MINNESOTA ■

MACALESTER COLLEGE
Macalester Gays, Lesbians and Bisexuals United
Macalester College
St. Paul, MN 55105

■ NEW YORK ■

CITY UNIVERSITY
CUNY Lesbian and Gay People
c/o Wolfe, Environmental Psychology Program
33 W. 42nd Street
New York, NY 10036
Phone: 212 251 6310

COLUMBIA UNIVERSITY
Columbia Gay and Lesbian Alliance
303 Earl Hall
Columbia University
New York, NY 10027
Phone: 212 854 1488

CORNELL UNIVERSITY
Cornell Lesbian, Gay and Bisexual Alliance
207 Willard Straight Hall
Ithaca, NY 14853
Phone: 607 255 6482

NEW YORK UNIVERSITY
Gay and Lesbian Union at NYU
Loeb Student Center
566 LaGuardia Place, #810
New York, NY 10012
Phone: 212 598 7056

VASSAR COLLEGE
Vassar Gay People's Alliance
Box 271
Vassar College
Poughkeepsie, NY 12601

■ OHIO ■

OBERLIN COLLEGE
Oberlin College Lesbian, Gay and Bisexual Union
Wilder Hall, Box 88
Oberlin, Ohio 44074
Phone: 216 775 8179

OHIO STATE UNIVERSITY
Gay and Lesbian Alliance of OSU
1739 High Street
Columbus, OH 43210
Phone: 614 292 9212

■ PENNSYLVANIA ■

TEMPLE UNIVERSITY
Temple University Lambda Alliance
Box 116, SAC
Temple University
Philadelphia, PA 19122

UNIVERSITY OF PENNSYLVANIA
Lesbian, Gay and Bisexual Alliance
Houston Hall, Room 243
3417 Spruce Street
Philadelphia, PA 19104
Phone: 215 898 5270

■ RHODE ISLAND ■

BROWN UNIVERSITY
Brown Lesbian/Gay Alliance
Box 1930
Student Activities Office
Providence, RI 02912

UNIVERSITY OF RHODE ISLAND
URI Gay Task Force
346 Memorial Union Building
University of Rhode Island
Kingston, RI
Phone: 401 792 2398

■ VERMONT ■

UNIVERSITY OF VERMONT
Gay, Lesbian and Bisexual Alliance
B-164, Billings
University of Vermont
Burlington, VT 05405

■ WISCONSIN ■

UNIVERSITY OF WISCONSIN
The Ten Percent Society
Box 614, Memorial Union
Madison, WI 53706
Phone: 608 262 7365

CANADA

■ ONTARIO ■

UNIVERSITY OF TORONTO
Committee on Homophobia
c/o Students' Administrative Council
12 Hart House Circle
University of Toronto
Toronto, ON M5S 1A1

■ QUEBEC ■

CONCORDIA UNIVERSITY
Lesbians and Gay Friends of Concordia
c/o Concordia University Student Association
1455 de Maisonneuve Boulevard West
Montreal, QU H3G 1M8

SAMPLE COLLEGE AND UNIVERSITY NONDISCRIMINATION STATEMENTS

OBERLIN COLLEGE: In 1977 the Board of Trustees passed an affirmative action policy. Included was a nondiscrimination statement: "Nondiscrimination means administering programs and treating all persons without regard to race, color, national origin, religion, creed, age, sex, **sexual orientation**, marital status, family relationship, physical handicaps, or veteran status except where such a distinction is required by law or proved to be a bona fide occupational qualification."

NEW YORK UNIVERSITY: "New York University is committed to a policy of equal treatment and opportunity in every aspect of its relations with its faculty, students, and staff members, without regard to sex, **sexual orientation**, marital or parental status, race, color, religion, national origin, age, or handicap."

▼ *The Standing Committee for Lesbian, Gay and Bisexual Awareness of the American College Personnel Association* helps campus professionals deal with gay issues on campus. Their newsletter, *Out on Campus,* while one of the best resources in the field, is available only to members. That membership, though, isn't restricted. The cost is $15.00 ($7.50 for students) and benefits include other publications in addition to *Out on Campus.* For information:

Joan Campbell
Campus Housing (M/C 579)
University of Illinois at Chicago
818 S. Wolcott Avenue, Room 317 SRH
Chicago, IL 60612

▼ Many large gay and lesbian organizations have internship programs that give students the opportunity to work in their offices during vacations or work/study breaks. College students often use these internships to examine the possibilities of a career in gay and lesbian activism. These two groups have especially developed young leaders programs, but they are not the only ones. Any student interested should feel free to approach other organizations as well.

Human Rights Campaign Fund
1012 14th Street, NW, Suite 607
Washington, DC 20005
Phone: 202 628 4160

and

National Gay and Lesbian Task Force
1517 U Street NW
Washington, DC 2009

George Segal's famed sculpture *Gay Pride* was originally meant to sit in Sheridan Square in New York City, across the street from the site of the Stonewall Riots. When some community activists objected, and the sculpture was threatened with being defaced, the Mariposa Foundation, which had commissioned the piece, worked to find it a new home.

It now stands on the campus of University of Wisconsin–Madison.

PHOTO BY ROBERT LUCIK. REPRINTED WITH THE PERMISSION OF THE MARIPOSA FOUNDATION.

GAY STUDIES

Gay studies are increasingly important on college campuses. Probably the most extensive gay studies program in the country is at San Francisco Community College in California, but many smaller institutions are introducing classes at the undergraduate level.

The following is a syllabus developed by Scott Lennon for Fairhaven College in Bellingham, Washington. It gives an idea of the scope of these new courses and examples of the kinds of resource material they use. It's reprinted with his permission:

CULTURAL STUDIES: AN INTRODUCTION TO GAY AND LESBIAN STUDIES

Class 1 Introduction; in-class quiz; lecture: Minority Politics in the United States.

Class 2 Discussion on sex and sexuality; definitions, continuum model, taboos. Readings: *Longest War;* "Interview with an Analyst." *Joy of Gay Sex; Joy of Lesbian Sex.*

Class 3 Homophobia and heterosexism discussed. Readings: *Male Homophobia,* "Homophobia in the Classroom."

Class 4 Language, identity and coming out discussion. Readings: *Another Mother Tongue.* "What We're Rollin' around in Bed with."

Class 5 Lecture on gay/lesbian political history. Reading: *A Reporter at Large: The Castro I.*

Class 6 Film: *The Times of Harvey Milk.*

Class 7 Discussion: Contemporary lesbian/gay culture—the ghetto institutions and its members.

Class 8 Film: *Silent Pioneers* and *Before Stonewall.*

Class 9 Lecture and discussion: AIDS and American Society. Reading: *And the Band Played On.*

Class 10 Film: *Parting Glances.*

Class 11 Discussion: Nature versus Nurture (or "How did they get that way?"). Reading: "The science of strange females."

Class 12 Guest lecturer on the church and the homosexual. Reading: *Christianity, Homosexuality and Social Tolerance.*

CLASSICS OF LESBIAN AND GAY STUDIES

Academic, critic, and publisher Jeffrey Escoffier created this list of the "classics" of gay and lesbian studies. These are the books he found to be most seminal in the development and articulation of gay and lesbian intellectual discourse.

BOSWELL, JOHN. *Christianity, Social Tolerance and Homosexuality.* Chicago: University of Chicago Press, 1980.

D'EMILIO, JOHN. *Sexual Politics, Sexual Communities: The Making of the Homosexual Minority.* Chicago: University of Chicago Press, 1983.

DOVER, K. J. *Greek Homosexuality.* Cambridge: Harvard University Press, 1980; reprinted by Vintage Books, 1978.

FADERMAN, LILLIAN. *Surpassing the Love of Men.* New York: William Morrow, 1981.

FOUCAULT, MICHEL. *A History of Sexuality,* vol. 1. New York: Pantheon, 1978.

FREEDMAN, ESTELLE, BARBARA C. GELPHI, SUSAN L. JOHNSON, AND KATHLEEN M. WESTON, EDS. *The Lesbian Issue: Essays from Signs.* Chicago: University of Chicago Press, 1985.

GRAHN, JUDY. *Another Mother Tongue: Gay Words, Gay Worlds.* Boston: Beacon Press, 1983.

KATZ, JONATHAN. *Gay American History.* New York: Thomas Y. Crowell, 1976.

LOURDE, AUDRE. *Zami: A New Spelling of My Name.* Trumansburg, New York: The Crossing Press, 1982.

MORAGA, CHERRIE. *Loving in the War Years.* Boston: South End Press, 1983.

———, AND GLORIA ANZAIDÚA, EDS. *This Bridge Called My Back.* New York: Kitchen Table Press, 1981.

NEWTON, ESTHER. *Mother Camp: Female Impersonation in America.* Englewood Cliffs, N.J.: Prentice-Hall, 1972; reprinted University of Chicago Press, 1985.

PLUMMER, KENNETH, ED. *The Making of the Modern Homosexual.* London: Hutchinson, 1981.

PONSE, BARBARA. *Identities in the Lesbian World.* Westport, Conn.: Greenwood Press, 1978.

RUSSO, VITO. *The Celluloid Closet: Homosexuality in the Movies.* New York: Harper and Row, 1981.

SNITOW, ANN, CHRISTINE STANSELL, AND SHARON THOMPSON, EDS. *Powers of Desire: The Politics of Sexuality.* New York: Monthly Review Press, 1983.

VANCE, CAROL, ED. *Pleasure and Danger.* Boston: Routledge & Kegan Paul, 1984.

WEEKS, JEFFREY. *Coming Out: Homosexual Politics in Britain from the Nineteenth Century to the Present.* London: Quartet Books, 1977.

COPYRIGHT © 1990 JEFFERY ESCOFFIER. THIS LIST ORIGINALLY APPEARED IN *OUT/LOOK* AND IS REPRINTED WITH PERMISSION OF THE AUTHOR AND *OUT/LOOK.*

TRAINING TOMORROW'S LEADERS

The New Pacific Academy for Lesbian and Gay Community Service and Activism opened in June of 1990. The primary activity of the academy is a one-month intensive instructive program called "Basic Training." The goal is to provide young lesbians and gay men between the ages of eighteen and thirty with the knowledge, practical skills, and peer support necessary for effective leadership.

All costs for participants are covered by fund-raising, except for transportation to the California campus, and there are some scholarship monies available for that expense as well. The student population is split equally between men and women and half of the places in the program are reserved for persons of color.

In addition to organizational development and community organization skills, the academy will offer students exposure to a range of interests from gay culture and film to AIDS work.

For more information, contact:

New Pacific Academy
2338 Market Street
San Francisco, CA 94114
Phone: 415 252 1690

NEWSLETTERS

Gay studies courses have been rapidly added to many college curricula. Four of the centers for such academics have newsletters through which others can follow the evolution of the discipline:

Gay and Lesbian Studies Department Newsletter
City College of San Francisco
50 Phelan Avenue
San Francisco, CA 94112

LEGACY: Newsletter of the Lesbian and Gay Studies Center at Yale
Box 2585, Yale Station
New Haven, CT 06520

News from CLAGS
The Committee for Lesbian and Gay Studies at City University of New York
Center for the Study of Women and Society
University Graduate Center
33 W. 42 Street
New York, NY 10036

Centre/Fold
Toronto Centre for Lesbian and Gay Studies
2 Bloor Street, Suite 100–129
Toronto, ON M4W 3E2

STUDENT ORGANIZATIONS

HOW DOES A STUDENT GROUP OPERATE ON CAMPUS?

Stanford University boasts one of the most complete gay and lesbian presences in North America, with a community center as its centerpiece. Here's a brief description of how its gay and lesbian presence is handled, provided by member David Cruz:

"Although the Lesbian, Gay, and Bisexual Community Center at Stanford University (LGBCC) was created in September 1986, visible gay activity on campus goes back at least as far as 1968, when the first gay student/gay rights organization at Stanford was founded. The Gay Student Union, a direct predecessor of the Gay and

Lesbian Alliance at Stanford (GLAS), was recognized as a voluntary student organization in 1971 and gay student groups have used the second floor of the Fire Truck House as an unofficial community center since 1974.

"The Mission Statement of the community center states that it is to meet the special needs of the lesbian, gay, and bisexual population at Stanford, and to reach out to the community at large to foster increased understanding. The LGBCC coordinates a number of discussion and support groups that assist people in coping with the difficulties of life as a lesbian, gay, or bisexual person in society. These weekly groups include a 'coming out' discussion group, a student men's group, another gay and bisexual men's group, a graduate student and community men's group, and two women's discussions groups. In addition, the center lends its planning capabilities to GLAS in helping organize its Wednesday and Thursday night Socials, Monday movie nights, a spirituality discussion group, community forum, and quarterly dances. The staff provide information, referrals, and counseling by phone, walk-in, and correspondence, not only to students, but also to members of the mid-peninsula community who find it difficult to obtain information elsewhere. The center maintains a large resource library that includes books, periodicals, and videotapes addressing such concerns as sexuality, health issues, coming-out processes, the role of the family in gay life, and other topics. We also receive and post flyers and newsletters from gay and lesbian student groups, religious organizations, professional organizations, and political and social groups, both local and nationwide.

"The center also maintains the Gay and Lesbian Archives Project, which chronicles the lives of lesbian, gay, and bisexual people in San Mateo and Santa Clara counties, with an emphasis on Stanford. This record is and will continue to be a source for scholarly as well as casual research into our history.

"The center, in addition to its office phone, maintains an information tape. This recorded announcement, updated frequently, supplies the caller with referral numbers, a list of special and weekly events, and information about the center and its resources.

"The center also provides support to the Lesbian, Gay and Bisexual Speakers' Bureau, a very successful and popular volunteer organization that conducts discussion groups within university residences."

LIFE ON A SMALL COLLEGE CAMPUS

Most active gay organizations are on larger campuses, and most of them in urban areas, but gay life isn't absent at small liberal arts colleges. Here's a brief description of the activities of the Macalester Gays, Lesbians and Bisexuals United sent in by Co-Coordinator Lisa Lipner:

"Our campus is a great place to be gay, as colleges go, and we're always happy to see new gay faces in our classes and dorms. Our organization is about five or six years old and is open to all bisexual, lesbian, and gay Macalester students. We also have some members who are students at other area colleges that don't have support groups. Our primary purpose is four-fold: support, education/campus outreach, social and community-oriented. Along with weekly group meetings, we sponsor a gay awareness week on campus every year, along with speakers and entertainers from the Twin Cities area. Out of a college of approximately 1,700 students, we have a mailing list of fifty members and thirty or so friends and supporters, a high percentage for a small school.

"Truthfully, we do occasionally have incidents of verbal harassment and our curriculum is not very gay-sensitive, but we're working on it! Mac is a safe, fairly supportive, and often fun place to be gay. Same-sex couples raise few eyebrows here, and the school administration is very sensitive to and supportive of our concerns."

It isn't always easy to set up such organizations in a small school. When he was a student at Colby College in Waterville, Maine, Tom Hagerty opened a gay information line with administration support and kept it open every Wednesday night of his junior year in 1988. No one ever called the highly publicized number. But his activities did lead to a campus group at Colby, one that's now as active as Macalester's.

HELP IN STARTING A GAY CAMPUS GROUP

The National Gay and Lesbian Task Force has available a *Student Organization Packet.* The packet includes all the basic information you might ever need to start up a campus group of your own. Included is advice on how to begin the group, models of other campus organizations, and a comprehensive bibliography.

The packet also has listings of gay studies courses and programs throughout the United States. There are also sample syllabi.

The NGLTF also publishes *Organizing for Equality,* a newsletter for people organizing on campus.

For information:

The National Gay and Lesbian Task Force
The Campus Project
1517 U Street NW
Washington, DC 20009
Phone: 202 332 6483

▼ People at Rutgers University have produced a video that will be helpful for any college group interested in dealing with gay issues on campus.

A Little Respect: Gay Men, Lesbians & Bisexuals on Campus is a twenty-four-minute tape that helps promote provocative discussions of homophobia, racism, and sexism. It explores the experience of being a lesbian or gay student in a culturally diverse environment.

The video is ideal for new-student orientation, faculty/staff development, student leadership programs, and general classroom use.

The cost is $20, which includes a facilitator's guide. To order, or to get more information:

Rutgers—The State University
Sexual Health Program
249 University Avenue, Room 202
Newark, NJ 07102

▼ *The NGLTF Campus Project* works with college and university groups interested in establishing campus organizations. Through a newsletter, and many publications providing advice on subjects ranging from the reporting of violence on campus to the orchestration of gay and lesbian film festivals, the Campus Project provides resources for students and faculty who are engaged in gay activism in academia.

For more information:

The NGLTF Campus Project
The National Gay and Lesbian Task Force
1517 U Street NW
Washington, DC 20009
Phone: 202 332 6483

▼ There are lots of different reasons for college organizations to form leagues. Resources can be pooled and shared, for one. There can be more lobbying power, for another. Various compacts of college and university organizations exist around the country. If you're interested in finding out how such a confederation can work, The Coalition of Lesbian/Gay Student Groups in Texas is a fine model. The various campuses in the state share a lending library for research and topic discussion, sponsor an annual conference, and are establishing a scholarship fund for lesbian/gay/bisexual studies.

For more information, write:

Coalition for Lesbian/Gay Student Groups
Box 190712
Dallas, TX 75219
Phone: 214 621 6705
Fax: 214 528 8436

I came out my first year in college. I'd previously told a few close friends in high school that I was gay, but I had my first sexual experience, beheld my first roomful of gays, and developed my sense of gays as a community my freshman year at U.C.L.A. I met my first open, out gays at the Gay Student's Union on campus. The meetings were held Tuesday evenings, and I tried never to miss one. There was something about sitting in a room with fifty, a hundred or more other gays that gave me a feeling of belonging the likes of which I'd never felt before. The organization is now called the Gay and Lesbian Association (GALA), but I'll always remember the GSU.

—*LARRY DUPLECHAN,*
author

DELTA LAMBDA PHI: A PROGRESSIVE SOCIAL FRATERNITY

With gay acceptance comes all forms of gay social organization. In addition to the politically motivated gay student groups, there is now a gay fraternity, modeled on the time-honored model of frat row, complete with songs and cheers.

Delta Lambda Phi is the brainchild of Vernon Strickland III, Esq., who clearly felt that being gay wasn't a reason to have to give up the fraternal bond on campus. The national organization has over a dozen active chapters with more being established all the time. An individual at a school without a chapter can petition to become a member by applying to the national office, which can work out an individual program.

National Headquarters
Delta Lambda Phi Fraternity
Box 57184
Washington, DC 20037
Phone: 202 857 8026

■ CALIFORNIA ■

UCLA CHAPTER
Delta Lambda Phi Fraternity
118 Men's Gym
405 Hilgard Avenue
Los Angeles, CA 90024
Phone: 213 825 6322

CALIFORNIA STATE UNIVERSITY AT SACRAMENTO CHAPTER
Delta Lambda Phi Fraternity
Box 59
6000 J Street
Sacramento, CA 95819

SAN DIEGO CHAPTER
Delta Lambda Phi Fraternity
3783 Wilson Avenue, #2
San Diego, CA 92104

SAN FRANCISCO STATE CHAPTER
Delta Lambda Phi Fraternity
584 Castro Street
Box 383
San Francisco, CA 94114

■ DISTRICT OF COLUMBIA ■

DELTA LAMBDA PHI FRATERNITY
Box 18862
Washington, DC 20036

■ FLORIDA ■

FLORIDA STATE UNIVERSITY CHAPTER
Delta Lambda Phi Fraternity
1321 Rumba Lane
Tallahassee, FL 32304

■ MINNESOTA ■

UNIVERSITY OF MINNESOTA CHAPTER
Delta Lambda Phi Fraternity
Box 9691
Minneapolis, MN 55458
Phone: 612 336 4196

■ TEXAS ■

UNIVERSITY OF HOUSTON CHAPTER
Delta Lambda Phi Fraternity
University Center
4800 Calhoun C.A. Box 219
Houston, TX 77204

The chapters on these campuses do not have addresses available at press time. They may be contacted through the national office.

Northwestern University

University of California at Davis

University of California at Berkeley

California State University at Northridge

San Jose State University, California

University of Nevada at Las Vegas

© 1987 BY VERNON STRICKLAND. REPRINTED WITH PERMISSION.

DELTA LAMBDA PHI FRATERNITY CHEER

Lambda Men one time
Lambda Men two times
Lambda Men all the damn time

Brothers embracing fellow brothers;
Strong the circle we

Lambda Men! Lambda Men!
The best fraternity!

DELTA PHI FRATERNITY SONG

Lambda men are gathering
I know the sight so well;
There's a clap of thunder,
I hear the centaurs yell!

With a bond of friendship forever strong,
Preserving justice whenever called;

LAMBDA MEN ARE MAKING THEIR PRESENCE KNOWN.

There once was mighty Lambda man
    Who lived by the sword;
Defending the kingdom's honor,
    He crushed the rogue horde.

With a whirl of steel he took the fight
And won the prince's heart that night.

LAMBDA MEN ARE MAKING THEIR PRESENCE KNOWN.

Out on the mountain range
Lambda men do roam;
Depending on instinct and luck,
He makes the land his home.
Respecting the Indian for the life he made
And teaching young braves his worldly ways.

LAMBDA MEN ARE MAKING THEIR PRESENCE KNOWN.

COPYRIGHT 1987 BY VERNON STRICKLAND. REPRINTED WITH PERMISSION.

GAY ALUMNI ORGANIZATIONS

The social goals of gay alumni associations go beyond academic organizing. Two lovers who are both alumni of the University of Illinois successfully fought to have the announcement of their relationship printed in the marriage columns of the university's *Alumni News.* They've been joined by other gay male couples to fight the cost of membership to the larger alumni organization, demanding the right to pay the same $25 fee that heterosexual couples pay, rather than two separate $20 individual memberships. While these types of battles might not seem important, they are the kinds of activities that force the establishment to be conscious of gay issues.

If you went to college, what does your school's alumni organization have to say about announcements concerning your life or the fees they charge you, as opposed to those they charge heterosexual marrieds? The best way to find out is to ask.

The University of Illinois GALA members give these suggestions, if you do want to have your relationship with your lover mentioned:

1. Have both partners sign the announcement.
2. Use a substitute word for married (such as "united").
3. Send your notice registered mail, so there's no argument about whether or not it arrived at the proper office.

BAYLOR UNIVERSITY GALA
c/o S. Taravella
P.O. Box 1862
Santa Monica, CA 90406

BOWDOIN GALA
c/o M. Rebic
1641 Third Avenue, #19J
New York, NY 10128

UNIVERSITY OF CALIFORNIA GALA
Box 3415
Oakland, CA 94609

COLUMBIA UNIVERSITY GALA
c/o Rick Shur
Box 790
New York, NY 10108

DARTMOUTH GALA, INC.
P.O. Box 7745, FDR Station
New York, NY 10150-1914

GEORGETOWN UNIVERSITY GALA-GU
P.O. Box 19326
Washington, DC 20036

GRINNELL COLLEGE GALA
c/o R. Rose
1320 Rhode Island Avenue NW
Washington, DC 20005

HARVARD UNIVERSITY
Gay and Lesbian Caucus
Box 1809
Cambridge, MA 02238

UNIVERSITY OF ILLINOIS GALA
Box 53336
Washington, DC 20009

JOHNS HOPKINS UNIVERSITY LAGA
c/o Josh Einhorn
175 Bleecker Street, #14
New York, NY 10012

LAWRENCE UNIVERSITY GALA
P.O. Box 234, Old Chelsea Station
New York, NY 10011

UNIVERSITY OF MASSACHUSETTS GALA
P.O. Box 15141
Washington, DC 20003

MIAMI UNIVERSITY OF OHIO GALA
P.O. Box 382
Oxford, OH 45056

OHIO STATE UNIVERSITY GALA
c/o Bryan Knedler
703 Devonshire Road
Takoma Park, MD 20912

UNIVERSITY OF PENNSYLVANIA PENNGALA
110 Houston Hall
3417 Spruce Street
Philadelphia, PA 19104-6306

PRINCETON UNIVERSITY FUND FOR REUNION
P.O. Box 1481
Princeton, NJ 08542

RUTGERS UNIVERSITY RUGALA
Box 160
New Brunswick, NJ 08903

STANFORD UNIVERSITY/IVY LESBIANS & GAYS OF LOS ANGELES
P.O. Box 70221
Ambassador Station
Los Angeles, CA 90070

STANFORD UNIVERSITY LESBIAN AND GAY ALUMNI
Box 460632
San Francisco, CA 94146

TRINITY COLLEGE GALA
Office of Alumni Relations
330 Summit
Hartford, CT 06106

WILLIAM & MARY GALA
Box 15141
Washington, DC 20003

YALE GALA/NEW YORK
Box 2119
New York, NY 10185

This list was compiled with the help of *NetGALA*, the association of gay alumni/ae organizations. For information on how your own college gay alumni group can become part of this national network, write:

NetGALA
Box 15141
Washington, DC 20003

One of the goals of many alumni organizations is to provide support for gay students and gay studies at the alma mater. *The Open Gate* is a foundation formed by Harvard alumni and Radcliffe alumnae. The fund gives money for special forums and research projects.

The fund is open to any individuals or groups with an affiliation with Harvard, including employees and undergraduate and graduate students.

The Carpenter Foundation is a private not-for-profit trust that provides funding to improve the quality of life for gay and lesbian students at Dartmouth University. Originally funded by a bequest from Dr. Ralph Elias, a Dartmouth alumnus, it's organized independently of the university structure and is ruled by a board composed of students, faculty, and alumni.

Contact either group through its university's alumni organization.

One researcher who was using a number of gay-themed books through inter-library loan from university libraries began to see a definite pattern in the volumes he'd receive from around the country. At least half the volumes in his random survey had been donated to the school collection by the gay student organization. He pursued his unscientific investigation and discovered that one of the most common—and most worthy—undertakings of the student groups was adding titles of gay and lesbian books to their school libraries.

Such donations to any library are effective means of adding to the community's base of knowledge. At least as important is pressuring your community or college library to add titles on their own. For advice on how to do just that, get "Censored, Ignored? Overlooked? Too Expensive? How Library Users Can Get Gay Materials into Libraries." The brochure is available for a small charge from:

GLTF Clearinghouse
American Library Association
50 E. Huron Street
Chicago, IL 60611

PART FIVE

HOW WE LEAD OUR LIVES

How we lead our lives and with whom are the questions that each of us has to answer. How do we come out—and to whom? How do we form our intimate relationships—and how do we find our partners? What do we choose to do for work—and how do we negotiate with our employers?

The evolution of the gay world has given us more options and more problems to face, but it's also given us more support systems to turn to when the predicaments present themselves.

GAY MEN IN THE WORKPLACE

PROFESSIONAL ORGANIZATIONS

There are many professional organizations specifically for gay men and lesbians. Almost all the groups produce a newsletter, work within their larger professional field for recognition of gay and lesbian issues and as advocates for better education on gay issues. The organizations listed here are in alphabetical order by their organizational name. If the group is the gay and lesbian special interest section of a larger organization, it's listed under the name of the parent association.

AMERICAN ASSOCIATION FOR COUNSELING AND DEVELOPMENT
Association for Gay, Lesbian and Bisexual Issues in Counseling
Box 216
Jenkintown, PA 19046

AMERICAN ASSOCIATION OF LAW LIBRARIANS
Gay and Lesbian Concerns Subdivision
Paul George
1361 N. Laurel Street, #18
West Hollywood, CA 90046

AMERICAN ASSOCIATION OF LAW SCHOOLS
Section on Gay and Lesbian Legal Issues
Arthur Leonard
New York Law School
57 Worth Street
New York, NY 10013

AMERICAN ASSOCIATION OF PHYSICIANS FOR HUMAN RIGHTS
Box 14366
San Francisco, CA 94144

AMERICAN ASSOCIATION OF SEX EDUCATORS, COUNSELORS AND THERAPISTS
Gay, Lesbian and Bisexual Caucus
418 Elk Street
Albany, NY 12206

AMERICAN FEDERATION OF TEACHERS
National Lesbian and Gay Teachers Caucus
3328 Edgemont Street
Philadelphia, PA 19134

AMERICAN FOLKLORE SOCIETY
Gay and Lesbian Folklore Section
Joseph Goodwin
Ball State University
Muncie, IN 43706

AMERICAN HISTORICAL ASSOCIATION
Committee on Lesbian and Gay History
John Fout
Bard College
Annandale-on-Hudson, NY 12504

AMERICAN LIBRARY ASSOCIATION
Gay and Lesbian Task Force
50 E. Huron Street
Chicago, IL 60611

AMERICAN MEDICAL ASSOCIATION
Lesbian and Gay People in Medicine
1910 Association Drive
Reston, VA 22091

AMERICAN MEDICAL STUDENT ASSOCIATION
Lesbian, Gay, and Bisexual People in Medicine Task Force
1890 Preston White Drive
Reston, VA 22091

AMERICAN MENTAL HEALTH COUNSELORS ASSOCIATION
Gay/Lesbian Task Force
c/o Moon Valley Counseling Associates
502 E. Tam-o-Shanter Drive
Phoenix, AZ 85022

AMERICAN NURSES ASSOCIATION
Gay Nurses Alliance
214 Market Street
Wilmington, DE 19801

AMERICAN ORTHOPSYCHIATRIC ASSOCIATION
Committee on Lesbian and Gay Concerns
1200 17th Street NW
Washington, DC 20036

AMERICAN PSYCHOLOGICAL ASSOCIATION
Society for the Psychological Study of Lesbian and Gay Issues
1200 17th Street NW
Washington, DC 20036

AMERICAN PUBLIC HEALTH ASSOCIATION
Gay Public Health Workers Caucus
1801 Clydesdale Place NW
Washington, DC 20009

COLLEGE ART ASSOCIATION
Gay and Lesbian Caucus
Joseph Ansell
7023 Cipriano Woods Court
Landham, MD 20706

COUNCIL ON SOCIAL WORK EDUCATION
Donald W. Beless
1744 R Street NW
Washington, DC 20009

GAY PILOTS ASSOCIATION
Box 1291
Alexandria, VA 22313

(Men in professional aviation, including commercial and corporate pilots as well as air traffic controllers, mechanics and others.)

HIGH TECH GAYS
Box 6777
San Jose, CA 95150

(Men and women working in high-technology industries.)

MODERN LANGUAGE ASSOCIATION
Gay and Lesbian Caucus
English Department
7 Kings College Circle
University of Toronto
Toronto, ON M5S 1A1

NATIONAL ASSOCIATION FOR LESBIAN AND GAY GERONTOLOGY
1853 Market Street
San Francisco, CA 94103

NATIONAL ASSOCIATION OF LESBIAN AND GAY ALCOHOLISM PROFESSIONALS
204 W. 20th Street
New York, NY 10011

NATIONAL ASSOCIATION OF SOCIAL WORKERS
National Committee on Lesbian and Gay Issues
7981 Eastern Avenue
Silver Spring, MD 20910

NATIONAL EDUCATION ASSOCIATION
Gay and Lesbian Caucus
2023 Lemyne Street
Los Angeles, CA 90026

NATIONAL LAWYERS GUILD
Gay Rights Subcommittee
c/o Lambda Legal Defense and Education Fund
666 Broadway, 12th floor
New York, NY 10012

Publishing Triangle

NATIONAL ORGANIZATION OF GAY AND LESBIAN SCIENTISTS AND TECHNICAL PROFESSIONALS
Box 14138
Chicago, IL 60614
or
Box 91803
Pasadena, CA 91109

(Gays and lesbians in science, engineering, data processing, and high-technology.)

NEW YORK ADVERTISING AND COMMUNICATIONS NETWORK
496A Hudson Street, Suite 149
New York, NY 10014

(This organization also has a special interest group for professionals in video.)

PUBLISHING TRIANGLE
248 W. 17th Street, Suite 605
New York, NY 10011

(Men and women working in publishing.)

SOCIETY FOR LESBIAN AND GAY PHILOSOPHY
John Pugh
Department of Philosophy
John Carroll University
University Heights, OH 44118

SOCIETY OF AMERICAN ARCHIVISTS
Lesbian and Gay Archives Round Table
Steven Wheeler
195 10th Avenue, 5-F
New York, NY 10011

SOCIETY OF LESBIAN AND GAY ANTHROPOLOGISTS
Arnold Pilling
Department of Anthropology
Wayne State University
Detroit, MI 48202

SOCIOLOGISTS LESBIAN AND GAY CAUCUS
Box 415
Claremont, CA 91711

SPEECH COMMUNICATION ASSOCIATION
Caucus on Gay and Lesbian Concerns
R. Jeffrey Ringer
Speech Communication Department
St. Cloud State University
St. Cloud, MN 56301

This list was compiled with the help of "Directory of Gay and Lesbian Professional Groups," a publication of the Gay and Lesbian Clearing House of the American Library Association. For a complete listing of publications write to them at 50 E. Huron Street, Chicago, IL 60611.

TEACHERS ORGANIZATIONS

UNITED STATES

AMERICAN FEDERATION OF TEACHERS
National Lesbian and Gay Teachers Caucus
3328 Edgemont Street
Philadelphia, PA 19134

■ CALIFORNIA ■

BANGLE
584 Castro Street
San Francisco, CA 94114

GALE/LA
Box 10024
Glendale, CA 91209

GALE/ORANGE COUNTY
Box 4511
Garden Grove, CA 92642

■ MARYLAND ■

GAY TEACHERS OF MARYLAND
Box 5604
Baltimore, MD 21210

■ MINNESOTA ■

TEACHER EMPOWERMENT
GLCAC
Sabathani Center
Room 204
310 E. 38th Street
Minneapolis, MN 55409

■ NEW YORK ■

GAY TEACHERS ASSOCIATION OF NEW YORK CITY
Box 150435
Van Brunt Station
Brooklyn, NY 11215

Being the only openly gay teacher on my campus gives me the chance to be a role model for gay students and to dispel a few myths for straight students.

—*ARNIE KANTROWITZ,*
college professor

THE TEN BEST PLACES TO WORK

After *Black Enterprise* published the results of a survey of the best places for blacks to work, *BLK,* the black gay magazine, used their results as a basis for their own survey. Here, based on the responses they received, is *BLK*'s list of the best places to work.

1. IBM. "Although low key about having a policy against discrimination based on sexual orientation, IBM does have one covering both hiring and advancement. IBM encourages its employees to become involved in labor organizations, loaning consultants to AIDS organizations, universities and government agencies at full salary." *BLK* also notes that IBM has a very advanced AIDS policy for its employees and does extensive AIDS education in the workplace.

2. Apple Computers. "Apple has a strong anti-discrimination policy regarding its lesbian and gay employees, and supports *Apple Lambda,* a gay employee group within the company."

3. American Telephone and Telegraph Company. AT&T's nondiscrimination clause states, in part, "An individual's sexual orientation is strictly personal, and information about this matter should not be sought by company personnel."

4. Bristol-Myers. "Bristol-Myers maintains a commitment to nondiscrimination based on sexual orientation and HIV-status, and holds its management responsible for behavior 'abusing the dignity of any individual.' "

5. Chevron. The oil company has an exceptional policy toward employees with AIDS and HIV-infection and donates hundreds of thousands of dollars a year to AIDS groups.

6. Adolph Coors Company. "After years of battle with labor, minority groups and the gay community, Coors committed itself in a major way to being an equal opportunity employer, including protection based on sexual preference in 1986. . . . Many activists in the community are still wary of Coors, based on past differences between the company on one hand and both gays and people of color on the other. One gay Latino AIDS activist in Denver quietly notes that Coors is not only that state's largest employer but the *only* one with protection for lesbian and gay employees, and a corporate leader in Denver area AIDS fund-raising.

"The quandary is, Coors *the brewery* has become socially responsible to its employees and the communities where its products are marketed, yet Coors *the family*—which still owns the brewery and funds the ultra-conservative Coors Foundation—still gives out money to anti-gay individuals and groups."

7. Equitable Company (insurance). "Equitable has a formal policy prohibiting discrimination based on sexual preference. Already one of the largest corporations investing in minority communities, Equitable donated over $25,000 to gay and lesbian organizations in 1988.

"Medical programs include specialists who will help determine what accommodations may be necessary for employees with HIV complications. AIDS education is provided for all Equitable employees."

8. Ford Motor Company. "Ford includes an anti-discrimination policy for both sexual orientation and AIDS. The company maintains a disability program and has invested heavily in an employee AIDS education program."

9. General Mills. "General Mills has been exemplary in providing corporate leadership in the Midwest" in terms of AIDS funding.

10. USWest. "USWest has encouraged the development of employee resource goals for women, Native Americans, and lesbians and gays. They have sponsored a regional conference for its lesbian and gay employees in Seattle in 1989, a first by any major corporation. USWest has a high recognition of the various ways in which race or sexual orientation may be used as cause for discrimination, and recognized awareness of homophobia as a critical element in training for employees."

Some companies that are generally well regarded did not answer the *BLK* survey. They include MacDonald's, Bank of America, Levi Strauss & Co., Merck & Co., and Avon Products.

COMMENTS ARE TAKEN FROM "10 BEST PLACES TO WORK" BY MARK HAILE, *BLK*, NO. 14 (JANUARY 1990). © BLK PUBLISHING COMPANY. REPRINTED WITH PERMISSION.

▼ Many employees are organizing within their own companies. The most extensive internal gay employee organization is inside Digital Electronics Corporation, the largest private employer in both Massachusetts and New Hampshire. The members of *DECplus* communicate extensively with one another through in-house electronic mail and make public appearances at events including Boston's Gay Pride parade, where they march as a unit.

DECplus
Box 331
Maynard, MA 01754

THE GAY EMPLOYMENT PROTECTION PROJECT

GEPP is a Washington, D.C.–based group that helps gay and lesbian employees in that metropolitan area by securing the voluntary commitment of employers to the prevention of anti-gay discrimination within their organizations. GEPP simply asks employers to amend their Equal Employment Opportunity (EEO) statements to include "sexual orientation."

When an employer does make that move, GEPP believes the benefits are real and substantial.

■ Gay and lesbian employees already hired will see their protection noted in the personnel manual and will be reassured that their sexuality may not be used against them.
■ Gay men and lesbians applying for employment will know that their applications are to be judged solely on their qualifications.
■ Non-gay employees and applicants need no longer fear that their status would be jeopardized by "accusations" or "suspicions" of homosexuality by hostile supervisors or coworkers.
■ Employees harboring anti-gay prejudice might be deterred from acting out their homophobia on the job.

■ In many firms, employees who feel they have been victimized by anti-gay prejudice are able to seek redress through the firm's internal grievance process to resolve allegations of EEO policy violations.

The GEPP effort has been handled by only a few volunteers. How much good can they do? Firms that have joined the GEPP campaign have included Control Data Corporation, C&P Telephone Company, National Public Radio, The Times Journal Company, the *Washington Post,* and the Washington Gay Light Company. This is an effort that could be easily replicated in any city. For more information:

Gay Employment Protection Project
Box 7382
Gaithersburg, MD 20898

HOMOPHOBIA IN THE WORKPLACE

How can you get your company and coworkers to understand the pressures of being gay in the workplace? Gay educator Brian McNaught has developed a day-long workshop that's been held in many major corporations around the country.

The objectives of "Homophobia in the Workplace: What Is It? Can It Be Changed" are to work with employees to:

■ Understand the corporate commitment to, and policy on non-discrimination toward, homosexual employees (where applicable);
■ Examine and articulate their feelings about homosexuality and homophobia;
■ Replace myths with accurate information about homosexuality;
■ Explore effects of homophobia on all employees;

■ Identify strategies for eliminating destructive homophobic behaviors from the workplace.

For more information on this workshop, including costs and possible applicability to your situation, contact:

Brian McNaught
5 St. Louis Avenue
Gloucester, MA 01930
Phone: 508 281 5805

Homohatred exists throughout the world—just be prepared for it but don't let it detract from your pride in who or what you are.

—*DANIEL L. OTERO,*
bookstore owner

▼ *The Alliance for Gay and Lesbian Artists in the Entertainment Industry* (AGLA) publishes a newsletter, holds meetings (actually, they "take" meetings in Hollywood talk), and sponsors an annual award event, where people in The Industry are acknowledged for their work toward gay community, gay rights, and positive gay images.

If you want to know more about our lives in Tinseltown:

AGLA
Box 69A18
Los Angeles, CA 90069
Phone: 213 273 7199

▼ The American Library Association Social Responsibilities Round Table Gay and Lesbian Task Force has compiled a *Directory of Gay and Lesbian Library Workers,* which is a complete listing of names and addresses.

For more information:

GLTF Clearinghouse
American Library Association
50 E. Huron Street
Chicago, IL 60611

▼ *Lesbian and Gay Labor Network* is involved with providing support for workers, especially by working with labor unions to which gays and lesbians belong.

While its activities are currently limited to the metropolitan New York area, the Network is interested in working with individuals and groups throughout the country. They publish a newsletter and a booklet, *Organizing for Lesbian and Gay Rights in Unions.*

Lesbian and Gay Labor Network
Box 1159, Peter Stuyvestant Station
New York, NY 10009

▼ *International Gay Travel Association* is a network of gay travel agents. They publish a newsletter, *IGTA Today,* that announces familiarity trips for members and which carries news about current travel publications and special events. The organization also arranges for cooperative advertising for members in major gay publications and does special mailings for gay resorts and guesthouses to IGTA members.

For more information, write:

International Gay Travel Association
Box 18247
Denver, CO 80218
Phone: 303 467 7117

> *I especially like being a gay entrepreneur. I don't have to put up with the pressures of the non-gay, often anti-gay, corporate world. I'm my own boss. And my personal success is directly proportional to the good that I do in creating life-affirming gay culture.*
>
> —*TOBY JOHNSON*

THE GAY MILITARY

While many gay men and lesbians serve their country in the military, the U.S. government continues to fight against them. In recent, highly publicized cases, students who joined ROTC or enrolled in the military academies have been asked to return money paid for their education when they disclosed their sexual identities. Court cases continue to challenge the federal bureaucracy while individuals continue to be hurt and devastated in the process.

Some gay activists who have progressive political agendas wonder about the wisdom of arguing for people's right to join the military. They hold out the ideal of a society that's not involved in militaristic ideals. There's one element that's often lost in these arguments: The military is not only one of the arenas in our society where people of color are most able to rise in rank, prestige, and income, it's also a place where people from the lower classes, no matter what their racial or ethnic backgrounds, find they can secure significant instruction and work experience that can translate into wider educational horizons and higher income. Barring a group of people from the military also bars them from what is traditionally one of the most impressive means of upward mobility accessible by the lower classes.

Two major organizations are fighting military prejudice:

The Gay and Lesbian Military Freedom Project, spearheaded by the National Gay and Lesbian Task Force in conjunction with The ACLU Lesbian/Gay Rights Project, the National Lawyers Guild Military Law Task Force, the National Organization for Women, and Women's Equity Action League, is working for repeal of all criminal sanctions against gay people in the armed forces. The Project works through lobbying, legal challenges, and public education. The Project also conducts educational and outreach programs to gays and lesbians in the military to inform them of their legal rights during an investigation.

Gay and Lesbian Military Freedom Project
National Gay and Lesbian Task Force
1517 U Street NW
Washington, DC 20009
Phone: 202 332 6483
Fax: 202 332 0207

▼ *Gay, Lesbian and Bisexual Veterans of America* is a coalition of many individuals and some local gay veterans organizations that are fighting for many of the same results with a slight bend toward the individual who needs counseling or other help to fight discrimination, harassment, and less-than-honorable discharge. The group is also networking with gay and lesbian student groups who are fighting ROTC recruitment on their campuses.

The Veterans have established a "Witch Hunt Strike Force" to provide legal observers on military installations where witch hunts against gay men and lesbians are taking place.

The national office:

Gay, Lesbian and Bisexual Veterans of America
1350 N. 37th Place
Milwaukee, WI 53208
Phone: 414 342 6543

These are member organizations:

NEW ENGLAND GAY, LESBIAN AND BISEXUAL VETERANS
Lesbian and Gay Service Center
338 Newbury Street
Boston, MA 02116

SAN DIEGO VETERANS ASSOCIATION
Jim Woodward
Box 89196
San Diego, CA 92138

TEXAS GAY VETERANS
Tarrant County Gay Alliance, Inc.
Box 11044
Ft. Worth, TX 76110

VETERANS C.A.R.E.
Redwood Empire Council
Box 3126
Rohnert Park, CA 94927

GAY, LESBIAN & BISEXUAL VETERANS OF AMERICA

▼ *Citizen Soldier* is another group working against prejudice in the military. It's not a gay-specific organization, but a progressive political organization that works in many areas of importance to gay soldiers, sailors, and marines. Citizen Soldier is especially concerned with the military policy on HIV-status and testing. They welcome inquiries from people who want to know more about military homophobia or who have personal problems related to those policies.

Citizen Soldier
175 Fifth Avenue, Suite 808
New York, NY 10010
Phone: 212 777 3470

Three books—two nonfiction, one a novel—highlight the stories of gay men and women in the military:

My Country, My Right to Serve: Experiences of Gay Men and Women in the Military, World War II to the Present by Mary Ann Humphrey (New York: HarperCollins, 1990) is the result of years of research and interviews.

Coming Out Under Fire: The History of Gay Men and Women in World War Two by Allan Bérubé (New York: The Free Press, 1990; Plume, 1991) is a highly readable account of the integration of gay servicemen and servicewomen into the American armed forces during that period. The record of the military's horrendous response to their courage and sacrifice is here too.

Hold Tight by Christopher Bram (New York: Donald Fine, 1988; Plume, 1989) is a novel about a sailor trapped by naval security during World War II and forced to become a spy, trading his body for secrets in a New York City bordello. The plot is based on real events and the story carries the weight of some of the real pain and confusion felt by gay men in the war.

GAY LEGIONNAIRES

The Alexander Hamilton Post 448 is the only predominantly gay and lesbian post in the American Legion. Members do not have to live in the San Francisco area to take part in the Post's activities—or to have their membership listed. In fact, other gay American Legion members are encouraged to transfer their membership to Alexander Hamilton to increase the visibility of gay numbers in the Legion.

If you're a veteran and are interested in taking part, contact:

Alexander Hamilton Post #448
The American Legion
Veterans Building
401 Van Ness Avenue, Room 128
San Francisco, CA 94102
Phone: 415 431 1413

GAY AND LESBIAN VETERANS ASSOCIATIONS

NATIONAL ORGANIZATION OF GAY & LESBIAN VETERANS
c/o P.O. Box 69961
West Hollywood, CA 90069
Phone: 213 662 4862

ALEXANDER HAMILTON AMERICAN LEGION POST #448
401 Van Ness Avenue, Room 128
San Francisco, CA 94102
Phone: 415 431 1413

GAY VETERANS ASSOCIATION, INC.
346 Broadway, Suite 814
New York, NY 10013
Phone: 212 689 0499

LAVENDER VETERANS FOR PEACE
650 Shrader
San Francisco, CA 94117
Phone: 415 386 7364

NEW ENGLAND GAY & LESBIAN VETERANS
P.O. Box 1392, Back Bay Annex
Boston, MA 02117
Phone: 617 263 8846

SAN DIEGO VETERANS ASSOCIATION
P.O. Box 89196
San Diego, CA 92138
Phone: 619 267 6664/619 299 2373

TEXAS GAY VETERANS
c/o Tarrant County Gay Alliance
P.O. Box 11044
Fort Worth, TX 76109
Phone: 817 870 8920

VETERANS C.A.R.E. NORTHERN CALIFORNIA, REDWOOD EMPIRE
P.O. Box 3126
Rohnert Park, CA 94928
Phone: 707 829 5393

VETERANS C.A.R.E. SOUTHERN CALIFORNIA
P.O. Box 69961
West Hollywood, CA 90069
Phone: 213 662 4862

THE BEST PLACE TO LIVE

San Francisco and New York have traditionally been thought of as *the* gay cities. Their large and visible gay ghettos made the presence of large numbers of gay men visible and obvious to many.

There have always been other gay neighborhoods in larger cities: Boston's Beacon Hill was long well known for its gay population, though the South End is probably better recognized as the gay neighborhood in that city today; Minneapolis's Loring Hill, Chicago's Near North Side, Houston's Westheimer area, and Denver's Capitol District all have their own place in the lexicon of gay geography. West Hollywood, most often associated as the gay neighborhood of Los Angeles (it used to be called Boys' Town), has taken all that a step further and incorporated as a separate municipality.

Provincetown, Key West, Guerneville, California (the center of the Russian River region), Saugatuck, Michigan, and other gay resort towns have also attracted year-round residents who want to live in what they think will be a gay culture.

Where's the best place for a gay man to live? All of the above would be on a short list of the assumed capitals of gay life, but the rules have changed since Stonewall. What are the essentials of a decent gay community?

It should be well organized. There should be support groups for any conceivable gay life-style. There should be legal protection from the state and/or the city. There should be a vibrant cultural life, complete with concerts, gay theater, gay television and gay radio programs. There should be a sustaining foundation for communal activities including gay sports, gay parenting, and gay studies.

Taking into account the whole range of possibilities for gay men, looking around at quality-of-life issues, including the safety of the streets, the sense of acceptance and promotion among gay men themselves, though perhaps eliminating sexual options as a major factor, the surprising answer to the question What's the Best Gay City is *Columbus, Ohio.*

The Stonewall Union of Columbus offers one of the most inclusive and active umbrella organizations for any gay community in the country. Through it, or with its cooperation, there is a cable television program, a newspaper, a political action committee, and nearly as many organizations as a city many times more its size.

Ohio State University and its energetic student and faculty organizations bring annual waves of new vigor to the city. But Columbus is not simply a university town. Many of those—Bloomington, Indiana; Santa Cruz, California; Ann Arbor, Michigan; Amherst, Massachusetts; and Boulder, Colorado, to name only a few—appear to be fine places for some gay men to live. However, the student populations in those situations lead to a certain sense of instability, with the make-up of the community changing every autumn.

Columbus is the state capital and a business center in its own right. It may not be as large or even as cosmopolitan as some of the cities that come to mind when one thinks of gay life, but it's proven itself to be a place where gay men can settle, construct their lives, and feel productive members of a larger community.

For more information on what Columbus has to offer, contact:

The Stonewall Union
Box 10814
Columbus, OH 43201
Phone: 614 299 7764

▼ *Moving?* Finding a comfortable place to live is often a difficulty for gay men. Not everyone wants to begin a relationship with a realtor by announcing his sexual identity, but that very identity often means that certain neighborhoods and cities are preferred, or to be avoided. There are many local apartment-hunting firms that advertise in the gay press. They can help you out if you're looking to rent.

If you want to purchase a house, a simple call to Gayrelo can help you locate a realtor familiar with the local gay community. Ten percent of any commissions earned by this service (no direct charge is made to you) will be given to an AIDS service organization, which you can designate. For more information, call the toll-free number between 8 A.M. and 11 P.M. any day of the week: 800 673 9093.

MAKING RELATIONSHIPS WORK

For many of us, this is what it's all about. Falling in love and finding a life partner is the foremost goal for many gay men. But, once you find someone with whom you want to establish a relationship, then what do you do? There haven't been many models for gay love affairs till recently. But now there are organizations and other support groups to offer you advice, legal counsel, and good humor as you try to set up your new relationship.

A CEREMONY OF COMMITMENT

Many people want to ritualize their relationships with a ceremony. Any such rite can be created and performed in any way that the individuals choose. They certainly can opt for either a private or a public statement. Many men who are in relationships particularly want to have a ceremony that fits their beliefs and their church traditions. *Lutherans Concerned* provides samples of such rites. The

Ceremony of the Three Cups which follows is one. The references to the LBW are to the Lutheran Book of Worship. Obviously, other denominational worship guides can be substituted. George D. Knudson wrote this particular service and provides a foreword giving its meaning and history:

BACKGROUND

The sources of inspiration for this ceremony include the Jewish wedding ritual, the Japanese tea ceremony, and, of course, the Christian Eucharist, the latter having the greatest influence. Yet the ceremony itself is not borrowed from any of these traditions, but is composed to meet the needs of gay people living in North America in the late Twentieth Century.

Although the Christian wedding ritual has had an influence on this ceremony, it is not intended to be a marriage ceremony. My philosophy is that marriage is a special relationship for heterosexual couples, a relationship focusing on reproduction, raising a family, and so on. Gay men, too, have a special relationship, a relationship that stands on its own merits, rather than trying to mimic heterosexual marriage. It is this special gay relationship that the Ceremony of the Three Cups seeks to sanction and to celebrate.

You will find some political language in the text of this ritual. This stems from my belief that "coming out" is unavoidably a political act, and making a public pledge of gay love is surely a way of coming out at some level. Gay people need to be reminded that their personal affairs, especially insofar as they are "gay" affairs, are perceived by many as having a good deal of social significance for good or ill, depending on the point of view. To ignore this is, I believe, both dangerous and irresponsible. Thus, I have written some softly worded political commitments into this ritual.

I have tried to avoid sexist language. I have also tried to avoid the use of words like *gay* or *homosexual,* since different people often think of themselves as adjectivally different. There is no *blatant* reference in the rite to sex or sexuality.

Remarks on the rubrics of the rite: Different presiders could be used for the different sections of the service. But when the rite is used in a Lutheran context the presider at the Cup of Salvation should be ordained. The various tasks in the service should be divided, so that there are several readers, acolytes, musicians, and so on.

The music should be high quality, befitting the nobility of the occasion. Common sense, combined with good liturgical sense, should be the order of the day.

The three cups used in the ceremony are the Cup of Bitterness, the Cup of Sweetness, and the Cup of Salvation. The Cup of Salvation is, of course, the Communion chalice. The other cups or chalices (please, no coffee cups) could be made or decorated appropriately for the occasion. During the service the three cups should stand in a line, in plain view, with the Cup of Salvation in the middle. After a cup is used, it is put back with the others for the remainder of the service. The Cup of Bitterness should contain some slightly bitter-tasting substance to add to the symbolism: tonic water, perhaps, or salt water, lemon juice, or very strong tea at room temperature. The Cup of Sweetness might contain sweet wine, fruit juice, a soft drink, flavored milk, or a sweet cream.

—George D. Knudson

CEREMONY OF THE THREE CUPS

1. *Processional. This should preferably be a hymn. At this point, the couple, the worship leaders, banner bearers, the crucifer, and so on, process to the front of the assembly. The presider takes a place at the front of the assembly. The rest are seated at the end of the hymn.*

2. *Prayer of Invocation.*

Let us pray.

Holy Spirit, creator of all things, and giver of every good and perfect gift: we thank you for the gifts of love and companionship that fill our hearts with gladness. We thank you for *name* and *name,* who have come before this assembly to pledge themselves to each other in love. We ask you to come and be with us, and bless us, as we witness their vows and celebrate their life together. We ask this in the name of Jesus Christ, our Savior. Amen.

3. *Readings. These should be selections from the gay and lesbian literature, poetry, theology, and so on. One or two readings should suffice, depending on the length of the service.*

4. *The Lesson. This is a reading from the Holy Scriptures. Possible selections include St. Paul's love chapter in I Corinthians 13, a reading from the story of David and Jonathan, one of Jesus' warnings that his followers would be persecuted, or a section about love from I John.*

5. *Sermon.*

6. *Special Music.*

7. *The Cup of Bitterness. The couple move to the front of the assembly and face the presider.*

Name and *name,* we rejoice in your decision to give yourselves to each other. Yet it is important for you, and all of us, to be reminded of the sober realities you will face as you lead your life together in the world.

Be aware that there are many who will oppose your relationship and seek to destroy it. Be aware that you will suffer insult and indignity on every side. Remember our frightening history of past oppression, and know that your personal struggle together against injustice will continue to be a way strewn with danger and difficulty. Remember that these are burdens you will bear together in addition to the usual sorrows and disappointments in life.

Since you have decided to support each other in every circumstance, and to help each other bear the burdens of life, I ask you now to pledge accordingly, in the making of vows, and in partaking of the Cup of Bitterness.

8. *The presider takes the Cup of Bitterness and hands it to the couple. Both grasp the cup together, facing each other, and clasping each other's hands. The presider addresses the first member of the couple.*

Repeat after me: *Name,* I promise to share with you the bitter things of life as well as the sweet, to stand by you in times of trouble, and to help you bear your burdens. Together with you, I promise to strive against prejudice and misunderstanding, and to seek justice and peace for all people. In all this, I ask God to help and guide me.

9. *The first member of the couple repeats the vows.*

10. *The presider addresses the second member of the couple in the same fashion, who then repeats the vows. When the vows are complete, each drinks in turn from the cup, both of them still grasping the cup. They then hand the cup back to the presider.*

11. *The Cup of Sweetness.*

How glad we are that, in spite of all the suffering we find in the world, the sweetness of life far outweighs the bitterness. *Name* and *name,* your very presence here is testimony that love is stronger than hatred, hope stronger than despair, and faith in God's goodness stronger than some narrow belief in divine malevolence.

Your life together will be graced with all the sweets of love: the joy of companionship, the exhilaration of intimacy, the freedom of being accepted completely.

You will also enjoy the company and support of your special community, and know the privilege of helping to blaze new trails for church and society.

Since you have decided to share the sweets of life together, I ask you now to pledge accordingly, in the making of vows and in partaking of the Cup of Sweetness.

12. *The presider takes the Cup of Sweetness and hands it to the couple. Both grasp the cup together, facing each other, and clasping each other's hands. The presider addresses the first member of the couple.*

Repeat after me: *Name,* I promise to share with you the sweet things of life as well as the bitter, to love you and enjoy you, to respect you and encourage you, to listen to you and forgive you. Together with you, I promise to strive for a life of courage, faithfulness, and dignity, and to seek understanding among all people. In all this, I ask God to help and guide us.

13. *The first member of the couple repeats the vows.*

14. *If rings are exchanged, the vows continue with these words:* Receive this ring as a token of my love and faithfulness.

15. *The presider addresses the second member of the couple in the same fashion, who then repeats the vows. When the vows are complete, each drinks in turn from the cup, both of them still grasping the cup. They then hand the cup back to the presider.*
16. *Special music may be performed at this point, while the couple moves to the back of the assembly to collect the bread and wine for the Eucharist.*
17. *The Cup of Salvation.*
18. *Communion Hymn. During the hymn, the couple brings gifts of bread and wine to the altar, where the presider is preparing for the Eucharistic celebration.*
19. *At the conclusion of the hymn, the presider begins the sacramental liturgy with the offertory prayer, "Blessed are you," in the first setting at the top of page 68 of the* LBW. *From that point the service follows the liturgy in the* LBW *until just before the distribution of the bread and wine. At that point, the presider lifts the cup, displaying it to the people, and says these words:*

This, at last, is the Cup of Salvation, the blood of our Savior, Jesus Christ. In this cup, all of our joy and sorrow, sweetness and bitterness are mingled together. From this cup, we draw strength to withstand the sorrows of life. Yet, here we taste of our highest joy.

This cup is for all who believe. Come, drink of the cup. Eat of the bread. For when we eat of this bread and drink of this cup, we are all one in Jesus Christ.
20. *The couple receives the Sacrament together with all the people, although it is appropriate for them to receive it first. They may also help in the distribution. Special music or hymns may be performed during the distribution. After all have received, the post-communion hymn is sung, according to* LBW *until the post-communion prayer, top of page 74 in the* LBW. *At this point, the following prayer is substituted:*

Let us pray. Our loving God, grant that the grace you have given to us in this sacrament may strengthen *name* and *name* in their love for each other. Send down your blessing of their life together. Comfort them when life is bitter. Make your presence known to them when life is sweet. And through all the changes and chances of life, preserve them in faith by the power of your Holy Spirit. We pray in the name of Christ our Savior. Amen.

21. *The service concludes as in the* LBW, *but the presider may choose to use another benediction. The service may finish with a recessional hymn.*

REPRINTED WITH PERMISSION FROM *CREATING WORSHIP THAT WELCOMES AND INCUDES* BY LUTHERANS CONCERNED/NORTH AMERICA, CHICAGO. COPYRIGHT 1988 LUTHERANS CONCERNED.

Permission to reprint this ceremony must be gotten from Lutherans Concerned. Copies of *Creating Worship* are available in the United States from Lutherans Concerned/North America, Box 10461, Fort Dearborn Station, Chicago, IL 60610, and in Canada from Lutherans Concerned/North America, 304 Broadway, Box 22171, Winnipeg, MB R3C 4KS. Write for cost and ordering information.

COUPLES: A SURVEY

Partners: Newsletter for Gay and Lesbian Couples presents itself as a resource and forum supporting committed same-sex relationships. They recently did a survey of couples to learn more about how we relate and how we keep our relationships going. Here are just a few of the provocative results:

WHAT DO YOU CALL HIM?

NAME MOST OFTEN USED TO IDENTIFY PARTNER:

Partner/Life Partner	27%
Lover	40
Spouse	9

Roommate/friend	5
Mate/Life Mate	6
Boyfriend	2
Husband/Wife	1
Multiple Responses	8
Other	4

WHERE DID YOU MEET HIM?

WHERE MALE COUPLES MET:

Bar	22%
Friends	19
Social Event	13
Religious Event	7
Work	7
Park/public space*	6
Classified ad	6
Baths/cruising*	5
Political event	4
School*	3
Support group*	2
Other	6

** Write-in responses. The questionnaire didn't offer these choices; they had to be offered by the respondents, indicating that these places are, in fact, very common ones at which men who meet each other go on to form relationships.*

WHO HELPS THE RELATIONSHIP KEEP ON GOING?

Men were asked to rate where they found support for their relationship. The answers were based on a scale of 1 to 7. 1 = strong support, 7 = hostility. The lower the final number, then, the more likely men found it a good place to look for help in their relationships; the higher the number, the more likely they found people unhelpful and unsupportive.

Gay friends	1.65
Lesbian/gay couples group	1.77

Other gay organizations	1.91
Gay church	1.99
Other friends	2.09
Coworkers	2.55
Boss	2.78
Siblings	2.80
Mother	2.98
Other relatives	3.34
Father	3.37
Church	4.54

WHAT ARE THE BIGGEST CHALLENGES?

Respondents were asked to name the two greatest challenges they thought they faced in their relationship. Here were the biggest problems that the men themselves saw:

Communications	49%
Career	30
Money	28
Sex	22
Relatives	18
Health	12
Coworkers	2
Neighbors	1
Other	13

HOW DO COUPLES HANDLE THE LEGAL ARRANGEMENTS?

Since gay relationships have no standing in the law, or at least very little, the partners have to work out some other arrangement. It becomes especially important when there's significant property shared by the two that might be in dispute in case of death, or in case of a break up. These are the agreements the respondents have come up with:

	Done (%)	*Planned* (%)
Will	39	40

Power of Attorney	27	29
Partnership/Living Together Arrangement	10	13
Other	3	1

BUT ARE THEY HAPPY BEING TOGETHER?

The respondents were asked to rate the quality of their relationships. 1 = highest quality; 7 = lowest quality.

Rating	*Percentage*
1	36%
2	39
3	15
4	4
5	3
6	3
7	1

The only generalization from the data that the editors could make shouldn't come as any surprise: The higher the family incomes, the higher the quality rating. They caution us not to overinterpret that information. It may be that more money means fewer problems, but it could just be that people who are more wealthy are more inclined to pronounce their relationships pleasant.

COPYRIGHT PARTNERS 1990. REPRINTED WITH PERMISSION.

These and more results appeared in the May/June 1990 issue of *Partners.* This issue can be ordered from:

Partners: Newsletter for Gay and Lesbian Couples
Box 9685
Seattle, WA 98109

Also ask for a listing of other back issues, as well as a current subscription. Most issues focused on a specific topic and can be used as a valuable resource.

▼ As relationships between gay men become more visible and are more strongly supported by the community in which they live, a new etiquette has come about. How does a couple announce the milestones of their connection? Well, any way they want to! Up to and including throwing themselves a formal reception, as these two men in Brooklyn did on their tenth anniversary.

In celebration of
ten years together
Timothy P. Martin
and
Donald W. Morlan
request the pleasure
of your company at
An Open House
Sunday, February eleventh
Nineteen hundred and ninety
three p.m. to eight p.m.
5151 Vanderbilt Avenue
Apartment 6 B
Brooklyn, New York

R. S. V. P.

How do you know this is the one? There don't seem to be many easy answers, but many men are turning to astrology to find out if they're compatible with a possible mate. If you're intrigued, *Gay Signs: An Astrological Guide for Homosexual Men* by J. E. Kneeland, foreword by Louise Hay (Los Angeles: Hay House, 1990) is a resource for you.

"ON FAMOUS GAY AND LESBIAN RELATIONSHIPS: WALT WHITMAN AND HIS 'REBEL SOLDIER FRIEND' PETER COYLE—TOGETHER 8 YEARS." DRAWING BY DEMIAN. © 1987 DEMIAN. REPRINTED WITH PERMISSION OF *PARTNERS NEWSLETTER FOR GAY AND LESBIAN COUPLES.*

This should be an inspiration for all gay employees in the retail business:

Woodward and Lothrop, a Washington, D.C.–based department store whose divisions include John Wanamaker in Philadelphia, gave in to union and gay activist pressure that was applied after a gay employee complained that his lover wasn't eligible for a store discount. The activism worked and now all branches of the retail giant honor gay lovers. Check out your local store. If these DC and Philadelphia activists can pull off this kind of equality, so should you be able to as well.

—*Reported by*
Philadelphia Gay News

These cities now recognize domestic partnerships, a legal status for gay, lesbian, and unmarried heterosexuals that parallels marriage.

Berkeley, California
Los Angeles, California
Santa Cruz, California
West Hollywood, California
Takoma Park, Maryland
Ithaca, New York
Seattle, Washington
Madison, Wisconsin

REPORTED IN *GAY COMMUNITY NEWS.*

AN AGREEMENT FOR LIVING TOGETHER

Relationships need work, and they need clarity. Relationships that involve living together and sharing money together also need contracts. The heterosexual marriage license in the United States and Canada covers many of the legal obligations between the parties. Gay couples don't have those bonds—or those restrictions. You and your partner need to reconstruct them with a written contract.

A place to begin is with *A Legal Guide for Lesbian and Gay Couples* written by attorneys Hayden Curry and Denis Clifford, edited by attorney Robin Leonard. The book is a treasure of insight and lucidity, offering examples of the many different forms of agreement that a gay couple might need. The following is only one example of a contract presented as an option by the authors. It is reprinted with permission from *A Legal Guide for Lesbian and Gay Couples,* published by NOLO Press, 950 Parker Street, Berkeley, CA 94710; telephone 415 549 1976.

Living Together Agreement:
Sharing Most Property

We, ______ and ______, agree as follows:

1. This contract sets forth our rights and obligations toward each other, which we intend to abide by in a spirit of joy, cooperation, and good faith.

2. All property earned or accumulated prior to this date belongs absolutely to the person who earned or accumulated it and cannot be transferred to the other except in writing. Attached is a list of the major items of property we own separately.

3. All income earned by either of us while we are living together and all property accumulated from that income belongs in equal shares to both of us, and should we separate, all accumulated property shall be divided equally.

4. Should either of us receive real or personal property by gift or inheritance, the property belongs absolutely to the person receiving the gift of inheritance and cannot be transferred to the other except by writing.

5. We agree that neither of us has any rights to, or financial interest in, any separate real property of the other, whether obtained before or after the date of this contract, unless that right or interest is in writing.

6. Either one of us may terminate this contract by giving the other a one-week written notice. In the event either of us is seriously considering leaving or ending the relationship, that person shall take at least a three-day vacation from the relationship. We also agree to at least one counseling session if either one of us requests it.

7. In the event we separate, all jointly owned property shall be divided equally, and neither of us shall have any claim for support or for any other money or property from the other.

8. We agree that any dispute arising out of this contract shall be arbitrated under the terms of this clause. If we both choose, we shall first try to resolve the dispute with the help of mutually agreeable mediator(s). Otherwise, either one of us may: (1) initiate arbitration by making a written demand for arbitration, defining the dispute and naming one arbitrator; (2) within five days from receipt of this notice, the other shall name the second arbitrator; (3) the two named arbitrators shall within ten days name a third arbitrator; (4) within seven days an arbitration meeting will be held. Each of us may have counsel if we choose, and may present evidence and witnesses pertinent; (5) the arbitrators shall make their decision within five days after the hearing. Their decision shall be in writing and shall be binding upon us; (6) if the person to whom the demand for arbitration is directed fails to respond within five days, the other must give an additional five days' written notice of his or her intent to proceed. If there's no response, the person initiating the arbitration may proceed with the arbitration before the arbitrator he or she has designated, and his/her award shall have the same force as if it had been settled by all three arbitrators.

9. This agreement represents our complete understanding regarding our living together and replaces any and all prior agreements, written or oral. It can be amended, but only in writing, and must be signed by both of us.

10. We agree that if the court finds any portion of this contract to be illegal or otherwise unenforceable, that the remainder of the contract is still in full force and effect.

Signed this ______ day of ______ at ______

______ ______

(Signature) (Signature)

There should be three exhibits attached to this agreement:

Exhibit A should list the personal property of the first partner.

Exhibit B should list the personal property of the second partner.

Exhibit C should list jointly owned property.

▼ These four books are among those recommended for gay couples by ***Partners,*** with their abbreviated comments on the volumes:

The Male Couple: How Relationships Develop by David McWhirter and Andrew Mattison. Englewood Cliffs, N.J.: Prentice Hall, 1984. A male couple studies 156 male couples. (McWhirter and Mattison have also developed videotapes and other programs on male couples. Check your local bookstore for availability.)

The Male Couple's Guide to Living Together: What Gay Men Should Know about Living Together and Coping in a Straight World by Eric Marcus. New York: Harper & Row, 1988. Practical, clear, complete, and supportive.

Man to Man: Gay Couples in America by Charles Silverstein. New York: William Morrow and Co, 1981. Psychologist's sexually frank report, based on 190 cross-cultural/country interviews.

Mendola Report: A New Look at Gay Couples in America by M. Mendola. New York: Crown, 1980. Looks at coupling from first encounters to widowhood, based on a national survey and interviews.

Two other books that are useful are:

Intimacy Between Men by John Driggs, M.S.W., and Stephen E. Finn, Ph.D. New York: Plume, 1991; and ***Permanent Partners*** by Betty Berzon. New York: E. P. Dutton, 1988.

A GAY WEDDING RING

A wedding usually calls for a ring. A plain gold band is always permissible, but Pride Products has an option. The joined male symbols are one of the many high-quality products of gay jewelry this gay, lesbian, feminist company provides. For their catalog:

Pride Products
3449 Orchid Trail
Calabasas, CA 91302
Phone: 818 710 9292
Fax: 818 716 6276

▼ *Male Couples Facing AIDS* is a videotape produced by the authors of *The Male Couple.* The videotape comes as a complete learning package with a discussion guide and extensive bibliographies that a discussion leader or an individual or a couple can consult for additional information.

Male Couples Facing AIDS
The Mariposa Education and Research Foundation
4545 Park Boulevard, Suite 207
San Diego, CA 92116
Phone: 619 542 0088

When it comes to marriage manuals, you can't do much better than reading *Wendel,* the creation of cartoonist Howard Cruse. Long serialized in *The Advocate,* Wendel's gone on to find a new home in books. His and Ollie's constant battles with intimacy and relationship can be utterly inspiring. The most accessible form of Wendel is: *Wendel on the Rebound* by Howard Cruse (New York: St. Martin's Press, 1989).

COPING WITH DOMESTIC VIOLENCE

Even relationships with the best intentions go wrong. Domestic violence is a reality in the gay world, just as it is in the heterosexual majority. If you or someone you know is in an abusive relationship, get help. More and more organizations are working in our community to deal with domestic violence.

Lambda Project Oasis is a model program designed to aid gay men and women who are victims of domestic abuse. Trained counselors are available to talk with you about your problems and the different ways in which you can work toward resolving them. The services are free. Call 718 447 5577, in the New York City metropolitan area for more information.

Another resource is *The New York City Gay and Lesbian Anti-Violence Project.* They publish an excellent brochure, "Behind Closed Doors: Battering and Abuse in Relationships: Information for Gay Men."

New York City Gay and Lesbian Anti-Violence Project
208 W. 13th Street
New York, NY 10011
Office: 212 807 6761
Hot line: 212 807 0197

"ON DOMESTIC VIOLENCE." DRAWING BY DEMIAN. © 1988 DEMIAN. REPRINTED WITH PERMISSION OF *PARTNERS NEWSLETTER FOR GAY AND LESBIAN COUPLES.*

THE FAMILY

The family has come to mean new things in the gay world. There is the perpetual issue of how to deal with one's biological family—to receive support from them or to deal with the pain of their rejection—and there are new questions about family that involve adoption and other ongoing relationships with children.

WHAT DO YOU DO ABOUT YOUR PARENTS?

That's one of the eternal questions of adult life, in general, but it seems to be one that particularly haunts gay men. *The Federation of Parents and Friends of Lesbians and Gays, Inc.* (P-FLAG) is one place to look for answers. The organization, one of the favorites of gay pride marches and one of the most formidable forces when dealing with homophobia in the press and church, is composed of parents and other relations and friends who have come to, not only understand, but support our life-styles.

They have many publications that can help a parent cope with a child's homosexuality and also help a young person contend with the issues of how to relate one's homosexuality and gay life-style to the rest of social life.

P-FLAG asks for a donation with every request of material. For a publication list and a referral to one of their hundreds of local chapters, contact the national office:

Federation of Parents and Friends of Lesbians and Gays, Inc.
Box 27605
Washington, DC 20038
Phone: 202 638 4200

PHOTOGRAPH © P-FLAG. REPRINTED WITH PERMISSION.

QUESTIONS YOU NEED TO CONSIDER BEFORE COMING OUT TO YOUR PARENTS

1. *Are you sure about your sexual orientation?* Don't raise the issue unless you're able to respond with confidence to the question, "Are you sure?" Confusion on your part will increase your parents' confusion and decrease their confidence in your judgment.

2. *Are you comfortable with your gay sexuality?* If you're wrestling with guilt and periods of depression, you'll be better off waiting to tell your parents. Coming out to them may require tremendous energy on your part; it will require a reserve of positive self-image.

3. *Do you have support?* In the event your parents' reaction devastates you, there should be someone or a group that you can confidently turn to for emotional support and strength. Maintaining your sense of self-worth is critical.

4. *Are you knowledgeable about homosexuality?* Your parents will probably respond based on a lifetime of information from a homophobic society. If you've done some serious reading on the subject, you'll be able to assist them by sharing reliable information and research.

5. *What's the emotional climate at home?* If you have the choice of when to tell, consider the timing. Choose a time when they're not dealing with such matters as the death of a close friend, pending surgery, or the loss of a job.

6. *Can you be patient?* Your parents will require time to deal with this information if they haven't considered it prior to your sharing. The process may last from six months to two years.

7. *What's your motive for coming out now?* Hopefully, it is because you love them and are uncomfortable with the distance you feel. Never come out in anger or during an argument, using your sexuality as a weapon.

8. *Do you have available resources?* Homosexuality is a subject most non-gay people know little about. Have available at least one of the following: a book addressed to parents, a contact for the local or national Parents and Friends of Lesbians and Gays, the name of a non-gay counselor who can deal fairly with the issue.

9. *Are you financially dependent on your parents?* If you suspect they are capable of withdrawing college finances or forcing you out of the house, you may choose to wait until they do not have this weapon to hold over you.

10. *What is your general relationship with your parents?* If you've gotten along well and have always known their love—and shared your love for them in return—chances are they'll be able to deal with the issue in a positive way.

11. *What is their moral societal view?* If they tend to see social issues in clear terms of good/bad or holy/sinful, you may anticipate that they will have serious problems dealing with your sexuality. If, however, they've evidenced a degree of flexibility when dealing with other changing societal matters, you may be able to anticipate a willingness to work this through with you.

12. *Is this your decision?* Not everyone should come out to their parents. Don't be pressured into it if you're not sure you'll be better off by doing so—no matter what their response.

FROM "READ THIS BEFORE COMING OUT TO YOUR PARENTS" © 1984 T. H. SAUREMAN. REPRINTED WITH PERMISSION OF PARENTS AND FRIENDS OF LESBIANS AND GAYS, INC.

▼ *Parents and Friends of Integrity* is an organization for the relatives and friends of gay men and lesbians. The organization is specifically directed to members of the Episcopal Church, but its resources and experiences would be applicable to any religious person who wants to be supportive of the goals and aspirations of his or her gay family members or others.

Parents and Friends of Integrity
Box 19561
Washington, DC 20036

DEFINING OUR OWN FAMILIES

Gay men and lesbians have been redefining the concept of family for years. The delineation of "family" as television explains it to us—mother, father, 2.5 children—doesn't fit our social reality or our most intimate and personal needs. Forms of ceremonies of commitment help with part of the problem by making public our vows to our emotional partners, but there are even larger definitions of family that we've come to know need to be recognized.

The Human Rights Campaign Fund has come up with a innovative option. They have established ***The Lesbian and Gay National Family Registry.*** The Registry is a centralized record of lesbian and gay families in the United States. It broadly interprets family as a person's primary affectional and support system of close relationships. It may include any number of adults and children.

When you register, your family will receive a certificate as a symbol of your commitment. Just as important, your registration will become part of the organization's database, a way to quantify for lawmakers and policy developers just how important our native family systems are to us. You can be part of this program and still remain anonymous; your information will be stored in the database in a confidential record system for statistical purposes only.

If you're willing and able to be more public, the Registry is also putting together a photo album of gay and lesbian families that will be used to educate legislators and the public.

The cost is a donation to cover the expense of the Registry. There's no fixed sum, participants are asked to contribute what they can afford, as little as $5 or more, as their means allow.

For more information, contact:

Human Rights Campaign Fund
Lesbian and Gay National Family Registry
1012 14th Street NW, Suite 607
Washington, DC 20005
Phone: 202 628 4160

Human Rights
CAMPAIGN FUND

Family Registry Certificate

We hereby certify that on ________________ 19___, the Board of Directors of the Human Rights Campaign Fund recognized that the persons listed below registered as a family with the National Family Registry.

The Registry will identify this family by the family name of ________________
and record that the family residence is ________________.

SIGNATURES OF FAMILY MEMBERS

________________ ________________
Laura Altschul, *Co-chair of Board*

________________ ________________
Charles Q. Forester, *Co-chair of Board*

____
WITNESSED BY

________________ (1) ________________

________________ (2) ________________

▼ Adoption is a loaded issue for many people for many reasons. *Chain of Life* is a newsletter for gay, lesbian, and feminist adoptees that supports full access to information about people's birth heritage. Past issues explore many provocative topics, including the ethics of semen donation and articles such as "Some Random Thoughts on Being Gay, Being Male, and Being Adopted." For more information, send a self-addressed, stamped envelope to:

Chain of Life
Box 8081
Berkeley, CA 94707

▼ As more gay men and lesbians have children in their lives, a need for a special literature has been developed. *Alyson Wonderland* is the name of a new line of kids' books designed for boys and girls who live in a gay family.

Alyson Wonderland Books
40 Plympton Street
Boston, MA 02118

GAY FATHERS AND MOTHERS

Gay & Lesbian Parents Coalition International's statement of purpose:

"We are a group of parents who are gay or lesbian. Our experiences are varied but we are united in our determination to integrate these two aspects of our lives. In the past, our roles have been viewed incompatible, both by society at large and, all too often, by ourselves as well. We believe that we can love and nurture children and provide them with a safe environment in which they can mature into loving, productive men and women.

"We have formed this organization to help ourselves and others in similar situations to grow and continue to develop in ways which draw upon the rich experiences in both aspects of our lives. We do this by forming supportive groups that help in building positive self-images, by networking with other gay and lesbian parents and by educating professionals and the general public to our special strengths and special concerns."

In addition to a newsletter, GLPCI sponsors an annual convention. It provides support for local groups through packets of information on how to establish and maintain a variety of services.

It has organized a speakers bureau for interested organizations and the media as one part of its outreach to the general public, legislators, and the gay and lesbian community.

For information:

Gay & Lesbian Parents Coalition International
Box 50360
Washington, DC 20004

▼ *Gay Fathers Winnipeg* and *Gay Fathers Toronto* are two Canadian organizations that provide support and information for gay fathers in that country. If there's an organization like theirs near you, they'll be able to direct you to it:

Gay Fathers Winnipeg
Box 2221
Winnipeg, MB R3C 3R5

Gay Fathers Toronto
Box 187, Station F
Toronto, ON M4Y 2L5

If you have children through a heterosexual marriage, want to adopt a child, want to father a child, or become a foster parent, or in any other way desire to become permanently involved in the life of a child, the legal obstacles you face and protections you need are immense and complex.

One of the best resources you can find is *A Legal Guide for Lesbian and Gay Couples* by Hayden Curry and Denis Clifford, edited by Robin Leonard (Berkeley: NOLO Press Self-Help Law, 1988), which investigates all these situations and more.

CLOSETS ARE FOR KID'S TOYS

Closets are for kid's toys — not for the lifestyles of Gay and Lesbian parents. Come out and be proud, you are not alone!

The Gay and Lesbian Parents Coalition International, is a world-wide advocacy and support group for lesbian mothers and gay fathers. We have over 50 chapters in large and small communities and a network of area contacts to help you be the parent you want to be — more open, loving and understanding. For more information, contact:

Gay and Lesbian Parents Coalition International
Post Office Box 50360
Washington D.C. 20004
(703) 548-3238

Only the most willful blindness could obscure the fact that sexual intimacy is a sensitive, key relationship of human existence, central to family life, community welfare, and the development of human personality. . . . The fact that individuals define themselves in a significant way through their intimate sexual relationships with others suggests, in a nation as diverse as ours, that there may be many "right" ways of conducting those relationships, and that much of the richness of a relationship will come from the freedom an individual has to choose *the form and nature of these intensely personal bonds.*

—FROM JUSTICE HARRY A. BLACKMUN'S MINORITY DISSENT IN *HARTWICK* V. *BOWERS.*

COMING OUT

How public to be about our identity? Who should we tell and how should we tell them? It's one of the continuing considerations in gay life.

The basic imperative of being a gay man today is to be out as far as you can. To move a little step further each moment you have an opportunity. It seems hard, especially when you're just beginning to accept your gay identity yourself, but it's the way you have to go to achieve a full life for yourself and to make the best relationships possible.

COMING OUT IDEAS

- Take a lover/partner home for the holidays.
- Come out to your family—parents, brothers and/or sisters.
- Circulate a petition in your office in support of a gay rights initiative.
- Put your lover's photo on your desk at work.
- Consider leaving the *Joy of Lesbian Sex* in your bookcase when mom visits.
- Move your favorite "fantasy" man's poster to a prominent place in your house.
- Stop lying to your fraternity brother about all the women you've had.
- Go to your local jeweler with your lover to shop for matching rings.
- Register your china pattern when you and your partner make a commitment.
- Send flowers to someone special and don't use initials on the card.
- Acknowledge that those roses are not from your mother.
- Wear an openly gay symbol or button for an entire week.

■ Call a radio talk show and introduce a gay/lesbian topic.
■ Tell a friend you are going climbing with a gay hiking club.
■ Read a gay paper on the bus or in a restaurant.
■ Write a letter to the editor of your local newspaper commenting on gay coverage or lack of coverage.
■ Contact your local university and offer to answer questions for the Human Sexuality class.
■ Call him a him and her a her when talking about your love life.
■ Write a check to a gay organization using the full name of the organization.
■ Write a letter to your senator or congressperson in support of lesbian/gay rights.
■ Take a straight friend to a lesbian/gay event.
■ Invite your straight and gay friends to the same party.
■ Hold hands publicly.
■ Have both of your names on your magazine subscriptions.
■ Check into a hotel under Mr. and Mr. or Ms. and Ms.
■ Speak the truth when asked, "So are you engaged yet?"
■ Tell three people that you are gay.
■ Visit a basically straight bookstore that sells lesbian/gay titles and openly browse.
■ Include your gay family in traditional family or religious functions.
■ Come out to your landlord, neighbors, and coworkers.
■ Be affectionate with your lover or partner upon arrival or departure at the airport.
■ Put a "National Coming Out Day" bumper sticker on your car.
■ Confront your coworkers about a bigoted joke or comment.
■ Recognize that moms and dads aren't all straight—become a foster parent.
■ Volunteer to be a Big Sister or Big Brother.
■ Organize a march or demonstration for lesbian/gay rights.
■ Boycott a company or organization that discriminates.

FROM *THE FRONT PAGE*, REPRINTED WITH PERMISSION.

WHAT DOES IT MEAN TO BE "OUT"?

The emotional significance of the coming out experience to lesbians and gay men is suggested by the extraordinary response to a query published in *Out/Look,* issue #8. The results of the poll follow:

Realizing and Acting on Homosexual Feelings
Most people seemed to become aware of their homosexual feelings quite early. The median age at which respondents realized that their "feelings toward other people of the same gender were sexual in nature" was age 12 for men and 14 for women. By age 17 for men and 19 for women, half of our respondents had acted on their sexual feelings. By age 20 for men and 24–25 for women, at least 90 percent of them had realized that their feelings were homosexual.

Different Meanings of "Out"
Being "out" means a variety of things. . . . Its most important meanings were these:

I use certain opportunities with some people to bring up the subject of homosexuality	55%
I conceal nothing about myself when the subject of homosexuality comes up	32
I bring up the subject at every opportunity	4
Other	7

The importance of being "out" also varied widely:

Very important	67%
Somewhat important	25
Neither important nor unimportant	6
Somewhat unimportant	>1
Very unimportant	>1

Who Are Our Readers "Out" To:
Family: Seventy-four percent of the respondents are "out" to all of their siblings, 76 percent to their mother, and 59 percent to their father. Forty-seven percent are out to most of their relatives, while only 2 percent are out to all their relatives.

Friends and Acquaintances: 72 percent are out to all their friends, 38 percent are out to all of their coworkers, and 24 percent are out to all their neighbors.

Sexual identity is the aspect of our readers' identity that they are *most likely* to tell family friends and acquaintances about:

Sexual orientation	48%
Favorite hobby	20
Political party identification	19
Religious preference	8

When it comes to those aspects of our readers' identity that others are *least likely* to know, gayness takes a definite backseat to other things:

Religious preference	45%
Favorite hobby	25
Political party identification	17
Sexual orientation	11

Straightening Up/Straightening Out:
How many of our readers "straighten up" their homes when relatives, friends, and acquaintances come to visit?

	Always	*Usually*	*Rarely*	*Never*
Parents visit	16%	24%	10%	42%
Other relatives visit	20	22	15	36
Coworkers visit	10	26	15	45
Neighbors visit	5	21	22	48

COMPILED BY KENNETH SHERRILL, HUNTER COLLEGE AND THE GRADUATE SCHOOL OF THE CITY UNIVERSITY OF NEW YORK. COPYRIGHT 1990 OUT/LOOK. REPRINTED FROM *OUT/LOOK*, ISSUE #10, WITH PERMISSION.

NATIONAL COMING OUT DAY

October 11 has fast become one of the major days of celebration for gay men and lesbians in the United States and Canada.

The holiday was designated by a group of community leaders in 1988. It was chosen to commemorate the 1987 March on Washington, one of the great political and communal successes of the gay movement. The goal is to increase the visibility of gay people.

Here are the reasons the organization believes we need a National Coming Out Day:

- If the AIDS epidemic has taught us anything, it has made it clear that we will achieve equality under the law only if we are out and visible. We will be treated with respect and dignity only if we expect and demand it. This cannot be done from the closet.
- We have been fighting one legislative battle after another, many regarding AIDS funding or oppressive AIDS measures, both nationally and in many states and provinces. These have cost us enormous amounts of time, money, and energy. We are virtually always on the defensive, and responding to someone else's agenda.
- Research has indicated that the vast majority of people who report that they know someone who is gay overwhelmingly support our rights. Conversely, the vast majority of people who don't think that they know anyone who is gay oppose us on every one of the issues important to our rights and to our survival.
- Our ability to "pass" and to hide has perhaps been our greatest liability. Most people don't think that they know anyone who's gay, and that's what we get for hiding.
- It is clear that gay-related issues will not be taken seriously, or given adequate consideration, until it is known who we are. Gay men and lesbians are not some distant stereotypical group of people. We are not out of the mainstream, but we are part of the mainstream. It is up to us to let the world know that.
- People come up with a wide variety of reasons to justify not discussing homosexuality. These reasons are perpetuated by lesbians

and gays as well as by heterosexuals. It is essential that we engage actively and constructively in this discussion and raise our national consciousness about this issue.

For information on how you can take part in National Coming Out Day:

National Coming Out Day
Box 15524
Santa Fe, NM 15524
Phone: 505 982 2558

There are other days of the year that should be on every gay man's calendar.

■ *June 29* is the anniversary of the Stonewall Riots in 1969.
■ *The last Sunday in February, National Day of Remembrance,* is a time set aside to honor black gay and lesbian people who have passed on. Sponsored by the National Coalition for Black Lesbians and Gays, groups and individuals are asked to send information on how they've recalled and celebrated the lives of people who were a vibrant part of our lives before they passed on. Write to NCBLG, Box 19248, Washington, DC 20036.
■ *July 7* is set aside as the day to remember Charlie Howard, a young man who was killed in an unprovoked homophobic attack in 1984. Howard has come to be the symbol of the victims of gay-bashing. A memorial is held every year in Bangor, Maine.
■ *June 30* is the day when gay and lesbian activists remember that, in 1986, the United States Supreme Court upheld sodomy laws. In *Hartwick* v. *Bowers,* the Court declared that sexual acts between adults in private were not constitutionally protected, and it upheld the conviction of an Atlanta man who was arrested for having oral sex in his own bedroom.

GAY YOUTH

If you believe seriously that there is a gay world, and that it is a good addition to our society, and if you have seriously benefited from the organizations and institutions of that world, you must, at some point, turn around and ask what you can do for those who will follow you.

Youth was the most painful part of most of our lives. It's the time when the isolation and doubt about our lives were the most grinding and hardest to accept.

Organizations that exist to support gay youth have to be recognized as among the most important in our community. They take many forms. You can check with your local gay community center, gay hot line, or political group to see if one exists in your town or city.

Here are some examples. You can contact any of them for more information about their experiences and for advice on how you might structure a youth group in your own area:

BAGLY (Boston Alliance of Gay and Lesbian Youth)
Box 814
Boston, MA 02103
Phone: 617 523 7363

BAGLY is one of the oldest gay and lesbian youth groups in the country, and one of the most activist. It's formed on principles of youth liberation, with power and organization firmly in the hands of the youths themselves.

Sexual Minority Youth Assistance League
1228 17th Street NW
Washington, DC 20036
Phone: 202 296 0221

SMYAL, like most other youth organizations, provides social meetings, referrals, and training sessions for people interested in working on its hot line and publications.

SMYAL also is involved in research concerning issues of sexual minority youth and in training parents and adult professionals on how to deal with those youths' special issues.

Lesbian/Gay Youth Program
ECOH Community Center
826 Euclid Avenue
Syracuse, NY 13210
Phone: 315 422 9741

This is a program of the local Metropolitan Community Church. Staffed by adults, it provides support groups, counseling, and community education.

Lesbian/Gay Youth Program

"The cost of feeling alone is too high"

Temenos
The Gay and Lesbian Community Services Center
1213 N. Highland Avenue
Los Angeles, CA 90038
Phone: 213 464 7400
For the hearing impaired: 213 464 0029
Youth Talkline: 213 462 8130

Temenos mixes principles of youth empowerment with an active social work outreach program run by adults. Financed in part by a grant from the State of California Health and Welfare Agency, Department of Alcohol and Drug Programs, it is a program of the Youth Services Department of the LA Gay and Lesbian Community Services Center.

The name Temenos comes from the Greek for "safe space." In this case, safe space isn't just adults providing for youngsters, but the larger agency providing a safe space within which youths are able to work with one another.

▼ The National Gay Alliance for Young Adults can offer you help if there's no youth organization in your home area. Its Organizing Assistance Programming is set up to help grass-roots youth organizations with advice, a "Facilitator's Handbook," and a "Facilitator's Guide." There may even be limited financial support to help you get started.

For more information:

National Gay Alliance for Young Adults
Box 1904226
Dallas, TX 75219
Phone: 214 701 3455

▼ *The National Gay Youth Network,* which has members in both the United States and Canada, has existed for more than ten years. They assist local activists, both in the regular population and on college campuses.

The Network produces *We Are Here,* a resource guide for gay men and lesbians, containing over 600 resources for youth. The guide costs $3 and is available from:

National Gay Youth Network
Box 846
San Francisco, CA 94101

> *For you who are just coming out; you are neither the first nor last to journey along this uncommon and wondrous way. Still, you are extraordinary. Welcome.*
>
> —*JAMES CARROLL PICKETT, playwright*

SUPPORTING GAY YOUTH

Gay youth groups are seldom funded. They're one place where a very little money can go a long way. One of the better things I've done in my own life was to give the local group a few dollars and to make myself available for advice, only when they sought it, and on their terms, not mine. Helping out gay youth is one of the most important activities we have and older members of the community should seek them out and lend a helping hand. They are our future, and they shouldn't have to face all the problems we did.

Adults in Minnesota have come up with a unique way to reward gay and lesbian youth. The Minnesota Gay/Lesbian Task Force, the local chapter of Parents and Friends of Lesbians and Gays and the members of Teacher Empowerment, an organization of gay and lesbian educators, have combined to establish awards given annually to three youths.

According to Lyle Rossman, one of the people involved in the program, there are several desired results:

First, $500 stipends are a financial boost to worthy young students. Second, the awards are viewed as a positive supportive statement to express belief in our community. When we invest in our youth, we're saying we belong to a community that deserves a future. Third, local school administrators are involved, which helps to further legitimize the efforts of those acknowledging and supporting gay and lesbian youth in the school systems.

The criterion for the award relates to youth who have demonstrated comfort with their sexual identity. They must be graduating from high school or must have received their GED or be in their first or second year of post-secondary school. They need to have displayed pride and they must have shown that they are going to make valued contributions to the community.

Because so many talented gay and lesbian students have suffered severe academic and social stresses with the awareness of their sexual orientation and the tension of coming out, the adult organizers have chosen to focus on an award rather than a scholarship, recognizing that there are many talented youths whose grades have plummeted and who may have dropped out of school. The organizers want to express their belief in these young adults when they have been working for the good of the community in spite of academic difficulties, not just those who are achieving in a usually recognized fashion.

Gay/Lesbian Youth Award
c/o Rossman
15 First Street, A420
Minneapolis, MN 55401

▼ Sex between youths and adults is one of the most difficult issues in the gay movement. When does a youngster have the right and the power to make his own sexual decisions? How are laws against intergenerational sex used specifically to target gay men? What are the issues that make the romantic image of the Greek teacher and his student in times of antiquity turn into something ugly and forbidden in the modern age?

If you want to explore these issues, North American Man Boy Love Association is the organization that will supply you with brochures, thought-provoking books, and booklets.

NAMBLA
537 Jones Street, #8418
San Francisco, CA 94102

PROJECT 10

Resolution adopted on July 7, 1988, at the National Education Association Convention:

"The National Education Association believes that all persons, regardless of sexual orientation, should be afforded equal opportunity within the public education system. The Association further believes that every school district should provide counseling for students who are struggling with their sexual/gender orientation."

Most school systems—public and private—ignore the existence of gay youth among their populations. Because they are less visible than those minorities based on skin color, national heritage, or religion, they remain the most underserved minority within the educational system. Their status as a stigmatized group places them at considerable risk.

Project 10 is an exception. An on-campus counseling program organized in 1984 at Fairfax High School, it's become a model program within the Los Angeles and other school districts. The focus is on education, reduction of verbal and physical abuse, suicide prevention, and accurate AIDS information.

Project 10 is committed to keeping students in school, off drugs, and sexually responsible. Services include workshops and training sessions for administrators and staff personnel, informal drop-in counseling for students, outreach to parents and significant others, peer counseling, substance abuse and suicide prevention programs, and coordination of health education programs.

Friends of Project 10 is a nonprofit educational organization established in 1986 to assist schools and school districts in setting up counseling programs modeled after Project 10 in Los Angeles. Included in the mission of this organization is the distribution of nonjudgmental materials which provide accurate information about human sexuality and which stress personal responsibility and risk-reduction behavior. Friends of Project 10 works with parents, community members, teachers, school administrators, elected officials, and other professionals.

For more information on how this fine public education model might apply to your locality, write:

Virginia Uribe
7850 Melrose Avenue
Los Angeles, CA 90046

or

Friends of Project 10, Inc.
11684 Ventura Boulevard, Suite 348
Studio City, CA 91604

> *Some day, maybe, there will exist a well informed, well considered and yet fervent public conviction that the most deadly of all possible sins is the mutilation of a child's spirit.*
>
> —*ERIC ERIKSON*

GAY YOUTH PEN-FRIENDS

The National Gay Alliance for Young Adults has a special service where isolated gay youths can correspond with one another. The service is free to members of the organization or its chapters, an easy condition to meet.

A pamphlet on the project explains how to make it work for you, including securing postal delivery if it's a problem in your own home. Answering a simple questionnaire and writing an introduction of yourself are the only other requirements.

For more information:

The National Gay Alliance for Young Adults
Box 190426
Dallas, TX 75219
Phone: 214 701 3455

THE HETRICK-MARTIN INSTITUTE

One of the best known and most advanced programs for gay and lesbian youths is *Harvey Milk High School.* Sponsored by *The Hetrick-Martin Institute, Inc.* (HMI), Harvey Milk is a special high school that's part of the New York City School system.

With supplemental funds from the gay and lesbian community, the purpose of Hetrick-Martin is not just to provide adequate schooling for those gay and lesbian youths who can't survive in regular schools, where many are subjected to brutal harassment and prejudice, but to make Harvey Milk one of the finer public education institutions.

In addition, HMI runs Project First Step, an outreach program that provides counseling and crisis intervention to over 2,600 homeless teens on the streets of New York. They also coordinate a counseling and referral program that matches young clients with professional help. A drop-in center serves as an after-school program for adolescents, not all of whom attend the Milk school.

HMI also runs a major AIDS awareness program for adolescents in New York City.

For more information on HMI programs and how they might be a model for activities in your city, contact:

Hetrick-Martin Institute
401 West Street
New York, NY 10014
Phone: 212 633 8920

My novel, Blackbird, *concerns a 17-year-old black high school boy, coming to terms with his gayness. It's based on my own experiences. I remember when I was a 17-year-old black high school boy, coming to terms with my own gayness, and the horrible feeling that I was utterly alone, that no one else was going through what I was going through. A decade later,* Blackbird *was published, and I began receiving letters from people—blacks and whites, in the United States and England and Africa; men my own age, college students only a couple of years older than my protagonist, men a generation older than myself—all of whom had written to tell me how much they'd enjoyed my book, and how much they'd identified with it. I had made them laugh and cry and remember their own experiences, when they'd felt as if no one else was going through what they were going through. I realize it's not as if I've cured AIDS or something; still, it's a real good feeling.*

—*LARRY DUPLECHAN,*
author

▼ "I think I might be gay. . . . Now what do I do?"

That's the title of a brochure for young men written by Kevin Cranston and Cooper Thompson with help from members of BAGLY, Boston Area Gay and Lesbian Youth. The pamphlet is an excellent, clearly written introduction to the issues facing any young gay man, with quotes and real questions from others who have faced the same problems.

The brochure is available from the Campaign to End Homophobia. Organizations and individuals interested in distributing copies of the brochure can secure a sample and written permission by writing:

Campaign to End Homophobia
Box 819
Cambridge, MA 02139

It is within your reach to be among the first generations of whole, healthy, undamaged gay men in this society. Embrace that freedom and carry it forward. You can dazzle the world!

—*NEIL WOODWARD,*
bookstore owner

SOME FACTS ON SUICIDE AND GAY YOUTH

The U.S. Department of Health and Human Services' Report of the Secretary's Task Force on Youth Suicide indicates that gay and lesbian youth are in need of special consideration and programs to reduce their risk of suicide. "The root of the problem of gay youth suicide," the Task Force states, "is a society which discriminates against and stigmatizes homosexuals while failing to recognize that a substantial number of its youth has a gay or lesbian orientation."

Among the Task Force's findings are:

- Lesbian and gay teenagers are two to three times more likely to attempt suicide than are their heterosexual counterparts.
- Lesbian and gay teenagers may comprise up to 30 percent of completed youth suicides annually.
- Lesbian and gay youth face problems in accepting themselves due to the lack of accurate information about homosexuality during adolescence.
- Lesbian and gay youth face extreme physical and verbal abuse, rejection and isolation from family and peers.
- Lesbian and gay youth are more vulnerable than other young people to psychosocial problems including substance abuse, chronic depression, school failure, early relationship conflict, being forced to leave their families, and having to survive on their own prematurely.

COPYRIGHT 1990 THE HUMAN RIGHTS CAMPAIGN FUND. REPRINTED WITH PERMISSION.

READING AND GAY YOUTH

"I thought I was the only one in the world . . ."

That sentiment, in one form or another, continues to be one of the themes of gay life in North America. Especially if we come out as youth, the facts of gay life are so often hidden from view that, even in this modern age of gay liberation, too many people think they're all alone.

Youth organizations and others work to overcome that isolation and loneliness. For many people, books are the first connection they can make with others, particularly people their own age.

Dr. Steven Berg is an educator who has written this introduction to the importance of reading for gay youth and has compiled a bibliography as well:

"Reading can be an important activity for gay teenagers if the books and articles they read treat real-life situations in a realistic fashion. As long as reading materials are chosen with care and gay youth are able to discuss the readings with their peers or a caring adult, books can be an effective tool to help them deal with the coming out process.

"A youth who reads gay-positive literature has the opportunity to go through a four-stage process. First he . . . is able to identify with the characters . . . or situations described. . . . As a result he is able to acknowledge feelings which he has about the issues in his life. After [he] begins to recognize himself in the literature, he begins the second stage—examination. In this stage, [he] focuses on his reaction to the text, reactions which lay the groundwork for the third stage where he compares his experience with the experience of others. . . . The literature also offers him positive role models by which he can pattern his life and it gives him alternatives which he can incorporate into his daily affairs. . . . In [the final] stage, the young man evaluates his life and then integrates his new insight and understanding into his daily affairs.

"Because [ours] is a homophobic society, youth encounter much misinformation about homosexuality. As a result, it is extremely important to educate gay youth about sexual orientation by introducing them to the fact that sexuality is a continuum and not a dichotomy (homosexual/heterosexual) or trichotomy (homosexual/bisexual/heterosexual). Such education will help them better accept their sexual identity and permit them to make decisions with which they can be comfortable. . . ."

Dana Finnegan and Emily McNally's *Dual Identities* (Center City, Minn.: Hazelden, 1988) has been effectively used to educate youth on sexual orientation issues. Although the book is directed at therapists who work with gay and lesbian clients, the first section includes one of the most easily understandable descriptions of sexuality that exists.

Reading *Dual Identities* can help young people understand that many of the ideas they had about sexuality were invalid—especially the "fact" that one same-sex fantasy makes them homosexual.

In addition to knowing the facts of sexuality, gay teenagers need to know they are not alone. *One Teenager in Ten: Writings by Gay and Lesbian Youth,* edited by Ann Heron (Boston: Alyson, 1983), is a collection of first-person stories by gay and lesbian youth. In addition to *One Teenager in Ten, Young, Gay and Proud* (Boston: Alyson, 1985) can also be used to help teenagers confront issues which they face in their lives.

Another factual book is Aaron Fricke's *Reflections of a Rock Lobster.* In this book, Fricke focuses on the discrimination he faced when he tried to take a male date to his senior prom as well as the support he received from classmates and the court system that ruled he and his date could attend.

Fiction is especially important in helping gay teenagers increase their self-esteem. However, in recommending fiction to a gay youth, a few simple guidelines should be followed.

First, it is necessary to remember that there are a variety of experiences in the gay community. No one set of experiences should be presented as *the* gay experience.

Second, what is appropriate for one individual is not necessarily appropriate for another.

Third, it is important to be conscious of the length of the material and the individual's reading level as well as the person's chronological and emotional maturity.

Finally, the individual youth's specific problems or issues need to be considered as do the individual's reading preferences.

SUGGESTED READING FOR GAY YOUTH

The following is a selected list by Dr. Steve L. Berg of other books that might be especially interesting to gay teenagers. This is not meant to be a listing of all the good books available, but it is an introduction to good gay literature.

Cody by Keith Hale. Boston: Alyson, 1987.

Set in Little Rock, Arkansas, this is the story of two friends who are trying to make sense of the world in which they live. The difficulty in "being different" is not only seen in the main character's homosexuality, but also in the fact that his mother is a socialist who loses her teaching position as a result of her beliefs.

Night Kites by M. E. Kerr. New York: Harper & Row, 1987.

The main character in this book is a non-gay teenager whose

brother has AIDS. Although neither the brother nor homosexuality is the focus of this book, the young man does need to confront the homophobic feelings of his family and the small community in which he lives.

Franny: The Queen of Provincetown by John Preston. Boston: Alyson, 1983.

Although the book is not specifically directed at gay youth, it does a superb job of showing the diversity found within the gay male community.

Sweet Dreams by John Preston. Boston: Alyson, 1984.

This is the first of six volumes of the story of Alex Kane, a gay Rambo whose lover had been killed by American soldiers in Vietnam because he was gay. As a result of this experience, Kane serves as a vigilante for gays who are being exploited. In this first adventure, Kane breaks up a group of men who are forcing gay teenagers into drugs and prostitution. Danny, the key teenager in *Sweet Dreams,* becomes Kane's lover and takes a prominent role in the series.

Lucky in Love by Don Sakers. Boston: Alyson, 1987.

In this sequel to *Act Your Part Well,* Keith, after moving to a new city, falls in love with a member of the basketball team. The book traces the development of their relationship and the reaction of family and friends. It is one of the few gay youth books that has a prominent black character and deals with interracial relationships.

Bridges of Respect: Creating Support for Lesbian and Gay Youth by Katherine Whitlock. Philadelphia: American Friends Service Committee, 1988.

Whitlock provides information on a variety of issues faced by gay youth. Resources for additional information are included.

© STEVE L. BERG 1990. REPRINTED WITH PERMISSION. DR. BERG SERVES ON THE BOARD OF DIRECTORS OF THE NATIONAL ASSOCIATION OF LESBIAN AND GAY ALCOHOLISM PROFESSIONALS AND IS THE COAUTHOR OF *THE NALGAP ANNOTATED BIBLIOGRAPHY: ALCOHOLISM, SUBSTANCE ABUSE AND LESBIANS/GAY MEN.* HE IS CURRENTLY COORDINATING A BIBLIOGRAPHY PROJECT ON SPIRITUAL ISSUES IN RECOVERY. HE MAY BE CONTACTED AT 675 OYSTER ROAD, ROSE CITY, MI 48654.

GAY AGING

Just as we take care of our young, we also have to respect those who came before us. As we progress, there will be more and more of us who have spent all our lives as gay people. We need to work to construct ways our elderly can continue to lead constructive, fulfilling, and gay lives.

▼ *S.A.G.E.* (Senior Action in a Gay Environment) is one of the most wonderful organizations in the country. Established and run by older gay men and lesbians, S.A.G.E. has regular social events for its members, but it goes far beyond that usual model. A History Project is involved in producing a stage show, *You Must Remember This,* made up of the true stories of S.A.G.E. members' lives. It also tapes oral histories and stores them as a vibrant memory of our recent past.

The Friendly Visitor Program pairs up younger volunteers with S.A.G.E. members to help them maintain an independent life-style, while the volunteers learn about the dignity of our past.

For more information:

S.A.G.E.
208 W. 13th Street
New York, NY 10011
Phone: 212 741 2247

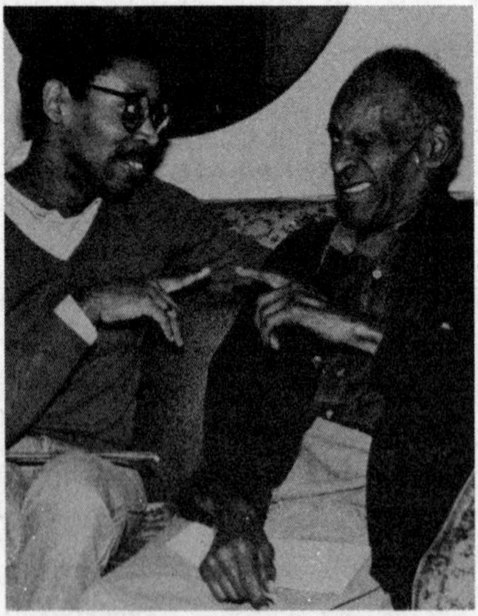

© 1989, S.A.G.E. PHOTO BY WENDY JANE WORKMAN. REPRINTED WITH PERMISSION.

▼ Other groups like S.A.G.E. are being formed around the country as the issue of gay aging becomes more obvious to the community. While an extensive listing of such associations hasn't been compiled, here are some others:

Prime Timers
Box 59071
Jackson, MS 39284

G.L.O.E.
1853 Market Street
San Francisco, CA 94103

▼ For resources and advice on how to establish such an organization, *The National Association for Lesbian and Gay Gerontology* produces *The Resource Guide: Lesbian and Gay Aging.* The book is available for $15 from:

National Association for Lesbian and Gay Gerontology
1853 Market Street
San Francisco, CA 94103

▼ The stories of older gay men are an important part of our history. Understanding how others lived before us informs our contemporary understanding of ourselves.

One resource for this kind of vernacular history is *Quiet Fire: Memoirs of Older Gay Men* by Keith Vacha, edited by Cassie Damewood. Freedom, Calif.: Crossing Press, 1987.

▼ *Chiron Rising* is a magazine for gay elders, especially those who are not interested in packing up their sexual lives with their retirement. The journal includes stories, informational essays, and lively letters and personal sections.

Chiron Rising
Box 2589
Victorville, CA 92393

GAY FINANCES

The larger the gay world becomes, the more questions we need to ask about funding. How do we pay for all of these services and organizations? How do we watch our investments and other monetary interests in a way that can benefit the gay world?

SIGNIFICANT FUNDERS OF GAY ORGANIZATIONS

GENERAL GUIDELINES FOR SEEKING FOUNDATION MONEY

Before spending a lot of time and effort on a grant request, your organization would do well to follow these helpful hints. Call or write foundations to determine their guidelines, restrictions, and application procedures before submitting any formal requests. Follow their instructions carefully, but feel free to ask for help through the process (some progressive funds offer technical assistance). Most of the foundations listed here do not fund individuals or direct political work (lobbying or labor organizing). Several make grants only in certain cities or regions.

This preliminary listing does not concentrate on funding the struggle against AIDS, although all the funds listed here have given AIDS-related grants. There are a large and growing number of sources for such funding, and several resources for information on seeking it. Two references are:

AIDS Funding: A Guide to Giving by Foundations and Charitable Organizations. The Foundation Center, 79 Fifth Avenue, New York, NY, 10003.

National AIDS Information Clearinghouse—800 458 5231. (They have started a database on AIDS grants; printouts are available, able to be sorted by category, region, etc.)

Read up on fund-raising skills and funding sources. Three good references are:

Shellow, Jill R., and Nancy C. Stella, eds. *Grant Seekers Guide,* 3d rev. ed. Mt. Kisco, N.Y.: Moyer Bell Ltd., 1989. (Colonial Hill/RFD 1, Mt. Kisco, NY 10549.)

Klein, Kim. *Fundraising for Social Change.* Inverness, Calif.: Chardon Press, 1985. (P.O. Box 101, Inverness, CA 94937.)

Finding Funding: A Beginner's Guide to Foundation Research. Somerville, Mass.: RESIST, 1990. (Very short, good start; available from RESIST, One Summer Street, Somerville, MA 02143.)

There are regional associations of grantmakers throughout the country, and resource libraries elsewhere; recent lists are published in the *Grant Seekers Guide,* pp. 741–54, and the RESIST guide *Finding Funding* (see above). The Working Group on Funding Lesbian and Gay Issues of the National Network of Grantmakers has been assembling information and making educational presentations since 1983; it may be contacted through Kathy Acey at the Astraea Foundation or Bob Crane at the Joyce Mertz-Gilmore Foundation (see addresses below). Finally, while being aware of the perhaps slim chances of receiving funding, groups should consider applying to their local, more mainstream funds, at least to raise consciousness of a wider group of funders. For instance, local community foundations (such as the New York Community Trust) are beginning to recognize and fund institutions in their gay and lesbian communities.

EXCLUSIVELY GAY AND LESBIAN FUNDERS

Paul Rapoport Foundation
220 E. 60th Street
New York, NY 10022
Phone: 212 888 6578

Contact: Jane Schwartz, Executive Director

Purpose and Guidelines
The Foundation was established under the will of Paul Rapoport. It supports "(1) organizations that provide care, support and services, primarily within the gay community, to individuals with HIV infection and (2) organizations that aid the lesbian and gay community by promoting and supporting the community's development, social and legal rights, identity and well-being."

Grant Limitations
Primarily funds in the New York City area; does not fund "political or legislative activities."

Financial Data
Awarded $162,500 in its Fall 1989 cycle.

Application Process and Meeting Times
The Foundation has four cycles a year; grant decisions are made by a committee of the board.

Colin Higgins Foundation
1388 Sutter Street
San Francisco, CA 94109
Phone: 415 771 4308

Contacts: Ellen Friedman, Manager
John Konowalski, Grants Manager

Purpose and Guidelines
Established in 1986 by Mr. Higgins, continued after his death. It supports organizations which "provide a variety of services directed at meeting the needs of individuals, particularly lesbians and gay men; residential care and hospice programs for people with AIDS; programs which address the spiritual growth and development of individuals." It funds nationwide.

Grant Limitations
Average grant size falls between $5,000–$15,000.

Financial Data
Awarded $75,000 in its Fall 1989 cycle.

Application Process and Meeting Times
One grant cycle per year; decisions are made by the Board of Directors.

Horizons Foundation
604 Mission Street, Suite 306
San Francisco, CA 94105
Phone: 415 546 5226

Contact: Doug Braley, Director

Purpose and Guidelines
Established in 1979 by Golden Gate Business Association (San Francisco's gay and lesbian "chamber of commerce"). Its purpose is to "improve the quality of life of lesbians and gay men." Funding is made in the following categories: Education, Health, Services, Arts and Culture, AIDS, and Rights. The Foundation attempts to balance funding of women-only, men-only, and mixed-gender organizations. Individual donors may restrict their donation to a specific issue area, but not to a specific group.

Grant Limitations
Funds in Bay Area; other areas only if those groups impact the Bay Area.

Financial Data
Distributes approximately $50,000 per year.

Application Process and Meeting Times
The Foundation has two open cycles a year, and a restricted one in which the board solicits specific proposals. Applications are reviewed by staff and board members; decisions are made by full board.

Pride Foundation
1535 11th Avenue, Suite 202
Seattle, WA 98122
Phone: 206 323 3318

Contact: Jolly Sue Baker, Executive Director

Purpose and Guidelines
Established in 1985, the Foundation provides technical assistance, in-kind services, and outright grants to "non-profit organizations serving lesbians, gay men, and their friends." Specific issue areas of grantmaking are: Health/Social services, Arts/Culture, Advocacy/Legal/Education, and Recreation. It seeks groups which have limited appeal to traditional funding sources. Although it fund-raises only in the Seattle area, it considers grants from around the country. It has recently started a special credit card through the Seafirst Bank which will channel money to the Foundation.

Grant Limitations
Does not fund direct lobbying or political work.

Financial Data
Awarded $30,000 in grants in 1989.

Application Process and Meeting Times
Three cycles a year; grant decisions are made by a committee of the board.

Philanthrofund Foundation
607 Marquette Avenue, Suite 101
Minneapolis, MN 55402-1709
Phone: 612 339 7121

Contact: Karen Wright, President

Purpose and Guidelines
Established in 1987 to provide support to "organizations and individuals that seek to serve the needs and enhance the quality of life of the gay and lesbian community." Contributions are placed in a permanent endowment, the interest from which is used as the grant pool. The Foundation's issue areas include health and AIDS organizations, social service groups, legal services, education, and cultural and social organizations.

Grant Limitations
Gives priority to Minnesota organizations, though it has also funded conferences of national organizations which have met in the area.

Financial Data
Currently, some $3,500 is projected as total grantmaking for 1990.

Application Process and Meeting Times
Grant decisions are made by the board of directors; there is one funding cycle per year.

OUT—A Fund for Lesbian and Gay Liberation
The Funding Exchange
666 Broadway, Suite 500
New York, NY 10012
Phone: 212 529 5300

Contact: Charlie Fernandez

Purpose and Guidelines
OUT recognizes "the crucial role of lesbian and gay organizing within a broader movement for progressive social change." It

primarily supports projects working against the oppressions of heterosexism and homophobia in our society. It will support emerging issues and new organizations, either of which have little access to other sources of funding. Within the broad spectrum of lesbian and gay organizing, OUT will look for projects organizing in communities of color, lesbian projects, projects building coalitions within the community, and projects working with particular communities (the elderly, youth, etc.) or in isolated areas (rural areas, prisons, etc.).

Grant Limitations
OUT will generally not fund social service organizations, and it does not fund individuals. Independent film/video projects should be submitted to the Paul Robeson Fund at the above address.

Financial Data
Unavailable; OUT's first grantmaking cycle will be in early 1991.

Application Process and Meeting Times
Grant decisions will be made by a diverse, national board of community activists.

Note: In addition, there are other community foundations around the country which either serve as fund-raising mechanisms for specific organizations or are grantmaking foundations themselves. Among these are the Stonewall Community Foundation (New York City), Cream City Foundation (Milwaukee), Grass Roots Gay Rights Fund (Boston).

Further Note: For lesbian organizations, note should be given of the many women's foundations around the country, other significant women's funders (such as the MS. Foundation for Women, Inc., 141 Fifth Avenue, Suite 68, New York, NY 10010 [212 353 8580]), and in particular of the Astraea Foundation (666 Broadway, Suite 520, New York, NY 10012 [212 529 8021]), a national grantmaker which funds lesbian groups exclusively. See also the *Grant Seekers Guide.*

GENERAL FOUNDATIONS THAT HAVE SIGNIFICANT LESBIAN AND GAY FUNDING

Chicago Resource Center
53 W. Jackson Boulevard, Suite 315
Chicago, IL 60604
Phone: 312 461 9333

Contact: Mary Ann Snyder, Director

Purpose and Guidelines
Support of lesbian and gay organizations is one of three primary issue areas, the other two being domestic violence and AIDS. It has been the major public funder of gay and lesbian organizing in recent years. Within the latter area, the Center focuses on "direct services, health care issues and education, civil and legal rights, programs serving lesbians and gay men of color, coalition building, and outreach to educational and community institutions." Preference is given to organizations which focus exclusively on gay and lesbian issues, and those with limited funding resources.

Grant Limitations
All grants are for one year's funding only, although organizations may reapply in subsequent years.

Financial Data
In 1988, the Center distributed $324,533 in grants to gay and lesbian organizations.

Application Process and Meeting Times
There are three funding cycles per year.

Publications
No annual report; annual list of grants is available.

Joyce Mertz-Gilmore Foundation
218 E. 18th Street
New York, NY 10003
Phone: 212 475 1137

Contact: Robert Crane, Vice-President, Program

Purpose and Guidelines
Within its broad program areas of Human Rights and Democratic Values, the Environment, Alternative Defense and Common Security, and New York City Programs, the Mertz-Gilmore Foundation has increasingly prioritized gay and lesbian civil rights work, within New York and nationwide. It has made significant grants to organizations within the community.

Grant Limitations
The Foundation does not make grants for endowments, maintenance, construction, political purposes, individuals, film or television production, publications, or annual fund appeals. Within New York City, it does not provide funds for direct social services.

Financial Data
In 1987, Foundation grants in all program areas totaled over $3,000,000. In 1988, it granted some $62,500 to gay and lesbian groups (and considerably more to the AIDS struggle).

Application Process and Meeting Times
There are no application deadlines, though applications are considered in spring and fall board meetings.

Publications
The Foundation distributes grants lists, brochures, and other information concerning its programs.

RESIST
One Summer Street
Somerville, MA 02143
Phone: 617 623 5110

Contact: Nancy Wechsler

Purpose and Guidelines
Founded in 1967 as a political organization in opposition to the draft and the Vietnam War, RESIST began soliciting money to help

these movements and evolved into a foundation whose grantmaking became quite broad, and now supports organizations generally working "for peace and social justice." It has long committed a significant share of its funding to gay and lesbian organizing as a part of the movement.

Grant Limitations
Does not fund film or video production, legal defense costs, individuals, social service organizations, material aid campaigns, projects outside the United States, or travel expenses. Gives priority to groups with budgets under $100,000 and those with few options for other funding. It also considers loans and "emergency" grants.

Financial Data
Total grants in 1989 were over $63,000; of that, some $5,000 was given to gay and lesbian groups (further categories include AIDS-related funding and women's groups).

Application Process and Meeting Times
The board considers grants eight times a year; grants range between $100–$600.

Publications
An excellent brief introduction to grant-seeking (*Finding Funding*), funding guidelines, and an excellent newsletter published several times a year.

The Funding Exchange
666 Broadway, # 500
New York, NY 10012
Phone: 212 529 5300

Contact: Charlie Fernandez, Program Officer

Purpose and Guidelines
The Funding Exchange is a national network of fifteen progressive community foundations working for fundamental social change that fund in specific geographic areas. All have commitments to funding gay and lesbian issues. In addition, National Community Funds is the

grantmaking component of the Funding Exchange and considers applications from national organizations and those in areas not covered by the individual funds. All these funds incorporate significant grant decision making by community activists, and are often valuable sources of networking information for further sources of funding (especially for individual donors in various parts of the country).

THE REGIONAL FOUNDATIONS

Appalachian Community Fund, 517 Union Avenue, #206, Knoxville, TN 37902 (Region: Southwest Virginia, West Virginia, East Kentucky, East Tennessee).

Bread and Roses Community Fund, 924 Cherry Street, 2d floor, Philadelphia, PA 19107 (Region: Philadelphia and Camden, New Jersey).

Chinook Fund, 2412 W. 32nd Avenue, Denver, CO 80211 (Region: Colorado).

Crossroads Fund, 3411 W. Diversy Avenue, #20, Chicago, IL 60647 (Region: Chicago metropolitan area).

Fund for Southern Communities, 552 Hill Street SE, Atlanta, GA 30312 (Region: Georgia, North and South Carolina).

Haymarket People's Fund, 42 Seaverns Avenue, Jamaica Plain, MA 02130 (Region: New England).

Headwaters Fund, 122 W. Franklin Avenue, #110, Minneapolis, MN 55404 (Region: Minnesota).

Liberty Hill Foundation, 1320 C Santa Monica Mall, Santa Monica, CA 90401 (Region: Los Angeles County and San Diego).

Live Oak Fund, P.O. Box 4601, Austin, TX 78765 (Region: Texas).

McKenzie River Gathering Foundation, 454 Willamette Street, Eugene, OR 97401 (Region: Oregon).

North Star Fund, 666 Broadway, Suite 500, New York, NY 10012 (Region: New York City).

The People's Fund, 436 Piikoi Street, Honolulu, HI 96814 (Region: Hawaii).

People's Resource of SW Ohio, P.O. Box 6366, Cincinnati, OH (Region: Southwest Ohio).

Vanguard Public Foundation, 14 Precita Avenue, San Francisco, CA 94110 (Region: San Francisco Bay Area).

Wisconsin Community Fund, 222 S. Hamilton, #4, Madison, WI 53703 (Region: Wisconsin).

COMPILED BY DAVID P. BECKER AND CHARLIE FERNANDEZ. REPRINTED WITH PERMISSION.

▼ Gay banks were a sometime fad in California in the early 1980s, but it was sometimes hard to discern just what constituted a gay bank in the highly competitive San Francisco and Los Angeles markets. And, besides, what was more "gay," the savings and loan association whose charter members were gay men, or the Castro Street branch of the large Hibernia National Bank? A shake-out of the savings industry ended the debate as the gay banks were merged into other institutions or disappeared.

Probably the only "gay bank" left in the United States is the *Dallas Gay Alliance Credit Union.* Membership in the Dallas Gay Alliance is a requirement for membership, along with a small fee. For more information:

Dallas Gay Alliance Credit Union
4012-B Cedar Springs
Dallas, TX 75219

MAKING YOUR MONEY SERVE THE GAY COMMUNITY

Working Assets is not a gay company, but gay people who use its many services are able to help many of our organizations. Every year, the pool of donation money from the company is divided according to a poll of members. The National Gay and Lesbian Task Force and the Lambda Legal Defense Fund are two of the progressive nonprofits who have shared in the donations pool from Working Assets.

There are many ways to use Working Assets:

The Working Assets MasterCard or VISA Card is an affinity card; a portion of the membership fee and a very small percentage of each purchase is put into a fund that is shared by the designated organizations.

Working Assets US Sprint service allows you to use the long-distance phone carrier and to have 1 percent of the charges added to the donations pool.

Working Assets Travel Service will put 2 percent of any travel purchase (airline tickets bought by phone with a credit card, for instance) into the pool for donations.

Working Assets Money Fund and other investment funds not only share some of their profits with nonprofits, but the various funds follow different levels of social consciousness in making their investments. You can be sure that your money isn't being put into a company that has a homophobic policy, for instance.

For more information on these and other Working Assets operations:

Working Assets
230 California Street
San Francisco, CA 94111

For information on Working Assets Long Distance: 800 669 8585.

For information on Working Assets credit cards and travel service: 800 522 7759.

For information on Working Assets Money Fund: 800 533 3863.

▼ *Christopher Street Financial, Inc.*, was founded in 1981 by gay Wall Street professionals as a fully registered broker/dealer and investment adviser. From the beginning, the firm's singular target market has been the gay community and its intent to provide prudent financial planning and brokerage services to gay men and women. The firm offers a safe and open environment for clients to discuss any element of their lives which they might not be willing to divulge in a mainstream financial firm.

The firm has learned that the most pressing issues for their clients are HIV-related financial planning, trust and estate planning, and protection of assets for their life partners. The company has geared itself to an individual analysis of each client.

The firm is also aware that many of its gay and lesbian clients are interested in socially conscious investments, especially in terms of companies' gay-related employment and other policies. Christopher Street Financial has investigated a number of mutual funds, for instance, where gay-awareness is one of the criteria for inclusion.

For more information:

Christopher Street Financial, Inc.
80 Wall Street
New York, NY 10005
Phone: 212 269 0110

PAYING ATTENTION TO WHERE YOUR MONEY GOES

Many of us give money to organizations that wouldn't welcome us in any other role but donor. *The Other Side,* an activist Christian magazine, polled many religious and other nonprofit organizations and asked them about their internal policies on a number of social justice issues, including gay hiring. The complete results have been published in *A Giver's Guide: Special Issue for 1989–90,* which is available from *The Other Side,* 300 W. Apsley, Philadelphia, PA 19144, for $7.50 plus $2 postage and handling. Subscriptions to *The Other Side* are available for $27.95 per year.

Akewesane Notes, a Native American newspaper, and Habitat for Hunanity, a favorite charity of Jimmy Carter and his family, were among those that said their hiring decisions are affected if an applicant is gay or lesbian. Among the nonprofit organizations that openly welcome gay and lesbian employees are the American Civil Liberties Union, the American Friends Service Committee, Greenpeace, the Minneapolis American Indian Center, Oxfam America, and the Sierra Club.

You have the right to ask any organization soliciting your money about its policies on hiring—and serving—gay men and lesbians. If you don't make an issue of these questions, they'll have every right to assume you don't care.

▼ The most contention between gay activists and a progressive nonprofit is in our relationship with Amnesty International. While Amnesty will take on cases of people who are prosecuted for advocating gay rights, they will not champion people who have been imprisoned for homosexual activity. That stance, which does not recognize the activity as a form of speech which should be protected, has made Amnesty the target for numerous complaints and attacks. Gay donors should think very carefully before responding to appeals from Amnesty International and, if you choose not to support this organization, it's important that you tell them exactly why. Without that pressure, nothing will change.

▼ *The Pride Foundation:* An example of lesbian and gay philanthropy.

The Pride Foundation was organized in the early 1980s as the philanthropic arm of the Greater Seattle Business Association and was incorporated in 1985.

The foundation's principal objectives include:

- Encouraging philanthropic activism in the community of gay men and lesbians.
- Promoting futuristic thinking and planning in and for the lesbian/gay community by promoting unity and cooperation.
- Providing technical assistance to nonprofit organizations serving lesbians and gay men.
- Serving as an umbrella organization for those gay and lesbian nonprofit organizations that wish to participate in workplace-giving campaigns.
- Providing significant financial assistance to nonprofit organizations serving lesbians and gay men through an endowment fund.

WHY A LESBIAN AND GAY FOUNDATION?

■ Self-sufficiency strengthens and empowers our community.
■ Local and national foundations award less than 1 percent of their grants to lesbian and gay projects. Local and national governments provide only minimal support for lesbian and gay services. The local United Way awards less than .5 percent to gay/lesbian agencies, despite generous contributions from lesbian and gay employees through payroll deduction.
■ Most lesbian/gay projects have limited appeal to traditional funding agencies.
■ We understand our own needs as no one else can. We must continue to demonstrate our responsibility to one another.

COPYRIGHT PRIDE FOUNDATION, 1988. REPRINTED WITH PERMISSION.

▼ Many gay and lesbian business associations have spawned such foundations. Another example, founded by San Francisco's Golden Gate Business Association:

The Horizon Foundation
6004 Mission Street, Suite 306
San Francisco, CA 94105
Phone: 415 546 5226

▼ Other gay community philanthropic activities are coupled with celebrations of contributions made by local gay and lesbian citizens. *The Nicky Awards* are a major fund-raiser for *San Diego Friends, Inc.* The annual award presentation not only recognizes the work of individuals, it also is a money-making proposition of its own. The proceeds from the dinner benefit gay and lesbian organizations and AIDS groups in the San Diego area. For information:

Eagle Productions
Box 33915
San Diego, CA 92103

THE NICKY AWARDS ARE AN ANNUAL EVENT FOR THE SAN DIEGO GAY COMMUNITY.

▼ Social clubs have also propagated charitable funds. ***Brother Help Thyself*** was founded eleven years ago by a group of leather/Levi's and motorcycle clubmen who wanted to assist the Whitman-Walker Clinic. The group continued its work by helping the DC Sports Club get started.

Like many other community-based organizations, Brother Help Thyself is volunteer-run. They have no staff. Money is collected by asking businesses and other organizations to set up and run fund-raisers. The proceeds go to those nonprofit organizations that benefit the gay and lesbian community.

Here's a list of one year's recipients of Brother Help Thyself funds, and example of where gay money goes when it's properly directed:

Alexandria Gay Community Association: A volunteer, member-based organization working to provide a supportive community to northern Virginia gays and lesbians. AGCA operates telephone services, a speakers bureau, a monthly newsletter, library project, and media campaign to educate the public on gay and lesbian issues.

Baltimore Men's Chorus: An organization formed 3½ years ago with the purpose of bringing a musical voice to the gay community of Baltimore. The BHT grant will assist in the purchase of new music and the chorus's attendance at the GALA Choral Festival in Seattle.

Chase-Brexton Clinic: A gay community-based health facility in the city of Baltimore providing SDI testing, psychological services, substance abuse counseling, and HIV testing and evaluation.

D.C. Different Drummers: A Washington-based gay and lesbian concert and marching band.

Episcopal Caring Response to AIDS: A coalition of Episcopal parishes and related organizations in the Washington area offering a Christian response to the AIDS crisis. ECRA provides funding for the Michael Haas House as well as pediatric care, parish outreach, and an AIDS chaplaincy.

Gay & Lesbian Community Center of Baltimore: Provides cultural and social service support to the Baltimore gay and lesbian community.
Gay & Lesbian Switchboard of Washington: A telephone information and referral service which supplies information about community events and activities. Switchboard offers peer counseling and a roommate referral service.
Gay Community Center of D.C.: An organization providing a wide variety of cultural and social services to the gay and lesbian community in Washington including substance abuse programs, peer counseling, youth programs, a monthly newsletter, and meeting space for other organizations.
Grandma's House: A housing provider for children with HIV- and AIDS-related illnesses. The organization creates a living environment for children and provides educational programs in the community.
H.E.R.O.: An organization providing patient and legal services to PWAs in Maryland. HERO also operates a hot line and conducts educational outreach programs. The grant will benefit the Patient Assistance Fund.
Hospice of Northern Virginia: A program designed to meet the needs of terminally ill patients and their loved ones. The hospice provides residence health care to people with AIDS and offers a variety of counseling and bereavement programs. The grant will assist people with AIDS who cannot afford the cost.
Lifelink: A PWA coalition in Washington who provides peer support and advocacy, AIDS education, a monthly newsletter, and assistance with social services.
Maryland AIDS Foundation: An organization providing AIDS education and outreach in Montgomery County, Maryland, particularly to youth and young adults. The Foundation operates a speakers bureau, counseling program, and teen hot line.
Northern Virginia AIDS Ministry: A church-based ecumenical program for PWAs. NoVAM provides direct financial assistance to PWAs and educational programs to churches, clergy, and youth groups. The grant will assist in direct patient assistance.
Parents & Friends of Lesbians and Gays: A coalition committed to educating the public on gay and lesbian issues relating to discrimination, civil rights, and AIDS-related matters. P-FLAG provides peer

counseling, community outreach, and a monthly newsletter. The grant will benefit the Washington and Baltimore chapters.

St. Francis Center/Community of Hagar: An organization providing support to PWAs and their families through peer counseling, bereavement programs, and direct financial assistance and housing to visiting families.

Sexual Minority Youth Assistance League: A youth services and advocacy agency based at the Gay Community Center of D.C. whose mission includes the prevention of the abuse, neglect and self-hatred of lesbian and gay young adults. SMYAL provides direct outreach, peer counseling, telephone information and referral, and public education.

Washington Women's Center: An organization which provides a variety of cultural and social events for women including workshops and a newsletter.

Whitman-Walker Clinic/AIDS Foundation: An organization which provides direct financial assistance to PWAs in need of short-term aid.

Whitman-Walker Clinic AIDS Legal Services: A program which assists PWAs in addressing legal matters such as bankruptcy, wills, power of attorney, and guardianship issues.

Whitman-Walker Clinic/Biker's Fund: A direct financial assistance program created by the Capital Area Board of leather/Levi's clubs and BHT to assist PWAs.

Whitman-Walker Clinic Schwartz Housing Service: A program to provide housing for displaced PWAs in Washington. The service encourages independent living and provides a variety of services for its residents.

Brother, Help Thyself
P.O. Box 23499
Washington, DC 20026

▼ Seattle's *Pride Foundation* has launched the first gay and lesbian credit card. In an agreement with Seafirst Bank, Pride solicits customers for the bank's MasterCard and VISA cards. The organization receives $15 of the $18 annual membership fee and also a small percentage of the charges made on the cards. If you want to sign up for one of the credit cards, call 206 323 3318 or write for an application:

The Pride Foundation
1535 Eleventh Avenue, Suite 202
Seattle, WA 98122
Phone: 206 323 3318

▼ One of the major ways institutions build up financial security is through bequests. You may not like the idea of planning for what happens to your money after you're gone, but you should think about the possibilities that your insurance policies or any savings might create for a gay group.

For more information on how you can make a bequest, get a free copy of "Taking Care of Our Own . . . Where There's a Will, There's a Way." Write or call the Pride Foundation at the address above.

▼ Giving is important, but that doesn't mean you should give your money away foolishly. The Council of Better Business Bureaus, Inc., works with local Better Business Bureaus and sponsors the Philanthropic Advisory Service, which monitors and reports on national and international soliciting organizations and conducts counseling and educational activities to aid contributors and nonprofit groups. Their many publications are useful, not only to individual donors, but to nonprofit organizations that are interested in conscientious and legal fund-raising programs.

For a list of publications, many of them free, a few for a small fee, send a stamped, self-addressed envelope to:

Philanthropic Advisory Service
Council of Better Business Bureaus, Inc.
4200 Wilson Boulevard
Arlington, VA 22203

GAY HEALTH

It sometimes seems as though health has overtaken all other aspects of gay life. The AIDS crisis has become one of the defining elements of the gay experience in the past years. There has been a kind of nobility in our response to AIDS, the way our community eventually came to recognize the severity of the epidemic and the way it's been devastating our population. It took too long, and the price of the learning we've accomplished has been too high as thousands of gay men have died around the world.

There is now a complex and efficient organizational response to AIDS. There are groups all around the United States and Canada that can offer you help, or a way for you to help.

NATIONAL ORGANIZATIONS DEALING WITH AIDS

UNITED STATES

AIDS ACTION COUNCIL
2033 M Street, 8th floor
Washington, DC 20036
Phone: 202 547 3101

AMERICAN FOUNDATION FOR AIDS RESEARCH
1515 Broadway, Suite 3601
New York, NY 10036
Phone: 212 719 0033

AMERICAN PSYCHOLOGICAL ASSOCIATION
AIDS Community Training Project
1200 17th Street NW
Washington, DC 20036
Phone: 202 955 7740

BLACK AND WHITE MEN TOGETHER
National Task Force on AIDS Prevention
National Office
Urban Life Center
1101 O'Farrell Street
San Francisco, CA 94109
Phone: 415 673 8133

GAY AMERICAN INDIANS/AIDS OUTREACH PROGRAM
1347 Divisidero Street, # 312
San Francisco, CA 94115
Phone: 415 431 9437

NATIONAL ASSOCIATION OF PEOPLE WITH AIDS
2025 I Street NW
Suite 415
Washington, DC 20066
Phone: 202 429 2856

NATIONAL COALITION OF GAY STD SERVICES
Box 239
Milwaukee, WI 53201
Phone: 414 277 7671

NATIONAL COALITION OF HISPANIC HEALTH AND HUMAN SERVICE ORGANIZATIONS
1030 15th Street NW
Suite 1053
Washington, DC 20005
Phone: 202 371 2100

NATIONAL COUNCIL OF LA RAZA
20 F Street NW, 2d floor
Washington, DC 20001
Phone: 202 628 9600

NATIONAL JEWISH AIDS PROJECT
1082 Columbia Road
Suite 32
Washington, DC 20009
Phone: 202 387 3097

NATIONAL LAWYERS GUILD
AIDS Network
211 Gough Street
Suite 311
San Francisco, CA 94102
Phone: 415 861 8884

NATIONAL LEADERSHIP COALITION ON AIDS
1150 17th Street NW
Suite 202
Washington, DC 20036

NATIONAL LESBIAN AND GAY HEALTH FOUNDATION
Box 65472
Washington, DC 20035

NATIONAL MINORITY AIDS COUNCIL
714 G Street SE
Washington, DC 20003
Phone: 202 544 1076

CANADA

CANADIAN AIDS SOCIETY/LA SOCIÉTÉ DU SIDA
1101–170 ouest
Laurier West
Ottawa, ON K1P 5V5
Phone: 613 230 3580
Fax: 613 563 4998

LOCAL AND REGIONAL AIDS ORGANIZATIONS

UNITED STATES

■ ALABAMA ■

Hot lines:
205 930 0440
800 445 3741

AIDS TASK FORCE OF ALABAMA
Box 55703
Birmingham, AL 35255
Phone: 205 322 0757

■ ALASKA ■

Hot lines:
907 276 4880
800 478 2437

ALASKA AIDS PROJECT
Box 200070
Anchorage, AK 99520
Phone: 907 276 4880

■ ARIZONA ■

Hot lines:
Phoenix and northern Arizona: 602 420 9396
Tucson and southern Arizona: 602 322 6226

ARIZONA AIDS PROJECT
919 N. First Street
Phoenix, AZ 85004
Phone: 602 420 9396

■ ARKANSAS ■

Hot lines: 501 224 4020

ARKANSAS AIDS FOUNDATIONS
Box 5007
Little Rock, AR 72225
Phone: 501 224 4020

■ CALIFORNIA ■

Hot lines:
Los Angeles and southern California: 213 876 2437
San Diego: 619 543 0300
San Francisco and northern California: 800 367 2437

AIDS PROJECT LOS ANGELES
6721 Romaine
Los Angeles, CA 90038
Phone: 213 962 1600

General information:	800 922 AIDS
Spanish information:	800 222 SIDA
Hearing impaired:	800 553 AIDS
Multi-language:	800 922 2438

SAN DIEGO AIDS PROJECT
Box 89049
San Diego, CA 92138
Phone: 619 543 0300

SAN FRANCISCO AIDS FOUNDATION
Box 6182
San Francisco, CA 94101
Phone: 415 864 4376

SHANTI PROJECT
525 Howard Street
San Francisco, CA 94105
Phone: 415 777 CARE

■ COLORADO ■

Hot line:
303 837 0166

COLORADO AIDS PROJECT
Box 18529
Denver, CO 80218
Phone: 303 837 0166

■ CONNECTICUT ■

Hot lines:
General information: 203 247 2437
Spanish information: 203 951 7432

AIDS PROJECT HARTFORD
30 Arbor Street
Hartford, CT 06106
Phone: 203 523 7699

■ DELAWARE ■

Hot lines:
302 655 5280
800 422 0429

DELAWARE LESBIAN AND GAY HEALTH ADVOCATES
214 N. Market
Wilmington, DE 19801
Phone: 302 652 6776

■ DISTRICT OF COLUMBIA ■

Hot lines:
General information: 202 332 2437
Hearing impaired: 202 332 5295

WHITMAN-WALKER CLINIC/AIDS PROGRAM
1407 S Street NW, 4th floor
Washington, DC 20009
Phone: 202 332 5295

■ FLORIDA ■

Hot lines:
General information: 305 634 4636
800 443 5046
Spanish information: 305 324 5148
Hearing impaired: 305 545 5151

AIDS PREVENTION CENTER
513 Whitehead Street
Key West, FL 33040
Phone: 305 292 6701

HEALTH CRISIS NETWORK
Box 42-1280
Miami, FL 33242
Phone: 305 326 8833

TAMPA AIDS NETWORK
Box 8333
Tampa, FL 33674
Phone: 813 237 8683

■ GEORGIA ■

Hot lines:
General information: 404 876 9944
800 551 2728
Hearing impaired: 404 876 9950

AID ATLANTA
1132 W. Peachtree NW
Atlanta, GA 30309
Phone: 404 872 0600

■ HAWAII ■

Hot lines:
808 924 2437
808 531 4888

LIFE FOUNDATION
Box 88980
Honolulu, HI 96830
Phone: 808 924 2437

■ IDAHO ■

Hot line:
208 345 2277

IDAHO AIDS FOUNDATION
Box 421
Boise, ID 83701
Phone: 208 345 2277

■ ILLINOIS ■

Hot line:
800 243 2437

GAY COMMUNITY AIDS PROJECT
Box 713
Champaign, IL 61820
Phone: 217 337 2928

AIDS FOUNDATION OF CHICAGO
1332 N. Halsted Street, Suite 303
Chicago, IL 60622
Phone: 312 642 5454

HISPANIC HEALTH ALLIANCE
1608 N. Milwaukee, Suite 912
Chicago, IL 60647
Phone: 312 252 6888
(Primarily oriented to the Hispanic community)

HOWARD BROWN MEMORIAL CLINIC
945 W. George Street
Chicago, IL 60657
Phone: 312 871 5777

KAPONA NETWORK
4611 S. Ellis Avenue
Chicago, IL 60653
Phone: 312 536 3000
(Primarily oriented to the black community)

■ INDIANA ■

Hot line:
317 257 4673

MARION COUNTY AIDS COALITION
1350 N. Pennsylvania Street
Damien Center
Indianapolis, IN 46220
Phone: 317 634 1441

■ IOWA ■

Hot line:
800 445 2437

CENTRAL IOWA AIDS PROJECT
2116 Grand Avenue
Des Moines, IA 50132
Phone: 515 274 6700

■ KANSAS ■

Hot lines:
913 232 3100
800 255 1382

TOPEKA AIDS PROJECT
Box 118
Topeka, KS 66601
Phone: 913 232 3100

■ KENTUCKY ■

Hot line:
800 654 2437

AIDS CRISIS TASK FORCE
Box 11442
Lexington, KY 40575
Phone: 606 281 5151

AIDS VOLUNTEERS OF LEXINGTON
1628 Nicholasville Road
Lexington, KY 40503
Phone: 606 276 2865

■ LOUISIANA ■

Hot lines:
504 522 2437
800 992 4379

NO/AIDS TASK FORCE
Box 2616
New Orleans, LA 70176
Phone: 504 891 3732

■ MAINE ■

Hot lines:
207 775 1267
800 851 2437

THE AIDS PROJECT
22 Monument Square, 5th floor
Portland, ME 04101
Phone: 207 774 6877

■ MARYLAND ■

Hot lines:
General information: 301 685 1180
800 638 6252
Hearing impaired: 800 553 3140

HEALTH EDUCATION RESOURCE ORGANIZATION (HERO)
101 W. Read Street
Suite 812
Baltimore, MD 21201
Phone: 301 685 1180

■ MASSACHUSETTS ■

Hot lines:
General information: 617 536 7733
800 235 2331
Latino AIDS Hot line: 617 262 7248
Hearing impaired: 617 536 7733

AIDS ACTION
131 Clarendon Street
Boston, MA 02116
Phone: 617 437 6200

AIDS PROJECT WORCESTER
305 Shrewsbury Street
Worcester, MA 01604
Phone: 508 755 3773

■ MICHIGAN ■

Hot line: 800 872 2437

MIDWEST AIDS PREVENTION PROJECT
660 Livernois
Ferndale, MI 48220
Phone: 313 545 1435

WELLNESS NETWORKS, INC.
Box 438
Flint, MI 48501
Phone: 313 232 0888

GRAND RAPIDS AIDS RESOURCE CENTER
42 S. Division
Grand Rapids, MI 49516
Phone: 616 459 9177

■ MINNESOTA ■

Hot lines:
612 870 0700
800 248 2437

MINNESOTA AIDS PROJECT
2025 Nicollet Avenue S
Suite 200
Minneapolis, MN 55404
Phone: 612 870 7773

■ MISSISSIPPI ■

Hot lines:
General information: 800 537 0851
Hearing impaired: 800 243 7889

MISSISSIPPI GAY/LESBIAN ALLIANCE
Box 8342
Jackson, MS 39284
Phone: 601 353 7611

■ MISSOURI ■

Hot lines:
Kansas City: 816 561 8784
St. Louis: 314 367 8400

Help us read to someone who can't.

One in ten Massachusetts residents won't read this ad. They can't. They're functionally illiterate. So how can you expect them to read about AIDS prevention? You can't. But you can read to them. For information and literature, call 1-800-235-2331.

AIDS ACTION
COMMITTEE
661 Boylston Street, Boston, MA 02116

GOOD SAMARITAN PROJECT
3030 Walnut, 2d floor
Kansas City, MO 64108
Phone: 816 367 2382

ST. LOUIS EFFORT FOR AIDS
4050 Lindell Boulevard
St. Louis, MO 63108
Phone: 314 531 2847

■ MONTANA ■

Hot lines:
406 252 1212
800 537 6187

BILLINGS AIDS SUPPORT NETWORK
Box 1748
Billings, MT 59103
Phone: 406 252 1212

■ NEBRASKA ■

Hot line:
800 782 2437

NEBRASKA AIDS PROJECT
3624 Leavenworth
Omaha, NE 68105
Phone: 402 342 4233

■ NEVADA ■

Hot line:
702 329 2437

NEVADA AIDS FOUNDATION
Box 478
Reno, NV 89109
Phone: 702 329 2437

■ NEW HAMPSHIRE ■

Hot line: 603 595 0218

NEW HAMPSHIRE AIDS FOUNDATION
Box 59
Manchester, NH 03105
Phone: 603 595 0218

■ NEW JERSEY ■

Hot line:
800 433 0254

HYACINTH FOUNDATION AIDS PROJECT
211 Livingston Avenue
New Brunswick, NJ 08901
Phone: 201 246 0925

■ NEW MEXICO ■

Hot line:
505 524 4471

COMMON BOND
Box 26836
Albuquerque, NM 87125
Phone: 505 266 8041

NEW MEXICO AIDS SERVICES
124 Quincy NE
Albuquerque, NM 87131
Phone: 505 266 0911

■ NEW YORK ■

Hot lines:

Albany:	518 445 2437
Buffalo:	716 847 2437
Long Island:	516 385 2437
New York City:	212 807 6664
Rochester:	716 232 4430
Syracuse:	315 475 2437

AIDS COUNCIL OF NORTHEASTERN NEW YORK
750 Broadway
Albany, NY 12210
Phone: 518 434 4686

WESTERN NEW YORK AIDS PROGRAM
220 Delaware Avenue, Suite 512
Buffalo, NY 14202
Phone: 716 847 2441

GAY MEN'S HEALTH CRISIS
129 W. 20th Street
New York, NY 10011
Phone: 212 807 6655

AIDS ROCHESTER
20 University Avenue
Rochester, NY 14605
Phone: 716 232 3580

AIDS TASK FORCE OF CENTRAL NEW YORK
675 W. Genesee Street
Syracuse, NY 13204
Phone: 315 475 2430

■ NORTH CAROLINA ■

Hot lines:

Asheville:	704 252 7489
Charlotte:	704 333 2437
Winston-Salem:	919 723 5031

NORTH CAROLINA AIDS SERVICE COALITION
Box 187
Rocky Point, NC 28457
Phone: 919 675 9222

AIDS TASK FORCE OF WINSTON-SALEM
Box 2982
Winston-Salem, NC 27102
Phone: 919 723 5031

■ NORTH DAKOTA ■

Hot line:
701 224 8378

■ OHIO ■

Hot lines:

General information:	800 332 3889
Hearing impaired:	800 332 3889
Cleveland:	216 621 9723
Dayton:	513 223 2437

COLUMBUS AIDS TASK FORCE
1500 W. Third Avenue, Suite 329
Columbus, OH 43212
Phone: 614 488 2437

■ OKLAHOMA ■

Hot line:
405 525 2437

OASIS COMMUNITY CENTER/AIDS SUPPORT PROGRAM
2135 N.W. 39th Street
Oklahoma City, OK 73112
Phone: 405 525 2437

■ OREGON ■

Hot line: 800 777 2437

CASCADE AIDS PROJECT
408 S.W. Second Street
Suite 412
Portland, OR 97204
Phone: 503 223 5907

■ PENNSYLVANIA ■

Hot lines:

Philadelphia:	215 732 2437
Pittsburgh:	412 363 2437

PHILADELPHIA COMMUNITY HEALTH ALTERNATIVES
Box 53429
Philadelphia, PA 19105
Phone: 215 732 2437

PITTSBURGH AIDS TASK FORCE
141 S. Highland Avenue
Suite 304
Pittsburgh, PA 15206
Phone: 412 363 6500

■ RHODE ISLAND ■

Hot line:
401 277 6502

RHODE ISLAND PROJECT AIDS
Roger Williams Building
22 Hayes Street
Providence, RI 02908
Phone: 401 277 6545

■ SOUTH CAROLINA ■

Hot line:
803 736 1171

SOUTH CAROLINA AIDS EDUCATION NETWORK
2768 Decker Boulevard
Columbia, SC 29206
Phone: 803 736 1171

■ SOUTH DAKOTA ■

Hot line:
605 332 4599

SIOUX EMPIRE GAY AND LESBIAN COALITION
Box 220
Sioux Falls, SD 57101
Phone: 605 332 4599

■ TENNESSEE ■

Hot lines:

Chattanooga:	615 265 2273
Knoxville:	615 523 2437
Memphis:	901 726 1690
Nashville:	615 385 1510

CHATTANOOGA CARES
Box 8402
Chattanooga, TN 37411
Phone: 615 265 2273

MEMPHIS AIDS COALITION
1400 Central Avenue
Memphis, TN 38104
Phone: 901 726 1690

NASHVILLE CARES
Box 25107
Nashville, TN 37202
Phone: 615 385 1510

■ TEXAS ■

Hot lines:

Austin:	512 472 2437
Dallas:	214 539 2437
El Paso:	915 533 5003
Houston:	713 524 2437
Lubbock:	806 794 1757
San Antonio:	512 821 6218

AIDS SERVICES OF AUSTIN
Box 4874
Austin, TX 78765
Phone: 512 472 2273

DALLAS GAY ALLIANCE AIDS RESOURCE CENTER
4012 Cedar Springs
Dallas, TX 75219
Phone: 214 521 5124/214 528 4233

SOUTHWEST AIDS COMMITTEE
916 E. Yandell
El Paso, TX 79902
Phone: 915 533 5003

AIDS FOUNDATION HOUSTON
3927 Essex Lane
Houston, TX 77027
Phone: 713 623 6796

■ UTAH ■

Hot lines:
801 531 8238
800 366 2437

UTAH AIDS FOUNDATION
450 S. 900 East, Suite 205
Salt Lake City, UT 84102
Phone: 801 359 5555

■ VERMONT ■

Hot line:
802 863 2437

VERMONT CARES
Box 5248
Burlington, VT 05402
Phone: 802 863 2437

■ VIRGINIA ■

Hot lines:
804 355 4428
800 533 4148

TIDEWATER AIDS CRISIS TASK FORCE
814 W. 41st Street
Norfolk, VA 23508
Phone: 804 423 5859

RICHMOND AIDS INFORMATION NETWORK
1721 Hanover Avenue
Richmond, VA 23219
Phone: 804 358 6343
Hot line: 804 358 2437

AIDS COUNCIL OF WESTERN VIRGINIA
Box 496
Roanoke, VA 24003
Phone: 703 985 0131
Hot line: 703 982 2437

■ WASHINGTON ■

Hot line: 206 329 6923

NORTHWEST AIDS FOUNDATION
1818 E. Madison
Seattle, WA 98122
Phone: 206 329 6923

■ WEST VIRGINIA ■

Hot line: 304 696 7132

HUNTINGTON AIDS TASK FORCE
816 Twelfth Avenue, # 12
Huntington, WV 25701
Phone: 304 525 7801

■ WISCONSIN ■

Hot lines:
Milwaukee: 414 273 2436
Statewide: 800 334 2436

MADISON AIDS SUPPORT NETWORK
Box 731
Madison, WI 53701
Phone: 608 255 3349

MILWAUKEE AIDS PROJECT
Box 92505
Milwaukee, WI 53202
Phone: 414 273 2437

■ WYOMING ■

Hot line:
307 237 7833

WYOMING AIDS PROJECT
Box 9353
Casper, WY 82602
Phone: 307 237 7833

CANADA

■ ALBERTA ■

Hot line:
403 228 0155

AIDS CALGARY AWARENESS ASSOCIATION
300–1021 Tenth Avenue, SW
Calgary, AB T2R 0B7
Phone: 403 228 0198
Fax: 403 229 2077

AIDS NETWORK OF EDMONTON SOCIETY
10704 108th Street, 2d floor
Edmonton, AB T5H 3A3
Hot line: 403 429 2437
Phone: 403 424 4767

■ BRITISH COLUMBIA ■

AIDS VANCOUVER
Box 4991, Vancouver Main Post Office
Vancouver, BC V6B 4A6
Hot line: 604 687 2437
Phone: 604 687 5220
Fax: 604 687 4857

■ MANITOBA ■

THE VILLAGE CLINIC
Winnipeg Gay Community Health Centre, Inc.
668 Corydon Avenue
Winnipeg, MB R3M 0X7
Hot line: 204 453 2114
Phone: 204 453 0045
Fax: 204 453 5214

■ ONTARIO ■

Hot lines:
613 545 1414
416 926 1626
613 238 4111

KINGSTON AIDS PROJECT
Box 120
Kingston, ON K7L 4V6
Phone: 613 545 3698

AIDS COMMITTEE OF LONDON
304 York Street
London, ON N6B 1P8
Phone: 519 434 1601
Fax: 519 434 1843

AIDS COMMITTEE OF OTTAWA/COMITÉ DU SIDA D'OTTAWA
201–267 Dalhousie Street
Ottawa, ON K1N 7E3
Phone: 613 238 5014
Fax: 613 238 3425

AIDS COMMITTEE OF TORONTO
202–464 Yonge Street
Toronto, ON M4Y 1W9
Phone: 416 926 1626

■ QUEBEC ■

Hot line:
418 687 3032

LA COMITÉ SIDA AIDE MONTREAL
3600 Hôtel-de-Ville
Montreal, QU
Phone: 514 282 9888
Fax: 514 282 0072

MOUVEMENT D/INFORMATION ET D'ENTRAIDE DANS LA LUTTE CONTRE LE SIDA À QUÉBEC
575 ouest, boulevard St-Cyrille
Quebec, QU G1S 1S6
Phone: 418 687 4310

■ SASKATCHEWAN ■

Hot line:
800 667 6878

AIDS REGINA
2221 Fourteenth Avenue
Regina, SK S4P 0X9
Hot line: 306 525 0905
Phone: 306 525 0902
Fax: 306 525 0904

AIDS SASKATOON
Box 4062
Saskatoon, SK S7K 1L9
Phone: 306 242 5005

U.S. NAMES AND ADDRESSES FROM THE FILES OF THE AIDS PROJECT, PORTLAND, MAINE. CANADIAN NAMES AND ADDRESSES COURTESY OF THE CANADIAN AIDS SOCIETY/LA SOCIÉTÉ CANADIENNE DU SIDA.

LIVING WITH AIDS

PWA coalitions are organizations made up of people who are living with AIDS. The groups sponsor many different programs, all initiated by the members and not by outside "experts." These associations provide inestimable support for people with HIV-infections and often perform valuable community education services as well.

In the United States, the coordinating body of the PWA Coalitions is:

National Association of PWAS
2025 I Street, NW, Suite 1101
Washington, DC 20006
Phone: 202 429 2856
Fax: 202 429 0404

UNITED STATES

■ ALABAMA ■

BIRMINGHAM LIVING WITH AIDS COALITION
Phone: 205 934 3262

■ ALASKA ■

ALASKANS LIVING WITH HIV
Box 2040805
Anchorage, AK 99524
Phone: 907 338 0835

■ ARIZONA ■

PHOENIX PWA COALITION
Phone: 602 264 5486

TUCSON PACT FOR LIFE
Box 2488
Tucson, AZ 85702
Phone: 602 322 9808

■ CALIFORNIA ■

PWA COALITION (SAN FRANCISCO)
519 Castro Street
Box M-46
San Francisco, CA 94114
Phone: 415 553 2560

BEING ALIVE (WEST HOLLYWOOD)
4222 Santa Monica Boulevard, Suite 105
Los Angeles, CA 90029
Phone: 213 667 3262
Fax: 213 667 2735

■ COLORADO ■

PWA COALITION (DENVER)
Phone: 303 837 8214

■ CONNECTICUT ■

PWA COALITION
Box 636
New Haven, CT 06503
Phone: 203 624 0947

■ DISTRICT OF COLUMBIA ■

LIFELINK
300 I Street, NE, Suite 107
Washington, DC 20002
Phone: 202 833 3070
Fax: 202 546 3451

■ FLORIDA ■

PWA COALITION (BROWARD COUNTY)
130 East Mocnab Road
Pompano Beach, FL 33060
Phone: 305 784 0314

PWA COALITION (DADE COUNTY)
187 N.E. 36th Street
Miami, FL 33137
Phone: 305 576 1111
Fax: 305 576 0604

PWA COALITION (JACKSONVILLE)
Box 5789
Jacksonville, FL 32247
Phone: 904 396 2562

PWA COALITION (KEY WEST)
709 Olivia Street
Key West, FL 33040
Phone: 305 296 5701

PWA COALITION (PALM BEACH)
Box 8755
West Palm Beach, FL 33407
Phone: 407 845 0800

■ GEORGIA ■

PWA COALITION (ATLANTA)
98 6th Street
Atlanta, GA 30308
Phone: 404 874 7926

■ ILLINOIS ■

KAPONA WELLNESS NETWORK (CHICAGO)
4611 S. Ellis Street, Floor #2
Chicago, IL 60653
Phone: 312 536 3000
Fax: 312 536 8355

■ INDIANA ■

PWA COALITION (INDIANAPOLIS)
1034 N. Takoma Street
Indianapolis, IN 46201
Phone: 317 637 2720

■ MAINE ■

PWA COALITION
377 Cumberland Avenue
Portland, ME 04101
Phone: 207 773 8500

■ MARYLAND ■

PWA COALITION (BALTIMORE)
Phone: 301 625 1677/301 625 1688

■ MASSACHUSETTS ■

PWA COALITION (WESTFIELD)
Phone: 413 562 8465

■ MICHIGAN ■

FRIENDS PWA ALLIANCE (DETROIT)
Box 211048
Detroit, MI 48221
Phone: 313 543 8310

■ MINNESOTA ■

THE ALIVENESS PROJECT (MINNEAPOLIS)
730 E. 38th Street
Minneapolis, MN 55407
Phone: 612 822 7946

■ MISSISSIPPI ■

PWA COALITION (JACKSON)
Box 8342
Jackson, MS 39284

■ MISSOURI ■

HEARTLAND AIDS RESOURCE COUNCIL (KANSAS CITY)
110-A E. 43rd Street
Kansas City, MO 64111
Phone: 816 753 3215

■ NEW JERSEY ■

PWA COALITION (BERGENFIELD)
Phone: 201 944 6670

■ NEW MEXICO ■

NEW MEXICO ASSOCIATION OF PEOPLE WITH AIDS
105 E. Marcy, Room 111
Santa Fe, NM 87105
Phone: 505 982 5995

■ NEW YORK ■

NIAGARA FRONTIER AIDS ALLIANCE (BUFFALO)
367 Delaware Avenue
Buffalo, NY 14202
Phone: 716 852 6778

PWA COALITION (LONG ISLAND)
1600 New Highway, Suite 22
Farmingdale, NY 11735
Phone: 516 324 2076

PWA COALITION (NEW YORK CITY)
31 W. 26th Street
New York, NY 10010
Phone: 212 532 0290

■ OHIO ■

PWA COALITION
1500 W. Third Avenue, Suite 329
Columbus, OH 43212
Phone: 614 488 2437

■ PENNSYLVANIA ■

WE THE PEOPLE (PHILADELPHIA)
425 S. Broad Street
Philadelphia, PA 19147
Phone: 215 545 6868

■ SOUTH CAROLINA ■

HEALING CIRCLE SUPPORT GROUP
Phone: 803 771 7300

■ TENNESSEE ■

PEOPLE LIVING WITH AIDS
Box 25107
Nashville, TN 37202
Phone: 615 385 1510

■ TEXAS ■

PWA COALITION (AUSTIN)
Phone: 512 448 4357

PWA COALITION (DALLAS)
c/o AIDS Services of Dallas
Box 4338
Dallas, TX 75208
Phone: 214 941 0523

PWA COALITION (HOUSTON)
1475 W. Gray
Houston, TX 77019
Phone: 713 522 5428

PWA COALITION (PORT ARTHUR)
Phone: 409 724 2437

PWA COALITION (SAN ANTONIO)
Box 12543
San Antonio, TX 78212
Phone: 512 821 6218

■ UTAH ■

PWA COALITION OF UTAH (SALT LAKE CITY)
Box 2843
Salt Lake City, UT 84110
Phone: 801 359 9619

CANADA

■ BRITISH COLUMBIA ■

PWA COALITION (VANCOUVER)
1447 Hornby Street
Vancouver, BC V6Z 1W8
Phone: 604 683 3367

THIS LIST IS FROM *AIDS TREATMENT NEWS.* REPRINTED WITH PERMISSION.

AIDS ACTIVISM

AIDS has produced a fury of activism in the gay community and in other affected populations. *ACT-UP* is the most visible, and often the most militant, group fighting for the rights of people living with AIDS. The activist coalition has spread rapidly across the country. If you don't find an ACT-UP group in your hometown, call another, one close by you, and the chances are you'll find a chapter of that organization or another activist AIDS group right there beside you.

UNITED STATES

■ CALIFORNIA ■

ACT-UP (LOS ANGELES)
Box 26607
Los Angeles, CA 90026
Phone: 213 668 2357

ACT-UP (SAN DIEGO)
1043 University Avenue, #271
San Diego, CA 92013
Phone: 619 233 9337

ACT-UP (SAN FRANCISCO)
2300 Market Street, #68
San Francisco, CA 94114
Phone: 415 563 0724

ACT-UP/GOLDEN GATE
347 Dolores Street, Room 119
San Francisco, CA 94110

■ COLORADO ■

ACT-UP (DENVER)
Phone: 303 830 0730

■ FLORIDA ■

CURE AIDS NOW (COCONUT GROVE)
7543 Biscayne Avenue
Miami, FL 33138
Phone: 305 667 7278

■ ILLINOIS ■

ACT-UP (CHICAGO)
Phone: 312 509 6802

■ MASSACHUSETTS ■

ACT-UP (BOSTON)
Box 483
Kindelbrook Station
Cambridge, MA 02142
Phone: 617 492 2887

■ NEW JERSEY ■

ACT-UP (ORANGE)
Phone: 201 836 8645

■ NEW YORK ■

ACT-UP (NEW YORK)
135 W. 29th Street, 10th Floor
New York, NY 10001
Phone: 212 533 8888
Fax: 212 389 1797

■ OREGON ■

ACT-UP (PORTLAND)
Phone: 503 284 0262

■ WASHINGTON ■

ACT-UP (SEATTLE)
Phone: 206 726 1678

CANADA

■ ONTARIO ■

ACT-UP (TORONTO)
Phone: 416 591 8489

THESE LISTS ARE BASED ON INFORMATION PROVIDED, WITH PERMISSION, BY *AIDS TREATMENT NEWS.*

AIDS NEWSLETTERS

Newsletters have become the best source of information about AIDS research and treatment. Here are some of the best:

▼ *AIDS Treatment News* appears biweekly. It keeps abreast of experimental and alternative treatments.

ATN Publications
Box 411256
San Francisco, CA 94141
Phone: 415 255 0588

▼ *Body Positive* is the publication of an organization formed specifically for those people who have tested positive for the HIV virus but who are not ill.

Body Positive
263A W. 19th Street
New York, NY 10011
Phone: 212 633 1782

▼ *Focus: A Guide to AIDS Research* is a monthly publication of the AIDS Health Project, a group affiliated with the University of California at San Francisco. Its purpose is to provide AIDS research information to health care providers.

Focus
UCSF AIDS Health Project
Box 0884
San Francisco, CA 94143
Phone: 415 476 6430

▼ *Medical Treatment Issues* is the medical publication of the Gay Men's Health Crisis. It monitors research and alerts readers to new treatment possibilities as they emerge. It's published ten times a year.

Medical Treatment Issues
The GMHC Newsletter of Experimental AIDS Therapies
Department of Medical Information
129 W. 20th Street
New York, NY 10011

▼ *PI Perspective* monitors drug research, especially those therapies which are in the experimental stage and which can be made available to people who meet certain entrance criteria for studies.

Project Inform
347 Dolores Street, Suite 301
San Francisco, CA 94110
Phone: 415 558 8669

There's also a drug hot line available from the organization. Locally, call: 800 334 7422; nationally, call: 800 822 7422.

▼ *PWA Coalition Newsletter* is written for and by people with AIDS and other HIV-related illnesses. It's available free for people with AIDS or ARC; a donation is requested of others.

The PWA Coalition Newsline is the monthly publication of the national PWA Coalition. It contains information, articles, personal testimony, and more. *The Newsline* is available for $35, but is free to anyone with AIDS.

PWA Coalition, Inc.
31 W. 26th Street
New York, NY 10010
Phone: 212 532 0290

▼ *ATIN* (*AIDS Targeted Information Newsletter*) publishes a regular search of medical journals around the world. Heavily technical, it's an unsurpassed resource for those who are attempting to follow AIDS research around the world.

Williams & Williams
Box 23291
Baltimore, MD 21203
Phone: 800 638 6423

The first seventy-five issues of *AIDS Treatment News* have been collected in one volume, edited by John S. James (Berkeley: Celestial Arts, 1990).

ON A POSITIVE NOTE

▼ Most AIDS service organizations have a newsletter or other means to regularly communicate with their clients, volunteers, and supporters. If you're interested in starting such a newsletter on your own, *On a Positive Note,* published by the AIDS organizations of Palm Beach County is one fine example. You can get a sample copy by writing:

PWAC/PBC
Newsletter Committee
Box 8755
West Palm Beach, FL 33407

Michael Callen is one of the founders of the PWA Coalition. A long-term survivor of the disease, He's written an inspirational book, *Surviving Aids* (New York: HarperCollins, 1990), about his life, his fight against AIDS, and the organizations that have worked to empower and work with people living with AIDS.

▼ Raising money is one of the biggest problems for the new and always hungry AIDS organizations. Many of us want to help, but aren't sure how. One group has emulated one of the classics of American fund-raising: *Stamp Out AIDS* is in the tradition of Easter Seals and Christmas Seals. You buy the stamps, then put them on your correspondence, or use them in any other way you choose. Organizations around the country receive your help, and you are able to spread a visible concern about the disease.

Stamp Out AIDS
240 W. 44th Street
New York, NY 10036

▼ Many people living with AIDS have turned to the arts to document their lives and express their experiences. *James White Review,* a gay men's literary journal, sponsored workshops for people with AIDS. As a result of those workshops, they've published *Save It All: A Journal of Creative Writing by People with AIDS and Caregivers.*

Copies are available for a minimum donation of $3. Any profits from the sale of this booklet will be used to promote more workshops.

PWA Journal Workshop
James White Review
Box 3356, Traffic Station
Minneapolis, MN 55403

▼ AIDS has turned the medical establishment in this country on its head. It's not just that AIDS represents a major crisis for our medical care system, it's also changed many of the rules about how health care is delivered and what is considered safe health care.

One way this is manifest is the number of people who have turned to *clinical trials* for their primary health care. While clinical trials were originally perceived as a way to test drugs, they are now seen as a major way for expensive and untried AIDS drugs to be gotten to people who may benefit from them.

Clinical trials present many questions that anyone should examine before he commits himself to them. For more information on the process, how the trials work, and referrals to more resources, read *AIDS Clinical Trials: Talking It Over.* It's available free from:

NIAID Office on Communication
National Institutes of Health
Building 31, Room 7A32
Bethesda, MD 20892

▼ Nothing has drawn gay men and lesbians closer together than AIDS. Lesbian response to the first wave of the disease, which devastated gay male communities, has been compassionate, strong, and unfailing.

Some lesbians articulate the need for gay men to reciprocate in some way, taking more care about women's issues and listening more clearly to what women have to say about sexism in our society.

You can begin by understanding just what women have gone through because of AIDS. There's no better starting point than *AIDS: The Women,* edited by Ines Rieder and Patricia Ruppelt (Pittsburgh: Cleis Press, 1989).

NATIONAL AIDS INFORMATION CLEARINGHOUSE

The National AIDS Information Clearinghouse, a project of The Centers for Disease Control (CDC), will provide you with a printout of all the information in their computers on any specific field having to do with AIDS. You can ask them for posters designed for homosexual men, legal projects—anything that might have been collected in their archives can be retrieved through computers and delivered to you, free, in a presentation folder. They'll send you a "Considerations for Field Review" to help you figure out how to pose your inquiry most effectively.

For more information:

National AIDS Information Clearinghouse
Box 6003
Rockville, MD 20850

▼ Videotapes are an important part of AIDS education. Most of the local AIDS organizations will have a library of tapes, or will have some other means to procure them for you.

The Shanti Project has an extensive offering of such tapes, which can be purchased directly from them. The topics range from "Facing Death and Dying" to "How to Facilitate a Support Group" to "Patient Advocacy."

For a complete listing of these tapes and many other Shanti educational materials:

Shanti Project
Public Education Department
525 Howard Street
San Francisco, CA 94105

▼ If you need more information on AIDS, contact your local organization, or else write to Gay Men's Health Crisis. The New York–based organization has a publication to deal with almost any situation. The list of publications is free:

Gay Men's Health Crisis
129 W. 20th Street
New York, NY 10011

▼ Another major source of AIDS information material is *AIDS Educator,* a catalog produced by *The San Francisco AIDS Foundation.* For a copy, write to:

San Francisco AIDS Foundation
Box 6182
San Francisco, CA 94101

Both organizations have materials available in Spanish.

JUST WHAT IS THE TEST?

When HIV (human immunodeficiency virus) enters the body, the body produces antibodies in response to the virus. "The Test" detects the presence of these antibodies in a small sample of your blood. "The Test" *does not detect AIDS* (acquired immunodeficiency syndrome), it only tells you if your body has produced antibodies in response to the virus that causes AIDS.

For more complete information, contact your local AIDS organization, or write to Gay Men's Health Crisis for their brochure "The Test: Understanding HIV antibody testing."

Gay Men's Health Crisis
129 W. 20th Street
New York, NY 10011

I began to volunteer for Gay Men's Health Crisis early in 1982. At that time GMHC was a very *small organization, and none of us had any idea of what we were in for regarding AIDS. But all of us did know that what was at that time just beginning to happen to men in our community frightened us terribly, and we couldn't simply stand on the sidelines and do nothing. The people I met there profoundly influenced my life.*

Having become involved in AIDS volunteer work with GMHC is one of the things in my life that I am most proud of. The experiences I have had as a result of volunteering with people who have AIDS has caused me to profoundly grow personally, professionally, interpersonally, and spiritually.

—MICHAEL SHERNOFF,
therapist

AIDS AND THE LAW

AIDS presents many legal problems. To educate yourself about the issues and the policies as they affect you, the American Civil Liberties Union (ACLU) and Lambda Legal Defense Fund both have brochures and other publications that you should read. Contact them for more information on the services they offer you.

The ACLU has model laws that you can advocate when lobbying your legislature or city council.

American Civil Liberties Union
AIDS and Civil Liberties Project
132 W. 43rd Street
New York, NY 10036

Lambda Legal Defense and Education Fund, Inc.
666 Broadway
New York, NY 10012

TEN PRINCIPLES FOR AIDS AND THE WORKPLACE

1. People with AIDS or HIV infections are entitled to the same rights and opportunities as people with other serious or life-threatening illnesses.

2. Employment policies must, at a minimum, comply with federal, state, and local laws and regulations.

3. Employment policies should be based on the scientific and epidemiological evidence that people with AIDS or HIV infection do not pose a risk of transmission of the virus to coworkers through ordinary workplace contact.

4. The highest levels of management and union leadership should unequivocally endorse nondiscriminatory employment policies and education programs about AIDS.

5. Employers and unions should communicate their support of these policies to workers in simple, clear, and unambiguous terms.

6. Employers should provide employees with sensitive, accurate, and up-to-date education about risk reduction in their personal lives.

7. Employers have a duty to protect the confidentiality of employees' medical information.

8. To prevent work disruption and rejection by coworkers of an employee with AIDS or HIV infection, employers and unions should undertake education for all employees before such an incident occurs and as needed thereafter.

9. Employers should not require HIV screening as part of general pre-employment or workplace physical examinations.

10. In those special occupational settings where there may be a potential risk of exposure to HIV (for example, in health care, where workers may be exposed to blood or blood product), employers should provide specific, ongoing education and training, as well as the necessary equipment to reinforce appropriate infection control procedures and ensure that they are implemented.

▼ "Ten Principles for AIDS and the Workplace" was developed by The Citizens Commission on AIDS for New York City and Northern New Jersey, 51 Madison Avenue, Room 3008, New York, NY 10010. As of January 15, 1990, more than 425 corporations and organizations had endorsed "Ten Principles for AIDS and the Workplace." Write to the Commission for a complete listing.

AIDS and the workplace is also a priority issue for *The National Leadership Coalition on AIDS,* an organization that includes private corporations as well as AIDS service providers and other health groups.

National Leadership Coalition on AIDS
1150 17th Street NW, Suite 202
Washington, DC 20005

▼ Native Americans and Native Canadians have special issues concerning AIDS, how it's perceived in their communities, and how prevention programs must be structured.

The National Native American AIDS Prevention Center maintains a hot line for information: 800 283 2437. It also has other material and support services to offer.

National Native American AIDS Prevention Center
6239 College Avenue, Suite 201
Oakland, CA 94618
Phone: 415 658 2051

BUT WHAT CAN I *DO*?

With something as overwhelming as AIDS, the most difficult problem is often trying to find a way to help. The issue seems so immense, the problems so enormous, that we can't always see what help we can be.

The Howard Brown Memorial Clinic is one of the oldest and most complete gay medical operations in the country. It predates the AIDS crisis and has provided important care for the gay and lesbian communities for years. They have an entire pamphlet called "Volunteer Opportunities." Even if you aren't in the Chicago area, you can write and get hold of the publication, then see what a wide range of specific help is necessary and perhaps then you can find a niche for yourself.

Howard Brown Memorial Clinic
945 W. George Street
Chicago, IL 60657

▼ You could also read *You Can Do Something About AIDS.* This inexpensive book ($1.00 a copy) is available at most bookstores. A project of concerned people in the publishing industry whose companies underwrote most of the costs, there are many chapters by celebrities and just people on the street talking about individual projects that can serve as models for community service for people with AIDS in your community. The book is available for bulk purchase by organizations *only* from the publisher:

Alyson Publications
40 Plympton Street
Boston, MA 02118

Please don't write to them for single copies. The expense of handling those orders is too great.

▼ *The Names Project* took one of the most basic forms of American art and produced an epic memorial with it. *The Quilt* has become the major memorial for people who have died of AIDS. Each panel tells a story of a person's life, made by people who pledge to remember.

After touring The Quilt throughout North America, The Names Project is now building a permanent home for it. A whole set of products has evolved to help in fund-raising; a book, postcards, posters, and T-shirts are only a few examples.

For more information:

The Names Project
Box 14573
San Francisco, CA 94114

MYTHS AND FACTS ABOUT FEDERAL AIDS SPENDING

Myth The federal government spends $1.6 billion on AIDS, and only $1.5 billion on cancer.

Fact The National Cancer Institute (NCI) will spend $1.5 billion on cancer research this year (not including AIDS-related cancer research). The total AIDS budget of the National Institutes of Health (NIH) in this fiscal year is $750 million (including AIDS-related cancer research at NCI)—less than half the budget for cancer research.

The federal government will spend $1.6 billion this year on all AIDS activities in the Public Health Service, including the Centers for Disease Control, the Food and Drug Administration, the Health Resources and Services Administration, and the Alcohol, Drug Abuse, and Mental Health Administration. Comparison figures are not available for other diseases.

Myth The government is spending a disproportionate amount on AIDS, compared to other diseases with a high mortality rate.

Fact The death toll from AIDS is growing rapidly, while that from other "major" diseases is relatively static. At the present rate of growth, AIDS will be the number one cause of early death—measured in years of life lost before age 65—in the U.S. by mid-decade; by next year it will be on par with cancer and heart disease as a major killer.

The potential for further growth of AIDS cases is far greater than that of other major killers because AIDS is communicable. Other sexually transmitted diseases have shown alarming growth in the last decade with no sign of slowing down. Thirty million Americans are estimated to carry genital herpes infections. If HIV infection—which is spread in the same ways—were to become as prevalent as genital herpes, its toll in death, suffering, and lost productivity would dwarf the present cost of cancer and heart disease.

Myth AIDS research is wasted money because most infected people will die anyway. The money would be better spent on prevention.

Fact Prevention and research both are necessary. Even if effective treatments for HIV infection are found soon, their expense still will make prevention efforts critical.

Nonetheless, millions of lives worldwide depend on the discovery of effective treatments for people who are already infected. Our investment in medical research has produced startling progress in a very short time. The National Institutes of Health released study results in January of 1990 showing that treatment improvements have produced substantial increases of life expectancy from time of AIDS diagnosis; the prospects for those infected but not sick are even better.

Myth If the government spends more on AIDS, it cannot increase spending for other medical research or other health needs.

Fact The government could spend more on AIDS *and* cancer—and other critical domestic needs—by cutting military spending. Polls show that the American people want to do just that.

The entire National Institutes of Health is funded at $7.6 billion in fiscal 1990. For the same year Congress provided more than that for just two weapons systems: $3.8 billion for the Strategic Defense Initiative and $4.3 billion for the B-2 bomber. (The Persian Gulf crisis is only escalated these defense expenditures.)

COPYRIGHT 1990 THE HUMAN RIGHTS CAMPAIGN FUND. REPRINTED WITH PERMISSION.

NATIONAL AIDS RELIGIOUS CONTACTS

AMERICAN BAPTIST CHURCHES/USA
Coordinating Committee on AIDS
ABC in the USA
Box 851
Valley Forge, PA 19482
Phone: 215 768 2000

CHURCH OF THE BRETHREN
HIV/AIDS Ministries Network
1451 Dundee Avenue
Elgin, IL 60120
Phone: 312 742 5100

THE EPISCOPAL CHURCH
Joint Commission on AIDS
The Episcopal Church Center
815 Second Avenue
New York, NY 10017
Phone: 212 867 8400

EVANGELICAL LUTHERAN CHURCH IN AMERICA
The Reverend Adele Reamer
8765 W. Higgins Road
Chicago, IL 60631
Phone: 312 380 2682

MENNONITE HEALTH ASSOCIATION
H. Ernest Bennett, Executive Director
Box 370
Elkhart, IN 46515
Phone: 219 294 7523

NATIONAL CATHOLIC AIDS NETWORK
Lazzaro Center
Box 30926
New York, NY 10011
Phone: 212 779 0450

NATIONAL EPISCOPAL AIDS COALITION
The Reverend Canon Earl Conner
540 E. 36th Street
Indianapolis, IN 46205
Phone: 317 632 0123

PRESBYTERIAN AIDS NETWORK
The Reverend Jim Hedges
John Calvin Presbyterian Church
6501 Nebraska Avenue
Tampa, FL 33604

PRESBYTERIAN CHURCH (U.S.A.)
The Reverend David Zuverink
100 Witherspoon Street
Louisville, KY 40202
Phone: 502 569 5793

UNION OF AMERICAN HEBREW CONGREGATIONS
Rabbi Richard Sternberger, UAH
2027 Massachusetts Avenue NW
Washington, DC 20036
Phone: 202 232 4242

UNITARIAN UNIVERSALIST ASSOCIATION
Rev. Scott Alexander
25 Beacon Street
Boston, MA 02108

UNITED CHURCH OF CHRIST
The Reverend Bill Johnson
UCBHM AIDS Program
475 Riverside Drive
New York, NY 10115
Phone: 212 870 2100

UNITED METHODIST CHURCH
Health and Welfare Ministries
General Board of Global Ministries
The United Methodist Church, Room #350
475 Riverside Drive
New York, NY 10115
Phone: 212 870 3871

UNIVERSAL FELLOWSHIP OF METROPOLITAN COMMUNITY CHURCHES
The Reverend A. Stephen Pieters
5300 Santa Monica Boulevard
Los Angeles, CA 90029

This listing has been provided by the Ministers and Missionaries Benefit Board of the American Baptist Churches, 475 Riverside Drive, Room 1700, New York, NY 10115.

A listing of state and regional religious organizations and task forces and AIDS ministries is available from *The AIDS National Interfaith Network,* 475 Riverside Drive, 10th floor, New York, NY 10115; telephone: 212 870 2100.

What can churches do about AIDS? The American Baptist Benefit Board of Ministers and Ministries has put together *AIDS: A Ministry Resource.* Designed for pastors, the kit is available free in limited quantities from: The American Baptist Benefit Board of Ministers and Ministries, 475 Riverside Drive, Room 1700, New York, NY 10115.

A PRAYER IN A TIME OF AIDS

Lord Jesus, this prayer is offered up within a place where we feel safely separated from sins whispered under our breath. This is our place of quiet rest, where we feel near to the heart of God. And like Peter, we confess that this is a wonderful place, a needed time of renewal, and here we would gladly stay.

We cannot, and must not, remain in this holy isolation. So, we are praying because we know what awaits us when we depart. We need not tell you about AIDS, but we cannot represent your love for those who suffer from AIDS unless you grant us this moment to say that we are confused and confounded by such suffering.

Here we rejoice that all men and women have value in your sight so that all can be redeemed. Out there we give in quickly to emotional responses of condemnation which provide us with the needed excuse to refrain from applying the healing touch of acceptance to persons who have AIDS.

Here we proclaim that all things are possible for God. Out there we quickly lose hope, and resign ourselves to the finality of disease. Fearing death ourselves, we fail to give those who are suffering the presence of a needed friend.

Here we think about God. Out there we think about what other people will think of us if we get too close to someone with AIDS.

Here we pray for healing. Out there we won't even lend our voice as an advocate for a social commitment necessary for healing so that a cure may take place.

Like disciples of many generations, we ask you humbly, "Why don't we have greater results out there because of these sacred moments spent in here?" And we hear you say again, "These cases are only solved by prayers that are put to disciplined work."

Lord Jesus, hear our prayer in this place of quiet reflection, so that there, amid loud and contradictory voices, we might have the power to touch, care, love, and heal. Amen.

FROM THE AMERICAN BAPTIST BENEFIT BOARD OF MINISTERS AND MINISTRIES. USED WITH PERMISSION.

Most religious bodies have made special provisions for prayer in the lives of people who live with AIDS and the rest of the society that lives in a time of AIDS. Here are two examples:

Praying with HIV/AIDS: Collects, Prayers, and Litanies in a Time of Crisis by Randolph Lloyd Frew. Available from an Episcopal publishing house: Forward Movement Publications, 412 Sycamore Street, Cincinnati, OH 45202.

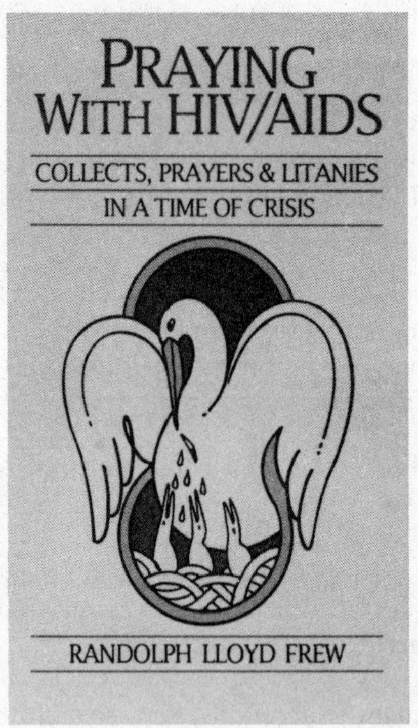

Nothing Can Separate Us from the Love of God: Help from the Scriptures for Coping with AIDS. Available from the American Bible Society, 1865 Broadway, New York, NY 10023.

▼ What to do when someone you know has AIDS is often a confusing and disturbing question. What's appropriate? How do you help without intruding? How can you be supportive without invading someone's privacy? The list of responses on the following page was put together by the staff of a hospital in Illinois. It's one of the most useful and to-the-point set of directions you can find.

TWENTY-FIVE PRACTICAL TIPS FOR CAREGIVERS OF THOSE FACING A SERIOUS ILLNESS

1. Don't avoid me. Be the friend . . . the loved one you've always been.

2. Touch me. A simple squeeze of my hand can tell me you still care.

3. Call to tell me you're bringing my favorite dish, and what time you are coming. Bring food in disposable containers so I won't have to worry about returns.

4. Take care of my children for me. I need a little time to be alone with my loved one. My children may also need a little vacation from my illness.

5. Weep with me when I weep. Laugh with me when I laugh. Don't be afraid to share this with me.

6. Take me out for a pleasure trip, but know my limitations.

7. Call for my shopping list and make a special delivery to my home.

8. Call me before you visit, but don't be afraid to visit. I need you. I am lonely.

9. Help me celebrate holidays (and life) by decorating my hospital room or home, or bringing me tiny gifts of flowers or other natural treasures.

10. Help my family; I am sick, but they may be suffering. Offer to come stay with me to give my loved ones a break. Invite them out. Take them places.

11. Be creative! Bring me a book of thoughts, taped music, a poster for my wall, cookies to share with my family and friends . . . an old friend who hasn't come to visit me.

12. Let's talk about it. Maybe I need to talk about my illness. Find out by asking me: "Do you feel like talking about it?"

13. Don't always feel we have to talk. We can sit silently together.

14. Can you take me or my children somewhere? I may need transportation to a treatment . . . to a store . . . to the doctor.

15. Help me feel good about my looks. Tell me I look good, considering my illness.
16. Please include me in decision making; I've been robbed of so many things. Please don't deny me a chance to make decisions about my family . . . in my life.
17. Talk to me of the future. Tomorrow, next week, next year. Hope is so important to me.
18. Bring me a positive attitude. It's catching!
19. What's in the news? Magazines, photos, newspapers, verbal reports keep me from feeling the world is passing me by.
20. Could you help me with some cleaning? During my illness, my family and I still face dirty clothes, dirty dishes, and a dirty home.
21. Water my flowers.
22. Just send a card to say . . . I care!
23. Pray for me and share your faith with me.
24. Tell me what you'd like to do for me and when I agree, please do it!
25. Tell me about support groups like the AIDS Support Group so I can share with others.

CONDENSED FROM THE BROCHURE "25 TIPS TO HELP THOSE FACING A SERIOUS ILLNESS," ST. ANTHONY'S HOSPITAL, ALTON, ILLINOIS. SPECIAL THANKS TO ST. ANTHONY'S MAKE TODAY COUNT FOR REPRINTING PERMISSION. ADDITIONAL COPIES AVAILABLE, WRITE TO ST. ANTHONY'S HOSPITAL, ST. ANTHONY'S WAY, ALTON, IL 62002.

HOW DO YOU CHOOSE A THERAPIST?

According to Michael Shernoff, ACSW, who's in private practice in New York City, "The Process of looking for the right therapist should be no more mysterious than choosing an accountant or attorney. At all times in your search for a therapist you should remember that you are a consumer—and proceed in an informed and intelligent manner. A good psychotherapist is not someone who possesses some absolute truth, but rather a trained professional who should always have your own best interests at heart."

Here's a list of questions Shernoff suggests you ask any prospective therapist:

1. Is the therapist licensed? By whom?
2. What kind of training has this individual completed?
3. What is the therapist's fee?
4. Is there a sliding fee scale?
5. How is payment to be made—weekly or monthly?
6. Is the therapist qualified to receive medical insurance reimbursement?
7. Does this therapist have experience in treating people with similar problems?
8. How often does the therapist suggest you meet?
9. How long are the sessions?
10. How available will he or she be to you during emergencies at odd hours or over weekends?
11. Is there any bias about affectional or sexual orientation?
12. Does the therapist treat other lesbians or gay men?
13. Does the therapist treat any non-gay people?
14. What are the therapist's feelings about the validity of gay and lesbian life-styles?
15. Is the therapist skilled in working with couples?
16. Is the therapist willing to work with you and your lover if the need arises?
17. Does the therapist conduct therapy groups?
18. If not a psychiatrist, is the therapist affiliated with one in case there is a need for medication or hospitalization?

WHAT ARE THE DIFFERENT KINDS OF THERAPISTS?

Who can practice therapy is determined by laws that vary greatly from one state to another. Here is a quick glossary of the more common and legitimate forms of therapy:

A Psychiatrist is an M.D. who has completed at least four years of specialty training in psychiatry. A psychiatrist is the only kind of therapist who can prescribe medications. Psychiatry is the most likely kind of therapy to be covered by health insurance.

A Psychologist needs either a Ph.D. or Ed.D. to be licensed in most states. Not all psychologists have clinical training. It's important to ask a prospective psychologist about the kind of training he or she has completed.

Social Workers can usually enter therapy practice after earning an MSW or other master's degree and, in some states, passing a certifying examination. ACSW after a social worker's name means he or she is nationally accredited as a member of the Academy of Certified Social Workers and is qualified to conduct a self-regulated practice by the National Association of Social Workers.

Psychiatric Nurses sometimes practice therapy. They should have at least an RN degree as well as training in therapy.

Pastoral Counselors are current or former members of the clergy. Some have extensive training in counseling and therapy, but it's important to inquire, since some may only have theological training.

Peer Counselors have no training in therapy. They usually work for community organizations such as gay community centers or rape centers where an empathetic relationship is considered important to a counseling situation.

Psychoanalysis is a specific method of psychotherapy. Any of the above professionals may become psychoanalysts. In order to use the designation legitimately, one must have completed a postgraduate training program at a certified psychoanalytical institute. This is often the most traditional form of therapy and usually the most expensive since it calls for at least two visits a week, and often one a day.

THIS INFORMATION HAS BEEN ADAPTED WITH PERMISSION FROM MICHAEL SHERNOFF'S "HOW TO CHOOSE A PSYCHOTHERAPIST" © 1988 MICHAEL SHERNOFF, 80 EIGHTH AVENUE, NEW YORK, NY 10011.

▼ While the fact that a therapist, counselor—or any other

professional—is gay or lesbian isn't proof that he or she is competent, you might like to make contact with someone who has this empathy with you. Most of these organizations have the means to make a referral for you.

All also have an interest in working with people interested in entering their fields, and sponsor informational meetings, seminars, and other activities for students and trainees.

These groups also work to affect the policy and procedures of the larger organizations within which they operate.

Association of Gay and Lesbian Psychiatrists
1439 Pineville Road
New Hope, PA 18938

Association of
Gay & Lesbian
Psychiatrists

Committee on Lesbian and Gay Concerns
American Psychological Association
1200 17th Street NW
Washington, DC 20036

The Committee on Lesbian and Gay Concerns produces an exceptionally wide range of publications. In addition to a Therapist Roster, listing the names and address and interests of individual therapists, they also provide listings of graduate faculty interested in gay and lesbian issues and abstracts of many research programs. Write to them for a complete list of papers.

Association of Lesbian and Gay Psychologists
2336 Market Street, #8
San Francisco, CA 94114

Gay/Lesbian/Bisexual Interest Group
Society for the Scientific Study of Sex
Box 208
Mt. Vernon, IA 52314

Gay/Lesbian/Bisexual Interest Group
American Association of Sex Educators, Counselors and Therapists
11 Dupont Circle NW, Suite 220
Washington, DC 20036

OTHER GAY HEALTH ISSUES

While AIDS is certainly the overwhelming health concern of gay men, it is of course not the only health issue. Even before the AIDS crisis, the gay community had begun to build a series of health clinics and resources that could respond to unique issues in our lives. If many of them have now become AIDS clinics, in fact, they also continue to provide other comprehensive services. Three of the most prominent gay and lesbian specific clinics are:

Whitman-Walker Clinic, Inc.
1407 S Street NW
Washington, DC 20009
Phone: 202 797 3500

The Chase-Brexton Clinic
241 W. Chase Street
Baltimore, MD 21201
Phone: 301 837 2050

Howard Brown Memorial Clinic
945 W. George Street
Chicago, IL 60657
Phone: 312 871 5777

THE CHASE-BREXTON CLINIC

▼ *The Fenway Community Health Center* is a model of a clinic in a gay neighborhood that serves an entire geographic neighborhood, but recognizes as its main service group the gay men and women who live in that area and those from all over New England who look to Fenway for special health care.

Fenway Community Health Center
93 Massachusetts Avenue
Boston, MA 02115
Phone: 617 267 0900

▼ *The National Lesbian and Gay Health Foundation, Inc.*'s major activity is putting on a large annual national conference. NLGHF coordinates interests in every possible health care arena that might affect gay people. In addition to the conference, it publishes a *Sourcebook on Lesbian/Gay Health Care* which provides extensive resources concerning gay health services for the consumer and for the provider.

National Lesbian and Gay Health Foundation, Inc.
Box 65472
Washington, DC 20035
Phone: 202 797 3708

▼ *Education in a Disabled Gay Environment, Inc.*, is a nonprofit organization devoted to providing support services for the physically disabled members of the gay and lesbian community. Founded by people who were themselves disabled, EDGE holds regular meetings in its New York base and works with groups in other areas dealing with the same issues.

EDGE
Box 305, Village Station
New York, NY 10014

MYTHS AND FACTS ABOUT THE GAY DISABLED

Myth: Gay disabled people are not sexual.

Fact: Disabled people have the same sexual and emotional needs as everyone else. We are sexual, we can give and receive love and establish relationships. Many disabled gays and lesbians are in loving, adult relationships.

Myth: The disabled are deformed and unattractive.

Fact: Many of us do not have visible signs of disability and not all visible disabilities are unattractive. Beauty is in the eye of the beholder.

Myth: There are no disabled gay men or women.

Fact: Ten percent of the population is gay and lesbian. Therefore it is common sense to assume a percentage is physically disabled.

Myth: Disabled lesbians and gays isolate themselves by choice.

Fact: Isolation is rarely a matter of choice. Physical barriers and society's prejudices can cause isolation and withdrawal.

Myth: The disabled are unable to make their own choices or decisions.

Fact: Disabled individuals are often not asked what they want; it is assumed their dependencies are across the board. Just because someone cannot do what they want does not mean they don't know what they want.

Myth: The disabled are an embarrassment.

Fact: The public response to the disabled is often one of embarrassment and discomfort. We are an embarrassment of riches and have the same variety of skills and talents as everyone else. Disabled does not mean un-abled!

Myth: The disabled have nothing to offer and cannot be helpful.

Fact: Many disabled people hold valuable positions in all walks of life regardless of our balance and posture.

REPRINTED WITH THE PERMISSION OF EDGE.

▼ A special health concern for many gay men comes after surgery that results in a colostomy, an ileostomy, or a urostomy. There's now a special committee of the *United Ostomy Association* that helps gay men and lesbians who've had this surgery. For information:

GLCC
United Ostomy Association
36 Executive Park, Suite 120
Irvine, CA 92714

SAFE SEX

WEARING CONDOMS SAVES LIVES!

The virus that is believed to trigger Acquired Immune Deficiency Syndrome (AIDS) is carried in semen. Tests have shown that, used properly with a water-soluble lubricant, a latex condom is an effective way to stop transmission of the virus. Condoms are readily available, inexpensive, and—when used properly—are good protection. Learn to use them. It takes practice.

- Practice while jerking off, before you use them in sexual encounters.
- Don't give up after one try. It takes a while to get used to them.
- Squeeze the air out of the tip before you start putting it on.
- Don't place the head of the penis all the way into the end of the condom. Let about ¼ – ½ inch of the condom extend beyond the tip of the penis.
- Unroll the condom until it is as close as possible to the pubic bone.
- Only buy condoms made of latex (lambskin-membrane condoms break more easily). Condoms in airtight packages are usually best.
- Use a good lubricant and lots of it. Use only water-soluble lube (like K-Y). Petroleum-based lubricants damage latex condoms.
- Use a condom every time you have sexual intercourse.
- Put the condom on early in your sex play and before any penetration is made.
- To avoid leakage, pull out soon after ejaculating (holding firmly onto the end of the condom).
- If you want to be absolutely safe, pull out before ejaculating.
- Wash your hands and genitals immediately after having sex.
- Don't carry unpackaged condoms around in your wallet.

PLAY SAFELY!

FROM *THE FRONT PAGE.* REPRINTED WITH PERMISSION.

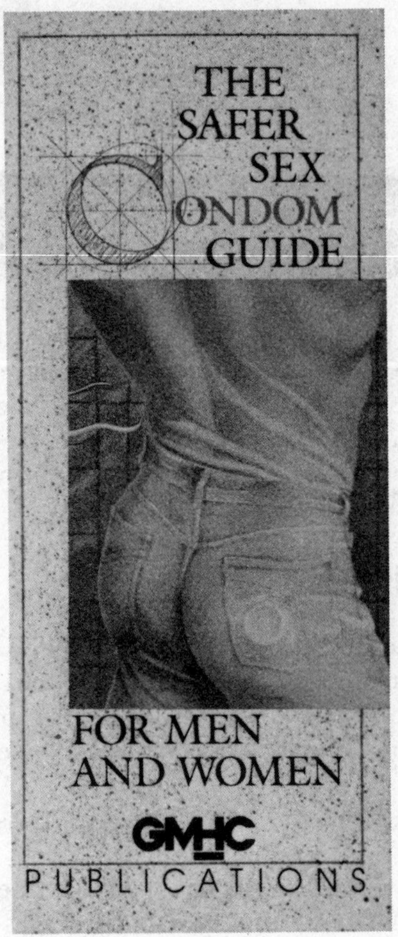

▼ Louise Hay has become one of the most persistent faces in the AIDS crisis. A survivor of cancer herself, she's taken her learning about healing and delivered it to people living with AIDS through books, audio cassettes, workshops, and public-speaking appearances.

For a complete catalog of her materials contact:

Hay House, Inc.
501 Santa Monica Boulevard
P. O. Box 2212
Santa Monica, CA 90406
Phone: 213 394 7445

▼ Chastity during the health crisis might be the choice of some people, but there's no reason for sex to die. Gay men have a history of sexual deprivation from our pre-liberation days and there's a will to keep it alive, safely, during the AIDS epidemic.

If there's resistance in your community to the idea of safe sex, you should consider putting on *safe sex workshops*. For information on how they might work, contact Gay Men's Health Crisis and order a copy of *Eroticizing Safe Sex: A Facilitator's Guide* by Luis Palacios-Jiminez and Michael Shernoff.

Gay Men's Health Crisis
129 W. 20th Street
New York, NY 10011

▼ Safe sex education programs are among the most important activities of AIDS organizations. Of course we need to take care of people who are ill, but we also need to work on prevention.

One of the most innovative and successful programs has been *Friends for Life,* organized by a group in North Carolina. For more information on their distribution of materials and instructional information, write to them:

NCHRF
Box 26284
Raleigh, NC 27611

PART SIX

GAY SPORTS

It wasn't too long ago that the locker room was the symbol of everything gay men were supposed to hate about the world, and ourselves. If an old pioneer were to suddenly come back to life in present-day gay America and Canada, possibly one of the most amazing things to him would be the development of gay athletics—not just the well-defined body that so many gay men now have, but the sight of the Gay Games and other major athletic competitions among gay men.

Coming out into athletics makes sense in terms of making all forms of activity available to us; that would be one of the goals of political and social equality. Gay sports have other reasons for existing, though. To hate our bodies was one of the repercussions of our position in society. We had been told so long that we were ugly, we believed it. Now that we're starting to see the worth in our lives, we can also reclaim our bodies. Many men now say that their pride in their torsos reflect the pride in themselves. Team sports have another function, as well: they are a means by which gay men have learned to bond with one another. Competitive sports—both individual and team activities—are a way for men to challenge themselves and learn their own strength and ability.

THE GAY GAMES

The Federation of Gay Games is the outgrowth of the founding organization of the Gay Games, San Francisco Arts & Athletics, Inc.

The Federation was founded to coordinate the Gay Games and Cultural Festival that are held every four years. The 1990 Gay Games were held in Vancouver; the 1994 games are scheduled for New York City.

THE FEDERATION OF GAY GAMES

The Federation helps host organizations and the international sporting world and major cultural organizations with communications, planning, promotional, and financial resources to ensure the success of the Gay Games.

For more information on the Gay Games in general:

The Federation of Gay Games
584 Castro Street, Suite 343
San Francisco, CA 94114

For information on Gay Games IV to be held in New York City in 1994:

New York in '94
Box 202, Times Square Station
New York, NY 10036

ATHLETIC ORGANIZATIONS

The Gay Games have led many cities to organize umbrella organizations. While a major purpose was to sponsor teams to the 1990 Gay Games in Vancouver, the organizations also act as communication and coordinating councils for activities year round. The teams for various specific sports—swimming, soccer, volleyball, etc.—are often difficult to locate, though the local gay newspaper is always a good source of information. These coordinating councils are another good bet on how to make contact with the team sports that you're most interested in.

UNITED STATES

■ ARIZONA ■

TEAM ARIZONA
c/o Mark Sandau
2945 N. 19th Avenue, #69
Phoenix, AZ 85015

TEAM GLENDALE
c/o S. Chamlius
13818 N. 47th Avenue
Glendale, AZ 85306

■ CALIFORNIA ■

TEAM LONG BEACH
c/o Dan Coles
1861 Britton Avenue
Long Beach, CA 90814

TEAM LOS ANGELES
c/o Kim McConnell
3641 W. 132nd Street
Hawthorne, CA 90250

PENINSULA AREA GAMES ASSOCIATION
c/o Margo Dutton
199 Buckthorn
Menlo Park, CA 94205

SACRAMENTO ATHLETIC GAMES ASSOCIATION
c/o Paul Coke
4610 Attawa Avenue
Sacramento, CA 95822

ATHLETES IN MOTION
c/o Barth Hopple
Box 33113
San Diego, CA 92103

TEAM SAN DIEGO
c/o Leslie Menitti
3841 Fourth Avenue, #255
San Diego, CA 92103

TEAM SAN FRANCISCO
c/o Nancy Warren
2215 R Market Street, #519
San Francisco, CA 94114

SAN JOAQUIN VALLEY SPORTS
Box 11490
Fresno, CA 93773

TEAM SAN JOSE
c/o Jan Williams
4469 Elmhurst Drive
San Jose, CA 95129

TEAM SANTA BARBARA
c/o Dale Teissier
2215 A.P.S.
Santa Barbara, CA 93103

■ COLORADO ■

COLORADO ATHLETIC EXCHANGE
c/o Dana Laessle
4571 Grove Street
Denver, CO 80211

■ DISTRICT OF COLUMBIA ■

TEAM DC
c/o Joseph Scheper
1745 Willard Street NW
Washington, DC 20009

■ GEORGIA ■

TEAM ATLANTA
c/o Larry Lucas
737-240 Peachtree Street
Atlanta, GA 30303

■ HAWAII ■

O.H.A.N.A.
c/o Bob Weaver
2222 Aloha Drive, #801
Honolulu, HI 96815

■ ILLINOIS ■

TEAM CHICAGO
c/o Peg Grey
809 S. Thurlow
Hinsdale, IL 60521

■ KENTUCKY ■

TEAM LOUISVILLE
c/o Rita Perkins
2427 Sherry Road
Louisville, KY 40217

■ MICHIGAN ■

TEAM DETROIT
c/o Esther Radgowski
3212 Belmont
Hamtramck, MI 48212

■ MINNESOTA ■

TEAM MINNEAPOLIS
c/o Ann DeGroot
310 E. 38th Street, Room 204
Minneapolis, MN 55409

■ MISSOURI ■

TEAM KANSAS CITY
c/o Sandy Hubbard
1008 W. 33rd St.
Kansas City, MO 64111

■ NEW YORK ■

TEAM NEW YORK
c/o Tom Cracovia
Box 902, Peck Slip Station
New York, NY 10127

■ NORTH CAROLINA ■

TEAM NORTH CAROLINA
c/o Mardy Carter
604 Chapel Hill Street
Durhan, NC 27701

■ OHIO ■

TEAM CINCINNATI
c/o Dennis Buttelwerth
Box 141102
Cincinnati, OH 45250

■ OREGON ■

CASCADE ATHLETICS
c/o Dan Brenton
527 E. Eighteenth Avenue
Eugene, OR 97401

TEAM PORTLAND
c/o Dave Corral
37 N.W. Trinity Place, #18
Portland, OR 97209

■ PENNSYLVANIA ■

FRONTRUNNERS PHILADELPHIA
Box 30115
Philadelphia, PA 19107

■ TEXAS ■

TEAM AUSTIN
c/o Paul Hallet
705 W. 32nd Street, Apt. A
Austin, TX 78705

TEAM DALLAS
c/o Jerry Strittmatter
4012-B Cedar Springs
Dallas, TX 75219

TEAM HOUSTON
c/o Felix Garcia
Box 542257
Houston, TX 77254

TEAM SAN ANTONIO
c/o Jack Green
Box 15933
San Antonio, TX 78212

■ UTAH ■

TEAM SALT LAKE
c/o Kris Justesen
95 S. Main, Box 306
Orangeville, UT 84537

■ WASHINGTON ■

TEAM SEATTLE
c/o Rick Petersen
2308 E. Lee Street
Seattle, WA 98112

CANADA

■ BRITISH COLUMBIA ■

METROPOLITAN VANCOUVER ATHLETIC AND ARTS ASSOCIATION
1170 Bute Street
Vancouver, BC V6E 1Z6
Phone: 604 684 3303

■ ONTARIO ■

TEAM TORONTO
5334 Yonge Street, Box 1214
Toronto, ON M2N 6M2

THIS LIST WAS DEVELOPED BY THE METROPOLITAN VANCOUVER ATHLETIC AND ARTS ASSOCIATION, THE HOSTS OF THE 1990 GAY GAMES. REPRINTED WITH PERMISSION.

IF YOU'D LIKE TO GET A NEW TAKE ON THE HISTORY OF GAY MEN AND SPORTS, FIND A COPY OF *THE ARENA OF MASCULINITY: SPORTS, HOMOSEXUALITY AND THE MEANING OF SEX* BY BRIAN PRONGER (NEW YORK: ST. MARTIN'S PRESS, 1990).

GAY SKI CLUBS

UNITED STATES

■ CALIFORNIA ■

ARRIBA (LOS ANGELES)
Phone: 213 393 2962

SAGA/LOS ANGELES
Phone: 818 994 2444

SAGA/NORTH (SAN FRANCISCO)
Phone: 415 995 2772

SAGA (SAN DIEGO)
Box 3203
San Diego, CA 92103

■ COLORADO ■

COLORADO OUTDOOR AND SKI ASSOCIATION
Phone: 303 470 9658

■ DISTRICT OF COLUMBIA ■

DC ADVENTURERS
Phone: 202 364 0985

DOWNHILLERS
3632 Wilson Place, NW
Washington, DC 20008
Phone: 202 364 0985

MASSACHUSETTS

CHILTERN MOUNTAIN CLUB
Phone: 617 266 3812

PENNSYLVANIA

GO (PHILADELPHIA)
Phone: 215 698 6617

TEXAS

OAKLAWN CLUB
Phone: 214 358 0427

CANADA

ONTARIO

OUT AND OUT (TORONTO)
Toronto's Gay and Lesbian Outdoors Club
Box 331, Station F
Toronto, ON M4Y 2L7
Phone: 416 694 8405

PHOTO © STONEWALL CLIMBERS. REPRINTED WITH PERMISSION.

▼ Rock climbing is *the* hot sport today. So, of course, there's already a gay group involved in it. *Stonewall Climbers* is a Boston-based association of gay men and lesbians who climb together on trips throughout the continent and the world.

Stonewall Climbers
Box 445
Boston, MA 02124

▼ Bowling is probably the single most popular organized sport among gay men. There are hundreds of recognized gay bowling leagues in the United States and Canada. The ruling body holds an international championship, publishes a magazine, and establishes standards for the various clubs.

International Gay Bowling Organization, Inc.
1730 Pendrell Street, #402
Vancouver, BC V6G 3A3
Phone: 604 689 5146

▼ There are many ways of participating in and enjoying sports and being part of the audience is certainly one of them. There are various—often hard to find—gay clubs around the country where the members are particular fans of a specific team or sport. *The Center,* New York's Community Center, has a wonderful structure, *Center Sports,* which organizes groups to attend professional and amateur sports in the New York metropolitan area. It's an easy and good way to encourage socialization.

Center Sports
The Center
208 W. 13th Street
New York, NY 10011

CENTER SPORTS

▼ Nudism is one form of outdoor activity. If you're interested in fun *au naturel,* you might want to contact this group that organizes special events in the Ohio area.

Ohio Gay Naturists Association
26500 Wildcat Road
Rockbridge, OH 43149

OUTDOORS ORGANIZATIONS

While there are always more leagues for organized sports, an effective and popular form of gay sports socializing is a simple communal pleasure in the outdoors. Loose gatherings of men who are interested in hiking, camping, bicycling, and other noncompetitive athletic events are among the easiest to establish.

Bob Terry of *Adventuring Outdoors,* a group in Austin, Texas, passes on these pointers from his group's experience, if you'd like to find others to share the outside with you:

"First, we try to be conscious of ourselves as a nonmembership organization whose purpose is networking and getting outings publicized, rather than a 'club,' or the pitfall of many gay organizations, a 'clique.' Anyone is welcome to participate (including a few token straights).

"Second, we have regular get-togethers—monthly potlucks and games parties—at which we socialize and hopefully plan outings. There is a real problem with inertia leading to some months when there is hardly anything listed in our newsletter but *indoor eating* events!

"Third, the all-important newsletter allows those who never come to meetings or who live in the country to stay in touch and appear now and then for the kind of event that interests them. Some guys only go on campouts, some will only play volleyball (which we usually do every Sunday in the summer), some will favor museum trips. We try to be multipurpose and encourage any idea for networking. Perhaps we are too broad, but when a great deal of interest pops up around one activity, there is usually a "spin-off"; people once associated with our group have gone on to devote most of their energies to organizing local bicycling, jogging, and bowling organizations. (We try to stay in touch with these other activity/athletic groups and cross-publicize certain things.)

"Fourth, related to concentrations on certain sports, I would recommend any group of a good size to do what a group in Houston has done: have a 'contact person' for each of several activities. I believe they have about ten such people listed in each newsletter, with their phone numbers, for spontaneous networking and event planning during a given month. This allows people to draw up plans after the newsletter deadlines. Often you can't realistically expect to know a month ahead of time that you will want to bike or canoe on a certain weekend.

"Fifth, I would also suggest a group to conduct themselves relatively democratically, with clear duties for the chore-maids and a 'term of office.' One group has five positions, elected yearly with duties like publicity, newsletter, meeting leader, event encourager, etc."

Following is a listing of gay outdoor organizations.

UNITED STATES

ARIZONA

TUCSON GREAT OUTDOORS
3750 Country Club Road, Suite 44
Tucson, AZ 85716

CALIFORNIA

ORANGE COUNTY GREAT OUTDOORS
Box 426
Garden Grove, CA 92642

LOS ANGELES GREAT OUTDOORS
Box 93247
Los Angeles, CA 90093

POMONA/SAN GABRIEL VALLEY GREAT OUTDOORS
Box 2943
Pomona, CA 91769

INLAND EMPIRE GREAT OUTDOORS
Box 56586
Riverside, CA 92517

CHANNEL ISLANDS GREAT OUTDOORS
Box 992
Samis, CA 93066

SAN DIEGO GREAT OUTDOORS
Box 82106
San Diego, CA 92138

SAN LUIS OBISPO GREAT OUTDOORS
Box 1512
San Luis Obispo, CA 93406

SANTA CRUZ GREAT OUTDOORS
Box 2143
Santa Cruz, CA 95063

■ MASSACHUSETTS ■

THE CHILTERN MOUNTAIN CLUB
Box 407
Boston, MA 02117

■ TEXAS ■

ADVENTURING OUTDOORS
Bob Terry
Box 345
Austin, TX 78767

HOUSTON OUTDOOR GROUP
Box 980893
Houston, TX 77082

CANADA

■ NOVA SCOTIA ■

OUT AND ABOUT
Phone: 902 423 7129

■ ONTARIO ■

OUT AND OUT
Toronto's Gay and Lesbian Outdoors Club
Box 331, Station F
Toronto, ON M4Y 2L7
Phone: 416 694 8405

ADDRESSES OF LOCAL GREAT OUTDOORS ORGANIZATIONS WERE PROVIDED BY CALIFORNIA GREAT OUTDOORS, INC.

▼ Philadelphia's *Humboldt Society* isn't a sports organization, but it is an outdoors group.

"In an effort to move toward a better understanding of natural history, and to reclaim our concealed past, lesbian and gay naturalists formed the Humboldt Society in 1983.

"The group is dedicated to the pursuit of increased awareness about our world and the phenomena that characterize it.

"The group participates in monthly educational/social meetings and frequent field trips for birding, botanizing, and related nature study."

The society is named for *Baron Friedrich Wilhelm Alexander von Humboldt* (1769–1859). The society's brochure explains:

"Though his fame and notoriety circled the globe, and people everywhere are acquainted with his endeavors, few know (or admit) that Humboldt was gay. His encyclopedic knowledge, remarkably handsome features, and capacity for developing deep friendships drew many gifted young scientists to his side. The famed Aimé Bonpland journeyed with Alexander throughout the wilds of South and Central America and they were, in Humboldt's words, "Connected by the most intimate ties of friendship."

"While Humboldt's gayness was no secret to his contemporaries, over the years this aspect of his life has been concealed by biographers and apologists. This conspiracy of silence has deprived gay men and women everywhere of a valuable part of their heritage."

The Humboldt Society
2030 Fitzwater Street
Philadelphia, PA 19146

LIBERATING THE WORKOUT ROOM

Probably the most amazing change in gay men's lives in the past two decades has been the invasion of the gym. While pre-Stonewall gays seemed to think the workout room was out-of-bounds to them, now gay men have turned the gymnasium into their new social center. The newcomer, though, may have a hard time maneuvering his way through the introductory stage. Even though most gyms have some form of training program for even the most uninitiated, men like to have some idea of what's involved, and many would like to begin their work in the privacy of their homes.

Bob Summer, coauthor of *Getting Strong, Looking Strong: A Guide to Successful Bodybuilding,* has agreed to give the following original presentation of the fundamental texts—and videotapes—of bodybuilding:

Stonewall was only five years past when Charles Gaines and George Butler's *Pumping Iron: The Art and Sport of Bodybuilding* stoked the rising fascination with all things physical by showing how the muscle subculture pursued the body beautiful. Single-handedly the surprising bestseller—which later became a popular movie starring Arnold Schwarzenegger—catapulted that subculture into the mainstream, and sent even pin-striped stockbrokers into sweaty gyms in pursuit of bulbous pecs, brawny arms, ribbed abs, and tight buns.

And gays, buoyed by the heightened consciousness stemming from Stonewall, latched onto bodybuilding as a route to improving our self-image and scurried to gyms in steadily growing numbers. Today "sets," "reps," "ripped," and "Nautilus machines"—lingo that came out of the bodybuilding gym—crop up in conversations among gays so frequently that the world first mapped by Gaines and Butler now seems almost quaint. Indeed the gay presence in bodybuilding has become so pronounced that despite the charade of bodybuilding's puritanical officialdom, physique competitions are often showcases for oiled-and-pumped muscular marvels who are gay. Mr. America, the National Physique Championships, Mr. Universe, Mr. Olympia (bodybuilding's own Superbowl)—you name the contest, and gays are among its roster of annual winners.

Nonetheless bodybuilding can seem pretty arcane to the guy just starting out to beef up and define his body. And much of the bogus printed material that has gushed out during the so-called fitness revolution of the past decade or so hasn't helped much. Most of the bodybuilding books published since *Pumping Iron*—which was revised in 1982 and is still in print from Simon and Schuster—are essentially photo collections with sparse uninformative texts as filler. And the magazines, though glitzier, are so notoriously sophomoric that a leading southwestern gym owner advises his trainees (especially beginners) to look only at the photos in most of the magazines, and pay no attention to the fluff pawned off as articles.

But there's always an exception that proves the rule. And among bodybuilding magazines, that's *Ironman,* which in its enlarged and redesigned format regularly beats the competition hands-down by getting out the news more promptly, using the best photographers in the bodybuilding shutter-fraternity, and in finding lively writers to convey credible information. The imaginative editors, for example, scored a breakthrough by publishing a perceptive article on homophobia in the gym and featured an interview in which the subject—Bob Paris, celebrated worldwide by physique aficionados for his rare combination of movie-star handsomeness, elegantly proportioned muscularity, and posing artistry—candidly talked at length for the first time about being gay. (By contrast, a rival magazine gave a forum to a multi-titled "star" frothing with an anti-gay diatribe.) *Ironman* is published monthly in the Southern California mecca of bodybuilding:

Ironman
13348 Beach Avenue
Marina Del Rey, CA 90292

When it comes to bodybuilding books, the situation is just the reverse of the proliferating magazine scene. At last count there were seven national bodybuilding magazines to choose from, plus two other lackluster general fitness magazines with bodybuilding information, for men on the nation's newsstands. But bodybuilding books seem to have worn out their welcome at publishers, many of whom elusively sought another *Pumping Iron* phenomenon during the seventies and early eighties. Much of what resulted, as previously noted, was dross or at best exploitative. Still, a few rose above that characteristically low level, and the best remain in print. These include the following, listed in order of the worth of their advice and completeness of content:

Beyond Built: Bob Paris' Guide to Achieving the Ultimate Look by Bob Paris. New York: Warner Books, 1991.

Long before he came out, Paris (Mr. America, Mr. Universe) captured the gay imagination with his sensational handsomeness, symmetrical muscularity, and artistry on the posing dias. For his legion of fans, he symbolizes the ultimate blending of aesthetics and athletics that is bodybuilding's unique allure. In this well-integrated paperback guide he covers the exercises, nutrition, and personal-care methods used to attain his harmonious perfection. Better rounded and less didactic than most bodybuilding manuals, its contents and superstar notes "are like a map and compass. They are the tools to help you find the way." The many photographs provide added inspiration for that journey of self-mastery.

The Nautilus Bodybuilding Book by Ellington Darden, foreword by Mike Mentzer. Chicago: Contemporary Books, 1989.

Darden, a Ph.D. in exercise science, evidences his abundant knowledge in a guide for bodybuilders at all levels that relates the history and concept of the pumping-iron game to the revolutionary workout machines he learned inside-out as director of Nautilus Sports/Medical Industries. Mentzer is the former Mr. Universe who once graced *The Advocate*'s cover. For its latest printing—the fourteenth—Darden revised his 1986 edition and added the most up-to-date information available on the Nautilus method of muscle building.

100 High Intensity Ways to Improve Your Bodybuilding by Ellington Darden. New York: Perigee Books, 1989.

Don't even think about buying the hefty *Encyclopedia of Modern Bodybuilding* by Arnold Schwarzenegger (with Bill Dobbins)—even at a bargain remainder price. Darden's succinct compendium of practical advice for productive bodybuilding is better organized, easier to use, and, yes, even more reliable. And the smashing photographs by Chris Lund of champion bodybuilders working out and in competition are positively inspiring. No wonder this handy training companion became a national bestseller within a month of publication.

Arnold: The Education of a Bodybuilder by Arnold Schwarzenegger and Douglas K. Hall. New York: Pocket Books, 1977.
Arnold's Bodybuilding for Men by Arnold Schwarzenegger and Bill Dobbins. New York: Simon & Schuster, 1984.

Arnold—his legion of fans called him "The Oak" during his long reign as bodybuilding's Top Man—has "gone Hollywood" since these two books were published. And that's a good thing for him, too; he has much more of an impact on the flickering screen than he does in an exercise book. But although each set of exercise instructions rarely rises above the basic and anecdotal, both are sound and will give the trainee a solid footing in principles and methods. And Arnold, unlike Darden, made it big by using free weights, which beginners most often associate with bodybuilding exercise.

Legendary Abs. Health for Life, 8033 Sunset Boulevard, Suite 483, Los Angeles, CA 90046.

Follow the easy-to-use manual's innovative instructions and watch that pudgy tummy turn to rock-hard muscle in a surprisingly short time. Talk about scientific principles applied to bodybuilding! This is a Class A example.

But books and magazines aren't the sole media aspiring bodybuilders can turn to for guidance. Taking a tip from the success of the Jane Fonda workout tapes, muscle-oriented entrepreneurs have achieved a fairly high level of sophistication with these popular methods of infotainment. The pick of the pack of bodybuilding video and audio cassettes now available are:

I Want to Pump You Up! Video starring Lee Labrada, Mr. Universe.

No, this isn't x-rated, although the perfectly developed Labrada is easy to look at. But he has the smarts to match the size of his muscles, and he's articulate, too. His intelligent dedication to bodybuilding will be highly motivating to the beginner. Order from:

Gym Rats
Box 691203
Houston, TX 77269

A Mr. Universe Physique . . . In Half the Time. Audio by Lee Labrada.

And you will listen, if you're savvy and want to turn your body into a work of art even half as exquisite as his. He talks you through a complete workout, and tells you about nutrition, programming for progress, and keeping motivated. Also order from Gym Rats, address above.

The Complete Man: Body Training Video. Francois Muse.

For beginners. If everyone had Muse—a popular California bodybuilder—as his personal instructor when he began bodybuilding, we might well be a nation of Mr. Americas. Visually he's a hard-to-top role model, and when he goes through his paces in the gym, he explains what he's doing so effectively that at the end of the hour-long cassette there's likely to be no questions asked—everyone, pumped up with excitement, will be making a beeline for the gym. Order from:

Video Pump
Box 1600
Rosemead, CA 91770

Both Labrada and Muse emphasize adding aerobic exercise to weight training (an anaerobic activity) for a healthily balanced bodybuilding regimen. Many bodybuilders use biking for this part of their program, and include *Bicycling,* the world's leading cycling magazine, in their monthly reading, along with the bodybuilding magazines. Others take the running route and become avid fans of *Runner's World,* claimed by many fitness buffs to be *the* outstanding fitness magazine today. And occasionally highly motivated athletes/ bodybuilders will cross-train in multi-sport forms to gear up for triathalon competitions; you're likely to see *Triathlete* sticking out of their gym bags. Bodybuilding has become so pervasive in fitness-oriented America that it has become a life-style. Ironically that—a life-style—is what it was to the coterie of muscle addicts featured in *Pumping Iron.* There's now a big difference, though; muscles are out of the closet. Even Macy's sells Gold's Gym T-shirts.

LIST © BOB SUMMER, 1990. REPRINTED WITH PERMISSION.

Arcadia Bodybuilding Society is a nonprofit corporation headquartered in San Francisco, where it holds the annual *International Lesbian and Gay Bodybuilding Championship* (it carries the name Physique [year]) on the day before the Lesbian and Gay Freedom Day Parade in June.

Arcadia Bodybuilding Society
1455A Market St.
San Francisco, CA 94103

JOSE ALVARADO AND RON ALVAREZ WON MEDALS IN THEIR DIVISIONS IN PHYSIQUE '89. PHOTO BY SAVAGE. REPRINTED WITH THE PERMISSION OF ARCADIA BODYBUILDING SOCIETY.

TOP TEN AEROBICS MUSIC

To do a decent aerobics exercise, you have to have the right background music. Sweaters and strainers around the country have their own favorites, but this list of the best was compiled by Wayland Garris, Club Aerobics Coordinator for Spa Health Clubs in Raleigh, North Carolina.

1. *Do You Want to Funk?* Sylvester. (Sylvester was and is the undisputed queen of elevated heart-rate maintenance. The child did no wrong. Flawless.)
2. *Call Me.* Sylvester.
3. *Loving Is Really My Game.* Sylvester.
4. *It's Raining Men.* The Weather Girls.
5. *Baby, I'm a Star.* Prince.
6. *Babe, We're Gonna Love Tonight.* Lime.
7. *New Attitude.* Patti LaBelle.
8. *Coming Out of Hiding.* Pamela Stanley.
9. *Rush Hour.* Jane Wiedlin.
10. *Tie:*
    Jump. The Pointer Sisters.
    Gloria. Laura Branigan.

Honorable Mentions:
Think/Respect Mix, Aretha Franklin; *So Excited,* The Pointer Sisters; *Rock into My Heart,* The Jets; *Jump to the Music,* Lila; *Breakdancing,* Irene Cara.

© 1990 WAYLAND GARRIS. REPRINTED WITH PERMISSION.

FRONT RUNNERS

Gay running groups are often the first organized sports organization to be set up in any city. A self-regulating sport that doesn't necessarily need heavy competition, running has also become a social occasion in much of the contemporary urban world. Running together can be an easy, low-pressure activity that gay men can share while they get in shape.

UNITED STATES

■ ARIZONA ■

TUCSON FRONT RUNNERS
3812 E. Pima
Tucson, AZ 85716

■ CALIFORNIA ■

EAST BAY FRONTRUNNERS
P.O. Box 5194
Berkeley, CA 94705

SHORELINE FRONT RUNNERS OF LONG BEACH
P.O. Box 13008
Long Beach, CA 90803

FRONT RUNNERS SAN DIEGO
P.O. Box 3633
San Diego, CA 92103

SAN FRANCISCO FRONT RUNNERS, INC.
1550 California Street
Suite 6200
San Francisco, CA 94109

FRONTRUNNERS TRACK CLUB OF GREATER LOS ANGELES
P.O. Box 5038
Santa Monica, CA 90405

■ COLORADO ■

DENVER FRONTRUNNERS
P.O. Box 18462
Denver, CO 80218

■ DISTRICT OF COLUMBIA ■

DC FRONT RUNNERS
P.O. Box 65550, Washington Square Station
Washington, DC 20035

■ FLORIDA ■

SOUTH FLORIDA FRONT RUNNERS
P.O. Box 100503
Ft. Lauderdale, FL 33310

■ ILLINOIS ■

FRONTRUNNERS/FRONTWALKERS CHICAGO
P.O. Box 148313
Chicago, IL 60614-8313

■ KENTUCKY ■

LOUISVILLE FRONTRUNNERS
1221 Bardstown Road
Louisville, KY 40204

■ MARYLAND ■

BALTIMORE FRONT RUNNERS
P.O. Box 22181
Baltimore, MD 21203

■ MASSACHUSETTS ■

FRONTRUNNERS BOSTON
P.O. Box 423, Back Bay Annex
Boston, MA 02117

■ MINNESOTA ■

FRONT RUNNERS TRACK CLUB OF MINNEAPOLIS/ST. PAUL, INC.
P.O. Box 3850
Minneapolis, MN 55403

■ MISSOURI ■

FRONTRUNNERS KANSAS CITY
c/o Ellis Thigpen
115 W. 68th Street
Kansas City, MO 64113

■ NEW YORK ■

FRONT RUNNERS NEW YORK, INC.
P.O. Box 363, Village Station
New York, NY 10014

FRONT RUNNERS NY
BOX 363, VILLAGE STATION, NEW YORK, NY 10014

■ OREGON ■

EUGENE FRONTRUNNERS
c/o Hank Alley
48 W. 26th Avenue
Eugene, OR 97405

PORTLAND FRONTRUNNERS
P.O. Box 2164
Portland, OR 97208-2164

■ PENNSYLVANIA ■

FRONTRUNNERS PHILADELPHIA
P.O. Box 30115
Philadelphia, PA 19103

■ TEXAS ■

FRONT RUNNERS HOUSTON
3327 W. Lamar
Houston, TX 77019

RIVER CITY FRONTRUNNERS
c/o Mark Ackerman
2102 W. Magnolia
San Antonio, TX 78201

■ WASHINGTON ■

SEATTLE FRONTRUNNERS
P.O. Box 70501
Seattle, WA 98107-0501

CANADA

■ ONTARIO ■

FRONTRUNNERS TORONTO
c/o Donald Walker
25 Maitland Street, Suite 810
Toronto, ON M4Y 2W1

ADDRESSES PROVIDED BY FRONT RUNNERS, NEW YORK.

PART SEVEN

GAY SPIRITS

Coming out has presented a host of options for gay men as we examine our spiritual lives. Our ability to find one another and build community has meant that we can explore the connections between ourselves. For many men the erotic and sensual is a spiritual experience all its own, and there's no need to invoke any structure or use other language to encounter a dimension beyond our individual experience; sex itself can become a religious event, now that it's not laden with the baggage of self-doubt and self-hatred.

Others have found their own comfort by re-creating in our culture the pattern of spirituality they honored in the straight world. There is a gay denomination, complete with its own seminary, now. Gay subgroups within traditional denominations and Jewish groups have also been established so that gay men, often with lesbians, are able to have what some consider the best of both worlds—a gay congregation within a historic religious context.

The support that gay life can provide us also allows some of us to exist proudly and happily within mainstream congregations, some of which are themselves reaching out to embrace the gay experience as a legitimate part of human life, one worthy of being consecrated and honored.

Religion was once seen as one of the most vicious negative forces working against the development of gay life. Now it is, for many, one of the foundations upon which a gay life can be constructed.

DENOMINATIONAL GAY CHRISTIAN ORGANIZATIONS

Most major denominations have gay and lesbian organizations, some of which have official standing in their respective churches. All these associations have many local groups affiliated with them. For a complete listing, contact their national offices, listed below.

These organizations are also wonderful sources of resources and networking. All have newsletters, some of them quite sophisticated.

The quotes accompanying some of the listings are from the organization's statement of purpose or mission.

American Baptist Churches, USA
American Baptist Concerned
2418 Browning Street
Berkeley, CA 94702
Phone: 415 841 4269

Christian Church (Disciples of Christ)
Affirming Disciples Alliance
Box 19223
Indianapolis, IN 19223

"Our goals include speaking with a prophetic voice calling the Church to break the silence and to name the reality that we are here; we are sons, daughters, brothers, sisters, parents, congregants, pastors, staff. We are created in God's image."

Church of Christian Science
United Lesbian & Gay Christian Scientists, Inc.
256 S. Robertson Boulevard
Box 7467
Beverly Hills, CA 90211
Phone: 213 656 9623

Church of Latter Day Saints (Mormons)
Affirmation
Box 26302
San Francisco, CA 94126
Phone: 415 641 4554

Church of the Brethren
Brethren/Mennonite Council for Lesbian and Gay Concerns
Box 65724
Washington, DC 20035
Phone: 202 462 2595

or

Box 2621
Kitchener, ON N2H 6N2

"We are a group of Brethren and Mennonite women and men who feel that the traditional attitude of the church towards lesbian and gay persons is inconsistent with the Christian ideal. Many members are gay or lesbian, but many are not. Because we value our faith and heritage, we seek to participate fully in the church family. Support from the church will strengthen our daily lives and relationships."

Episcopal Church
Integrity
Box 19561
Washington, DC 20036

Evangelical Lutheran Church
Lutherans Concerned/North America

In the United States:
Box 10461
Chicago, IL 60610

In Canada:
304 Broadway, Box 22171
Winnipeg, MB R3C 4KS

Evangelicals
Evangelicals Concerned
c/o Dr. R. Blair
30 E. 60th Street, Suite 1403
New York, NY 10022
Phone: 212 688 0628

Evangelicals Together, Inc.
7985 Santa Monica Boulevard
Suite 109, Box 16
West Hollywood, CA 90046

"The Mission of Evangelicals Together is to proclaim the Good News of Jesus Christ; and to be a nurturative community of faith where gay and lesbian persons can find affirmation, self-acceptance, healing and wholeness in Jesus Christ, and enablement for Christian ministry."

Jehovah's Witnesses
Jehovah's Witness Gay Support Group
c/o Jim Moon
Box 3744
St. Thomas, VI 00801

Pentecostal
National Gay Pentecostal Alliance
Box 1391
Schenectady, NY 12301
Phone: 518 372 6001

Presbyterian Church, USA
Presbyterians for Lesbian/Gay Concerns
c/o James D. Anderson
Box 38
New Brunswick, NJ 08903-0038
Phone: 210 846 1510

"If you are a Presbyterian . . . who knows and loves someone who is lesbian, gay, or bisexual . . . who believes in affirming the worth of lesbian and gay people and supporting their full participation in the Presbyterian Church . . . who believes that God has yet more light to break forth to inform our knowledge of sexuality and loving relationships . . . then PLGC's ministry is your ministry."

Roman Catholic Church
Dignity, Inc.
1500 Massachusetts Avenue NW
Suite 11F
Washington, DC 20005
Phone: 202 861 0017

"Dignity began as a small rap group in Los Angeles in 1969 . . . we now number approximately 5,000 full members. Dignity is an organization of gay and lesbian Catholics and their friends who believe that through Baptism we all share in the death and resurrection of Christ. As a result, we have an inherent dignity that is preserved and strengthened through the sacramental life of the Church, a life we rightfully share with all Catholics."

New Ways Ministry
4012 29th Street
Mount Ranier, MD 20712

"New Ways Ministry provides a ministry of advocacy and justice for lesbian and gay Catholics and the larger Christian community. It addresses inequalities within Church structures, promotes attitudinal change, and works for acceptance of gay and lesbian persons on all levels through research, education, and community awareness."

Seventh-Day Adventist
Seventh-Day Adventist Kinship International, Inc.
Box 3840
Los Angeles, CA 90078-3840
Phone: 213 876 2076

Society of Friends (Quakers)
Friends for Lesbian & Gay Concerns
Box 222
Sumneytown, PA 18084
Phone: 215 234 8424

"We are primarily gay/lesbian/bisexual people who gather for worship after the manner of Friends (Quakers). All are welcome. FLGC is a place where we help each other on our spiritual and personal journeys. Some come from Quaker meetings, some from other religious groups, some from no particular group. FLGC provides special opportunities to be gay among Friends and to be spiritual within the gay and lesbian community."

Unitarian Universalist Association
Unitarian Universalist Office of Lesbian/Gay Concerns
25 Beacon Street
Boston, MA 02108
Phone: 617 742 2100

"Unitarian Universalism is a religion where differences are respected. Unitarian Universalists thrive on diversity, defending freedom of belief and the worth of every individual. In Unitarian Universalism, lesbians, gays, bisexuals, and transsexuals find the unique opportunity to be a visible part of religious denomination in a positive, life-affirming way."

The United Church of Canada
AFFIRM
Box 1912
Winnipeg, MB R3C 3R2

United Church of Christ
United Church of Christ Coalition for Lesbian/Gay Concerns
18 N. College Street
Athens, OH 45701
Phone: 614 593 7301

United Methodist Church
Affirmation
Box 1021
Evanston, IL 60204
Phone: 312 475 0499

"We welcome to our family all persons who are committed to an inclusive church and society, and we seek to support others who work to bring about that inclusiveness. We affirm the message of the gospel through which all persons are reconciled to God and, through God, to each other. We join with all who seek to celebrate the fullness of God's creation. . . . All of us are at different places in our faith journeys and in the development of our personal identities. Our paths are unique; our abilities varied; our joys and sorrows individual. Yet none of us should have to face our experiences and challenges alone."

A GUIDE TO SPECIFIC MAINSTREAM CONGREGATIONS

A new trend among some liberal Christian denominations has been to identify those congregations that publicly and enthusiastically welcome gay and lesbian members. If you are a church member and your denomination doesn't have such a program, you should find out why. If you belong to one of the following denominations, you can find out more about these programs that already exist within your own tradition:

Evangelical Lutheran Church
Reconciled in Christ
12602 Park Street
Cerritos, CA 90701

"Reconciled in Christ congregations affirm that gay and lesbian people share with all others the worth which comes from being unique individuals created by God; that they are welcome within the membership of their congregation upon making the same affirmation of faith that all other people make; and as members of a congregation, are expected and encouraged to share in the sacramental and general life of their church."

Presbyterian Church, USA
More Light Churches
c/o Presbyterians for Lesbian/Gay Concerns
Box 38
New Brunswick, NJ 08903
Phone: 201 846 1510

"More Light Churches welcome lesbian and gay Christians into full membership in the Presbyterian Church, USA, which includes the opportunity and the responsibility to serve in leadership positions requiring ordination."

Unitarian Universalist Association
Welcoming Congregations
UUA Office of Lesbian Gay Concerns
25 Beacon Street
Boston, MA 02108
Phone: 617 742 2100

"A Welcoming Congregation is inclusive and expressive of the concerns of gay, lesbian, and bisexual persons at every level of congregational life, in worship, in program, and in social occasions, welcoming not only their presence but the unique gifts and particularities of their lives as well."

United Methodist Church
Reconciling Congregation Program
Box 23636
Washington, D.C. 20026
Phone: 202 863 1586

"Reconciling Congregations are local United Methodist Churches which affirm the participation of lesbians, gay men, their families, and friends. Heals the gulf between the United Methodist Church and its gay and lesbian members. Ministers to and with all persons, including lesbians and gay men."

UNIVERSAL FELLOWSHIP OF METROPOLITAN COMMUNITY CHURCHES

The Metropolitan Community Church (MCC) was founded by Rev. Troy Perry as an alternative denomination which would welcome all gay and lesbian people into its fold. MCC has evolved into a complete denomination on its own. It has international missions, a seminary (Samaritan College, 5930 Comey Avenue, Los Angeles, CA 90034), an extensive AIDS ministry and a prison ministry, and a Department of People of Color which, among other things, sponsors an annual conference.

There are hundreds of MCC congregations, missions, and clergy in North America. To make contact, write or call the District Office near you, or the international offices in Los Angeles.

Metropolitan Community Church
International Offices
5300 Santa Monica Boulevard, Suite 304
Los Angeles, CA 90029
Phone: 213 464 5100

UNITED STATES

GREAT LAKES DISTRICT
Judy Dale
1300 Ambridge Drive
Louisville, KY 40207
Phone: 502 897 3821

GULF LOWER ATLANTIC DISTRICT
Jay Neely
First MCC of Atlanta
Box 8356
Atlanta, GA 30306
Phone: 404 523 6823

MID-ATLANTIC DISTRICT
R. Adam DeBaugh
Box 7864
Gaithersburg, MD 20898
Phone: 301 670 1859

MID-CENTRAL DISTRICT
Rev. Bonnie Daniel
1364 Collins Avenue
Topeka, KS 66604
Phone: 913 233 4023

NORTHEAST DISTRICT
Rev. Jeffrey Pulling
Box 340529
Hartford, CT 06134
Phone: 203 296 6512

NORTHWEST DISTRICT
Rev. Edward Sherriff
Box 5795
Sacramento, CA 95817
Phone: 916 454 0170

SOUTH CENTRAL DISTRICT
Clarke Friesen
Box 262822
Houston, TX 77207

SOUTHEAST DISTRICT
Rev. Thomas Bigelow
625 Jefferson Avenue N
Sarasota, FL 34237
Phone: 813 334 4443

SOUTHWEST DISTRICT
Rev. Don Pederson
10913 Fruitland Drive, #117
Studio City, CA 91604
Phone: 818 760 3467

CANADA

EASTERN CANADIAN DISTRICT/DISTRICT DE L'EST DU CANADA
(Eglises communautaires métropolitaines [ECM])
Rod McAvoy
355 Wharncliffe Road, lower apt.
London, ON N6G 1E4
Phone: 519 348 9301

WESTERN CANADA
Bev Baptiste
270 Simcoe Street
Winnipeg, MB R3G 1W1
Phone: 204 775 4134

NAMES AND ADDRESSES SUPPLIED BY THE MCC INTERNATIONAL OFFICES.

▼ Brian McNaught has made a place for himself as an educator on issues of gay identity, especially within a religious context. McNaught, who grew up as an Irish Catholic—he describes his childhood as a time when he attempted to become a "saint"—went on to be an activist in many areas, including two years as the liaison between the gay community and the office of the mayor of Boston.

McNaught has combined his political and religious interests in an eighty-minute videotape that's often used by groups trying to explore issues of gay identity and persecution.

On Being Gay: A Conversation with Brian McNaught is available for $39.95 (plus $3.00 postage and handling) in either VHS or BETA format. For more information:

TRB Productions
Box 2362
Boston, MA 02107

▼ *The Second Stone* is a bimonthly magazine for gay Christians. While it has a noticeably evangelical bent, *The Second Stone* covers news and issues for all denominations. For subscription information:

The Second Stone
Box 8340
New Orleans, LA 70182

▼ Integrity, the gay Episcopal organization, has a publication on how to form an Integrity chapter. The lessons and advice are applicable to anyone wanting to start a local denominational organization. For a copy, write to:

Integrity, Inc.
Box 19561
Washington, DC 20036

GAY AND LESBIAN JEWISH GROUPS

> WHY A JEWISH GAY AND LESBIAN GROUP?
>
> *"Because Jewish gays and lesbians frequently face a complete lack of understanding, even hostility, when they come out to their parents and wider family; because gays and lesbians may be ostracized for not fitting into the expected pattern of marriage and parenthood, this can undermine previously warm family relationships and we know too well of the unhappiness that such a breach can cause; because even being Jewish in the wider gay and lesbian community can have its problems."*
>
> —*JEWISH GAY AND LESBIAN GROUP OF LONDON, ENGLAND*

The following are major congregations and social/political organizations that have been formed for gay and lesbian Jews in North America. Those marked with an asterisk are members of *The World Congress of Gay and Lesbian Jewish Organizations.*

UNITED STATES

■ ARIZONA ■

MISHPOCHAT AM*
P.O. Box 39127
Phoenix, AZ 85069
Phone: 602 249 3949

GAY GEZUNDT
P.O. Box 41684
Tucson, AZ 85717

■ CALIFORNIA ■

BETH CHAYIM CHADASHIM*
6000 W. Pico Boulevard
Los Angeles, CA 90035
Phone: 213 931 7023

CHAVURAH OF ORANGE COUNTY
Box 1444
Laguna Beach, CA 92652
Phone: 714 494 3806

YACHAD*
P.O. Box 3027
San Diego, CA 92104
Phone: 619 224 0202

SHA'AR ZAHAV*
220 Danvers Street
San Francisco, CA 94114
Phone: 415 861 6932

■ COLORADO ■

TIKVAT SHALOM
P.O. Box 6694
Denver, CO 80206

■ CONNECTICUT ■

AM SEGULAH*
P.O. Box 271522
West Hartford, CT 06127
Phone: 203 676 9245

■ DISTRICT OF COLUMBIA ■

BET MISHPACHAH*
P.O. Box 1410
Washington, DC 20013
Phone: 202 833 1638

■ FLORIDA ■

ETZ CHAIM*
19094 W. Dixie Highway
North Miami Beach, FL 33180
Phone: 305 931 9318

■ GEORGIA ■

BET HAVERIM*
P.O. Box 54947
Atlanta, GA 30308
Phone: 404 642 3467

■ ILLINOIS ■

HAVUROT ACHAYOT
P.O. Box 14066
Chicago, IL 60614

OR CHADASH*
656 W. Barry Avenue
Chicago, IL 60657
Phone: 312 248 9456

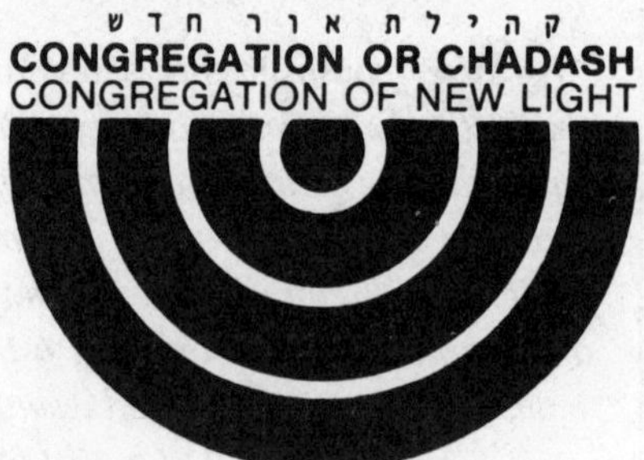

■ KENTUCKY ■

B'NAI SHALOM
c/o Jacobs
642 S. 2nd Street, #1004
Louisville, KY 40202
Phone: 502 583 0528

■ LOUISIANA ■

LAMBDA CHAI NEW ORLEANS
1401 St. Andrew, #122
New Orleans, LA 70130
Phone: 504 566 1361

■ MARYLAND ■

ADATH RAYOOT
c/o Gay Community Center
P.O. Box 22575
Baltimore, MD 21203

■ MASSACHUSETTS ■

AM TIKVA*
P.O. Box 11
Cambridge, MA 02238
Phone: 617 782 8894

■ MICHIGAN ■

SIMCHA*
P.O. Box 652
Southfield, MI 48037
Phone: 313 353 8025

■ MINNESOTA ■

BEYT G'VURAH*
P.O. Box 8503
Minneapolis, MN 55408
Phone: 612 870 1081

■ MISSOURI ■

L'CHA DODI
P.O. Box 32003
Kansas City, MO 64111

■ NEW YORK ■

BETH SIMCHAT TORAH*
P.O. Box 1270, G.P.O.
New York, NY 10116
Phone: 212 929 9498

ZIONIST UNION OF GAYS & LESBIANS, NY
c/o CBST
P.O. Box 1270, G.P.O.
New York, NY 10116

NAYIM*
P.O. Box 18053
Rochester, NY 14618
Phone: 716 546 1381

■ OHIO ■

CHEVREI TIKVA*
P.O. Box 18120
Cleveland, OH 44118
Phone: 216 932 5551

THE WORLD CONGRESS OF GAY & LESBIAN JEWISH ORGANIZATIONS

■ PENNSYLVANIA ■

BETH AHAVAH*
P.O. Box 7566
Philadelphia, PA 19101
Phone: 215 790 0603

■ TEXAS ■

BETH EL BINAH*
P.O. Box 64460
Dallas, TX 75206
Phone: 214 840 3553

■ VIRGINIA ■

BANOT U'VANIM
P.O. Box 11621
Norfolk, VA 23517

WASHINGTON

TIKVAH CHADASHAH*
P.O. Box 2731
Seattle, WA 98111
Phone: 206 329 2590

WISCONSIN

HAVA MACHMIAS
4944 N. Newhall
Milwaukee, WI 53217

CANADA

BRITISH COLUMBIA

THE JEWISH GAY/LESBIAN GROUP
P.O. Box 3556
Vancouver, BC V6B 3Y6

ONTARIO

CHUTZPAH*
P.O. Box 6103, Station A
Toronto, ON M5W 1P5
Phone: 416 323 3564

TORONTO GSH
c/o Wiseberg
15 Arrowstock Road
Willowdale, ON

QUEBEC

YAKHDAV
c/o Brody
3617 Marlowe Avenue
Montreal, QU H4A 3L8
Phone: 514 487 0644

If religion becomes too much for you, you can always get a respite by calling Dial A Gay Atheist: 713 880 4242. The twenty-four-hour-a-day recorded telephone commentary/information line has been in operation for over ten years. It's an outreach program of American Gay Atheists, Inc.

The same organization publishes a newsletter and provides a gay and lesbian presence at the national conventions of American Atheists.

For more information, write:

American Gay Atheists
Box 66711
Houston, TX 77266
Fax: 713 862 3283

OTHER PATHS

BUDDHISTS

From the statement of purpose of *The Buddhist Association of the Gay/Lesbian Community:*

"The purpose of the Buddhist Association of the Gay/Lesbian Community is to serve as a center for the spiritual growth and development of gay and lesbian Buddhists, and to act as a medium for the exchange of ideas and experiences of particular topicality to our place and role in the unfolding of the Buddhidharma. We welcome the participation of gay and lesbian Buddhists of all schools and traditions, however divergent in their practices and viewpoints of the 'Middle Way' and whatever their level of attainment and education in Buddhist thought and life. . . .

We believe that the Buddha, the Dharma and the Sangha have a special meaning and relevance to our community, and we to them. . . ."

For more information:

The Buddhist Association
Box 1974
Bloomfield, NJ 07003

THE GAY SPIRIT

The quest for a spiritual dimension in gay life takes many forms. *Gay Spirit: Myth and Meaning,* edited by Mark Thompson (New York: St. Martin's Press, 1987) is one of the most interesting books to explore the breadth and depth of the subject.

According to Thompson, the psychic and creative energies generated by people we now call gay have always existed on the outer shores of our culture's collective consciousness. In the past, gay people were labeled heretics, perversions of nature, or categorized pseudoscientifically. Gay people lived on the edge of the global village or worked within its mainstream in denial and disguise. But today that spirit has re-emerged and lives among us. *Gay Spirit* suggests ways in which we gay people might find a place and purpose in human culture unique to ourselves, starting with the questions asked nearly forty years ago by the Mattachine Society: Who are we? Where have we come from? Why are we here?

A NEW AGE OPTION

New Age is a movement that's been exploring options to traditional religious thought. Many parts of the New Age movement are gay-friendly though they're often hard to find since the very essence of the movement is antiorganizational. Here is one group that may be of interest to you if you want to examine a New Age option.

Earth Magic is an alternative spiritual path for gays who are interested in defining a new consciousness. According to Julian Spalding and Terry Brown, the major movers behind Earth Magic:

"During the past 5,000 years of history, humans have become isolated from each other and from the planet. Like a branch cut off from the tree, or a limb from the body, we have disconnected from our source of nurturance, forgetting that we are a vital part of the planet itself. We have strayed far from a harmonious relationship with one another, the other creatures, and the world we share.

"But now, the world is awakening. We are witnessing an increased awareness everywhere of the emergence of a new consciousness that all things are connected. . . . We are on the threshold of the next stage of human evolution. As we each awaken to ourselves as connected cells in the planetary body, we are re-membering the planetary body. All over the Earth, cells of the new body are being created by individuals who are bringing the magic back into their lives."

Earth Magic conveys its new perspective through workshops and seminars held around the country. Some of these are gay-specific. If you're interested in learning more, contact:

Earth Magic
Box 35160
Albuquerque, NM 87176
Phone: 505 268 8629

GAYLA

Gayla has been held at the Ferry Beach Association, a Unitarian Universalist campground, for over a decade. This annual gay men's conference welcomes "lovers, friends, fathers, many colors, couples, singles, PWAs/PWARCs, healers, survivors, flaming faggots and closet queens, leather queers, spiritual leaders, leather queens, sissies and jocks."

The week-long gathering is for spiritual connecting with the world, other men, and yourself. There are group encounters, sharing circles, support groups, and even a tea dance.

The event is open to all men interested in spiritual exploration. There's no pressure or presence that necessitates any allegiance to the Unitarian Universalist Church.

The costs are very reasonable; you can reduce them even more by cooking your own meals. Some limited scholarships are available.

For more information, write:

GAYLA Coordinators
c/o Executive Director
Ferry Beach Park Association
5 Morris Avenue
Saco, ME 04072

ART BY DAVID SOLTESZ, REPRINTED WITH PERMISSION.

A GAY THEOLOGY?

Rev. Malcolm Boyd, author of many books including *Gay Priest* and the famous *Are You Running with Me, Jesus?* made these remarks on the idea of gay theology at a meeting of the Unitarian Universalists for Lesbian and Gay Concerns in 1988:

"My first encounter with gay theology . . . took place twenty years ago. I was in Toronto being interviewed on a taped program to be seen on national Canadian television. The interviewer got on the subject of Jesus' humanity. . . . What did I mean that 'Jesus became fully human'?

'Well,' I said finally, 'I mean that he had a head, shoulders, chest, stomach, a penis, legs, and feet.' The next morning, hundreds of angry phone calls reached the media and church authorities. And one person called the Episcopal bishop of Michigan and wrathfully exclaimed, 'Jesus did not have a penis!' Well, as a matter of fact, he did. . . .

"The church is on the shakiest of ground theologically when it attempts to deny this, and also reveals its public embarrassment about not only Jesus' sexuality, but all sexuality. This has caused untold suffering for millions of people and engendered unnecessary guilt. The point is, a theologically untenable gulf has been set up between body and spirit. . . .

"Gay theology affirms that sex is valid and good as a form of bonding, of mutual support, and shared pleasure and fulfillment, as a means of receiving and giving respect, caring, and love. Gay theology calls for the blessing of gay and lesbian relationships. . . .

"Gay theology stands with feminist theology in invoking a new theology of the church which veers sharply away from institutional patriarchy. . . . The church has no right to place its own perpetuation and power over the struggles and needs of people. . . .

"Now gay theology emerges in creative counterpoint. It contributes gay insight and sensibilities, gay consciousness and experience to the study and practice of theology. More, it is a vessel containing expressions of gay spirit in the utterly highly diverse world of gay culture informed by many aspects of gay sensibility. Gay theology is a reflection of how vast numbers of lesbians and gay men view particular matters of the spirit. . . .

"I understand only too well that the fire burning inside me as a gay man and a gay priest cannot be extinguished by tears, alcohol, or semen. Gay theology informs me that the deep hunger and passionate yearning for coming home within one's self, within community, is holy, and the power bridging the gulf between soul and body, and life and death."

COPYRIGHT 1988 MALCOLM BOYD.

RECOVERY AND SELF-HELP

ALCOHOLICS ANONYMOUS AND OTHER 12-STEP PROGRAMS

It's sometimes hard to understand just what the role of Twelve-Step Programs is in the gay world.

There's no question about one thing. The Twelve Steps and the companion Twelve Traditions were developed by alcoholics for alcoholics. Their purpose is to help people stop drinking. That's all.

But from that root, the power of the Twelve Steps was taken further. People who identified other compulsions or problems in their lives took the Twelve Steps and applied them to themselves and their own lives. Al-Anon is one of the best known; it's an organization and movement for people who have relationships with alcoholics. From there the list goes on and becomes more controversial. There's Overeaters Anonymous for people who want to deal with eating compulsions. There's a Sexual Addicts Anonymous for people who think that sex is out of control in their lives. There's Adult Children of Alcoholics for people who grew up in alcoholic or other dysfunctional families.

All of these—and many more—raise still another aspect about the popularity of the Twelve Steps. In reality, the Twelve Steps are highly spiritual. AA and other Twelve-Step groups can be very attractive to people who want a spiritual component in their lives, but who are unwilling to take part in organized religion, as such.

That's not necessarily a problem, so long as you understand what your motives are and what the possible benefits and drawbacks might be for you if you enter one of these self-help groups.

THE 12 STEPS OF ALCOHOLICS ANONYMOUS

1. We admitted we were powerless over alcohol—that our lives had become unmanageable.

2. Came to believe that a Power greater than ourselves could restore us to sanity.

3. Made a decision to turn our will and our lives over to the care of God *as we understood Him.*

4. Made a searching and fearless moral inventory of ourselves.

5. Admitted to God, to ourselves, and to another human being the exact nature of our wrongs.

6. Were entirely ready to have God remove all these defects of character.

7. Humbly asked Him to remove our shortcomings.

8. Made a list of all persons we had harmed, and became willing to make amends to them all.

9. Made direct amends to such people wherever possible, except when to do so would injure them or others.

10. Continued to take personal inventory and when we were wrong promptly admitted it.

11. Sought through prayer and meditation to improve our conscious contact with God *as we understood Him,* praying only for the knowledge of His will for us and power to carry that out.

12. Having had a spiritual awakening as the result of these Steps, we tried to carry this message to alcoholics, and to practice these principles in all our affairs.

THE 12 TRADITIONS OF ALCOHOLICS ANONYMOUS

1. Our common welfare should come first; personal recovery depends upon AA unity.

2. For our group purpose there is but one ultimate authority—a loving God as He may express Himself in our group conscience. Our leaders are but trusted servants; they do not govern.

3. The only requirement for AA membership is a desire to stop drinking.

4. Each group should be autonomous except in matters affecting other groups or AA as a whole.

5. Each group has but one primary purpose—to carry its message to the alcoholic who still suffers.

6. An AA group ought never endorse, finance, or lend the AA name to any related facility or outside enterprise, lest problems of money, property, and prestige divert us from our primary purpose.

7. Every AA group ought to be fully self-supporting, declining outside contributions.

8. Alcoholics Anonymous should remain forever nonprofessional, but our service centers may employ special workers.

9. AA, as such, ought never be organized, but we may create service boards or committees directly responsible to those they serve.

10. Alcoholics Anonymous has no opinion on outside issues; hence the AA name ought never be drawn into public controversy.

11. Our public relations policy is based on attraction rather than promotion; we need always maintain personal anonymity at the level of press, radio, and films.

12. Anonymity is the spiritual foundation of all our Traditions, ever reminding us to place principle before personalities.

The 12 Steps and 12 Traditions are reprinted with permission of Alcoholics Anonymous World Services, Inc. Permission to reprint and adapt the 12 Steps and 12 Traditions does not mean that AA has reviewed or approved the contents of this publication nor that AA agrees with the views expressed herein. AA is a program of recovery from alcoholism. Use of the 12 Steps and 12 Traditions in connection with programs and activities which are patterned after AA, but which address other problems, does not imply otherwise.

▼ *Round Ups* are an important part of the gay and lesbian AA experience. These affairs, usually annual, are held in cities or regions. The weekend-long events include workshops, intensify twelve-step education and experiential programs and also usually have a major chemical-free dance and party, often one of the highlights of the social season.

For more information on when a gay and lesbian Round Up may be held in your area, contact any Alcoholics Anonymous organization. You'll find a number in your telephone book.

▼ *The International Advisory Council for Homosexual Men and Women in Alcoholics Anonymous* (IAC) is a service committee within the larger Alcoholics Anonymous organization. They provide experience, strength, and hope to gay and lesbian AA groups around the world. They also provide correspondence with gay and lesbian loners who have no other regular contact with the gay fellowship.

The AA program has tailored itself to the specific needs of its members. In this way special composition groups, such as gay and lesbian AA meetings, have evolved. Sharing each others' experience, strength, and hope with others of similar interests and backgrounds has always improved the chances of success. Lesbian and gay groups within AA permit freedom in communication that helps recovery from alcoholism.

To help gay and lesbian alcoholics, the IAC produces a directory of gay and lesbian groups and meetings. The cost is $2.50. There are other publications available from the office as well. Write:

IAC
Box 90
Washington, DC 20044

STARTING A NEW GAY OR LESBIAN GROUP OF ALCOHOLICS ANONYMOUS

The following advice comes from the IAC.

Dear Gay or Lesbian Sober Friends:

Do you feel a personal need for a new group in your home town where you can identify fully—sober in AA *and* homosexual? Have you at least one other like-minded associate also prepared to put in some faith and service? Then, congratulations, you have just founded an AA group. As our General Service Publication "The AA Group" makes clear: "Traditionally, any two alcoholics meeting together for purposes of sobriety may consider themselves an AA group, provided that, as a group, they are self-supporting and have no outside affiliation."

The beginning may feel a bit uphill; perhaps the following suggestions will help. The first requirement is a meeting place. Meetings have been started in members' homes—either at one place or rotated among members. While some successful meetings have been held in members' homes over a long term, there are pitfalls; somehow the meeting can seem to become "Frieda's meeting" or the "Tuesday Night Meeting at Tom's." In other words, personalities can get mixed with the principles. It is awkward to list home meetings in public directories so that newcomers can find them. If they can't attend, what's the point? Also, who looks after the meeting when Frieda or Tom is on vacation or sick? Can this really be a group? So, most meetings tend to be held in easily accessible public places—churches, clubs, community centers, and the like.

A word about honesty. It is essential that the landlord know exactly who you are. This avoids misunderstandings later and a possible—upsetting—need to move. So tell them who you are: a regular group of Alcoholics Anonymous, the majority of whose members will be gay and/or lesbian. Groups, like individuals, have tried to hide that fact, and have come to regret it.

Next, make a business-like agreement with your landlord regarding rent. Tradition Seven dictates that each group is self-supporting. It is essential that we pay fair rent for our facility, at least equal to what other outside groups are paying. This also helps ensure that the facility isn't juggling you around to accommodate the paying customers, a situation which is always disruptive to a meeting.

Once those basics are ironed out, you will need to decide on a format, that is, how are you going to run the meeting? This will have to be tentative; as new members join, they form part of members' needs. Be prepared to be flexible. The format of meetings varies widely in AA. You will probably be wise to use a format common in your area. What may work in one place seems very strange to sober members some place else, and vice versa. Some speaker meetings have readings from *The Big Book* and other AA literature followed by a thirty-minute speaker. Other places have three speakers qualify for ten minutes each. Another common format is twenty-minute "qualification" or personal history followed by sharing from the floor by people who raise their hands to be recognized by the speaker. There are also discussion meetings around a table. In these, a chapter from the "Twelve and Twelve" may be read aloud by the participants, one page each. Then, each person present shares his experience of this particular step. Other discussion meetings are held on a topic introduced by the chairperson, or simply "How was your week as it pertains to living the AA way of life?" If you would like more specifics on other formats, please write us.

Open or closed? Each AA group has the option of declaring itself open to anyone who chooses to attend or open to alcoholics only (and those who suspect they have a problem). Even a closed meeting of AA is open to any alcoholic. The Third Tradition overrides every other consideration or the meeting ceases to be AA and becomes something else.

Your next problem will be getting out the word. Here, your best bet is to announce, announce, announce. Your personal enthusiasm can hardly be duplicated by someone who has never attended your meeting. Once your meeting is an AA fact of life, you can list it locally with your Intergroup (or Central) Office. Also, please let IAC know so that we can support you with appropriate materials and list you in the next international directory of gay and lesbian groups in AA. This is also the time to write the General Service Office of AA for the form "New Group Information Record." Remember, IAC is an *as well as* service, not *instead of*.

© 1988 INTERNATIONAL ADVISORY COUNCIL FOR HOMOSEXUAL MEN AND WOMEN IN ALCOHOLICS ANONYMOUS, BOX 90, WASHINGTON, DC 20044. REPRINTED WITH PERMISSION.

▼ There are many private treatment centers dealing with alcohol and other chemical dependencies. Many are willing and able to deal with gay life-styles. You should feel free to approach any one of them to discover if it would, in fact, be able to cope with your or a loved one's sexuality in treatment.

Pride Institute is a gay- and lesbian-specific treatment center that offers special treatment programs for gay and lesbian clients. There are more and more such organizations around the country. Check with your gay hot line or gay community center to see what programs they might be able to refer you to.

For information on Pride:

Pride Institute
14400 Martin Drive
Eden Prairie, MN 55344
Phone: 612 934 7554

▼ *The Other Publishing Company* was founded by John Michael when he found that there was no easy way to distribute materials of interest that were needed for the gay recovering community.

Earlier, in 1977, when he couldn't find enough material to read, Michael had written *The Gay Drinking Problem—There Is a Solution* and *Sober, Clean and Gay* (both published by CompCare Publishers, Inc.).

Michael's interests and activities expanded from there until he decided in 1988 that he would establish his company, which produces an every-two-months newsletter and catalog.

According to Michael: "I hope to extend the range of materials beyond 'recovery' as we use that word in the 12-Step world, to encompass a gay population recovering from birth and life in this culture in this country.

"Not all the material offered will be by gay authors, nor will it all, at first glance, appear relevant. Yet I believe each selection will prove to be a valuable addition to someone's library, if not to the recovering alcoholic, to the adult child; if not to the substance abuser, to the sex or relationship addict; and if not for personal recovery, for all of us in our roles as true friends to our fellows in recovery and in living.

"It is my fervent wish to seek out such materials as presently are available and, where these do not exist, to seek out the men and women able and willing to create them. Then, when possible, I will publish them under *The Other Publishing Company* imprint or assist in getting them published elsewhere."

Contact:

The Other Publishing Company
Box 2151
San Diego, CA 92112

RESOURCES FOR GAY MEN INVOLVED WITH ALCOHOLISM AND CHEMICAL DEPENDENCY

Dr. Steven Berg, a professional in the field of substance abuse, has helped to construct this reading list for those who would like to explore further into issues around gay men and chemical dependency.

The NALGAP Annotated Bibliography: Resources on Alcoholism, Substance Abuse, and Lesbians/Gay Men by S. L. Berg, D. Finnegan, and E. McNally. Ft. Wayne, Ind.: National Association of Lesbian and Gay Alcoholism Professionals, 1987.

This annotated bibliography lists resources dealing with alcoholism and the lesbian and gay community. The book also serves as the guide for the NALGAP Collection at Rutgers University. The bibliography may be ordered from NALGAP, 204 W. 20th Street, New York, NY 10011.

Alcoholism in the Gay and Lesbian Community by C. Diamond-Friedman. Evanston, Ill.: National College of Education, 1989.

The author presents a holistic model for treating the gay or lesbian alcoholic. The booklet is written for counselors working with gay and lesbian clients and ends with a resources list and bibliography. Copies may be ordered from *Working It Out,* 9411 Overhill, Morton Grove, IL 60053.

Dual Identities: Counseling Chemically Dependent Gay Men and Lesbians by D. Finnegan and E. McNally. Center City, Minn.: Hazelden, 1987.

This book focuses on the special issues that people struggling with chemical dependency and homophobia must face and work through in order to recover. It examines the processes by which people come to terms with the stigmatized identities of being chemically dependent and homosexual. The book discusses the skills that counselors need in order to be helpful to their clients. In addition, the book includes resources, suggested readings, and an organizational audit for evaluating a program's sensitivity to gay and lesbian issues.

Franny: The Queen of Provincetown by John Preston. Boston: Alyson, 1985.

Franny is an ugly drag queen who makes her home in Provincetown. Each chapter in this book describes one of the men who have entered her life usually as friends, sometimes as lovers. Each man who comes into contact with Franny has his life transformed from his trapped existence into a productive, happy individual. For example, a professor sobers up through AA and eventually writes the gay novel which has been collecting dust in his desk drawer. The characters in *Franny* cover the range of individuals found in the gay community: drag queens, leather men, artists, bartenders, professors, hustlers, individuals just accepting their sexuality, et cetera.

Kevin by Wallace Hamilton. New York: New American Library, 1980. Out of print.

Kevin is a gay youth whose parents are both alcoholics. The book gives a realistic picture of some issues a child of an alcoholic may face.

The People of the Gay Grape: A Personal Investigation. San Diego: Other Publishing Company, 1988.

The People of the Gay Grape are gay and lesbian alcoholics in San Diego who are members of AA. By using a participant observer technique to study AA participation of gay men and lesbians, the anonymous Ph.D. who wrote this booklet provides a useful explanation of how AA works for gay people. It may be ordered from the Other Publishing Company, Box 2151, San Diego, CA 92112-2151.

Sweet Dreams by John Preston. Boston: Alyson Publications, 1984. Out of print.

This first book in the Alex Kane series has a strong anti-drug message. In it, Kane rescues Danny, a gay youth who has been forced into a life of prostitution and drug use.

Inside the Invisible Minority: Addressing the Special Issues of the Addicted Patient Who Is Gay/Lesbian by A. Swetnam. Park Ridge, Ill.: Parkside Publishing, 1989.

The pamphlet is written for therapists working with gay and lesbian clients. Issues of homophobia, spirituality, family, and AIDS are addressed in a sensitive manner. The cost is $2.50 and may be ordered by calling 1-800-221-6364.

Worthy of Recovery by A. Swetnam. Park Ridge, Ill.: Parkside Publishing, 1989.

Although it was written as a workbook for gay men and lesbians in treatment, this pamphlet would be valuable for any recovering gay man or lesbian. Such issues as family, homophobia, AIDS, and spirituality are addressed. The cost is $2.50 and may be ordered by calling 1-800-221-6364.

A Comfortable Corner by Vincent Virga. New York: Avon, 1982. Out of print.

The major theme in this novel is coaddiction in the gay community. Unfortunately, the book is out of print, but copies can still be found in used book stores.

The Way Back: The Stories of Gay and Lesbian Alcoholics. Washington, D.C.: Whitman-Walker Clinic, 1982.

The book includes the stories of five gay men and five lesbians who sobered up through AA. The stories are modeled after the stories of recovery which appear in the back of *Alcoholics Anonymous,* the basic text of AA which is also known as *The Big Book.*

Alcoholism and Homosexuality, edited by T. O. Zieboid and J. E. Mongeon. New York: Haworth Press, 1982.

This special issue of the *Journal of Homosexuality* has also been published under the title *Gay and Sober.* It includes theoretical and review essays which include information on treating gay alcoholics.

▼ An important pamphlet explains how lesbians and gay men have used AA to recover from their alcoholism. Copies can be obtained for 40 cents from:

AA World Services
Box 459
Grand Central Station
New York, NY 10163

A story of a gay man who recovered through AA can also be found in *Do You Think You're Different?* which is available from the same address for 30 cents.

SELF-HELP GROUPS

There are now so many self-help groups that it's been necessary to set up coordinating bodies. These organizations keep referral lists for all self-help organizations. You can call, let them know what you're interested in pursuing and where you live. They'll try to link you up with a group near you that has the same interests.

National Self-Help Clearinghouse
33 W. 42nd Street
New York, NY 10036
Phone: 212 642 2944

California Self-Help Center
405 Hilgard Avenue
Los Angeles, CA 90024
Call 800 222 5465 for referrals to groups.
Call 213 825 7990 for information about the Center, the regions, or operations.

The California group is more than a referral agency, though it does make referral to the over 3,500 such organizations in the state. It's also involved in helping Californians form and manage self-help support groups for a wide range of concerns. It works with five regional self-help centers to provide training to new state groups and give technical assistance to existing groups.

It has also produced an audio tape, *Common Concern,* which guides a newly forming group through its first twelve meetings.

Illinois Self-Help Center
1600 Dodge Avenue, Suite S-122
Evanston, IL 60201
Phone: 312 328 0470

Massachusetts Clearing-House of Mutual Help Groups
113 Skinner Hall
University of Massachusetts
Amherst, MA 01003
Phone: 413 545 2313

Minnesota Mutual Help Resource Center
919 Lafond Avenue
St. Paul, MN 55104
Phone: 612 642 4060

Self-Help Clearinghouse of Greater Washington
100 N. Washington Street
Falls Church, VA 22046
Phone: 703 536 4100

▼ *The Experience* is a workshop that presents itself as being "about love, truth, and being powerful in life." It began as The Advocate Experience, itself a takeoff on the est training that was very popular in the seventies.

Workshops are held around the country. You can find out more about "the training," as it's called, by contacting:

The Experience
3208 Cahuenga Boulevard W, #55
Los Angeles, CA 90068
Phone: 818 795 1833
Fax: 818 795 1833

PART EIGHT

ENTERTAINING OURSELVES

The many ways of celebration of gay life are among the great joys of our community. Yes, there are politics to be attended to. Yes, there is education that needs to be done. Yes, we need to deal with our spirituality.

But we also have to play.

Certainly gay resorts, gay travel organizations, and all forms of gay entertainment are important ways we go about this recreation. So too are our music, our songs, and our enjoyment of our sexuality.

CHORUSES

Gay choruses have become a major component of the social and aesthetic lives of the gay community. Their regular concerts are often important fund-raisers for the community and movement and their rehearsals and performances are part of an evolving quilt of many new ways for gay men and lesbians to get to know one another.

The national *Gay and Lesbian Association of Choruses* sponsors choral festivals for its member choruses. It holds annual conferences that provide a forum for networking, training, and information sharing. The workshops are held for both musical and administrative leadership. A central computerized library of musical holdings is being developed. It also publishes a newsletter, *GALA-GRAM.*

Here are the members of the GALA Choruses, with names and addresses provided by the national office:

UNITED STATES

■ NATIONAL ■

GAY AND LESBIAN ASSOCIATION OF CHORUSES
1617 E. 22nd Avenue
Denver, CO 80205
Phone: 303 832 1526

■ ARIZONA ■

TUCSON METROPOLITAN COMMUNITY CHORUS
P.O. Box 40036
Tucson, AZ 85717

■ ARKANSAS ■

LITTLE ROCK MEN'S CHORUS
124000 Southridge Drive
Little Rock AR 72212

■ CALIFORNIA ■

GAY MEN'S CHORUS OF LONG BEACH
P.O. Box 3566
Long Beach, CA 90803

GAY MEN'S CHORUS OF LOS ANGELES
7985 Santa Monica Boulevard, #109-134
West Hollywood, CA 90046

GOLDEN GATE MEN'S CHORUS
227 Congo Street
San Francisco, CA 94131

LESBIAN/GAY CHORUS OF SAN FRANCISCO
584 Castro, Suite 284
San Francisco, CA 94114

SACRAMENTO MEN'S CHORUS
P.O. Box 188726
Sacramento, CA 95818

SAN DIEGO MEN'S CHORUS
P.O. Box 33825
San Diego, CA 92103

SAN FRANCISCO GAY MEN'S CHORUS
P.O. Box 421491
San Francisco, CA 94142

SANTA CRUZ MEN'S CHORUS
400 California Street
Santa Cruz, CA 95060

SILICON VALLEY GAY MEN'S CHORUS
P.O. Box 62151
Sunnyvale, CA 94088

SOUTH COAST CHORALE
P.O. Box 92524
Long Beach, CA 90809

WEST COAST SINGERS
P.O. Box 46825
West Hollywood, CA 90046

■ COLORADO ■

DENVER GAY MEN'S CHORUS
P.O. Box 18251
Denver, CO 80218

GALA CHORUSES
1617 E. 22nd Avenue
Denver, CO 80205

■ CONNECTICUT ■

CONNECTICUT GAY MEN'S CHORUS
480 Winthrop Avenue
New Haven, CT 06511

■ DISTRICT OF COLUMBIA ■

GAY MEN'S CHORUS OF WASHINGTON, DC
P.O. Box 57043
Washington, DC 20037

LESBIAN & GAY CHORUS OF WASHINGTON
P.O. Box 65285
Washington, DC 20036

■ FLORIDA ■

GAY MEN'S CHORUS OF SOUTH FLORIDA
12555 Biscayne Boulevard, Suite 822
Miami, FL 33181

ORLANDO GAY CHORUS
P.O. Box 3103
Orlando, FL 32802

TAMPA BAY GAY MEN'S CHORUS
P.O. Box 20465
Tampa, FL 33622

■ GEORGIA ■

ATLANTA GAY MEN'S CHORUS
P.O. Box 77114
Atlanta, GA 30357

■ HAWAII ■

HONOLULU MEN'S CHORUS
P.O. Box 4076
Honolulu, HI 96812

■ ILLINOIS ■

CHAMPAIGN-URBANA MEN'S CHORUS
P.O. Box 889
Champaign, IL 61824

CHICAGO GAY MEN'S CHORUS
P.O. Box 14146
Chicago, IL 60614

WINDY CITY GAY CHORUS
606 W. Barry, #216
Chicago, IL 60657

■ INDIANA ■

CROSSROADS PERFORMING ARTS
P.O. Box 11512
Indianapolis, IN 46201

■ IOWA ■

DES MOINES MEN'S CHORUS
P.O. Box 2318
Des Moines, IA 50310

■ LOUISIANA ■

NEW ORLEANS GAY MEN'S CHORUS
P.O. Box 19365
New Orleans, LA 70119

■ MARYLAND ■

BALTIMORE MEN'S CHORUS
P.O. Box 2401
Baltimore, MD 21203

■ MASSACHUSETTS ■

ARS NOVA
27 Milford Street
Boston, MA 02118

BOSTON GAY MEN'S CHORUS
Box 1348, Back Bay Annex
Boston, MA 02117

© HOWARD CRUSE. REPRINTED WITH THE PERMISSION OF THE ARTIST.

■ MICHIGAN ■

DETROIT TOGETHER MEN'S CHORUS
P.O. Box 1381
Berkley, MI 48072

GREAT LAKES MEN'S CHORUS
P.O. Box 336
Royal Oak, MI 48068

LANSING GAY MEN'S CHORUS
733 W. Shiawassee
Lansing, MI 48915

■ MINNESOTA ■

ONE VOICE MIXED CHORUS
P.O. Box 2290
Minneapolis, MN 55402

TWIN CITIES GAY MEN'S CHORUS
528 Hennepin Avenue, Suite 208
Minneapolis, MN 55403

■ MISSOURI ■

GATEWAY MEN'S CHORUS
P.O. Box 14374A
St. Louis, MO 63178

HEARTLAND MEN'S CHORUS
P.O. Box 32374
Kansas City, MO 64111

■ NEBRASKA ■

RIVER CITY MIXED CHORUS
P.O. Box 315
Omaha, NE 68101

■ NEW MEXICO ■

NEW MEXICO GAY MEN'S CHORUS
8640 Horacio Place NE
Albuquerque, NM 87111

■ NEW YORK ■

CITY OF GOOD NEIGHBORS CHORALE
1313 McKinley Parkway
Buffalo, NY 14218

NEW YORK CITY GAY MEN'S CHORUS
P.O. Box 587
New York, NY 10156

ROCHESTER GAY MEN'S CHORUS
P.O. Box 1892
Rochester, NY 14603

STONEWALL CHORALE
P.O. Box 920
Old Chelsea Station
New York, NY 10011

■ NORTH CAROLINA ■

ASHEVILLE GAY MEN'S COMMUNITY CHORUS
P.O. Box 15321
Asheville, NC 28813

ONEVOICE
P.O. Box 9241
Charlotte, NC 28299

■ OHIO ■

DAYTON MEN'S CHORUS
1362 Harvard Boulevard
Dayton, OH 45406

■ OKLAHOMA ■

OKC METRO-MEN'S CHORUS
8332 N.E. 20th Street
Oklahoma City, OK 73141

■ OREGON ■

PORTLAND GAY MEN'S CHORUS
P.O. Box 3223
Portland, OR 97208

■ PENNSYLVANIA ■

HARRISBURG MEN'S CHORUS
P.O. Box 3302
Harrisburg, PA 17105

PHILADELPHIA GAY MEN'S CHORUS
P.O. Box 58842
Philadelphia, PA 19102

RENAISSANCE CITY CHOIR
P.O. Box 10282
Pittsburgh, PA 15232

SPRUCE STREET SINGERS
1236 Lombard Street
Philadelphia, PA 19147

■ TEXAS ■

ALAMO CITY MEN'S CHORALE
P.O. Box 120243
San Antonio, TX 78212

CAPITAL CITY MEN'S CHORUS
P.O. Box 50082
Austin, TX 78763

MONTROSE SINGERS
3407 Graustark, #16
Houston, TX 77006

TURTLE CREEK CHORALE
P.O. Box 190806
Dallas, TX 75219

■ WASHINGTON ■

SEATTLE LESBIAN AND GAY CHORUS
1501 Belmont Avenue
Seattle, WA 98122

SEATTLE MEN'S CHORUS
P.O. Box 20146
Seattle, WA 98102

■ WISCONSIN ■

FEST CITY SINGERS
P.O. Box 11428
Milwaukee, WI 53211

WISCONSIN CREAM CITY CHORUS, INC.
P.O. Box 1488
Milwaukee, WI 53201

CANADA

■ ALBERTA ■

ROCKY MOUNTAIN SINGERS SOCIETY
Box 34034, Westbrook P.O.
Calgary, AB T3C 3W0

■ BRITISH COLUMBIA ■

VANCOUVER MEN'S CHORUS
1270 Chestnut Street
Vancouver, BC V6J 4R9

■ NOVA SCOTIA ■

NOVA SCOTIA GAY MEN'S CHORUS ASSOCIATION
P.O. Box 7126
Halifax, NS B3K 5J5

■ ONTARIO ■

OTTAWA MEN'S CHORUS
P.O. Box 3010, Station D
Ottawa, ON K1P 6H6

TORONTO GAY MEN'S CHORUS
2 Bloor Street W, Suite 100
Toronto, ON M4W 3E2

BANDS

Like the choruses, *The Lesbian and Gay Bands of America* provide a wonderful alternative means of socializing. The bands also have a major role to play in Gay Pride celebrations around the country. Their good music, often accompanied by no-longer-repressed baton twirlers of truly professional ability, are a high point to the parades. Their serious recitals often take place in some of the most prestigious orchestra halls in both the United States and Canada.

To contact the bands:

Lesbian and Gay Bands of America
Box 57099
Washington, DC 20037

The following list of bands, with their names and addresses, was provided by the organization.

■ ARIZONA ■

DESERT OVERTURE
P.O. Box 16454
Phoenix, AZ 85011-6454

■ CALIFORNIA ■

SAN DIEGO'S FINEST CITY FREEDOM BAND
P.O. Box 34453
San Diego, CA 92103

BAY AREA GAY AND LESBIAN BAND
P.O. Box 280571
San Francisco, CA 94128-0571

SAN FRANCISCO GAY FREEDOM DAY MARCHING BAND & TWIRLING CORPS
1519 Mission Street
San Francisco, CA 94103-2512

GREAT AMERICAN YANKEE FREEDOM BAND OF LOS ANGELES
P.O. Box 46026
West Hollywood, CA 90046

■ COLORADO ■

MILE HIGH FREEDOM BAND
P.O. Box 9792
Denver, CO 80209-9792

■ DISTRICT OF COLUMBIA ■

D.C.'S DIFFERENT DRUMMERS
P.O. Box 57099
Washington, DC 20037

■ FLORIDA ■

FLAMINGO FREEDOM BAND OF SOUTH FLORIDA
P.O. Box 4986
Ft. Lauderdale, FL 33338

■ GEORGIA ■

PRIDE OF PEACHTREE BAND & CORPS
c/o Greer
4110-2 Hawthorne Circle
Smyrna, GA 30080

■ ILLINOIS ■

THE GREAT LAKES FREEDOM BAND
c/o Carlton
3950 N. Lakeshore Drive, #1504A
Chicago, IL 60613

■ MARYLAND ■

BALTIMORE'S STAR SPANGLED BAND
c/o Kammerer
6172 Chinquapin Parkway
Baltimore, MD 21239

■ MASSACHUSETTS ■

THE FREEDOM TRAIL BAND
P.O. Box 6598
Boston, MA 02102

■ MINNESOTA ■

MINNESOTA FREEDOM BAND
P.O. Box 300140
Minneapolis, MN 55403-5140

■ NEW YORK ■

LESBIAN & GAY BIG APPLE CORPS
123 W. 44th Street, Suite 12L
New York, NY 10036

■ OHIO ■

THE NORTH COAST FREEDOM BAND
c/o The Center
1418 W. 29th Street
Cleveland, OH 44113

■ PENNSYLVANIA ■

PHILADELPHIA FREEDOM BAND
c/o Woodyard
444 Olive Street
Philadelphia, PA 19123

■ TEXAS ■

OAK LAWN SYMPHONIC BAND
P.O. Box 190973
Dallas, TX 75219

LONE STAR SYMPHONIC BAND
P.O. Box 66613
Houston, TX 77266-6613

▼ *The Society of Gay and Lesbian Composers* was founded in 1981 to provide a body of literature for performing groups that spoke directly from, to, and for the gay and lesbian communities. It continues to provide composers with the opportunity to exchange ideas. Its further purposes are to encourage the composition of music that conveys the attitudes, ideals, and uniqueness of the gay and lesbian cultures, to provide opportunities for performances of this music and to disseminate this music to potential performers.

The Society publishes a catalog of members' works and sponsors concert series in the San Francisco area. While members are clustered in the Bay Area, many others come from all around North America.

To contact the Society:

Society of Gay and Lesbian Composers
2261 Market Street, #459
San Francisco, CA 94114

RESORTS

These hotels, motels and resorts welcome gay travelers and vacationers. If the resort promoted itself as wheelchair accessible, that fact has been noted. This listing includes everything from urban hotels to luxury resort complexes to simple country bed and breakfast inns. You should investigate the business before making a reservation, just to make sure it's something you'd be comfortable with. Almost all of these businesses have a brochure and price list available. If an 800 number is available for toll-free calling, it's been noted; however, most 800 numbers are not available for calls made within the state of the business. This listing is by state and then, within each state, by zip code.

UNITED STATES

■ CALIFORNIA ■

WEST ADAMS BED AND BREAKFAST INN
1650 Westmoreland Boulevard
Los Angeles, CA 90006
Phone: 213 737 5041

THE SELBY HOTEL
1740 North Hudson Avenue
Hollywood, CA 90028
Phone: 213 469 5320/800 537 3052

DMITRI'S GUESTHOUSE
931 21st Street
San Diego, CA 92102
Phone: 619 238 5547

HILL HOUSE BED AND BREAKFAST
2504 A Street
San Diego, CA 92102
Phone: 619 239 4738

BALBOA PARK INN
3402 Park Boulevard
San Diego, CA 92103
Phone: 619 298 0623

THE VILLA
67–670 Carey Road
Cathedral City, CA 92234
Phone: 619 328 7211
Wheelchair accessible.

HARLOW CLUB
175 E. El Alameda
Palm Springs, CA 92262
Phone: 619 323 3977

HACIENDA en SUEÑO

HACIENDA EN SUEÑO
586 Warm Sands Drive
Palm Springs, CA 92264
Phone: 619 327 8111
Wheelchair accessible.

VISTA GRANDE VILLA
574 Warm Sands Drive
Palm Springs, CA 92264
Phone: 619 322 2404

THE ATHERON HOTEL
685 Ellis Street
San Francisco, CA 94109
Phone: 800 227 3608

INN ON CASTRO
321 Castro Street
San Francisco, CA 94114
Phone: 415 861 0321

24 HENRY STREET
24 Henry Street
San Francisco, CA 94114
Phone: 415 864 5686

THE WOODS RESORT
16881 Armstrong Woods Road
P.O. Box 1690
Guerneville, CA 95446
Phone: 707 869 0111
Wheelchair accessible.

FIFES RESORT
16467 River Road
P.O. Box 45
Guerneville, CA 95446
Phone: 707 869 0656
Wheelchair accessible.

SIERRAWOOD GUEST HOUSE
P.O. Box 11194
Tahoe Paradise, CA 95708
Phone: 916 577 6073

■ COLORADO ■

THE BUNK HOUSE
P.O. Box 6
Breckenridge, CO 80424
Phone: 303 453 6475

■ DISTRICT OF COLUMBIA ■

CAPITOL HILL GUESTHOUSE
101 5th Street NE
Washington, DC 20002
Phone: 202 547 1050

■ FLORIDA ■

PARLIAMENT HOUSE MOTOR INN
410 N. Orange Blossom Trail
Orlando, FL 32805
Phone: 407 425 7571
Wheelchair accessible.

ALEXANDERS
1118 Fleming Street
Key West, FL 33040
Phone: 305 294 9919

BIG RUBY'S GUESTHOUSE
409 Appelrouth Lane
Key West, FL 33040
Phone: 302 296 2323

BLUE PARROT INN
916 Elizabeth Street
Key West, FL 33040
Phone: 305 296 0033

COCONUT GROVE GUEST HOUSE
817 Fleming Street
Key West, FL 33040
Phone: 305 296 5107

COLOURS KEY WEST
410 Fleming Street
Key West, FL 33040
Phone: 305 294 6977

CYPRESS HOUSE
601 Caroline Street
Key West, FL 33040
Phone: 800 525 2488

GARDEN HOUSE OF KEY WEST
329 Elizabeth Street
Key West, FL 33040
Phone: 305 296 5368

HERON HOUSE
512 Simonton Street
Key West, FL 33040
Phone: 305 294 9227
Wheelchair accessible.

LIGHTHOUSE COURT
902 Whitehead
Key West, FL 33040
Phone: 305 294 9588

SIMONTON COURT GUEST HOUSE
320 Simonton Street
Key West, FL 33040
Phone: 305 294 6386/800 338 9501

SOUTHWINDS TROPICAL INN
1321 Simonton Street
Key West, FL 33040
Phone: 305 296 2215
Fax: 305 294 0972
Wheelchair accessible.

SPINDRIFT
1212 Simonton Street
Key West, FL 33040
Phone: 305 296 3432
Wheelchair accessible.

BIG RUBY'S GUEST HOUSE
908 N.E. 15th Avenue
Fort Lauderdale, FL 33304
Phone: 305 523 7829
Wheelchair accessible.

WAYWARD WINDS GARDEN APARTMENTS
1499 N.E. 32nd Street
Fort Lauderdale, FL 33334
Phone: 305 563 2385

■ HAWAII ■

MAHINA KAI
Box 699
Anahola, Kauai, HI 96703
Phone: 808 822 9451

HOTEL HONOLULU
376 Kaiolu Street
Honolulu, HI 96815
Phone: 808 926 2766/800 426 2766
In Canada: 800 423 8733, ext. 660

▼ *Kalani Honua* is an intercultural conference and retreat center on the island of Hawaii. The resort has accommodations for the casual traveler looking for a room on the beach. It also organizes an array of special events including the Hawaiian Men's Gathering, a number of spiritual retreats, and Camp Camp-It-Up, a week-long celebration of gay life. For a brochure describing their regular accommodations as well as a complete schedule of their special happenings, contact them:

Kalani Honua, Inc.
Kalapana, HI 96778
Phone: 808 965 7823/800
367 8047, ext. 669

■ ILLINOIS ■

ABBOTT HOTEL
721 W. Belmont Avenue
Chicago, IL 60657
Phone: 312 248 2700

■ LOUISIANA ■

BON MAISON GUEST HOUSE
835 Bourbon Street
New Orleans, LA 70116
Phone: 504 561 8498

BOURGOYNE GUEST HOUSE
839 Bourbon Street
New Orleans, LA 70116
Phone: 504 524 3621/504 525 3983

THE FRENCHMEN
417 Frenchmen Street
New Orleans, LA 70116
Phone: 800 831 1781

ROYAL BARRACKS GUEST HOUSE
717 Barracks Street
New Orleans, LA 70116
Phone: 504 529 7269

URSULINE GUEST HOUSE
708 rue des Ursulines
New Orleans, LA 70116
Phone: 504 525 8509/800 654 2351

■ MASSACHUSETTS ■

OASIS GUEST HOUSE
22 Edgerly Road
Boston, MA 02115
Phone: 617 267 2262

CHANDLER INN
26 Chandler Street
Boston, MA 02116
Phone: 617 482 3450/800 842 3450

THE ANCHOR INN
175 Commercial Street
Provincetown, MA 02657
Phone: 508 487 0432

THE BEACONLITE GUEST HOUSE
12 Winthrop Street
Provincetown, MA 02657
Phone: 508 487 9603

THE BOATSLIP
101 Commercial Street
Provincetown, MA 02657
Phone: 508 487 1669

BRADFORD HOUSE
41 Bradford Street
Provincetown, MA 02657
Phone: 508 487 0173

CAPTAIN AND HIS SHIP
164 Commercial Street
Provincetown, MA 02657
Phone: 508 487 1850

CARL'S GUEST HOUSE
68 Bradford Street
Provincetown, MA 02657
Phone: 508 487 1650

CASABLANCA GUEST HOUSE
166 Commercial Street
Provincetown, MA 02657
Phone: 508 487 0858

DUNES MOTEL AND APARTMENTS
Box 361
Provincetown, MA 02657
Phone: 508 487 1956

1807 HOUSE
54 Commercial Street
Provincetown, MA 02657
Phone: 508 487 2173

▼ Owning your own inn or hotel in one of the gay resorts is a dream of many gay men. It's not just that you can enjoy a carnival atmosphere all the time—in fact, many innkeepers quickly tire of the pace of the resort life—but that you can live in a gay-supportive atmosphere in all parts of your life. Not only are the communities likely to be supportive, you don't have to worry about an employer and his or her attitudes. That was the dream of Jim Baer and George Berry when they bought *The Captain and His Ship* ten years ago. With no regrets, they saved everything they could from their professional salaries, aided and abetted by a diet that often was limited to peanut butter sandwiches, and bought the Victorian inn on Commercial Street. The freedom they earned made the sacrifice worthwhile, so far as they're concerned. It's a pattern that many others have followed.

ELEPHANT WALK
156 Bradford Street
Provincetown, MA 02657
Phone: 508 487 2543

HAVEN HOUSE
12 Carver Street
Provincetown, MA 02657
Phone: 508 487 3031

OCEAN'S INN
386 Commercial Street
Provincetown, MA 02657
Phone: 508 487 0358

THE SANDPIPER BEACH HOUSE
165 Commercial Street
Provincetown, MA 02657
Phone: 509 487 1928

SEA DRIFT INN
80 Bradford Street
Provincetown, MA 02657
Phone: 508 487 3686

TRADE WINDS INN
12 Johnson Street
Provincetown, MA 02657
Phone: 508 487 0138

TWELVE CENTER STREET GUEST HOUSE
12 Center Street
Provincetown, MA 02657
Phone: 508 487 0381

VICTORIA HOUSE
5 Standish Street
Provincetown, MA 02657
Phone: 508 487 1319

WESTWINDS
28 Commercial Street
Provincetown, MA 02657
Phone: 508 487 1841

WHITE WIND INN
174 Commercial Street
Provincetown, MA 02657
Phone: 508 487 1529

■ MAINE ■

THE EAST WIND INN & MEETING HOUSE
P.O. Box 149
Tenants Harbor, ME 04860
Phone: 207 372 6366

■ MICHIGAN ■

ACADEMY PLACE
Box 279
Saugatuck, MI 49453
Phone: 616 857 2271

SAUGATUCK LODGES
3291 Blue Star Highway
Saugatuck, MI 49453
Phone: 616 857 4269
Wheelchair accessible.

DOUGLAS DUNES RESORT
Box 365
Douglas, MI 49506
Phone: 616 857 1401

■ MINNESOTA ■

BRASIE HOUSE
2321 Colfax Avenue S.
Minneapolis, MN 55403
Phone: 612 377 5946

■ MONTANA ■

NORTH CROW VACATION RANCH
2360 N. Crow Road
Ronan, MT 59864
Phone: 406 676 5169

■ NEW HAMPSHIRE ■

HIGHLANDS INN
Box 118
Bethlehem, NH 03574
Phone: 603 869 3978

PAL'S GUEST HOUSE
Box 332
Madison, NH 03849
Phone: 603 367 8304

■ NEW JERSEY ■

KEY WEST HOTEL
109 Second Avenue
Asbury Park, NJ 07712
Phone: 201 988 7979

FRATERNITY HOUSE
18 S. Mt. Vernon Avenue
Atlantic City, NJ 08401
Phone: 609 347 0808

OCEAN HOUSE
127 S. Ocean Avenue
Atlantic City, NJ 08401
Phone: 609 345 8203

■ NEW MEXICO ■

TRIANGLE INN
Box 3235
Santa Fe, NM 87501
Phone: 505 455 3375

THE RUBY SLIPPER
Box 2069
Taos, NM 87571
Phone: 505 758 0613

■ NEW YORK ■

COLONIAL HOUSE INN
318 W. 22nd Street
New York, NY 10011
Phone: 212 243 9669

CHELSEA PINES INN
317 W. 14th Street
New York, NY 10014
Phone: 212 929 1023

INCENTRA VILLAGE HOUSE
32 Eighth Avenue
New York, NY 10014
Phone: 212 206 0007

▼ You have to become a member before you can use the *Hillside Campgrounds* facilities in the Endless Mountains of Pennsylvania, just over the border from Binghamton, New York. It's not a major issue: membership cards only cost $2 for the season, which runs from early May to mid-October. The campgrounds are available for adult men and comprise hundreds of acres of private woodlands. There's an in-ground pool, recreational hall, nature trails, and sunning area. Members put on stage shows on holiday weekends. There are sites for tents, some with electricity and water (remote sites are also available); there are hook-ups for electric and water for RVs and trailers. Trailers are also available for rent.

HILLSIDE CAMPGROUNDS
Box 726
Binghamton, NY 13902
Phone: 717 756 2833

BELVEDERE
Box 26
Cherry Grove, NY 11782
Phone: 516 597 6448
Wheelchair accessible.

KING HENDRICK MOTEL
Route 9
Lake George, NY 12845
Phone: 518 792 0418

RAINBOW GUEST HOUSE
423 Rainbow Boulevard S.
Niagara Falls, NY 14303
Phone: 716 282 1135

■ OHIO ■

SUMMIT LODGE RESORT
26500 Wildcat Road
Rockbridge, OH 43149
Phone: 614 385 6822
Wheelchair accessible.

■ PENNSYLVANIA ■

RAINBOW MOUNTAIN RESORT
R.D. 8, Box 8174
East Stroudsburg, PA 18301
Phone: 717 223 8484
Wheelchair accessible.

WYCOMBE INN
1073 Mill Creek Road
Wycombe, PA 18980
Phone: 215 598 7000
Wheelchair accessible.

■ PUERTO RICO ■

WIND CHIMES GUEST HOUSE
53 Taft Street
San Juan, PR 00911
Phone: 809 727 4153

■ RHODE ISLAND ■

BRINLEY VICTORIAN INN
23 Brinley Street
Newport, RI 02840
Phone: 401 849 7645

■ SOUTH CAROLINA ■

CHARLESTON BEACH B & B
Box 41
Folly Beach, SC 29439
Phone: 803 588 9443

■ TENNESSEE ■

LEE VALLEY FARM
Rt. 9, Box 223
Rogersville, TN 37857
Phone: 615 272 4068

■ TEXAS ■

MONTROSE GUESTHOUSE
501 Lovett Boulevard
Houston, TX 77006
Phone: 713 522 5224

LYLE'S DECK
Box 2326
South Padre Island, TX 78597
Phone: 512 761 5953

■ VERMONT ■

HOWDEN COTTAGE BED & BREAKFAST
32 N. Champlain Street
Burlington, VT 05401
Phone: 802 864 7198

MOUNTAIN BROOK INN
1505 Mountain Road
Stowe, VT 05672
Phone: 802 253 9983/800 553 3035

INWOOD MANOR
R.D. 1, Box 127
Barnet, VT 05821
Phone: 802 633 4047

▼ David Yoder is trying to build his own fantasy with *Timberfell Lodge.* He's taken his 250 acres of land in east Tennessee and turned it into a unique gay resort. There are accommodations for thirteen men in a bed-and-breakfast operation as well as provisions for RVs and camping on the grounds. Timberfell Lodge also acts as a social center for the region, hosting various conferences and special events.

Timberfell Lodge
Route 11, Box 94A
Greeneville, TN 37743
Phone: 615 234 0833

WASHINGTON

LANDES HOUSE
712 Eleventh Avenue NE
Seattle, WA 98102
Phone: 206 329 8781

CHAMBERED NAUTILUS BED & BREAKFAST INN
5005 22nd Avenue, NE
Seattle, WA 98105
Phone: 206 522 2536

Chambered Nautilus
Bed & Breakfast Inn

DUNCARE GUEST HOUSE
1509 S. Winthrop Street
Seattle, WA 98144
Phone: 206 324 4904/322 3818

GALET PLACE BED & BREAKFAST
318 W. Galet
Seattle, WA 98119
Phone: 206 282 5339

VIRGIN ISLANDS

SEA PARK
P.O. Box 2794
Frederiksted
St. Croix, VI 00841
Phone: 809 772 4219/800 537 6240

THE MARK ST. THOMAS
Blackbeard's Hill
Charlotte Amalie
St. Thomas, VI 00802
Phone: 809 774 5511/800 548 4452

CANADA

BRITISH COLUMBIA

THE WEST END GUEST HOUSE
1362 Haro Street
Vancouver, BC V6E 1G2

GABLES GUEST HOUSE
1101 Thurlow Street
Vancouver, BC V6E 1W9
Phone: 604 684 4141

OAK BAY GUESTHOUSE
1052 Newport
Victoria, BC V8S 5E3
Phone: 604 598 3812

ONTARIO

CATNAPS GUESTHOUSE
246 Sherbourne Street
Toronto, ON M5A 2S1
Phone: 416 968 2323

QUEBEC

AUX BERGES
1070 Mackay
Montreal, QU H3G 2H1
Phone: 514 876 9393

GUEST HOUSE 727
727 D'Aiguillon
Quebec, QU G1R 1M8
Phone: 418 648 6766

LE CHASSEUR GUEST HOUSE
1567 St-Andre Street
Montreal, QU H2L 3T5
Phone: 514 521 2238

LA CONCIERGERIE GUEST HOUSE
1019 rue Saint Hubert
Montreal, QU H2L 3Y3
Phone: 514 289 9297

THE CLASSIC BARS

Bars are no longer the only centers for gay social life, but they still are important for many people. The pubs listed below have been around for decades, most of them existed before Stonewall. As you travel through the country, you may want to make a stop and toast these long-time hubs of gay life. They aren't always the most popular place in town anymore and they aren't necessarily the most chic, but they are the sites of our history.

Café Lafitte in Exile
901 Bourbon Street
New Orleans, LA 70116
Phone: 504 522 8397

Lafitte's has been praised in gay literature for as long as there's been such a thing. The bar is in the middle of the famous French Quarter, right by the jazz spots and sleazy strip joints that have long made New Orleans a center for wonderfully perverted life. The most recent renovation doesn't really build on this history. Lafitte's now looks and feels like any other Yuppie bar with bare wood floors and white walls, but it's still a must during Mardi Gras, if you can get in.

Sporter's
228 Cambridge Street
Boston, MA 02141
Phone: 617 742 4084

Sporter's is on the foot of Beacon Hill's "wrong side" and just down the block from the first stop on the subway from Cambridge. The location provided a special mix of customers. The bohemians and the brahmins from the Hill merged with the students from Harvard and MIT (Cambridge didn't allow gay bars in those days; they didn't want to corrupt those very same students by allowing homosexuals too close to campus). You can still get some of the same mix at Sporter's today: A drag queen can be holding campy court while a Harvard student studies his Physics textbook at the next stool and a group of Yuppies stand just beyond him discussing the best roasted coffee beans.

Julius
159 W. 10th Street
New York, NY 10014
Phone: 212 929 9672

This was known as a polite men's bar for years before gay men came out of the closet. A hangout for theatrical types, it was known to the homosexual underground as a careful cruising spot as early as the fifties. One of the first organized gay protests took place in the sixties, before Stonewall, when the management tried to force the gay customers to be even more discreet. The protest was a lot different than any you'd expect today: All the regular gay customers showed up in coat-and-tie to show they were, indeed, respectable. It still serves a decent hamburger at not too great a cost.

Gay Nineties
408 Hennepin Avenue
Minneapolis, MN 55402
Phone: 612 333 7755

The Gay Nineties was the Twin Cities' for years. It began as a straight strip joint that tolerated gay activity in the small, out-of-the-way

Happy Hour cocktail lounge. Today it's all-gay and has expanded numerous times. There's a leather bar, a show bar, a country western bar and more in the expanded complex.

Twin Peaks
401 Castro Street
San Francisco, CA 04114
Phone: 415 864 9470

It may seem strange to single out just one bar in San Francisco's Castro District, but Twin Peaks deserves special mention. Most gay bars in this country used to hide behind blackened windows and signs that often had nothing more than the street address. Twin Peaks broke the syndrome. The bar, at the corner of Castro, Market, and 17th Streets, has large plate-glass windows so every passerby can look in and see gay men enjoying themselves and their famous Irish Coffees.

The Triangle
2036 Broadway
Denver, CO 80205
Phone: 303 295 9008

The Triangle was many gay men's first experience of an overtly masculine atmosphere. It wasn't so much that it was a leather bar in the old days (though leather does predominate now), it was more of a country western spot. That, alone, was enough to send visiting gays from the Coasts into ecstacy.

Mr. Henry's
601 Pennsylvania Avenue SE
Washington, DC 20003
Phone: 202 546 8412

This isn't even really much of a gay bar anymore. Yuppies of all forms make up the clientele. But it used to be the center of the District's gay life. The authorities weren't at all pleased and enforced the liquor laws as stringently as possible, which meant that a drink could only be served to a customer seated at a table and that customer couldn't stand up or move with the drink in his hands. It all made cruising very intricate, since your waiter had to move your drink for you when you deemed it time to make a move on the man who caught your eye. The servers made massive money in the extra tips they collected for that special duty.

Atlantic House
4–6 Masonic Street
Provincetown, MA 02657
Phone: 508 487 3821

Legend has it that this is the place where Nina Simone made her cabaret debut. The quiet bar with roaring fireplace—winter or summer—is on an alley off the main streets of the village. The music on the jukebox is pure nostalgia and the decor and ambience is old-time Provincetown, including the tradition of the bartender ringing a bell every time he's tipped.

TRAVEL GUIDES

Best Guide Series

Best Guide
Division of Eden Cross
P.O. Box 12731
NL-1100 AS
Amsterdam, The Netherlands

There are guides to four regions: Amsterdam (288 pages), Great Britain (384 pages), Asia, Australia, and Pacific Islands (240 pages), North Pacific and Orient (256 pages). Each volume contains regional maps of gay and lesbian bars, restaurants, nightclubs, political and service organizations. Coupons. Indices.

Gayellow Pages, National

Comprehensive, symbol-coded listings for United States and Canada of all entertainment, political, gay businesses. 256 pages.

Gayellow Pages, Northeast

Covers Ohio, West Virginia, D.C., Maryland, Delaware, Pennsylvania, Connecticut, Rhode Island, Massachusetts, New Hampshire, Vermont, and Maine. 64 pages.

Gayellow Pages, Southern/Midwest

Covers Alabama, Arizona, Arkansas, Florida, Georgia, Kansas, Kentucky, Louisiana, Mississippi, Missouri, New Mexico, North Carolina, Oklahoma, Puerto Rico, South Carolina, Tennessee, Texas, Virginia. 64 pages.

Gayellow Pages, NY/NJ
96 pages.

Renaissance House
Box 292
Village Station
New York, NY 10014
Phone: 212 674 0120

Gringo's Gay Guide to Tijuana
Entertainment listings, maps, political organizations, restaurants, hotels/motels, publications, drugstores. Separate section for scant gay life in Mexicali. Useful Spanish phrases. A 46-page pamphlet, illustrated with black-and-white photographs.

Dawn Media
4835 Voltaire Street
San Diego, CA 92107
Phone: 619 225 1700

10 percent of cover price goes to Tijuana Gay Hotline.

Guide to the Gay Northeast
Monthly travel magazine. Feature articles on regional travel destinations, fiction, AIDS updates. Columns on videos, entertainment, and nightlife. Regional listings of businesses, bars, clubs, and shows. Maps and classifieds. Approximately 150 pages.

Fidelity Publishing
P.O. Box 593
Boston, MA 02199
Phone: 617 266 8557

Inn Places

Accommodations worldwide catering to gays and lesbians. Brief description of nightlife, restaurants, and gay shopping in proximity to the listings. Tour operations, travel agents, reservation services, coupons. Index. 472 pages.

Ferrari Publications, Inc.
P.O. Box 37887
Phoenix, AZ 85609
Phone: 602 863 2408

The Just Out Pocket Book

Restaurants, hotels/motels, political organizations, health services, gay and lesbian businesspersons of all types in the state of Oregon. A 56-page pamphlet.

Just Out Pocket Book
P.O. Box 15117
Portland, OR 97215
Phone: 503 236 1252

Le Guide Gai du Quebec

Maps, drag shows, restaurants, services, hotels, gyms. Indexed. In French, gratuitous English section for Montreal only. 156 pages.

Les Editions Homeureus
CP 5245, Succ. C
Montreal, QU H2X 3M4
Phone: 514 523 9463

London Scene

Getting around, accommodations, nightlife, eating out, the arts, health and fitness, gay and lesbian groups, AIDS organizations, publications. Three historical walking tours. 240 pages.

GMP
P.O. Box 247
London, England N15 6RW

Odysseus '89

International accommodations with short descriptions of gay and lesbian nightlife in proximity to each location, preceded by general travel tips for each state, city, or country. Index. Extensive appendices including travel agents, tour operators, bookstores, gay publications. 499 pages.

Odysseus Enterprises
P.O. Box 7605
Flushing, NY 11357

Our World

Monthly magazine. Features travel articles on destinations around the world. News updates, travel tips. Classifieds. Approximately 50 pages.

Our World Publishing
1104 N. Nova Road
Suite 251
Daytona Beach, FL 32017
Phone: 904 441 5367

Pink Plaque Guide to London

Alphabetical sociobiographies of London's gay gliterati identifying homes and apartments of their residence. Illustrated with black-and-white photographs. Bibliography. Index. 234 pages.

GMP
P.O. Box 247
London, England N15 6RW

Places for Men, 1990

Symbol-coded state-by-state listings covering the United States, Canada, Mexico, Caribbean Islands, Australia, and New Zealand with short descriptions of accommodations, nightlife, gay shops, political and social organizations, preceded by extensive listings and descriptions of tours, cruises, outdoor adventures, and rodeos. 564 pages.

Ferrari Publications, Inc.
P.O. Box 37887
Phoenix, AZ 85069
Phone: 602 863 2408

Places of Interest with Maps, 1990

Lesbian and gay listings for U.S., Canada, Mexico, Caribbean, Australia, and New Zealand. Includes hotels, bars, restaurants, bookstores, and political organizations. Gay adventuring section includes rafting, kayaking, trekking, bicycling, exotic tours, cruises. Events calendar. Coupons. 334 pages.

Ferrari Publications, Inc.
P.O. Box 37887
Phoenix, AZ 85069
Phone: 602 863 2408

Spartacus

Coded country and city listings of every gay- and lesbian-oriented meeting spot in the world. Includes openly gay and lesbian public meeting places such as bars, nightclubs, political organizations, and others. Also includes gay-friendly or even gay-likely meeting places. Just reading through the obscure country listings is a treat. Quadralingual introductions to each country describe the general climate under which these establishments and meeting places operate. AIDS information. Index. 1,024 pages.

Bruno Gmunder
Lutzowstrasse 105-106
P.O. Box 301345
D-1000 Berlin 30
Germany

Sydney and Beyond '89

Listings and essays regarding nightlife, where to stay, getting around, the arts scene, the outdoors, sports, rights, and welfare. Split into regions of the city. Includes brief listings for other Australian cities. Index. 255 pages.

Southpaw Press
207 Oxford Street
Darlinghurst, New South Wales, 2010
Australia
Phone: (02) 331 4140

COMPILED BY JACK GARMOND, MANAGER OF LAMBDA RISING BOOKSHORE, BALTIMORE, MARYLAND.

LOCAL GUIDES

Many gay chambers of commerce and other local groups publish gay guides to their areas. While they are of obvious interest to tourists, they also list gay professional services and other departments of interest to year-round residents. The guides are free for the asking, unless a specific price is quoted.

UNITED STATES

■ CALIFORNIA ■

RUSSIAN RIVER: RESORT AREA AND WINE COUNTRY
Russian River Business Association
Box 1480
Guerneville, CA 95446

COMMUNITY YELLOW PAGES
($9.45 by mail; free at locations)
1604 Vista del Mar Avenue
Los Angeles, CA 90028
Phone: 213 469 4454

DBA DIRECTORY
Desert Business Association
Box 773
Palm Springs, CA 92263
Phone: 619 324 0178

THE REGISTER: BUSINESS AND PROFESSIONAL SERVICES IN SAN DIEGO
Greater San Diego Business Association
Box 33848
San Diego, CA 92103
Phone: 619 296 4543

■ FLORIDA ■

THE DIRECTORY
Greater Ft. Lauderdale Gay Business Association
Box 7341
Ft. Lauderdale, FL 33338
Phone: 305 357 4014/800 443 4084

KEY WEST MAP AND DIRECTORY
Key West Business Guild
Box 1208
Key West, FL 33041
Phone: 305 294 4603

■ HAWAII ■

POCKET GUIDE TO HAWAII
Pacific Ocean Holidays
Box 88245
Honolulu, HI 96830

■ MARYLAND ■

FOCUS
Baltimore Gaypaper
Box 22575
Baltimore, MD 21203

■ MASSACHUSETTS ■

PROVINCETOWN BUSINESS GUILD GUIDE
Provincetown Business Guild
Box 421
Provincetown, MA 02657
Phone: 508 487 2313

■ MICHIGAN ■

SAUGATUCK INFORMATION
($4.95)
Creative Information
Box 3173
Grand Rapids, MI 49501

■ NORTH CAROLINA ■

NC GAY AND LESBIAN DIRECTORY
NCHRF
Box 10782
Raleigh, NC 27605

■ OHIO ■

THE RESOURCE PAGE
KWIR Publications
Box 5426
Cleveland, OH 44101

LAVENDER LISTINGS
Stonewall Union
Box 10814
Columbus, OH 43201

■ OREGON, WASHINGTON, AND BRITISH COLUMBIA ■

THE NORTHWEST GAY GUIDE
($2.00)
Box 23070
Seattle, WA 98102
Phone: 206 323 7374

■ WISCONSIN ■

THE DIRECTORY
Madison Gay/Lesbian Resource Center
Box 1722
Madison, WI 53701

CANADA

■ ONTARIO ■

YOUR GAY GUIDE TO TORONTO
($1.00)
Xtra! Magazine
Box 7289, Station A
Toronto, ON M5W 1X9

▼ *FunMaps* are the new names for the regional maps that are created and distributed by the David James Press. Almost every major metropolitan area has an edition of one of these handy guides. Advertisers buy space in commercials that are put around a clear map of the city or region. The maps are available free in many gay businesses, or can be purchased by mail order from:

David James Press, Ltd.
Flushing Avenue and Cumberland Street
Building 280, Suite 603
Brooklyn, NY 11205
Phone: 718 797 1009

▼ *Our World* is a monthly magazine devoted to news about gay travel. There are constant reviews of international resorts and travel experiences. The advertisers are some of the most welcoming hoteliers for gay men. Feature articles highlight different gay resorts with even more specifics about those places than you'd generally find in publications.

For information:

Our World
1104 N. Nova Road, Suite 251
Daytona Beach, FL 32117
Phone: 904 441 5367

MARDI GRAS IN NEW ORLEANS

Probably no other mainstream holiday has the gay overtones of New Orleans Mardi Gras. The city's traditionally liberal mores become even more loose on this February week of celebration. Gay men from around the world have been attending Mardi Gras since long before there was a gay liberation movement.

Jared Campo, the secretary of one of the gay krewes, *The Lords of Leather,* describes some of the activity and some of the gay involvement:

"There are nine different gay Mardi Gras Krewes organized in New Orleans. Each krewe in the city (whether gay or straight) is a club with male and/or female members whose main purpose is to present a Mardi Gras Ball and/or Parade annually. There are currently over a hundred different krewes in the metropolitan area, all of which hold various types of fund-raising functions during the summer and fall to support the expenses of the event they will sponsor.

"For example, The Lords of Leather conduct a Mr. Leather New Orleans contest, American Bandstand Show and Dance Night and a stage production every year.

"A Mardi Gras Ball is much like a Las Vegas extravaganza with the presentation of returning royalty, costumed members, and special guests as well as the crowning of new royalty by the Captain of the Krewe and his Lieutenant.

"The average number of tickets available to a ball is 4,000 with marked distinctions between table seats on the floor of the hall and balcony seats above.

"A Mardi Gras Ball's expenses usually exceed twenty thousand dollars and some of the larger krewes run into a hundred thousand dollars.

"Mardi Gras season begins on the Feast of Epiphany (January 6) and continues through midnight Mardi Gras Day (the Tuesday before Ash Wednesday). Balls and parades are held during these six weeks or so, with a marked increase in the size and number toward the end of the season.

"Mardi Gras day itself is wild, with banks and stores closed; costume contests and parades all over the city; and tourists everywhere.

"Travel and hotel arrangements must be completed at least three months previous to Mardi Gras because of the heavy bookings.

"The Lords of Leather will try to respond to as many requests as possible for information about gay Mardi Gras, but people should talk to their tourist agents about travel and hotel reservations and so on."

For information:

The Lords of Leather
Box 71205
New Orleans, LA 70116

▼ *Bear Tooth Adventures* works out of a gay-owned and -operated location known as Fiddlehead Farm on British Columbia's famed Sunshine Coast. It's located in a secluded valley of warm lakes and thick forests. They offer comfortable dorms, gourmet organic cooking (both vegetarian and non-vegetarian), a sauna and other amenities.

From this location, retreats are organized for up to eighteen men, including individuals, couples, or groups. The activities vary and include hiking, canoeing, camping, fishing, swimming, boating, and mountaineering, all of which are guided.

For a full year's schedule, contact:

Bear Tooth Adventures
520 Victoria Drive
Vancouver, BC V5L 4E1
Phone: 604 251 2776

▼ *Adventure Bound Expeditions* was founded by David Johnson, a self-described avid traveler and outdoor sports enthusiast. The tour agency specializes in adventure trips for gays and their friends who enjoy the out-of-doors and who like to explore cultural and geographic diversity.

There is a basic backpack trip through the Rocky Mountains every year, a reflection of Johnson's love of his home state of Colorado. In addition to the Colorado Wilderness trip, a recent schedule included an Atlas Mountain Trek in Morocco, a trip to the volanic regions of Hawaii, and an Alpine Walk around Mont Blanc. A similar set of experiences is scheduled for each year.

Adventure Bound Expeditions
711 Walnut Street
Camage House
Boulder, CO 80302
Phone: 303 449 0990

CRUISES

RSVP Travel Productions, Inc., orchestrates cruises that have become a favorite gay male vacation. Runs from New York to Montreal make summer stops in such ports as Quebec and Provincetown. Caribbean voyages in the winter leave from Miami and St. Petersburg and call at ports in the Yucatán, Jamaica, and many of the Windward Islands. West Coast sailings leave from San Diego to Mexican destinations including Mazatlán and Puerto Vallarta.

RSVP charters cruise ships for their clients' exclusive use. There are some lesbians and a few straights who are aware of the scene on board, but the vast majority of customers are gay men. There are many special considerations including social groups for those who are HIV-positive or who have AIDS, and every cruise includes a daily gathering of The Friends of Bill W. (Alcoholics Anonymous).

Singles, couples, and groups all travel on RSVP's ships. There are unique parties to introduce single men to one another. More than that, while most regular cruises are priced with couples in mind, RSVP is willing to match up single people who are willing to share cabins—and expenses.

One of the most intriguing things is the way the men who take the cruises seem to bond with one another, not in any heavy New Age sense, but as though they all went to Boy Scout camp together. They greet one another on the street and at parties and seem to have had a unique experience they like to relive in their conversations. The company promotes just that kind of response with something called "The RSViP Club," an alumnilike organization that produces a newsletter for all former clients.

RSVP doesn't sell the cruises retail—a consumer has to go through a travel agent. If your travel agent doesn't know about these offerings, contact the ***International Gay Travel Association,*** a network of gay and gay-friendly travel agents. You can write to them at: Box 18247, Denver, CO 80219, or call 303 467 7117. The phone number is available twenty-four hours a day.

RSVP has a videotape to promote their cruises. You can get hold of a copy through your travel agent or else send RSVP $3.95 plus $1.05 for handling costs. They also have a free catalog of upcoming cruises. Send your order for the videotape or your request for the catalog to:

RSVP Travel Productions, Inc.
2800 University Avenue SE
Minneapolis, MN 55414

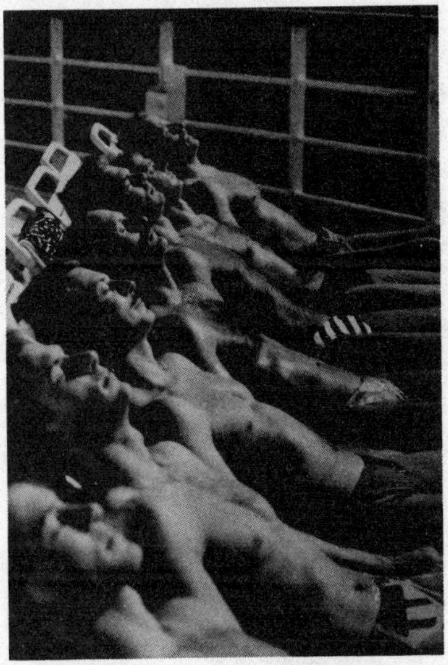

PHOTO © 1988. RSVP TRAVEL PRODUCTIONS, INC. REPRINTED WITH PERMISSION.

▼ *Hanns Ebensten* has been arranging extravagant gay vacations for decades. The company specializes in exotic adventures with a limited number of participants, such as cruises down the Nile and the Amazon or tours of the Himalayas and Morocco and group trips to Carnival in Rio de Janeiro.

The destinations change with the year. To find out what's planned in the near future, contact:

Hanns Ebensten Travel, Inc.
513 Fleming Street
Key West, FL 33040
Phone: 305 294 8174

▼ Frequent-flyer programs have become an important part of travel planning. You should be aware of your airline's policies toward these rewards when it comes to travel with "unrelated" people. Often an airline will only let you share your frequent flyer award with a member of your blood-family; others insist that you both live at the same address. This partial survey of frequent-flyer awards was compiled by Monte Pothlethwait for *The Washington Blade* and is reprinted with permission. You should check with each airline for an update on their policies. If they will not allow you to use your award with anyone but a family member, they're denying gay men access to these privileges and you should complain. "Yes" indicates that the airline restricts who can receive the award:

American	No
Continental	No
Delta	No
Eastern	No
Northwest	No
Pan American	Yes
Trans World (TWA)	Yes
United	No
USAir	No

HOTLANTA

The Hotlanta River Expo bills itself as the largest gay party in the world. Up to 5,000 gay men converge on Atlanta the first weekend in August. The event began in 1979 when a much smaller number of gay men took a float down the Chattahoochee River and made it into a party. By 1990 the weekend had expanded to include a mammoth dance event, a drag contest, and a "Mr. Hotlanta" competition that attracts gay body-builders from around the country in addition to the now traditional trip down the 'Hoochee.

This is the most highly organized of many similar summer events around the country that are popular with gay men. Others include Provincetown's *Carnival,* also held in August, and *Splash Day* in

Galveston on the official opening of the beaches in that city on the Gulf of Mexico.

For more information on Hotlanta, write:

Hotlanta River Expo
Box 8375
Atlanta, GA 30306

▼ In the midst of all the seriousness of gay life, there's also a place for some fun. Alpha Communications of Sarasota, Inc. has a whole line of role-playing gay games available. *Murder in Key West, Murder Is a Drag, Dial Gay for Murder,* and *Murder at Tara* are some of the titles.

Each game includes invitations and envelopes, complete host instructions, playing rules, name tags, a cassette to set the mood and start the game, and a sealed solution.

The games are available mail order at $17.95 apiece, plus $2.00 postage and handling. For more information:

ACOS, Inc.
Box 15192
Sarasota, FL 34277

TORCH SONGS

The wistful songs of the torch singers have informed gay men's sensibility since long before liberation. They still have an integral part in our lives. Michael Bronski has written a basic introduction to the best of the sad singers, complete with information on the classic recordings.

There you are. Sitting in a mostly empty bar, nursing your bourbon, feeling sorry for yourself. The man you loved just walked out of your life with your ex-boyfriend leaving you lovelorn and sex starved. You are about to be fired from your job because you sit at your desk and cry all day. And to make matters even worse you can't even stay at home because your roommate drags a steady line of tricks through the living room. Just when you think that your grief is beyond words, beyond comprehension, someone drops two-bits into the old juke-box and Billie Holiday's smokey, tormented voice begins to fill not only the emptiness of the room but the emptiness inside you. "Someday he'll come along, the man I love." And you thought that you had problems.

Women torch singers have long been an integral part of many gay men's culture. They sang from the heart and their songs were as much about survival as suffering. Life wasn't easy and love was harder but they never gave up. In a world that told gay men that their lives were pointless and their loves were wrong torch singers told a truth that was understood and taken to heart. From the great torchers of the '20s and '30s—Libby Holman, Ruth Etting, Fanny Brice, and Helen Morgan—to the new singers of today like Andrea Marcovicci, gay men have drawn sustenance and strength, as well as dozens of great songs to get themselves through everything from love affairs, to lazy afternoons or a quiet night at the bar. The following seven singers are in no particular order, but they are all great and deserve to be in your record collection. They are, however, in the pantheon of great women vocalists and gay male heros, the second tier. The first tier, Bessie Smith, Billie Holiday, Judy Garland, Ella Fitzgerald, Barbra Streisand, and Sarah Vaughn, are not great but incomparable; divine and inspired. We presume that you *already* have all of their records.

In a certain sense the singular hyper-emotional doom and gloom of torch singing is a pre-Stonewall phenomenon: Judy

Garland bemoaning "The Man Who Got Away." And it is probably no accident that the Stonewall Riots occurred the evening of Garland's funeral. The age which was ushered in allowed gay men to identify with more than emotional self-defeat and many of these singers are willing and able to get angry or get down as a way of getting over some lug who did them wrong. Although heartbreak and thwarted erotics are traditionally the meat and potatoes of these singers' repertory, there are also lighter moments: playful, sexy, and just plain fun. The contemporary torch singer is more than a simple victim, she is simply victorious.

Nancy Harrow is one of the great mistresses of understatement. When guitarist Jack Wilkins was late returning from a break Harrow went ahead with bass player Rufus Reid and recorded "Anything Goes" in late 1978 (*Anything Goes.* Audiophile Records AP-142). The result is tight and delightful, and calls to mind the time Barbra Streisand recorded "Autumn Leaves" with only a cello accompaniment. When she listened to the playback one of her technicians joked that it sounded like the cello was chasing Barbra around the room, which made her so insecure she rerecorded it with more instruments. This is what makes someone like Nancy Harrow all the more enchanting—she has a warm little instrument and she is quite at home with it. Having it chased around the room by a cello probably wouldn't bother her at all, if it was musically viable.

Harrow's accompaniment is not always this stripped down. Witness the album arranged and produced for her by impeccable jazz pianist John Lewis of the Modern Jazz Quartet (*The John Lewis Album for Nancy Harrow,* Finesse Records FW 37681). This is a lush jazz experience, with Nancy's spright little instrument riding above and playing with Lewis's piano, Joseph Kennedy's violin, Connie Kay's drums, and flute, bass, and guitar. She ends the set with Rodgers and Hart's "It Never Entered My Mind," one of the best interpretations of one of the best songs ever written. What more can you ask from a girl singer you've probably never heard of?

After Billie Holiday, the most exciting and enduring and intriguing singer ever to grace America is **Lee Wiley.** More or less Holiday's age peer (they were both born in the vicinity of 1915), she left her native Ft. Gibson, Oklahoma, in her teens, and went on to become one of the great nightclub chanteuses of the 1940s. Married for a brief while to jazz pianist Jess Stacy, she always maintained strong ties to great jazzmen, and this is as true for her final album (*Back Home Again,* Monmouth-Evergreen Records MES 7041) as it is for her legendary composer song books of the 1940s (on which she does definitive versions of many masterpieces by Cole Porter, the Gershwins, Rodgers and Hart, etc.). Here we will focus on *Night in Manhattan* (Columbia Records JCL 656) because it is still available, and it is ever-glorious. Recorded in the mid-1950s, it is smooth as Scotch and far more intoxicating; that gorgeous voice glides through beautifully simple arrangements of "I've Got a Crush on You," "Time on my Hands," "A Woman's Intuition," "Street of Dreams," "More than You Know," and others. She was Truman Capote's favorite singer, and Boston music critic George Frazier went gaga whenever he even so much as mentioned her, admitting at least once in print that he longed to go to bed with her. Straight men. I would have preferred to try on the gown she wears on the cover of her *West of the Moon* album, but I know what Frazier meant, for I've always felt that way about James Taylor (who owes part of *his* layback style to Peggy Lee).

Maxine Sullivan was one of the greats. Soprano Eileen Farrell hugs her in a photograph on one of Sullivan's many albums (thanks to George H. Buck, Jr., and other independent record producers, her final years were *very* prolific), and Maxine's friend Lady Iris Mountbatten once gave her a recording of "My Very Good Friend the Milkman," which subsequently became a Sullivan staple.

Maxine's voice was warm and full and very quiet. She was as far from Jennifer Holiday and Etta James as a singer can get. When the likes of Doc Cheatam would play trumpet for her, you can bet it's a muted accompaniment: and that dazzling little instrument just strutted its stuff in front of all those other carefully made sounds. She had a perfect ear, and exquisite taste. On one of her final albums, *It Was Great Fun* (Audiophile Records AP 185) she did "Skylark," "What Is There to Say?" "I Didn't Know About You," and "Just One of Those Things." One of those things—that was Maxine's voice and spirit.

Like Maxine Sullivan, **Alberta Hunter** became more recorded and more appreciated the older she got (fortunately they both got pretty old). Certainly the Alan Rudolph cult film *Remember My Name* helped the process in Hunter's case, as the soundtrack was a brilliant set of some of her best performances. She ranged from funky ("Workin' Man") to gentle as a lullaby ("The Love I Have for You") and she did it all with an artistry, a professionalism, that took your breath away. This is a musician who always had her ears open, even though she took a huge chunk out of the middle of her life to devote to nursing. The *Remember My Name* soundtrack is on Columbia Records (35553), and features several of the greats who worked with Sullivan, notably Doc Cheatham and Connie Kay. Hunter was embraced by the Baby Boomers before her death, and did several memorable television performances and a videotape. She's a hoot to watch, so don't stop with the soundtrack.

On first hearing, **Blossom Dearie's** voice may remind you of Minnie Mouse's: tiny and distinctly articulated it is a perfect, if miniature, instrument which Dearie uses meticulously, sacrificing neither style, form, or content as she makes her material hers alone. She has had an odd career—hugely popular in the '50s New York jazz scene, she has made a comeback these past fifteen years and can be heard on television doing commercials for the diary industry when she is not performing in New York industry. She has the smallest voice in the business—smaller than Astrud Gilberto's or Chet Baker's—and she is a musician par excellence. This perfection has stunned people into silence at her New York City recitals, always in small smoke-free places and no later than 6 P.M. People put up with these demands, because quite frankly no one else is remotely like her. Johnny Mercer penned one of his final masterpieces for her—a long, urbane, remarkably funny and hip song called "My New Celebrity is You," in which she plays "the uke with Vernon Duke so well in Dubuque that Vladimir Dukelsky said, 'Gee!' " (Daffodil Records, BMD 103). Although Susannah McCorkle later did an excellent cover of the song, only the Dearie magic can do a line like "I dig Modigliani, Jolson doing Swanee . . . several Maharanee are my intimates too/I played with Mantovani and that's a lot of strings to get through" and make you believe it. Her renditions of Leon Russell's "A Song For You" and "Killing Me Softly With His Song," made famous by Roberta Flack, are amazing creations of diminutive heartbreak. For most of her career she has recorded herself (Daffodil Records), ensuring that more than most she has always done it *her way.* A definite original.

Andrea Marcovicci is, like Barbra Streisand, an actress who sings, but unlike Streisand, Marcovicci still enjoys doing both. Her album *Andrea Marcovicci Sings Movies* (Philomel 1001) is one of the most brash and joyful performances I've heard since the very early Streisand (i.e., her pirated Hungry i concert from 1963). Like the early Barbra, Marcovicci lets it all hang out. She sounds positively drunk and sloppy on "Fanny," but she is after all a sailor in love with a girl, and she doesn't let you forget it as she swaggers about exhaling "Just a boy with no heart to give" as if the words are making her feel dirty, or laden down. When she does "Here Lies Love" you feel so wretched you just want to cry or jump out of a window of the York Hotel in San Francisco, where she recorded this set in 1987 with "just" the pianist Glenn Mehrbach. Anyone who appreciates the tension that can be maintained between the human voice and the piano has to experience this album. Her reading of Noel Coward's "Mad About the Boy" isn't as insane or hypersexual as Helen Merrill's, but like all the readings on this album it is so intelligent that you almost feel like all this material is new. And it's not. Marcovicci is new—with every song. Anyone who just *has* to see her can do so by renting Henry Jaglom's 1988 film *Someone to Love,* toward the end of which she sings the title song, included also on this album. If you enjoy the mesh of emotions and popular song, Marcovicci is a must.

Every now and then on television you might catch a whiff of a magnificent black female voice on a commercial for a certain cologne, informing you that her baby just cares for her. This is very likely the voice of **Nina Simone,** the mysterious genius diva of the jazz/pop world. If it weren't for her leftist politics and her anger and her admitted drug use she probably would have become a very famous singer, for God knows her contralto is at least as interesting an instrument as Sarah Vaughn's, and her classically trained piano provides sounds you can ride on (witness her piano on her haunting arrangement of Judy Collins's "My Father" on *Baltimore,* Creed Taylor, Inc. Records 7084). From her late 1950s recording of "I Loves You, Porgy" to her various and comparatively recent comebacks from Europe, Africa, and the West Indies (she is for many years now expatriate), she has never done a dull performance or an uninspired recording. She considers Bob Dylan the closest thing to a saint among white people, and she did right by him by recording several of his best songs in the late 1960s; on the other hand she steadfastly refuses to record "Bridge Over Troubled Waters," announcing, in concert, that Paul Simon stole it from her people. Her most legendary unrecorded performance is her painful and totally brilliant rewriting of Gilbert O'Sullivan's "Alone Again Naturally" which she takes out of the realm of self pity by making it a blow-by-blow account of her father's death by cancer. "And when he passed away, I drank and smoked all day," she says in a voice that could make Pirate Jenny herself shiver, and if I outlive Nina Simone, I'll drink and smoke all day in her memory, too. She is a goddess.

GAY TROUBADOURS

Romanovsky and Phillips are a gay singing duo who've toured the country since 1983. They're regulars at Gay Pride celebrations and rallies, in addition to the regular concert appearances you'd expect of singers and entertainers. Starting their touring career wasn't all that easy. According to their official biography:

Within the first week of their first tour, "their 1958 VW bus developed engine trouble in San Diego, spun 360° in the Rocky Mountains, and finally died in the cornfields of Iowa. . . . As the tour continued . . . they were confronted with more snowstorms and another (borrowed) VW bus which also broke down at regular intervals. When they narrowly survived rolling over twice off an icy Maine highway, they began to wonder if God was trying to tell them not to spread their message of gay pride. It wasn't until they completed their journey that they realized God was merely trying to tell them to buy a new car."

They've gone on to make three record albums and develop a coterie of fans so devoted that there's now even a newsletter, filling in details about their lives and their schedules.

For information on booking or mail order of records, tapes, and CDs:

Fresh Fruit Records
Box 4418
Berkeley, CA 94704

TOM WILSON WEINBERG. PHOTO BY SCOTT BURCH.

▼ Tom Wilson Weinberg is the composer, director, producer and, often, the star of *The Ten Percent Revue,* a theatrical production that's warmed the hearts of gay audiences all over the country. Contact *Aboveground Records,* which also distributes Wilson Weinberg's record albums, for schedules:

Aboveground Records
Box 2233
Philadelphia, PA 19103

▼ *Ten Percent Revue* has been published by Broadway Play Publishing Co., New York. Licensed productions are being handled by New Musical Theatre Library, 357 W. 20th Street, New York, NY 10011.

BEAUTY CONTESTS

You'll find advertisements and announcements for many "Mr." contests around the country. Gay men have flocked to the stage and stripped down to bikinis, jock straps, and G-strings. Often the competitions are simple local affairs; usually they're promotions for bars where the winners might get a small check for their efforts.

But many of the local affairs are hooked into one of the three big national competitions. If you're interested in entering one of these national events, you should contact the national offices to find out more about the rules and regulations. All three lead up to an annual all-star competition which often carries significant prizes, some of them cash, but you'll never get rich off your title.

Mr. Gay USA is a match up of clean-cut all-American types. Inexpensive franchises to the local events are sold by the national organization and most are bought by bars or other businesses. For more information on this (and the parallel contest track for transvestites: *Miss Gay USA*) contact:

USA Pageantry, Inc.
Box 1702
Pearland, TX 77588
Phone: 713 523 5293

KEVIN SCOTT WAS MR. GAY USA FOR 1987–1988. PHOTO COURTESY OF USA PAGEANTRY, INC.

MARK AMBROSY IS A PAST MR. GAY USA. PHOTO BY BRIAN CHAMPAGNE. REPRINTED WITH PERMISSION OF USA PAGEANTRY, INC.

▼ *Mr. International Leather* celebrates masculine men. The contest, more than a decade old, is climaxed with the national finals, always held on Memorial Day in Chicago. This is the one contest where individuals can apply to compete without having won a regional event, if they can secure sponsorship from a business or club. For more information:

Mr. International Leather, Inc.
5015 N. Clark Street
Chicago, IL 60640

MICHAEL PEREYRA, MR. INTERNATIONAL LEATHER OF 1988. COPYRIGHT 1988 RENSLOW FAMILY ENTERPRISES. REPRODUCED WITH PERMISSION.

THE INTERNATIONAL MR. LEATHER LOGO HAS BECOME ONE OF ARTIST ETIENNE'S MOST FAMOUS DRAWINGS. REPRODUCED WITH THE PERMISSION OF RENSLOW FAMILY ENTERPRISES.

4.95

DRUMMER

ISSUE 123

Jack Fritcher,
Scott O'Hara
and other experts on
SOLO SEX
Nobody Does It Better!

Contests!
Contests!
Match the Member contest:
pair up the beef and the sausage
Rex Story Contest:
your last chance

MR. DRUMMER 1988
RON ZEHEL

MR. DRUMMER

DISTRIBUTION TO MINORS PROHIBITED

▼ *Mr. Drummer* is another leather contest, this one sponsored by the San Francisco–based magazine. A series of regional contests is held, all of them highly publicized in the magazine, with the national finals held in the Bay Area, usually the same week as Gay Pride.

Drummer Magazine
Mr. Drummer Contest
Box 11314
San Francisco, CA 94101

THE CONTESTANT

What kind of person enters a male beauty contest and why does he do it?

The answer is often much different than what you might expect. While there are certainly some guys who are after a quick dollar and maybe a chance at starring in explicit videos, many others have more complex reasons.

Norman Guttman entered the International Mr. Leather Contest in 1988 when he was forty years old. Guttman is an attorney who's been politically active in the gay and lesbian movement for years. He's a past president of the Houston Gay/Lesbian Political Caucus and has been active in many other groups, from the Montrose Art Alliance to the Greater Montrose Business Guild. (He's not alone as a political activist who's entered—and won—national contests. Scott Tucker, Mr. International Leather of that year, is also a well-known politico and a regular contributor to many intellectual journals and newspapers.)

When I asked Guttman what his motivations were, he admitted that turning forty had been part of it. He wasn't about to give in to middle age without a struggle, especially since he'd spent long, hard months in the gym getting his body in shape.

If being in a beauty contest still isn't perceived as a politically correct act, there is also a sense among many competitors that they'd hidden their bodies and their sexuality for too long. Their coming out sometimes includes very public acts of sexual expression, and standing on the podium at the local Mr. Gay USA contest or one of the leather events is certainly one way to do that.

PHOTOGRAPH BY ROGER RUTHERFORD. © 1988, NORMAN GUTTMAN. REPRODUCED WITH PERMISSION.

A

B

INDEX

C

D

F

G

H

I

K

L

M

INDEX

O

R

S

T

INDEX

U

V

W

RD 11 W